Praise for

LADY COP
MAKES
TROUBLE

"*Lady Cop Makes Trouble* takes readers on a lively chase through a lost world. It's a colorful and inventive adventure tale that also contains a serious message at its core about the importance of meaningful work to women's identities and, in some cases, survival." —**Maureen Corrigan**, *Washington Post*

"[Constance's] days and nights come vividly to life. And although the real crimes are solved by the end of the novel, Stewart leaves the reader wondering about one mystery still developing unsolved: the relationship between Constance and her married boss, Heath . . . Readers will just have to wait—impatiently, no doubt—for book No. 3." —*Boston Globe*

"It's *True Grit*, New York style." —*New York Post*

"Constance and her sisters are every bit as enjoyable in this outing as their first. Stewart deftly combines the rough-and-tumble atmosphere of early twentieth-century New York City with the story of three women who want to live life on their own terms. The addition of supporting female characters who are also pushing societal boundaries is a welcome touch to the series."

— *Library Journal*, **starred review**

"Smart, atmospheric fun, with enough loose ends left dangling to assure fans there will be more entries in this enjoyable series."

— *Kirkus Reviews*

"The multiple players in the story provide wry situational humor and a backdrop for Kopp's unique, forceful character, while Sheriff Heath's surprisingly supportive regard lends a hopeful relational perspective. Stewart adeptly introduces details of early twentieth-century life in Hackensack, New Jersey, a burgeoning city on the outskirts of New York, and timely concerns such as jail reform and women's rights, rounding out this immensely satisfying mystery."

— *Booklist*

"Stewart's second volume in her Kopp Sisters series is a clever, suspenseful, and funny tale of a formidable woman facing crime, politics, social stigma, all while nailing evildoers . . . Fans of the first Kopp Sisters novel will find another treat in this follow-up."

— *Publishers Weekly*

Praise for

GIRL WAITS
WITH GUN

A National Bestseller
A *New York Times* Editors' Choice

A Best Book of the Year
NPR · *Washington Post* · *BookPage* · *St. Louis Post-Dispatch*

A Must-Read
People · *USA Today* · *New York Post* · *Cosmopolitan* · *Paste*

"An entertaining and enlightening story of how far one woman will go to protect her family."   —*Washington Post*

"Stewart has spun a fine, historically astute novel . . . The sisters' personalities flower under Stewart's pen, contributing happy notes of comedy to a terrifying situation . . . And then there is Constance: Sequestered for years in the country and cowed by life, she develops believably into a woman who comes into herself, discovering powers long smothered under shame and resignation. I, for one, would like to see her return to wield them again in further installments."   —*New York Times Book Review*

LADY COP
MAKES
TROUBLE

LADY COP
MAKES
TROUBLE

Amy Stewart

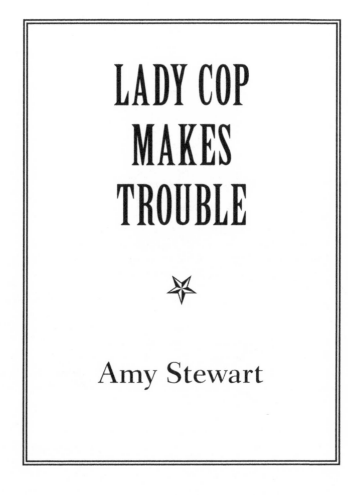

Mariner Books
Houghton Mifflin Harcourt
Boston   New York

First Mariner Books edition 2017

For information about permission to reproduce selections
from this book, write to trade.permissions@hmhco.com or to
Permissions, Houghton Mifflin Harcourt Publishing Company,
3 Park Avenue, 19th Floor, New York, New York 10016.

www.hmhco.com

Library of Congress Cataloging-in-Publication Data
Names: Stewart, Amy, author.
Title: Lady cop makes trouble / Amy Stewart.
Description: Boston ; New York : Houghton Mifflin Harcourt, 2017.
Identifiers: LCCN 2016004634 (print) | LCCN 2016010658 (ebook) |
ISBN 9780544409941 (hardback) | ISBN 9780544409620 (ebook) |
ISBN 9780544947139 (pbk.)
Subjects: | BISAC: FICTION / Historical. | FICTION / General. | FICTION /
Mystery & Detective / Women Sleuths. | GSAFD: Mystery fiction.
Classification: LCC PS3619.T49343 L33 2017 (print) |
LCC PS3619.T49343 (ebook) | DDC 813/.6—dc23
LC record available at http://lccn.loc.gov/2016004634

Book design by Greta D. Sibley

Printed in the United States of America
DOC 10 9 8 7 6 5 4 3 2 1

To Maria Hopper

Miss Constance Kopp, who once hid behind a
tree near her home in Wyckoff, N.J., for five hours
waiting to get a shot at a gang of Black Handers
who had annoyed her, is now a Deputy Sheriff
of Bergen County, N.J., and a terror to evildoers.

—New York Press, December 20, 1915

LADY COP
MAKES
TROUBLE

1

YOUNG GIRL WANTED — GOOD WAGE. Well-to-do man seeking a housekeeper who is matrimonially minded. Room and board offered. Reply to box-holder 4827.

I handed the newspaper back to Mrs. Headison. "I suppose you replied to the box-holder?"

She nodded briskly. "I did, posing as a girl who had just come to town from Buffalo, with experience not in housekeeping, but in dancing, and with aspirations for the stage. We can all imagine what he must have made of *that*."

I didn't like to imagine it, owing to the fact that a youthful aspirant to the stage lived under my own roof, but I had to admit that the trick worked. Sheriff Heath and I read the man's reply, which invited her to visit at her earliest convenience and promised an offer of marriage if she proved worthy of it.

"Any number of girls have auditioned for the job and are still awaiting that offer of marriage," she sniffed. "I've seen them going in and out of his house. As my position is only advisory in nature, I'm under instructions to report any suspicious findings to the police chief, who sends an officer to make the arrest. But this man lives out here in Bergen County, so we're handing the matter over to you."

Belle Headison was Paterson's first policewoman. She was a slight figure with narrow shoulders and hair the color of weak tea. Her eyes were framed by brass-rimmed spectacles that recalled the inner workings of a standing clock. Everything about her seemed upright and tightly wound.

I was New Jersey's first lady deputy sheriff. I'd never met another woman in law enforcement. The summer of 1915 felt like a brave and bright new age.

Mrs. Headison had arranged to meet us at the train station in Ridgewood, not far from the man's house. We stood on the platform, under the only awning that cast any shade. In spite of the late August heat, it gave me a bracing thrill to think about going after anyone who would so casually advertise for a girl in the newspaper.

The sheriff took another look at the letter. "Mr. Meeker," he said. "Harold Meeker. Well, ladies, let's go pay him a visit."

Mrs. Headison took a step back. "Oh, I'm not sure what use I'd be."

But Sheriff Heath wouldn't hear it. "It's your case," he said cheerfully. "You should get the satisfaction of seeing it through to the end." Nothing made him happier than the prospect of catching a criminal, and he couldn't imagine why anyone else wouldn't feel the same.

"But I don't usually go along with the officers," she said. "Why don't you go, and Miss Kopp and I will wait here?"

"I brought Miss Kopp along for a reason," the sheriff said, ushering us both off the platform and into his motor car.

Mrs. Headison stepped in with some reluctance and we drove through town.

On the way, Mrs. Headison told us about her work at the Travelers' Aid Society, where she helped girls who came to Paterson with no family or job prospects. "They get off the train and find no difficulty in making their way to the most disreputable boarding-houses and the tawdriest dance halls," she said. "And if she's a pretty girl, the saloons will give her supper and drink, free of charge. Of course, nothing comes free, but the girls aren't so easily convinced of that. It's their first time away from home and they've forgotten everything their mothers taught them, if they were taught anything at all."

Mrs. Headison, it developed, had been widowed in 1914. On the first anniversary of the death of her husband, a retired constable, she read about New Jersey's new law allowing women to serve as police officers. "It was as if John were speaking to me from the hereafter and telling me that I had a new calling. I went right to the Paterson police chief and made my application."

Sheriff Heath and I attempted to offer our congratulations but she continued without taking a breath. "Do you know that he hadn't even considered adding a woman to his force? I had to argue my case, and you can be sure I did. Do you know why he was so reluctant? The chief told me himself that if women start going about in uniforms, armed with guns and clubs, we would turn into little men."

I cast the sheriff a look of horror but he kept his eyes straight ahead.

"I assured him that my position in the police department would be exactly the same as that of a mother in the home. Just as a mother tends to her children and issues a kind word of warning or encouragement, I would carry out my duty as a woman and bring a mother's ideals into the police department. Wouldn't you agree, Miss Kopp? Haven't you become quite the mother hen at the sheriff's department?"

I hadn't thought of myself as a mother hen, but then again, I'd seen a hen peck an errant chick so sharply that she drew blood, so perhaps Mrs. Headison was right. For the last two months, I'd been riding along anytime a woman or a girl was caught up in some criminal matter. I'd served divorce papers to an estranged wife, investigated a charge of illegal cohabitation, chased down a girl attempting to run away on a train, put clothes on a prostitute who was found naked and half-dead from opium in a card room above a tailor's shop, and sat with a mother of three while the sheriff and his men ran through the woods looking for her husband, over whose head she had broken a bottle of brandy. The husband was returned to her, although she wouldn't let him inside until he promised, in front of the sheriff, to bring no more drink into her house.

It would be no exaggeration to say that the moments I have just described were among the finest of my life. The prostitute had soiled herself and had to be washed in the card room's dingy basin, and the girl running for the train bit my arm when I caught her, and still I assert that I had never been more content. Improbable as it may sound, I had, at last, found work that suited me.

I didn't know how to explain any of that to Mrs. Headison. To my relief, we arrived at Mr. Meeker's before I had to. The sheriff drove just past his house and parked a few doors down.

He lived in a modest shingled home with painted shutters and a small front porch that looked to have been added on recently. There was a window open in his living room and the sound of piano music drifted into the front yard.

"Someone's at home," Sheriff Heath said. "Miss Kopp, you'll knock at the door and we'll stay down here. If there's a girl in there now, I don't want to scare her off. Try to get her to come to you. We're not going to arrest her for waywardness, but she doesn't know that."

"That's fine," I said.

Mrs. Headison stared at the two of us as if we'd just proposed a safari to Africa.

"You aren't going to send her to the door unguarded, are you? What if—"

She stopped when she saw me take my revolver from my handbag and tuck it into my pocket. It was the same one the sheriff issued to me the previous year when my family was being harassed: a Colt police revolver, dark blue, just small enough to conceal in the pockets Fleurette stitched into all my jackets and dresses for that purpose.

"Do they have you carrying a gun? Why, the police chief—"

"I don't work for the police chief." I felt the sheriff's eyes on me when I said it. The fact that we were doing something the police chief wouldn't have dared gave me a great deal of satisfaction.

With my revolver in place, I marched up to the man's door. The two of them stayed just out of sight as the piano music stopped and the door opened.

Harold Meeker was a doughy man of about forty years of age. He came to the door in shirtsleeves and a tie, carrying a pipe in one hand and his shoes in the other. He had a flat forehead that rearranged itself into wrinkles when he saw me.

"Excuse me, ma'am," he said, looking down at his bare

feet. "The maid is in today doing some cleaning, and I was trying to stay out of her way."

He offered an abashed grin. I didn't want to waste any time lest the girl run out the back door.

"It's no trouble, Mr. Meeker," I said, loudly enough for the sheriff to hear. "In fact, I've come to see about that maid of yours. I believe I may have something that belongs to her."

I pushed my way in before he could stop me. Inside, I saw the worn carpets and shabby furniture that suggested a man who had never moved out of his mother's house. Every lamp shade was painted in pink roses. The upright piano was draped in doilies. There was even a needlepoint sampler on the wall, faded to brown and covered in dust.

Mr. Meeker jumped around in front of me. He was almost my height but of a slighter build. He might have hoped to intimidate me, but he couldn't.

"Lettie was just finishing," he said, looking back toward what I took to be the kitchen. "If you wouldn't mind waiting outside, she'll be out in a minute. Are you a relation, Mrs. . . . ."

I ignored him and went straight for the kitchen. "Lettie, is that you?" I called, pushing the door open.

There, at a little wooden painted table, sat a girl of fifteen with kid curlers in her hair and a cigarette between her fingers. She wore only a thin cambric gown and damask slippers of the kind Fleurette favored. It was an old kitchen with an iron stove and a washtub for a sink. It needed a good cleaning, but Lettie wasn't the one to do it.

She jumped up when she saw me.

"You don't look like a housekeeper," I said, and went alongside her to take her elbow.

"No, I'm just—I'm here visiting until . . ."

Harold Meeker hadn't followed us into the kitchen. I could only assume he'd realized that he was in trouble and tried to run. Sheriff Heath would grab him.

I kept a firm hold of her arm and said, "I'm from the sheriff's department, dear. You're not in any trouble, but we worry that you might have been misled by an advertisement Mr. Meeker placed for a housekeeper."

Lettie was defiant. She jutted out her lower lip and put her free hand on her hip. "I'm allowed to apply for work. There's no law against it."

I heard voices from the other room and knew that Sheriff Heath had caught his man and returned with him.

"We believe he's taking advantage of young girls, and there is a law against that. How long have you been here?"

She twisted around and looked toward the back door, but I pulled her firmly toward me. "When did you get to town, Lettie?"

She sniffed and dropped down to her chair. I eased down next to her. "Just last week." She fingered the sardine tin she used for an ashtray. "I came out on the train from Ohio. I was going to New York, but something got mixed up with my tickets and here I am, with no money and no one to take me in but Mr. Meeker."

Already I hated Mr. Meeker. What kind of man thinks he can just advertise for girls in the newspaper? "And what happened when he made it plain that he wasn't just looking for a housekeeper?"

She put her face in her hands and didn't answer.

I looked around for something for Lettie to wear and saw an old duster on a hook. "It's all right. I've brought a lady with me who can find a better place for you." I pulled the duster over her head and helped her up. She had a child's bony shoulders. "Have you any things upstairs you'd like to take with you?"

She wiped her eyes. "I lost everything on the platform. My bag went one way and I went the other."

"We'll see what we can do about that." I took her into the living room, where Harold Meeker stood in handcuffs alongside Sheriff Heath and a dazed Mrs. Headison. When Mr. Meeker saw us, he lunged for Lettie but could only rattle his chains at her.

"Did you call the sheriff?" he shouted. "You worthless little tramp, after all I've done—"

Sheriff Heath yanked him back, but they both lost their footing. Mr. Meeker kicked and fought and twisted out of the sheriff's grip. He was free for only a second, and tried to run between us and out the door. I threw myself at him and forced him into a corner. I had my fist around his collar but still he flailed around and tried to push past me. Mrs. Headison gasped and ran across the room to take hold of Lettie.

The sheriff came up behind me and grabbed Harold Meeker's arm. I pulled a little harder on his collar, forcing him to his tiptoes.

There was the tiniest flicker of a glance between me and the sheriff. Neither one of us wanted to let Mr. Meeker go. We were both enjoying ourselves. The man panted and seemed to wilt between us.

"I'll add avoiding arrest and assaulting an officer to your charges," Sheriff Heath said. "That'll keep you in jail a while longer."

I still had hold of his shirt. His neck had gone red where it pinched him.

"Get her hands off me!" Mr. Meeker gasped. "Who is she, your nurse?"

"She appears to be the deputy putting you under arrest," the sheriff said. "Speak to her if you have a complaint."

A little laugh escaped Lettie's mouth, but I heard nothing from Mrs. Headison.

It was an awkward ride back to Paterson with me, Lettie, and Mrs. Headison in the back, and the men together in the front. I didn't like to put a girl and her tormentor in the same auto, but we saw no other way to do it, as Mrs. Headison was too rattled to take Lettie back on the train alone and Sheriff Heath wanted me with him in case Mr. Meeker tried to escape.

The sheriff waited with his prisoner while I saw Lettie and Mrs. Headison back to the Travelers' Aid Office.

"I know you'll take good care of the girl," I said. "It was right of you to call us."

Paterson's first policewoman still seemed agitated. "I'll tell Mr. Headison all about you tonight in my prayers, but I don't think he'll believe me. The things they have you doing—well, I couldn't do it, even if they did pay me."

I stared down at her. Lettie was watching the two of us, open-mouthed.

"Don't they pay you?" My salary was a thousand dollars a year, the same as the other deputies.

"Ah—well, of course not," she said, slowly, still puzzling it out. "The chief expects me to serve out of a sense of duty and honor, and not to take a salary away from a policeman."

I couldn't think of a polite thing to say about that. I wanted only to get back into the wagon with my prisoner and to see him locked in jail where he belonged.

"Do call on us again if you need us, Mrs. Headison," I said, and ran back to Sheriff Heath.

AT THE JAIL, he handed Mr. Meeker off to Deputy Morris, a dignified older man who had become a family friend when he guarded our house against Henry Kaufman last year. Morris nodded stiffly and congratulated me on my work as he took the man away.

But when I went to follow him inside, the sheriff called me back.

"Miss Kopp."

There was something uneasy about the way he said it. He nodded toward the garage, a little free-standing stone building that had once been a carriage house and still had two stalls, matted with old hay, for keeping horses. He preferred it for private conversations because it had only one entrance, and there was no worry about someone slipping in a back door.

In the dim shadows under the eaves Sheriff Heath gave me a long and measured look and then said, "There's some trouble about your badge."

Something froze inside of me but I tried to make a joke out of it. "Have they run out of gold and rubies?" Sheriff Heath's badge held a single ruby, and he was always at pains to say that it had been purchased by his bondsmen, not the taxpayers.

He kept a large mustache that stretched when he smiled. It stayed perfectly still. When he spoke again it was in the manner of a speech he'd been rehearsing. "It has been brought to my attention by an attorney—who is a friend to the office of the sheriff and very much on our side—that I may stand on uncertain legal principle in the appointment of a female deputy sheriff."

My hands went nervously to my shirtfront. I patted myself down, smoothing my skirt and checking a button. "Haven't I been appointed already? Haven't I been doing the job since the middle of June?"

He took a step back and walked in a little circle, nodding. "You have. But it isn't official until the county clerk draws up the papers, and of course we don't yet have the badge itself. The trouble is that Mr.—our attorney friend . . ."

"Didn't the state pass a law allowing for the appointment of women police officers? Isn't that why you offered me the job?" There was a vibrato in my voice that I couldn't control. Even as I said it, I was beginning to understand what had happened.

"Yes. But that's the difficulty. The statute addresses police officers only. The sheriff is elected and governed under a different chapter of the law entirely. No mention was made of women deputies. In fact, the sheriff in New York City tried just such a scheme a few years ago, and had to abandon it because the law there requires that deputies be eligible voters in the county in which they serve, which means that women—"

I cut him off irritably. "Couldn't possibly qualify."

He was standing right in front of me again but I wouldn't look at him. Then he said, "We've no such troubles about voting in New Jersey. It isn't written into our laws that way. But if the lawmakers in Trenton had wanted women to serve as deputies, we can be sure they would have said so, and they didn't."

He had a higher opinion of lawmakers in Trenton than I did. "Couldn't it have been an oversight?" I was practically yelling.

"Yes. And I've been advised to write to all the other sheriffs in New Jersey and ask if any of them have appointed a lady deputy under the new law. It would give us precedence."

"And?"

"So far, no one has."

"And you don't want to be the first."

He lifted his hat, pushed his hair back, and set it down again. "Miss Kopp. I can fight the Freeholders over my budget and how I discharge my duties, but I cannot willfully break the law."

I turned away from him and tried to compose myself. I thought about the day, when I was about ten years of age, when I copied down a list printed in the newspaper under the title "What a Woman Can Do." I wrote down each item in a neat and careful hand, and then crossed most of them out after considered them. The Profession of Music was thus eliminated, as was Coloring Photographs and Women as Wood Engravers. Housekeeper was blotted out so thoroughly that the paper tore. Dressmaking met the same fate, as did Gardening. In fact, the paper was nearly in tatters under the force of my emphatic little hand.

Only The Profession of Law remained, along with A Lady Government Official, Women of Journalism, and Nursing. Each of those wore faint checks beside them.

I hid that list inside a white glove that needed mending and never showed it to anyone. On it were all the possibilities in the world.

No one, back in 1887, had dared to suggest Woman Deputy.

Now my profession was being taken away from me as quickly as it had been given. Already I'd grown accustomed to thinking of myself as one of the first to prove that a woman could do the job. I wasn't like Mrs. Headison. I wasn't just a chaperone for wayward girls. I carried a gun and handcuffs. I could make an arrest, just like any deputy. I earned a man's salary. People did find it shocking and I didn't mind that one bit.

A blue rectangle of sky lay beyond the garage's wide door. As soon as I walked out, I'd be ordinary again. I hadn't realized, until that moment, how much I hated being ordinary.

I still had my back to Sheriff Heath. I thought it best to leave without letting him see my face again. "Well. I suppose I'll go home."

"There's no need for that," the sheriff said quickly. "I've something else for you, if you'll take it."

That was enough to make me turn around.

"I won't be your stenographer." I wasn't about to sit in a room and take notes about what the other deputies had done.

Now he did smile a little. "It's not as bad as that. And it won't last long. Give me a month and I'll find a way."

I looked him in the eyes at last. They were sunken and soulful, and often carried dark circles around them. The man had a trustworthy face.

"A month?"

"That's all. One month."

⚜ 2 ⚜

"IT WON'T BE A MONTH," Norma said later that night.

I was sprawled across our divan, listening to my sister mutter at the newspaper. All I could see of her were her feet, crossed at the ankle on a tufted leather ottoman, and the tips of her stubby, chapped fingers gripping the paper by its edges. She kept at her side a portable gas lamp that made the room smell of Limburger cheese.

"Of course it will," I said. "This is only a legal difficulty and he's looking for a way."

"He should be looking for his own backbone." She rattled her paper again for emphasis. Norma was theatrical in her own way, a master of props, equipped with an impressive vocabulary of snorts, grumbles, and hisses, and always ready to bang a pot or slam a book shut to get her point across. In any disagreement, she could be counted upon to have a pencil and paper at the ready and to write down whatever outlandish and overheated claim the other party might be making, so that it could be entered into evidence and read back at a later date when it might favor her side.

When I didn't answer, she made another run at it. "If he hasn't any confidence in you, he should just say so. It may be true that most women lack the temperament, grit, and strength to enforce the law, but you have all three in abundance, and Sheriff Heath has no reason to doubt it."

"He doesn't doubt it," I said. "He's seen what I can do." He had, hadn't he? Norma had a way of speaking with such grim certainty that I could never truly dismiss those pronouncements of hers.

"Then why is he waiting for another sheriff to go first? Is he afraid of having his name in the paper? How the voters of Bergen County elected such a lily-livered man . . ."

"He's afraid of having Constance's name in the paper," Fleurette put in. She was coming downstairs in her stockinged feet, bouncing down the last few steps and spinning so the hem of her dress sailed around her knees.

Judging from her blue-and-white gingham and the milk pail on her arm, I took it that she was playing a farmer's daughter. She wore her hair in two braids, with fat pink bows tied around the tail of each, and carried white satin dancing shoes embellished with the kind of dainty beadwork that wouldn't last an hour on a farm.

"I'm auditioning for the fall play tomorrow," she said, hopping over to offer me a better look at her handiwork. "Helen wants to play my twin sister. We aren't supposed to come in costume, but it's no trouble to put a dress together and I think they'll have to cast us, don't you?"

I took the hem between my fingers and admired the stitching. Norma stared pointedly at her newspaper.

"I don't think you'll have any trouble getting the part," I said.

Having Fleurette perform for others—and not just for the two of us in our parlor—was a novelty in our household. When the sheriff first offered me a job two months ago, I knew better than to go to work without finding some way to keep Fleurette occupied as well. She thought she should go to New York, but Norma and I managed to convince her that eighteen-year-old girls didn't go to New York by themselves unless they were orphans working in factories, or society girls under the interference of a chaperone. We told her that Paterson would have to suffice and enrolled her at Mrs. Hansen's Academy of Music and Dance. Right away she made a friend in Helen Stewart, a red-headed Scottish girl who was as fine and fair as Fleurette was dark and dramatic. They both had ambitions for the stage that I hoped could be contained within the walls of Mrs. Hansen's school.

It pained me that Fleurette had never had a friend her own age before, a consequence of schooling her at home and our quiet life in the countryside. The isolation didn't bother me and Norma, but we were past the age when girls needed a friend with whom to share secrets. Our mother hadn't any friends either, but she never wanted any. She disliked strangers, the natural result of which was that she associated with very few people who weren't either known to her from birth or born to her.

We fled Brooklyn for New Jersey precisely to get away from the few people who did know us and might question how a baby had come to be added to our family. If Mother was forced to reveal anything about us at all to our neighbors out in Wyckoff, she gave only the general impression that her husband had died. This was explanation enough for anyone who might question why a woman in her forties was living alone on a farm with two nearly grown daughters, an adult son (our brother, Francis, now married and living in Hawthorne), and a baby girl.

Fleurette grew up believing me to be her sister. The only two people who knew the truth were Norma and Francis. It was a secret that held a terrible power over me when I was younger, but in the last few years, we'd survived my mother's death, the kidnapping threats that first brought Sheriff Heath to us, and, most recently, Fleurette's eighteenth birthday. For the first time, we were finding our way out into the world.

Even Norma had put herself on a new path. She ran an advertisement in the *Paterson Evening News* soliciting members for the New Jersey Society for the Deployment of Messenger Pigeons to Aid in Civic Affairs, an organization of her own creation whose name sprang wholly formed from her staid and stodgy imagination. Fleurette tried to suggest something more spirited, such as the Paterson Pigeon Fanciers, which was rejected on the grounds that we lived in Wyckoff, not Paterson. She then put forth Winged Messengers, which Norma thought sounded too mystical, and then she proposed my favorite, the Association of Intelligent Birds, on which Norma refused to pass comment.

"The name need only explain our undertaking," Norma argued, "and I don't want anything that attracts show breeders and fanciers. We've far more important work to do."

She had almost two dozen answers to her advertisement. The newspaper misprinted her name, calling her Norman Kopp rather than Norma, the result being that a few men dropped out when they understood a woman would be running the show. And there was never any question that Norma would have full charge of club affairs: she appointed herself both president and recording secretary and saw no need for any other officers or voting members.

"It isn't really a society, is it?" Fleurette said when she saw the circular Norma had neatly typed with her name in every leadership position. "It's more of a battalion, with you as the colonel."

Every Saturday fourteen people arrived at our house at dawn with their pigeons packed in baskets and ready to fly. There were half a dozen women in the group. (I hadn't any idea that there were so many other women raising pigeons in the barns of Bergen County.) A few of them brought a brother or father along. The rest of the group was made up of farmers who raised pigeons along with chickens, ducks, geese, guinea fowl, turkeys, and any other manner of bird that could be raised economically and sold at a profit.

None had any real experience in training pigeons to do what came naturally, which was to fly directly home after being transported a great distance. While all pigeons were possessed of this innate ability, Norma had lately come to believe that a methodical training program, begun at birth, would result in pigeons that flew at greater speeds and higher altitudes, making them of better use to doctors, police, and anyone else in need of a way of getting messages to far-flung places where telephone wires didn't reach.

It was a relief to see Norma and Fleurette both engaged in their own affairs. Francis used to fret over our ability to run our own lives, but he seemed resigned to the fact that we weren't about to let him take over. He still stopped by to deliver a pie from his wife, Bessie—for which we were endlessly grateful—and he would inspect the eaves or look around the barn with a proprietary air. Sometimes he made inquiries about our grazing land, which we leased to neighbors rather than keep our own livestock. We weren't bothered by his questions. We were taking care of ourselves, and my wages were just enough to keep Norma in pigeon feed and Fleurette in ribbons and buttons.

If only I could hold on to those wages.

Fleurette was admiring herself in the little oval mirror above the mantel. "If I'm cast in the play, I expect you both to come and see me every night of the run. We've two months of rehearsals and we open in late October. Plan accordingly."

Norma looked over the top of her paper with real dread in her eyes. "I'll send a representative."

"If you don't come, I'll have Constance arrest you."

Norma snorted. "Constance hasn't the authority to arrest a runaway dog."

Fleurette spun around and looked down at me, her hands on her hips. "If you're not allowed to arrest people, what are you going to do, exactly?"

❧ 3 ❧

"I'VE NEVER HAD a lady guard before," Mary Lisco said.

"They didn't have one in Newark?" Martha Hicks asked. Martha had been arrested for stealing hosiery from the department store where she worked.

"No, and they didn't have one in New Brunswick either, or in Yonkers."

"Gee, you've been in a lot of jails," Martha said.

"They don't keep me long. If they do, I find a way out."

Mary Lisco had escaped from the city jail in Newark and made her way to Hackensack, where she was caught putting her hand in the purse of the mayor's wife. She had glossy hair the color of honey and the figure of a chorus girl. I had an idea about how she slipped out of jail so easily, and it didn't involve a lady guard.

Mary might not have had the name for my job exactly right, but it was close enough. I was the jail matron, a perfectly legal job for a woman and the only position, other than stenographer, that Sheriff Heath could offer me after he stripped me of my duties as deputy. I had charge of the female section on the jail's fifth floor, which usually held only three or four inmates. The women tended to be better behaved than the men and rarely gave me trouble. I devised ways to keep them busy, oversaw their chores, and read to them if they didn't know how. It was simple work that any capable woman could have done—and I'd been doing it for longer than I should have.

I never liked to admit this, but Norma had been absolutely right. One month had stretched into two. It was late October and I was still without a badge. I had the authority to decide whether or not to let these two girl thieves out of their cells for a little fresh air, but I hadn't the authority to arrest them in the first place and I felt diminished because of it.

I swung open Mary's door and Martha's. Mary had only just been arrested the night before and this was her first time out of her cell. "You can walk around your cell block during the day and stretch your legs," I told her. "Did they let you do that in Newark?"

Mary raised an eyebrow but didn't answer. She and Martha stepped out of their cells at the same time and looked each other over, having only been acquainted through the sound of their voices thus far. Martha had thin lips and a narrow nose that had been broken, and the long, loosely jointed fingers of a piano player. I saw Mary look her up and down and decide if she could be put to use.

The jail was equipped with casement windows that could be cranked open by anyone who possessed a key. I gave the handle a half-turn, which was as far as the bars would allow it to go, and the noise from the street below rushed in: the rattle of motor cars, the ringing of trolley bells, and a man shouting something unintelligible at a horse.

The girls leaned against the window like two housewives

meeting over the back fence. A brisk autumn breeze sailed in and Martha took a long, deep breath. "Oh, I like that."

"It's the smell of civilization," Mary said.

Inmates loved to get a whiff of downtown Hackensack: the wet green wood from a cabinet shop, the long squat bakery behind Main Street that churned out loaves for the restaurants, and even the coal stacks and coughing, sputtering automobiles.

That smell had become part of my daily life as well. I'd always had charge of the female section, ever since Sheriff Heath first hired me, and it was customary for me to look after the women inmates when I wasn't out on a call. I never minded it and believed a jail matron to be necessary if the women were to be properly cared for. But now it was all I did, and with so few women in our custody, the days tended to drag.

I was beginning to suspect that Sheriff Heath was reluctant to mount a legal defense if he was challenged over appointing me deputy. Every day he faced some new criticism from the papers or the Board of Freeholders and he didn't need another. He also likely feared his wife's wrath if the papers got hold of a story about Bergen County's new female officer arresting a man or getting into some unfeminine scrape with a criminal. Mrs. Heath didn't care for her husband's progressive ideas, nor did she like the way they invited the ridicule of reporters. There would be a price to pay—at home and in the public eye—for giving me a badge and turning me loose on the streets of Hackensack.

Or did he harbor doubts as to whether I could do the job? He'd never said as much, but he might not have wanted to admit that he'd made a mistake. I thought over and over about the cases we'd worked together, and wondered where I might have gone wrong. I had strength enough—I was of a more substantial size than some of the other deputies—and he'd seen me handle a suspect. Surely he knew I wasn't prone to fright or hysteria. It was true that I was inexperienced, but where was my experience to come from if I didn't have the job?

Worries like these had a way of infecting my mind, especially with so much idle time on my hands. Had I enjoyed knitting, I would have kept the Red Cross in scarves all winter. Instead I watched Martha and Mary plant their elbows on the window-sill and press their foreheads against the glass, two conspirators planning mischief in low voices, and wondered what morally instructive activity I might contrive for them.

There were only two other inmates under my care: Ida Higgins, who'd been accused of setting fire to her brother's house over some family dispute we hadn't yet worked out, and a grandmother charged with neglect after her grandchildren were found locked in a barn and eaten up with lice. The grandmother was senile and possibly insane. She often mumbled to herself but had nothing to say to the rest of us. If we couldn't get her to tell us something soon, she'd almost certainly be committed to the asylum at Morris Plains and her grandchildren left under the permanent care of an orphanage.

Both she and Ida were snoring quietly in their cells. I was in danger of nodding off myself when Sheriff Heath called to me from the top of the stairs. He'd developed the habit of announcing himself before he entered the female section, which I thought strange considering that there had always been a man working on this floor before. But there he stood, modestly, his eyes on his shoes, so I excused myself and went to see him.

He carried his coat and hat. "Come and help me with a lady in Garfield."

I could tell from his tone that he didn't want to discuss it within earshot of the inmates. I put the girls back in their cells. "Do your cleaning," I told them.

"We clean every day," Martha protested. "I might like a little dust for company."

"You wouldn't have a cigarette, would you?" Mary called after me. That made Martha laugh.

"Did they give you cigarettes in Newark?" I asked.

"No. That's why I had to leave."

I let the girls have their joke and followed Sheriff Heath down the stairs and out to the garage. His mechanic had the wagon out and ready for us.

"We're just going over to Malcolm Avenue." He opened the door for me and ran around to the other side. "A lady shot her boarder."

"What for?" I asked.

"Something about the rent."

"Are you sure I should go along?" I hadn't been out with him on a case since the Harold Meeker arrest, two months ago.

He settled in behind the steering wheel and looked at me from under the brim of his hat. "Do you imagine I enjoy having lawyers tell me how to run my office?"

"You are a lawman. You're expected to follow the law, not just enforce it."

"This is a murder. It's the first one involving a female shooter this year. A lady deputy might get a confession where a man wouldn't."

He wasn't asking my opinion, but he did wait and watch me. "She might."

"Besides, she's already been arrested. That makes her my inmate. You have charge of the women, so you should come and collect her. That's how I see it."

That suited me just fine, so I didn't say another word. There rose up in me the peculiar thrill that goes along with a ghastly crime: a woman accused, a fallen victim, and reporters writing their lurid headlines. It was like being on a horse at the moment it broke into a gallop. I was in motion again, at last.

When we reached the corner of Malcolm and Clark, we found two police officers waiting for us on the front lawn of a run-down brick lodging-house. An upstairs window was broken and boarded over. Weeds sprouted from the roof. It looked like the kind of place where people were shot over the rent money.

On the front steps, a man's shoes sat marooned in a pool of blood. Tufts of clover and dandelion around the steps were smeared with it as well. The officers stood with their hands on their hips, staring down at the mess as if they were reading tea leaves. One of them, Stevens, was a man of about sixty who started working in Hackensack law enforcement when it was nothing but a volunteer protective league equipped with target rifles and draft horses. I hadn't met the younger officer and took him to be a new recruit.

"Where is she?" Sheriff Heath asked.

"Down in the basement, talking to the detective," Stevens said. "They just took the victim to the hospital."

"I take it those are his shoes," the sheriff said. "Is he still alive?"

The officer shrugged. "For now. She got him in the shoulder, and he sure did bleed. Looks like a goner to me."

Sheriff Heath sighed and nodded to me. I pulled a notebook out of my handbag. We had to be prepared for the possibility of a confession while she was under our supervision.

"What's the name of the victim?" I asked.

"Saverio Salino," the younger officer said. "Are you the new stenographer?"

"This is Miss Kopp," Sheriff Heath said. "She's the ladies' matron at the jail."

"There's a lady working at the jail? Inside, you mean?"

Officer Stevens interjected. "They've a lady police officer over in Paterson now, too. Looking after dance halls and the like. The mayor doesn't like to see paint on the girls' cheeks and she goes around with a handkerchief rubbing it off."

"If we can get to business," Sheriff Heath said.

"Salino worked at the munitions plant with Mrs. Monafo," Stevens said. "She rents rooms to some of the young fellows who work over there."

"Is that the shooter?" I said. "Munafo?"

"Monafo," the younger officer repeated, spelling it. "Given name is Providencia."

"Spanish?" the sheriff asked.

Officer Stevens shrugged. "Italian, more like."

"They don't like the war over there, but they come over here and make bullets and bombs," Sheriff Heath said. "What else do we know?"

"She claims Salino had a sister living with him but refused to pay any extra rent," Stevens said. "They got into a fight over it and he threatened to beat her up. That's when she shot him. She got scared and ran right out of here and jumped on a streetcar. Then I guess she thought better of it and came back."

"She came back?" the sheriff said. "Why?"

"Maybe she had nowhere else to go, or maybe she knew we'd finger her anyway. By the time she got back, Salino had dragged himself up the stairs, and there he lay, in full view. Someone saw him and telephoned."

"Where's the sister?" Sheriff Heath asked.

"Nobody's seen her."

"How do we know she was really his sister?" I asked.

"Who?" the younger officer said.

Stevens punched him in the arm. "Who do you think? She's asking if the sister was really his sister, or maybe she was a lady friend."

The officer rubbed his arm. "I hadn't thought of that."

"You don't think of much, do you?" Stevens said.

Sheriff Heath was looking restless. "We'd better go meet our prisoner. Who's down there with her?"

"John Courter." Stevens made a sympathetic face when he said it.

Sheriff Heath reached up and shifted his hat. "We'll manage. Let's go, Miss Kopp."

It was a popular saying around the Hackensack jail that no sheriff could keep the peace without disturbing it in equal measure. While Sheriff Heath possessed an agreeable and well-mannered disposition, he had more than his share of enemies. Since his election, he'd criticized the Board of Freeholders over the expensive but poorly constructed new jail he was given to run, feuded publicly with the county physician over medical care for the prisoners, and exposed the negligence of Detective John Courter in the newspapers.

This last dispute had been the most costly. A sheriff needed friends in the prosecutor's office if he wanted to see his cases tried and cleared. But Detective Courter refused to cooperate in any investigation involving the office of the sheriff, and contrived to lose evidence and miss court dates if it would put Sheriff Heath in an unfavorable light.

I was the cause of the trouble between them. When Mr. Courter refused to prosecute the man who was threatening my family, I aired my complaints against him in the newspapers. Since then he'd kept up a steady and persistent feud against the sheriff. I hadn't seen him in months and wasn't looking forward to doing so again.

The sheriff jumped over the doorstep to avoid the victim's shoes and the blood stain. He held his hand out to me, a gesture I generally refused on the grounds that I needed no help in getting around, but he took a firm grip on my elbow before I could say anything and pulled me across.

We stood together in the dim, wood-paneled entrance to the boarding-house. A staircase to the right led up to the second floor, and to our left was the door to a parlor apartment. An old gas lamp of yellow glass and tarnished brass swayed above us. A set of pigeon-holes on the wall were marked with the names of each tenant. Saverio Salino occupied a room on the third floor. Mr. and Mrs. Monafo lived in the basement.

I followed Sheriff Heath down to the end of the hall, where a narrow door opened into a makeshift stairwell. Although we could hear Detective Courter talking, there seemed to be no lights on below. He turned around to me.

"Can you see down there?"

"Of course." I wished he wouldn't be so careful with me.

He paused and tilted his head in the direction of John Courter's voice. "I guess I'd better do the talking."

"Please do." I couldn't think of a single civil word to say to that man.

At the bottom of the stairs the sheriff knocked on the door jamb and, without waiting for an answer, entered the shabbiest apartment I'd ever seen. The concrete floors were covered in overlapping rugs that looked like they'd been discarded once, pulled out of the garbage for someone else's use, and cast off again before being rescued by the Monafos. Mice had chewed holes through the rugs long before President Cleveland took office and returned again at some point during Mr. Roosevelt's tenure. The walls had been papered with what might have once been a pattern of red and white roses, but now looked like a patchwork of grease stains and nameless filth interlaced with the permanent ochre of tobacco smoke.

The room—and it was only a single large room with a boiler in the back—was incoherently crowded with furniture in the manner of people who could not afford a single nice thing and instead collected every broken and rotten thing that came their way. There were wooden chairs with three legs, pillows leaking their stuffing, tables with holes burned through the top, and a sagging iron bed whose posts were nearly rusted through. In one corner stood an old coal stove and a metal trough for a sink. Judging from the odor of spoiled milk, I gathered that the Monafos had no means of cooling their food. There was also no toilet, which suggested the possibility of an upstairs water closet shared with the boarders, or a privy out back.

In the middle of this mess stood John Courter, his hands in his pockets, looking down on a heap of scarves and rags that contained within it Providencia Monafo. Between the two of them, on a spot of bare floor, was another stagnation of blood. It had begun to attract flies.

"I hope this is the scene of the crime," I said.

The detective might have been expecting the sheriff to come and take her away, but he wasn't expecting me. He took a step back when he recognized me.

"Can't you leave your lady friends at home, Sheriff? This is an official matter."

"Miss Kopp is the matron at the jail," Sheriff Heath said stiffly. "She comes along when we have a female to transport. Is Mrs. Monafo to be placed in my custody?"

But Detective Courter hadn't unhitched himself from the topic. "It's not my business if you have a girl running a sewing circle at the jail, but this is a murder. I called for a deputy."

Last year I threw a man against a wall when he made me angry. I'd been trying not to do that anymore. Still, something about Detective Courter made me want to knock him around. The sheriff paid him no attention at all and I endeavored to do the same.

I knelt down in front of the woman. "Mrs. Monafo, we've come to take you to the Hackensack jail on the charge of shooting Saverio Salino. Have you anything to say before we go?"

She pulled a scarf away from her face and looked out at me. She was older than I'd expected, with loose folds of skin that wobbled about her chin as she moved, and pale, shriveled lips. A shock of gray hair fell across her eyes.

"I shoot him to protect me." She spoke English with the

Italian cadence common to the immigrants who worked in the factories. "He make threat to attack me and then to kill me, and he say my husband never know what happen."

Detective Courter jingled the coins in his pocket. "I'm pretty sure your husband would've noticed a dead wife, Mrs. Monafo." He was one of those men who spoke loudly to immigrants on the assumption that they only understood English if it was shouted at them. "I'd like to know the whereabouts of that husband of yours. If I don't find your fingerprints on the gun, I'll be wanting to have a look at his." He patted his coat pocket, where I supposed he had the gun tucked away.

Providencia Monafo gave a feeble shrug. Sheriff Heath nudged my shoulder and I said, "The detective is here to take your statement." I made sure each word came out slowly and clearly. "Mr. Salino may die at the hospital."

What I was trying to let her know, without saying so directly, was that if she confessed to shooting Salino, she might also be confessing to killing him. Sheriff Heath had a similar case go badly last year, when a man confessed to beating a night guard before he knew that the guard had died from the injuries. The confession was thrown out because the man had made it without realizing he was confessing to murder. That man went free. Sheriff Heath didn't want Mrs. Monafo to be acquitted for the same reason.

My warnings didn't seem to matter. She jutted out her shaky chin and said, "I shoot him. If he die, they bury him. It don't matter to me."

The detective smiled, his mustache stretching and wiggling as he repeated her statement to himself and jotted it down. He closed his notebook and nodded. "Now I've you two as witnesses to the confession. I hope you enjoy Mrs.

Monafo's delightful company. She'll be in your custody for a good long while."

"That'll be fine," I muttered, and reached into the pile of filthy rags that Mrs. Monafo had wrapped around herself. I took hold of an arm and pulled her to her feet. She was only five feet tall, the same as Fleurette. She cackled when she saw the way I towered over her.

"No wonder they make you police," she said.

⇥ 4 ⇤

PROVIDENCIA MONAFO CARRIED with her to jail hundreds of minuscule inmates of the six-legged variety, all latched to her skin and gulping down what was to be their final meal. We kept a separate prisoner entrance for this very reason. Inside, a brick- and concrete-lined hallway led to a tiled shower room that was furnished only with a metal chair and a wire bin.

The chair was for me. I sat just outside the range of the shower and ordered Mrs. Monafo to disrobe and stand under the stream of hot water. To my relief, she obeyed. I didn't particularly want to get into a struggle over the removal of her clothing. She scrubbed herself with naphtha soap until I told her she could stop. Then I handed her a towel and a cotton gown of the sort issued to hospital patients, and offered my chair to her. Once she was seated, I told her to hold the towel to her face while I combed her hair with mercurial ointment. The more tenacious inhabitants of her scalp came away in drifts, clinging to loose hairs that I dispatched into a jar of alcohol as I worked.

The ointment tended to raise blisters, so I sent her back to the shower for another assault with the soap and hot water. When she was finished I combed her hair again with petroleum oil to smother whatever stowaways remained.

The wire bin was for Mrs. Monafo's clothing, which would be taken directly outside and burned behind the garage. The hospital gown and towel would go into a bucket of hot water and borax that very night. I issued Mrs. Monafo a new set of underclothes and a house dress, along with a cap for her oily hair and a pair of knitted slippers. I assured her that we'd find her a more serviceable dress in the morning.

This was the method by which every inmate entered the Hackensack jail. It had become an ordinary matter to me. In fact, I took a strange satisfaction from it. I might not ever see these women cleansed of their crimes and misdeeds, and I might not keep them from misfortune and misery, but I could rid them of vermin and send them to sleep in a clean and quiet bed. For some of them, it was the first night they'd spent free of torment—of one kind or another—in years.

Mrs. Monafo had little to say to me that afternoon. I found it best to leave the women alone at first and to wait for them to come to me if they had something to confide. I put her in a quiet cell at the end of a block and brought her the usual Monday night supper of molasses, bread, and coffee. There was a little mutton stew left from lunch, so I spooned that into a cup as well. She sniffed it dubiously.

"Do you like to cook, Mrs. Monafo?" I asked.

She looked in my direction but didn't answer.

"The inmates do all the cooking here. It's a new program of Sheriff Heath's. Our cook used to make his living as a second-story man, but we've found he has a talent for stews and chops as well. Perhaps you'll cook for us one day."

She blinked and said nothing. Even in her clean cotton house dress she had the look of a bundle of rags about her. Sometimes the vestiges of a woman's old life hung on for weeks, and sometimes she never shed them at all.

I WOULD LET Mrs. Monafo rest for a few days and not bother her with the inmate work program. As jail matron I had charge of the women's duties, which were really nothing but a routine of cooking, laundry, and cleaning, and therefore familiar to them. It was the belief of Sheriff Heath and some of the other more reform-minded sheriffs in the state that the criminal mind could be rehabilitated by imposing order upon a disordered life. According to this line of thinking, women committed fewer crimes precisely because their days were filled with domestic duties.

But we always had a woman or two who managed to stay at home and do the cooking and cleaning while still finding time to commit a monstrous crime. Some of them stitched their drunken husbands into the sheets while they slept and beat them with broom handles. Some of them poisoned their mothers-in-law with spoonfuls of sugar laced with arsenic. Some of them set their houses on fire. They did all of this without ever leaving home.

I wasn't convinced that giving women the same chores they'd been doing right before they fired the gun or slipped the poison into the sugar would go very far in reforming their characters. I would've rather seen them take a course or learn a trade, but we had nothing like that on offer. Instead I tried to keep them busy throughout the day, with the exception of older women like Providencia, whom I permitted to lie down in the afternoon and rest their eyes, as I had known women of that age to do all my life. I could think of no advantage in depriving a stout, mature woman, who had been on her feet all day, of a little rest in the afternoon. And Providencia Monafo looked like she had been on her feet her entire life.

When I took the rags she'd been wearing out to the burn bin behind the garage, I stood for a minute under the gray and chilly sky. The steam heating had only just come on for the winter and it made the jail's top floor unseasonably warm. The wind stung as it came across the Hackensack River, but it was exactly what I needed. I shook my skirts out and loosened my collar.

The lights were just coming on in the Heath family's apartment. The sheriff, his wife, Cordelia, and their two children lived in an austere set of rooms on the first floor, facing the river and the drive by which all motor cars and inmates arrived. It couldn't have been a pleasant place to live, but the sheriff was required to reside at the jail and to supervise it around the clock.

I was about to go inside when I saw a young deputy named Thomas English walk around the corner with a man in chains. He must have been bringing him back from the courthouse next door, where the inmates often had to go for hearings or appeals. Being occupied with his inmate, he didn't notice that the Heaths' maid, a young girl named Grayce van Horn, had stepped out of the apartment to shake a rug. He was leading the man right to her.

I saw what happened next but I was too far away to stop it. The inmate turned to the girl and said something that made her shriek and drop the rug. She ran inside and the man made a move to go after her. Deputy English probably had him well in hand, but the sight was too much for me and I ran up the gravel drive and reached for the inmate. I stumbled as I took hold of him and knocked him over, taking the deputy with him. The three of us went down in an undignified heap.

"What did you say to her?" I shouted, my knee in his back and my skirts in disarray.

With his face in the gravel, his voice was faint and tinny.

"Fräulein Kopp, mein Engel."

I rocked back on my heels. It was Herman Albert von Matthesius, an old German who'd been in our custody since June. He had the dignified face of a scholar, with a high forehead, a sharply chiseled nose, and a strong chin with one dimple squarely in the center. He wore wire-rimmed spectacles that had become dislodged in the commotion.

"I'm not your angel," I said. I hated that he insisted on speaking to me in German. The situation in Europe was growing graver by the day and anyone caught speaking in the Kaiser's tongue could be accused of spying or disloyalty. But the sheriff knew that I'd grown up speaking French and German, so from time to time he called upon me to translate. One day von Matthesius heard me speaking in German to an old rail-yard worker who had been arrested for stealing coal. From then on, he considered me his confidante.

There was something sneaky and manipulative about the man, and hearing him speak to me in the old intimate language my mother taught me always made me feel exposed. English was the language of Sheriff Heath's jail. German was the language of our kitchen table and Mother's old bed and a closet under the stairs where Norma and I would hide as small children and listen to our parents fight in their mother tongues, before they realized that we had absorbed every language spoken under our roof.

Deputy English scrambled to his feet and jerked the inmate up by the shoulder. "What in hell do you mean by knocking us over? Aren't you supposed to be upstairs in your chicken coop?" That's what the guards called the female section. Two or three female inmates together was a hen party. Only Sheriff Heath and Deputy Morris called the fifth floor by its proper name.

I shook the gravel out of my dress. "What did he say to that girl?"

Deputy English squinted at me. He was one of those lean, wiry young men whose sharp and even features could make him look handsome if he tried, or brutal if he let anger get the better of him. He had brown eyes that were flat and expressionless, giving me the uncomfortable sense that he never meant what he was saying. He was too sure of himself and too certain that he knew more than Sheriff Heath or any of the rest of us.

"Leave that to me." He pulled at von Matthesius's handcuffs with one hand and put another hand on the man's back. "And try not to go stampeding over people like a circus elephant."

The inmate smiled and used his shoulder to push his glasses up on his nose. "I was only offering my greetings to Miss van Horn and her good brother who looks after her." His voice made a thin whistle through his teeth when he spoke. Deputy English yanked him away without another word and took him inside.

Now I understood. He'd found out something about Grayce and used it to rattle her and, through her, to intimidate the Heath family. Some inmates liked us to know that they had help outside—and that their helpers could find out more about us than we knew about them. It was an old trick, but none of us liked to see it played.

Von Matthesius had a habit of listening closely to the conversations that echoed up and down the jail's central rotunda and remembering everything he heard. I was careful not to speak of my family at work, but within a week he knew Norma and Fleurette by name, and understood that we lived alone in the countryside. He also knew about Sheriff Heath's family, and had the nerve to ask his brother Felix to deliver a bouquet of flowers to Mrs. Heath during one of his weekly visits. On the card was written, "To dear and gracious Cordelia, on the occasion of her birthday, with appreciation and good wishes from a friend and admirer, Rev. Dr. Baron Herman Albert von Matthesius."

Mrs. Heath had, in fact, celebrated her birthday only two days before. The delivery unnerved her so that she nearly took the children and moved back to her mother's. The sheriff spent an entire afternoon persuading her to stay.

I knocked on the door to the sheriff's apartment and called to Grayce. She opened the door, peeked out at me, and let me into the Heaths' sitting room, where she dropped into a chair with her arms folded across her chest and her chin tucked down into her collar. She was seventeen but had the fat cheeks of a child and a little pursed mouth that looked like it hadn't yet found much to say. Her hair hung down in two braids, both tied with blue ribbons. The ends were tattered from the Heath children pulling at them.

I sat down across from her. "I'm sorry about that old man. You shouldn't ever have to see the prisoners. I'll speak to the sheriff about it."

She sniffed and said, "My brother doesn't like me working here and I might agree with him. I don't know how Mrs. Heath tolerates it."

I leaned back and looked around the room. There was hardly an inch of fabric Cordelia Heath hadn't embellished with peacock feathers, butterflies, and damask roses. I'd always felt that one could read a woman's discontent in the amount of embroidery in her sitting room. It gave me a crowded and nervous feeling to sit among so much frantic stitchery.

"Mrs. Heath has made it very comfortable." It seemed like the only decent thing to say.

The baby cried from the next room. We both stood up as little five-year-old Willie stumbled into the doorway. He was a perfect miniature of Sheriff Heath, all dark hair and solemn brown eyes. His sister, the baby crying behind him, favored her mother, with a halo of golden curls and delicate well-bred features.

"Willie, go back to bed," Grayce said. "Mother wants you to have your nap."

The boy just stood and stared at us, tugging at his yellow nightshirt. I usually only saw him from a distance, when Mrs. Heath walked the children to a park across from the courthouse in the afternoons and let the boy clamber over a bronze statue of a general from the Revolutionary War. There was nothing for the baby to do but sit on the grass in fair weather and pull out tufts of it. We had no garden at the jail, or yard, or any other place for a child to play.

Willie reached his arms out mutely. Grayce sighed and picked him up. Just as she disappeared into the next room, a key rattled in the door and Mrs. Heath walked in. She was too distracted with her hat and coat to notice me at first, but when she did look up, she gave a startled cry, as if she'd disturbed a burglar.

"What in Heaven's name?" One birdlike hand flew to her neck and clutched at her collar. She favored old lace that had some sort of pedigree. I suspected a patrician English grandmother as the source.

I said, in what I hoped was a calm and officious tone, "Everything's fine, ma'am. One of the inmates shouted at Grayce when she stepped outside. It gave her a shock and I thought I should sit with her."

"I thought you were to stay on the women's floor."

Grayce came back into the room and said, "Miss Kopp rushed right over when she saw what happened. That man had no right to speak to me."

"I'm surprised by you, Grayce," Mrs. Heath said quietly, composing herself long enough to pull off her earrings and set them on the table. "I thought you were such a level-headed girl. Did anyone see you?"

Grayce looked puzzled. "See me? Outside?"

"I'm sure no one saw, Mrs. Heath," I said.

She would never say so directly in front of hired help, but she was worried that a courthouse reporter had wandered over and witnessed the scene. Mrs. Heath had an unnatural dread of newspapermen and believed them to be lurking about the jail at all hours, ready with a notebook if any opportunity arose to embarrass the sheriff over some mishap.

"Well, then," Mrs. Heath said. "You may go on upstairs, Miss Kopp."

Nothing suited me more. The door leading to the jail's interior corridor was of a solid and unyielding metal, and I had to put my weight against it to open it.

"Although . . ."

I turned, wearily, and waited. She pursed her lips and tilted her head as if the idea had just come to her. "Couldn't we have someone else guard the ladies at night? I recall something about you having a home to go to. I've never been myself, but I understand my husband spent quite a bit of time there last year when you had your troubles with those men."

She had the kind of fine, aristocratic face that one sees on porcelain cameos, and she knew how to arrange her features in such a way as to belie the meaning behind her words. I had to remember that I was on duty and should conduct myself as a member of the sheriff's staff.

"Yes, ma'am. I live out in the country and it's too far to go every night. Now that the days are getting shorter, I'd have a long walk in the dark. Sheriff Heath thought I should take a cell alongside the female inmates." I had only recently outfitted my cell with a lamp, a quilt, and a few books and magazines. It was not unusual anymore for me to fall asleep to the sobs of a girl pickpocket on her first night in, the mumbled prayers of a lonely woman afflicted with gout and a penchant for arson, and the symphony of snorts, groans, and whispers sent up from the men downstairs. It was never entirely peaceful, but I'd grown accustomed to it.

A shudder came over me as I heard myself tell the sheriff's wife that I'd been speaking to her husband about my sleeping arrangements. I hoped she couldn't see the flush creeping up my neck.

Her eyebrows lifted. "Well. If you're living under this roof, you must see quite a lot. You will remember not to speak of any disturbance at the jail. The reporters know you, and they will ask."

She made it sound disgraceful to be the kind of woman known to reporters. In my case, she might have been right. Some people aspired to the society page, but I'd only ever been found among the crime reports.

✦ 5 ✦

THE NEXT NIGHT a guard summoned me downstairs.

"Sheriff's outside, miss. Asked to speak to you."

I was about to call lights-out anyway, so I made sure everyone was in bed and went down. Sheriff Heath had just driven into the garage and was waiting for me there. It had been raining all afternoon and the path from the jail was nothing but a series of puddles with minor archipelagoes of gravel between them. I hopped from one to the next, my skirts hitched up as high as I was willing to take them, but I was entirely soaked by the time I reached the garage.

He was standing by the fire, talking to his mechanic. I ducked under the awning and breathed in the familiar smell of leather and motor oil, wood smoke and sweat.

"We need you at the hospital," the sheriff said. "Von Matthesius is raving in German. They had a German nurse to translate, but she's off-duty and they haven't been able to find her."

"I didn't know he'd gone to the hospital. What's the matter with him?" I worried suddenly that I'd knocked a rib loose when I threw him down.

He lifted his hat and rubbed his temples. "That's what we'd like you to tell us, Miss Kopp. He has a fever and a sweat, and his heart is weak, but the doctors haven't been able to find anything particularly wrong. They were about to release him when he coughed up blood and started shouting in German."

"He could tell them in English," I said as we settled into the sheriff's motor car. "He's perfectly capable of it."

"But he won't. He's making us do it his way. I don't like it either, but if he's got something of consequence to say, I'd like to hear it before they release him. After that business with Grayce yesterday, I'd just as soon leave him there." We rolled down the drive and I buttoned my coat against the cold.

"He didn't seem ill."

"But how are we to know? We can't do much longer without a jail physician." Sheriff Heath spoke under his breath, as if talking to himself. "It's unfair to the inmates. They're locked inside and can't very well send for a doctor themselves. They depend upon us. But I can't be the one to decide when to take a man to the hospital. And everybody who comes in here has a bunion and a loose tooth and gout or a fever or some damn thing or another. It's practically an infirmary already, except we've got no doctors, no nurses, and no druggist. We should fix them up a little while they're here, and not just because it's our Christian duty, but because we have an opportunity to put them on a path to clean living. Give a man a shower and a hot meal and a Bible to study and hard work to keep his hands busy—that's how you turn a criminal into a citizen. Not by locking him in a dungeon."

Sheriff Heath was a quiet man, but he knew how to make a speech. I studied his profile, which was already as familiar to me as my own brother's. It occurred to me that there was something admirable about a man in his late thirties. He was old enough to know his own mind and still young enough to do something about it.

"Those are fine ideas," I said. "It's why the voters put you here."

"I wonder. Cordelia says the voters didn't elect me to save souls and only want to see criminals put away. And she was none too pleased to see that business with Grayce make the papers. She says it makes us look like we can't control our inmates."

"How did it make the papers? No one saw."

He shrugged. "I think Grayce talked to a reporter, or her brother did. I told Cordelia not to worry about it. An inmate misbehaved. It's not even worth writing about, unless you're a reporter getting paid by the word."

Main Street was crowded, even in the rain, and it was slow going. We rode along in silence until I said, "What was von Matthesius's crime? I must have read about it at the time, but I don't recall."

It wasn't actually true that I didn't recall. In fact, I'd never been told. The crime had been scandalous in some way that had never been satisfactorily explained to me. None of the men—not the sheriff, not the deputies, not the guards—could bring themselves to tell me precisely why some of the men were in our custody.

Sheriff Heath coughed and didn't look at me. "Serious charges," he said.

This was the newspapers' way of hinting at a crime too aberrant to be described in a family newspaper. I'd never heard the sheriff use the term, but perhaps he'd never had cause to.

"He was running a sanitarium in Rutherford and three young men under his employment accused him."

"Accused him of . . ."

But the sheriff wasn't telling. "I don't believe he's any sort of doctor. You know he calls himself a reverend and a baron. He seems to collect titles whether he deserves them or not. I'm glad to be depriving New Jersey of his criminal mischief, but I don't know how we'll endure another year of it."

"Couldn't he pay the fine?" Any number of crimes in Bergen County were met with a sentence to be served only if the fine wasn't paid.

"There was a fine, but he doesn't have the money. I heard the sanitarium was filled with antiques and paintings. I don't know what's become of them." That was all the sheriff would say.

"Well, I'm glad to go out on some calls again," I ventured. "I hope this means you've found a way to return me to my old job."

"Is the position of jail matron too dull for you, Miss Kopp?" he asked distractedly, leaning forward to try to see through the glass. The rain made it impossible.

"I only mean to say that I've been out on two calls in as many days, and that's an improvement. I'm sure I can be of better use—"

"I'm sure you can," he said, but he was hardly listening. "What's happened up here?"

The Hackensack Hospital was a formidable six-story block of red brick and iron columns. The circular drive in front was so choked with carriages and hulking black automobiles that we couldn't find a place to stop. Nurses ran back and forth between them, shouting to drivers who could not hear and only blew their horns. Lanterns were being passed around, bobbing and swinging in the dark. By their light I caught a glimpse of a man being carried in by his feet and shoulders. Electric lamps blazed from the entrance to the hospital, but there were so many people crowding the doorway that I could only make out the silhouette of a mob in panic.

Deputy English had been watching for us. He ran out into the rain, dodging the vehicles and the doctors rushing to pull patients from them.

"Wreck on the train tracks," he said, leaning in through the window on Sheriff Heath's side. His eyes flickered up at me and away again. "A wagon loaded up with Italians coming in from one of those factories outside of Newark. Drove right through the crossing. They brought in eight men just now, but it looks like there's more."

Rain dripped off his hat and down the end of his nose. He looked at Sheriff Heath expectantly. Behind us a horn squawked and a man yelled for us to get off the street.

"Go tell that man to be civil and to drive around if he's got business at the hospital," the sheriff said. The deputy ran off.

While we waited, thunder rumbled in the distance. A crack of lightning illuminated the hospital's bulk against the sky, but it was so faint that only one chimney came into view and then disappeared again into blackness.

Sheriff Heath shook his head. "I can't post a man at every crossing," he said, mostly to himself. "If people can't listen to a whistle, then I don't know what else to do about it."

Deputy English's face appeared in the sheriff's window

again. "I'd better stay and help sort this out," Sheriff Heath said to him. "Take Miss Kopp to von Matthesius."

To me he added, "See what you can find out, and be quick about it. I'll be there in a minute."

"Find out about what?" Deputy English asked, a little petulant.

Sheriff Heath raised his arm against an onslaught of rain coming through the window. "Just get her in there!"

I gathered the collar of my coat around my neck. The deputy and I dashed through the rain, dodging puddles on the patchy lawn and skirting the nurses and orderlies carrying in the injured. At the entrance we had to duck behind a doctor setting a dislocated shoulder. The patient—one of the factory men, I assumed—was splayed across a stretcher. A nurse had hold of each leg and another had taken his right arm. The doctor gripped the left arm and made ready to pull. We ran behind him just before he made his move. I heard the patient's screams all the way up the stairs.

After the turmoil on the first floor, it was blessedly quiet on the second. Deputy English marched down a narrow hall lined with wooden benches, all of which were empty, and I hurried to keep up. The doors to the sick wards, each one numbered in gold lettering on a small window meant to allow a nurse to look in, were all closed. Above us, the electric lights flickered in their dusty shades.

"It's that damn storm," he said. "We're going to be stuck here all night."

At the end of the hall we turned the corner and found a nurse sitting at a desk. "Miss Kopp to see the prisoner," the deputy said. "Sheriff's orders."

The nurse was one of those steely, silver-haired women who tolerated no nonsense from patients or doctors. She looked up at me through wire-rimmed glasses and said, "Hurry up, then. And take him on out of here if you can. We're going to need that bed."

We turned the corner and jogged down another hallway to von Matthesius's room. At the end of the hall were two tall windows, and to one side was a doorway leading to some other passage. An orderly was slumped over on a metal chair outside the prisoner's door, half-asleep.

Thomas English kicked at the chair and the orderly jumped to his feet. "Get on downstairs."

He yawned and pushed a lock of sandy-colored hair out of his eyes. "I don't think anybody's looking for me quite yet."

"Then you should go and look for them." Deputy English spoke through gritted teeth. It was enough to make the orderly jump up and run off, leaving us alone in the hall. "If there's anything worse than being stuck on guard duty at the jail," he said, "it's having to spend an entire afternoon at this hospital, making sure that a man who can't get out of bed doesn't get out of bed. What did I bring you here to do?"

"Sheriff Heath asked me to speak to him and then we are to wait."

"You spoke to him yesterday and nearly knocked the wind out of him."

"If you can speak German, you can do the translation yourself."

He turned and spit on the floor. "We should put the Germans on a boat and send them home. This is a waste of my time. I belong down there bringing in the wounded, not standing around with a sick old man and the sheriff's lady friend."

"Then go."

I wasn't going to let him draw me into a fight. Sheriff Heath should never have given this boy a badge and a gun. He wasn't ready for it. Boys like him were already sneaking into France by way of the Canadian Army, so eager for a chance to shoot at someone that they would pledge fidelity to another nation to do it. Being hotheaded and careless, they were the first to be killed.

"But you're the ladies' matron. You can't guard a male inmate," he said, in a simpering, singsong voice, the way a little boy delivers taunts. "Sheriff won't like it."

"He doesn't mind," I said. "Go on."

He looked me up and down and then glanced at the door to von Matthesius's room. His face was all hard angles and calculations. "All right. He's yours now."

He turned on his heel and marched off just as the windows rattled at the end of the hall and hail thrummed against the glass. Soon there was another low rumble of thunder, and the lights flickered again. He broke into a run, glancing back only once as he rounded the corner and vanished.

At last I eased the door open and took a look inside. Von Matthesius lay flat on his back in an iron bed. He'd been confined to a windowless room not much larger than a closet. Such rooms were reserved for the insane, the highly infectious, and the criminals sent over from the jail. There was no chair and no table. A suit of clothes hung on a hook. A wool blanket had been kicked to the floor.

When the door opened wide enough to cast a panel of light across the bed, his eyes flew open and darted in my direction. His head didn't move, and he spoke out of the side of his mouth. *"Ich bin sehr schwach auf den Beinen und es zieht sich bis in die Schultern hoch. Ich ertrage das nicht mehr lange."*

It was a litany of symptoms: he couldn't move his legs, he was having trouble with his shoulders, and he thought he might not live much longer. The strange incantation continued: his toes had gone numb, the blood had left his ankles, his lips were dry, and he had lost the sensation in his fingers.

I leaned over the bed to get a better look at him, taking care to stay just out of arm's reach. His lips never stopped moving and his eyes rolled around wildly. Drops of sweat sprung from his forehead like leaks in a rubber hose. Something brown and tarry leaked from the corners of his mouth, and there was blood on the pillowcase where he'd been coughing.

"Sind Sie durstig?" I asked. He didn't stop his chanting or his mad eye-rolling, but he did nod slightly. I looked around for a drinking glass, but saw nothing.

"I'll go out in just a minute and get you some water," I told him. "The doctors find nothing wrong with you. What do you believe to be the matter? If you can't tell me, you'll go back to jail."

His eyes rolled up until I saw nothing but the whites, little half-moons laced in red like the hairline cracks in porcelain. A tremor came over him that made his teeth rattle. Then he went limp and his eyelids dropped shut.

I wanted to keep him awake and talking until the sheriff arrived. So I knelt down next to him and kept my voice low. "Isn't there any sort of treatment that could help you?"

"Es ist zu spat." It is too late for that.

I sat back on my heels and watched him breathe in the murky half-light. His breaths came in long, shallow stanzas, with rests between them so protracted that I wasn't sure he was still breathing at all. In his better days he had worn a neatly trimmed silver mustache, but someone at the hospital had given him a crude shave and chopped at his hair to keep it out of his eyes. He looked like he'd aged ten years overnight.

A rattle in his throat turned into the kind of racking cough that can send a man into a fit. "You need some water," I said. "I'll be right back."

I stepped into the hall but saw no one. There wasn't a sink or a water fountain in sight. I didn't dare go looking for one: the door to von Matthesius's room held a plain glass knob and a keyhole below it, but I didn't have a key and Deputy English hadn't said anything about one. I could hear someone running down the stairs just beyond the nurses' station, but thought it best not to call after them for a glass of water when there were so many patients in worse condition downstairs.

When I went back to his room, von Matthesius had risen up and put one bare leg on the ground. He looked up at me and put a hand to his throat, gasping for breath. It might have been the strange shadows in the room, but I could swear his face was going a little blue.

"Try to be still." I put a hand to his chest and eased him back into bed. "You can breathe. Someone will be here in a minute."

He did seem to settle into a raspy wheeze. I stepped back to the door to watch for anyone who might be of help, and I was rewarded almost right away by a clatter outside and the sound of footsteps. A crowd of nurses and doctors rushed past, pushing two carts. I didn't dare stop them and they disappeared around the corner. Through the window at the end of the hall I heard an even greater uproar from the street below. I closed von Matthesius's door behind me and dashed over to get a better look.

Beneath me was a scene that could have been a battlefield. The hospital's circular drive was entirely overrun with motor cars and nervous horses lashed to their carriages. At least another dozen victims must have arrived from the wreckage. Some were being carried in, but others were stretched out on the grass, shielded by umbrellas and makeshift tents. Every nurse, orderly, doctor, cook, and janitor must have been outside, fighting through the crowd to bring the wounded in.

I looked across the street to a row of automobiles and saw the sheriff's. He was down there somewhere, one of the black hats bobbing in the dark. From above, the rain fell in streaks that caught the light from the hospital windows.

I was back at von Matthesius's door when another clap of thunder shook the walls and the lights went out. A groan rose up from the crowd outside. They'd have to operate entirely on lanterns and candles.

I opened the prisoner's door. "Baron? The lights have gone out everywhere."

He mumbled something and I leaned in far enough to make out his figure on the bed. I could hardly see anything, so with some reluctance I reached out a hand and took hold of a bony kneecap. He jumped and I pulled away. At least he'd stopped coughing.

"I'll be right outside," I said, and stood in the darkened hall. There wasn't even the faintest glow from the window, which meant that the street lamps must have gone out, too, and the rest of Hackensack, as far as I knew.

From somewhere down the hall, a metal tray clattered to the floor and a nurse called out, "Go on! I'll get it."

"Leave it," a man shouted back, and they rushed away. The wheels of another cart rolled past, accompanied by the rumble of more footsteps. I pressed myself against the door and waited. Every few seconds there was the blur of a white uniform dashing by, and then I would hear a door bang open down by the windows, and another set of wheels would roll past.

A man's heavy step approached and I asked, "What's going on?"

"We had three surgeries under way downstairs, and men with crushed legs waiting their turn," he called without slowing down, just a dark figure rushing away.

"Isn't there anything I can do?" I called, but it was useless to ask. Someone had to guard the door, and I was the only one to do it.

Another roll of thunder was followed by a lightning strike so bright that the hallway was lit for a few seconds. A tray of metal instruments had been dropped and scattered. Some kind of bottle had broken and thrown chips of brown glass across the floor.

I ran across the hall to kick it all under a bench. The lightning was gone and the hospital once again plunged into darkness, so I couldn't be sure I'd removed everything. For a long while I did nothing but stand at my post, gripping the doorknob to von Matthesius's room and holding my breath as nurses and doctors ran past and patients cried out from distant rooms.

Finally I heard Sheriff Heath at the nurses' desk. "I'm

down here," I called, and soon he rounded the corner with a lantern swinging from his hand.

"Watch your step," I said. "There've been a few spills since the lights went out."

He cast a circle of light around and kicked a pair of scissors and a roll of bandages out of the way. "It's a real mess downstairs. Where's English?"

"He went down to help you," I said.

He was out of breath. A spatter of blood stains ran along the front of his coat, from one shoulder to the other. His hat was gone, probably lost in the commotion. He wore a look of shock I'd seen on him only once or twice before.

"Well, I don't know where he is," he panted. "I put him here to guard the prisoner. He shouldn't have left. I've got other deputies down there now."

"I'm sorry, I . . ."

"Never mind. How's von Matthesius?"

"He's resting. He said he's having trouble moving his legs and that he's losing sensation in his limbs. He has a terrible cough, too. Now that you're here, I'd like to get him some water."

More footsteps pounded toward us and the sheriff lifted his lantern to illuminate the passageway. It was a nurse with a baby in her arms, and two orderlies carrying more bandages and supplies. "We could use that lantern," she shouted as she ran past.

"I'll bring it to you," the sheriff said. Turning to me, he said, "You'll stay here until English turns up. We don't know when the lights will come back on. I've got a man out checking the wires now."

"That's fine," I said. "Let me look in on the Baron again before you take that lantern away."

My hand was still on the doorknob. I turned and swung it open. The sheriff lifted his lantern and we stared into an empty room.

⚔ 6 ⚔

"THIS ISN'T HIS ROOM."

The bed was stripped. We stared at the mattress's blue-and-white ticking. There was no blanket on the floor, and no suit of clothes on the hook.

I'd been holding the wrong doorknob. The inmate's room was next door.

We turned at the same time to reach for the other door. I knew before it opened that the room would be empty, and it was, save for the blanket and the dressing gown tossed across the bed. I'd never felt such horror at the sight of a vacant room.

Sheriff Heath lifted his lantern high and pitched it up and down the empty hall. "Didn't you see anything?"

"No! I—Of course not. I would have stopped him if I'd seen him."

"Check the rooms."

I started at one end of the hall and tried every door. The rooms were stripped bare. There was no sign that von Matthesius had been in any of them. The sheriff worked his way down the other side as I turned back to the inmate's room. I shook out the blanket and the dressing gown and pulled back the sheets on the bed. I bent down and looked in every corner of the room in case he'd dropped something—a scrap of paper, a button, anything at all. But von Matthesius had been quick and meticulous. Every time I'd stopped in to check on him, he must have been in the middle of readying himself, waiting for the right opportunity. I could picture him now, slipping his clothes on under the covers in case I walked in. When he heard the tray overturn and my footsteps running to clear the broken glass, he must have seen his moment and taken it.

He'd left nothing behind. I tossed the mattress over and looked under the bed. My fingers skipped along the grooves in the floor, as if there could be some trace of him in the dust.

Sheriff Heath and I met again in the hall.

"He's gone," I said, pushing down the thick dread in my throat. My forehead had broken out in a sweat. "I'll search the first floor in case—"

But he was already turning away. "Just stay here."

I should have chased after him but I was numb and rooted to the floor. I heard him running down the stairs and calling for his deputies. Then the electric lamps came on and under their glare I could see only the terrible truth of what I'd done: the empty white corridor, every door swung open now, revealing nothing.

The sheriff would be organizing a search party downstairs. I was of no use waiting outside an empty room. I went to the end of the hall and there, at the desk, was Deputy Morris speaking quietly to the nurse. They both looked up when I came around the corner. The nurse started to say something, but Morris shook his head and walked over to me.

So it would be Morris who handed me my fate. I stood and waited.

I couldn't look him in the face. My eyes were fixed on his feet. It took twenty-nine steps for him to reach me. When he got to me he said it as quietly and kindly as he could.

"Sheriff wants me to find you a taxicab."

THE HOUSE WAS DARK but they must have only just gone to bed. The charred remains of a log were still shifting and settling in the fireplace grate. I knocked something over as I stumbled across the sitting room: a theater prop of some kind, made from pasteboard and papier-mache. A floorboard groaned upstairs and Norma called out.

"What are you doing home?"

"Go back to bed." I couldn't bear to tell her.

She came down in her flannel gown and bare feet. "What's the trouble?" She stood at the bottom of the stairs with her arms folded over her chest. "You look stricken. I hope you're not about to tell me that Sheriff Heath has asked you to run off with him, because I've noticed him looking at you very strangely and it makes me wonder exactly what he's got on his mind. If he's taken any license, I'll go right over there and —"

"Norma, stop it!" I was still trying to untangle myself from the mess of paper and fabric Fleurette had left sitting in the middle of the room. She'd pasted some kind of false fur to it. I suppose it was meant to be a fox or a wolf.

"Then what's wrong?"

"What's wrong?" I kicked the thing away in frustration.

"Nothing's wrong, except that I was finally let out of that jail long enough to do a deputy's job and had some hope of earning my badge, but now that crazy old German has run off and it's my fault and I've gone and ruined everything."

"You've trampled the sheep dog," Norma said, clearing what was left of Fleurette's prop from the floor. She pulled a sweater off the divan and wrapped it around herself. "Did you say you're getting your badge?"

A door banged open upstairs and Fleurette called down. "What happened?"

"I'm afraid there's been a mishap with the sheep dog," Norma shouted.

"It's a goat," Fleurette said, and soon she was downstairs, too, eyeing the remains of her creation. She wore a shawl of red Japanese silk and gold fringe that hung down to her feet and brought to mind a very expensive piano drape.

"I'm sorry," I said. "It was dark and I didn't see it."

"You'll make it up to me." She bent down and patted it on what was left of its head. The creature had buttons for eyes and one of them dangled precariously, so she snapped it off. Then she looked up at me again.

"Why are you here in the middle of the night shouting about an old man?"

I put my hat on the rack and started to shake my coat off, then noticed how cold it was and thought better of it. "Never mind."

"Constance was just telling about some unpleasantness at work," Norma said.

"You work in a jail!" Fleurette said. "Of course it's unpleasant."

"What I was trying to say," I nearly shouted, making them

both take a step back, "was that I let an inmate escape tonight."

"You didn't!" Fleurette gasped.

"Of course she didn't," Norma said.

"I did."

"But it wasn't your fault," said Norma. "You haven't been given enough responsibility to have anything be your fault."

"I wish that were true."

"Sheriff Heath must be to blame," she continued, "or that other one we don't like. What was his name?" From Norma's pocket came a rustle of paper and I thought she was preparing to write it down.

"No one else is to blame. I was guarding an inmate at the hospital and the lights went out and in the confusion, he ran off. It's the worst thing I could have done."

They stared at me. I kept my eyes on my feet, which seemed very far away and looked like they belonged to someone else.

At last Norma cleared her throat. "Well. It isn't really the worst thing you could've done. Prisons do burn down, you know. There was that fire in Toronto last year that started with a guard's cigarette and a mattress on the floor, and . . ."

"Thank you, Norma," I said, dropping into a chair. "That lifts my heart. Letting a prisoner escape is far preferable to lighting the place on fire."

"Although Sheriff Heath might not think so at the moment." Norma perched on the arm of my chair.

"Of course he doesn't. He sent me right home. He wouldn't even speak to me himself. He had Morris do it."

"Mr. Morris was here? And you didn't ask him in?" Fleurette ran to the window to see if he'd left.

"He wasn't here," I said wearily. "He just put me in a hansom so I'd be out of the way."

I couldn't stand to listen to them anymore. I pushed Norma off my chair and started up the stairs to bed.

"Sheriff Heath had no cause to send you home," Norma said, following me upstairs. "Although in this case, there is one thing—"

"Not tonight," I said, and slammed my bedroom door.

⇥ 7 ⇤

"CONSTANCE!"

Norma was rapping on my door.

"Are you awake?"

She knocked again, louder this time. "Didn't you hear me? Sheriff Heath's outside."

I pulled the blanket around my shoulders and went over to the window. He was standing in the drive next to his motor car, talking to Fleurette.

Norma came in wearing her barn coat and boots. She disapproved of sleeping late and her expression let me know it.

"He's been out all night. You should've been out there with him."

"He sent me home." I looked down at the top of the sheriff's hat. He was stooped over slightly to listen to something Fleurette was telling him, his hands in his pockets.

Norma came and stood next to me at the window. "It's good that he's here, because I've made up my mind about what you ought to do and now you can go downstairs and tell him about it."

She waited for me to ask. I didn't.

"I've decided that if you had charge of the old German, then you ought to go find him yourself and bring him back. Why should you sit at home when you're the cause of all the trouble?"

Norma, who had never had a job, who rarely left the house except to run her pigeons down the road, was telling me to go out and hunt a fugitive.

"Thank you. It never occurred to me to just round him up."

She put her shoulder under the window sash and grunted until it gave way. The sharp bite of the wind came in, and the smoke from a distant chimney, and the odor of mud and wet leaves.

"What are you doing?" I tried to push the sash down again but it was too late. Fleurette heard us and looked up, and the sheriff followed.

"He's waiting for a word," Norma said, "and I don't like him skulking around here all day. Are you going down or aren't you?"

I was shivering in my nightgown and my bare feet had gone white. I climbed back into bed. "I'm not."

"She's coming down!" she shouted, and slammed the window shut before he could answer.

"I don't know why you're so eager to send me out on a manhunt. You used to consider it a fine idea to keep us all away from the criminal element."

Norma pushed me over with her knee and sat down next to me. "If it becomes known that you've disgraced yourself in your very first professional position, you won't find another. No one will hire the girl who let the prisoner escape."

"I hadn't realized."

"But if you're the girl who captured the fugitive, that puts the matter in a different light, doesn't it?"

She sat, breathing very noisily, awaiting my answer. I turned back to the wall and closed my eyes, then heard her walk over to my dresser. When she returned, there was a rustling of paper and she smacked me with something—a rolled newspaper, a heavy magazine. Then she pulled the blanket off my bed, sending a rush of cold air up my legs.

"Norma!" I tried to take it back but she was already folding it and seemed prepared to take it with her.

"You've got nothing else to do anyway. You're of no use to either of us. We dislike your cooking, and we've already hired a boy to do the vegetable garden. He's much better at it than you were. We're going to eat a cucumber for the first time in years." She clamped the blanket under her arm and went to work on the bedsheet.

I sat up and pushed my hair away. She stripped my bed of anything that might have made me comfortable, and then paused and looked down at me the way she looked at a broken fence board before she took a claw hammer to it.

"If you've no employment, then Fleurette won't get her singing lessons."

"Hand back that blanket."

"And if we can't keep body and soul together, I suppose we'll sell the farm after all. Francis might have some ideas about that."

I didn't want to know what our brother would say. There seemed to be no getting rid of Norma and she was bent upon making my bedroom uninhabitable. I went to the wardrobe and shoved my arms into an ugly old green dress that looked as terrible as I felt.

"Or we could find a husband for Fleurette and he'll look after us."

"That's just fine." My stockings tore at the ankle but I yanked them on anyway.

Norma stood in the doorway and watched me wrap my hair into a knot and stick pins in it. "Although our troubles are nothing compared to Sheriff Heath's," she said. "He'll go to jail for this."

My hair dropped all around my shoulders and the pins went everywhere.

"Jail?"

I MARCHED OUTSIDE and Norma followed me. "Is it true they'll put you in jail?" I shouted.

Sheriff Heath stood a little straighter in his coat and tipped his hat at us.

"Miss Kopp," he said.

Norma ran along behind me and called, "I was on my way to telling you last night but you had such a case of nerves you couldn't listen."

I came to a stop right in front of Sheriff Heath. Dark patches sagged under his eyes. His skin had that pasty cast that people get when they stay up all night.

"Is it true?" I asked him.

He swallowed and looked around at the three of us. "There is a law," he said, his voice a little hoarse, "that a sheriff can be jailed in place of a criminal he allows to escape. But it's rarely enforced and you needn't—"

"I should be the one to go to jail."

"You won't. It's the sheriff's responsibility if an inmate escapes."

"It certainly is," Norma said, recalling everything she knew on the subject with the brisk cheer of the well-informed. "It's one of the reasons a sheriff must furnish a bond. Your bondsmen are going to be very unhappy with you. They'll have to pay the prisoner's fine, and I'm not so sure you wouldn't face a trial and a jail term."

I took Sheriff Heath by the arm. He looked down in surprise but I held on to it. "You can't go to jail. What about Cordelia and the children?" I couldn't imagine the disgrace.

"We'll get him," the sheriff started to say, but Norma talked right over him.

"Well, Mrs. Heath couldn't stay in the sheriff's quarters if he was in jail. She'd have to find somewhere to go. Don't her parents live in Hackensack?"

Fleurette had been watching us from under the brim of a heavy velvet hat. "Would they really put a sheriff on trial?"

"Of course not," he said, but it was a quick and automatic answer and I didn't believe it.

"It's possible the prosecutor's office would take pity on you and spare you a trial," Norma said. "You have managed to keep at least one friend in the prosecutor's office, haven't you?"

Of course he hadn't. Sheriff Heath ran a hand over his mustache and I thought he might lose his patience with Norma. I sent her and Fleurette away, for which he gave me a little nod of gratitude.

When we were alone, he said, "I've put men at all the train stations. We're going around to the hotels, and asking anyone who—"

"I know. You're doing everything you can. But nobody really knows where to look."

He coughed into his fist. "We'll get him. Although the papers have it for the evening edition."

The papers. They would hound him for weeks over this. "I hoped you might catch him before the press got hold of it."

"We didn't."

I couldn't face him. I looked out at the barn and the dry meadow beyond it. "Let me go with you."

"Miss Kopp."

"I might be of some use. He'll speak to me."

He lifted his hat and pushed his hair aside. "I'm doing my best to keep your name out of it. You don't need another scandal in the papers, you and your sisters."

He was trying to protect us. His kindness only made it worse. "It doesn't matter about my name in the papers. But I won't sit out here while the rest of you go and . . ." I choked on the very idea of waiting around on our sleepy old farm while the other deputies were out searching.

"It's exactly what you'll do," he said. "Get some rest for a few days and then come back to the jail when you're ready to work."

"I'm unfit to work at the jail. I let a man go. You've no choice but to dismiss me."

He started to answer but thought better of it. I might have convinced him that I was right.

I took a step back toward the house. Something turned over inside of me. It had seemed impossible only a few minutes earlier when Norma put it before me, but now I could see it plainly. There was only one thing for me to do.

"Never mind. I'll go alone. I'll find him."

I took a few more steps backward in the gravel. He wore

a look of defeat and exhaustion and put a hand on the hood of his motor car to steady himself. "It isn't safe for you to go chasing after a fugitive. I won't allow it."

"But you sent the other deputies!"

"You're not a deputy." There was something definitive about the way he said it.

I should have stopped myself right there, but I couldn't. "That's your fault! It's been two months. I was a deputy before and I should be—"

He took off his hat and slapped it against his leg. "Damnit, Miss Kopp, I believe last night showed why you're not a deputy."

We stood only a few yards apart but the distance between us had never been greater.

"Pardon me," he said. "I didn't mean—"

But it was too late. Of course he meant it.

"They're not putting you in jail for something I did," I said quietly. "I won't have it." I stepped inside and slammed the door shut behind me.

Norma and Fleurette had been listening from the foyer. I leaned against the door and the three of us stared at one another. Sheriff Heath answered with a roar of his engine. His tires sprayed gravel behind them and he was gone.

Norma had my coat over her arm and my hat in her hand. When I took the hat from her I saw that she was also holding my revolver.

"I suppose you heard him," I said. "He's right."

Norma pushed my coat into my chest and waited until I'd put it on before handing me the gun.

"It's nonsense," she said.

"He hasn't any ideas about finding him."

"Yes, well, he's a man of limited intellect, and if he had more than one idea at a time they'd die from overcrowding." Norma was absolutely bristling with the sense of occasion that had come over her. She looked me over impatiently and reached up to take me by the shoulders. "You look wretched, but I know you'll put that to some advantage. Let's get you on a train."

❦ 8 ❧

THE GREAT OPEN waiting room at Pennsylvania Station received me the way a cathedral receives the lost and desperate. Even in the middle of a dreary late October day, with the sun fighting for a place between the broken clouds, there was a sanctity to the light. It gained something by its passage through the grand high windows, and when it fell on the faces of the brusque businessmen and fashionable young girls and haggard old working men in their crumpled hats, it bestowed upon all of them a generous glow that seemed to come not only from the glass above, but from the plaster and stonework all around. I turned my face up to it and closed my eyes. There, in that column of weak light, I felt revived.

But not forgiven. I didn't want forgiveness. I wanted nothing but my inmate, back in jail where he belonged.

Norma's notion of how to prepare for a manhunt consisted of tucking four ham and potato sandwiches into a hamper alongside three messenger pigeons, it being her idea that I would release the birds if I caught the man or if I needed rescuing. I tried to explain that it would do no good to send a message to my sister in the countryside if I was in urgent need of assistance, and, besides, the pigeons seemed intent on getting into the sandwiches and were quite likely to break out of the hamper and fly home on their own once they'd eaten my lunch. Nonetheless she packed all of this into the buggy and took me to the train station in Ridgewood, where I agreed to eat half a sandwich but take no more, and persuaded her to set the pigeons free.

I intended to go first to von Matthesius's brother's apartment on the chance that he might be hiding there. We all took turns signing in visitors to the jail, and Felix had been to see his brother often enough that I knew the address. Beyond that, I hadn't any sort of plan, and felt as shaky and skittish as a newborn colt as I wove through the train station, past the leather-skinned shoe-shine men snapping their rags and whistling, the newspaper boys with bags slung over their shoulders, a lunch counter where girls in hobble skirts perched on stools and ordered sandwiches and buttermilk, and a vast empire of ticket booths offering fares to San Francisco, Denver, and other unimaginably distant places.

On Seventh Avenue I was confronted by an icy wind for which I was ill-prepared. I gathered my collar around me and leaned against it, my head down, my cheeks stinging in the cold. I felt strangely conspicuous, as if everyone in New York knew that I was a disgraced former jail matron who had let a criminal escape.

Fortunately, no one even bothered to look at me. It was the great blessing of a busy city that one could be invisible in a crowd, but it was a blessing for the criminals, too. I forced myself to keep my head up and my wits about me as I marched uptown. After a few minutes I wondered if I should have looked around for a taxi or a trolley, but the blocks were short and the walk invigorating, so I kept to it.

When I reached the park, I walked around Columbus Circle, past the theaters and great dining halls and the enormous old carriage house that had already given way to a concern selling motor cars. Just to the west was a down-at-the-heel neighborhood of squat brownstones and dingy shops bearing the names of every Irish, French, and German family ever to sail across the Atlantic. There were derelict old saloons alongside fishmongers, dental parlors, and Yiddish tailors offering to buy old trousers.

I hurried past a puppeteer making wooden ostriches dance for a crowd of children, and a man with a banjo playing for pennies. A boy down the street bore woolen piecework in a pile over his shoulder, running it up the stairs of a workhouse and landing back on the sidewalk before I had even covered the block. On the corner a pair of skinny girls in braids sold matches and shoelaces to any young man who walked by. They ducked into an alley when a policeman blew his whistle and I wondered what else they might have been offering for sale. From some window above me, a trumpet played a popular melody and a bent old man sitting on a stoop banged out the rhythm on an ashcan.

Felix's building stood just off Ninth Avenue on a block that cowered under the shadow of the rickety and noisy elevated train. From the tracks came the perpetual drift of soot. It landed on hat brims and lodged in eyelashes and nostrils. Everyone kept their noses in their collars when they crossed under the tracks, and I did the same.

He lived in one of those skinny old buildings only two rooms wide. It had the appearance of having been dropped into place from above. The front door was locked and the shades pulled down over all the windows.

Before I could ring the bell, the door opened and a bony old woman in a house dress stepped out onto the stoop with a pail of murky water. I walked in as if I belonged there and she didn't stop me.

Just inside the door, a row of five mailboxes gave the names of the tenants on each floor. Felix von Matthesius was not among them, but there was a German name, Reiniger, on the top floor, so I decided to begin there and work my way down.

The stairs were as unreasonably narrow as the building itself. My skirt brushed both the wall and the iron railing as I climbed. At each landing I had to maneuver my shoulders and the brim of my hat to get around the corner with any kind of clearance. The walls were of a dingy old cracked plaster stained with tobacco smoke and, here and there, the black traces of a long-ago fire. The stair rail had given way and been propped up with wooden stakes that didn't look like they would hold the weight of a child, much less any person of more substantial size.

In the hall on each floor, wooden planks showed through layers of painted floor cloths of the kind that had been common when I was a child. All the doors were closed and I heard no noise from the occupants of the rooms as I climbed. From one of them I could smell coffee burning and from another came the odor of a pork chop in a pan.

At the fourth-floor landing I stopped to catch my breath. A bald man with an enormous belly opened his door and peered out at me. He had a pipe clamped between his teeth and a maimed hand, twisted and marred with a purple scar, tucked into his suspenders.

"Nobody home up there, miss," he said out of the side of his mouth not occupied with the pipe.

"That's fine. I mean to leave a note." I was still huffing from the climb.

"I told the men last night. He's not coming back." He sucked on his pipe until an ember in the bowl lit up and cast a little orange light.

"Which one of them was here last night?" I asked, trying to make it sound as if I didn't care one way or the other.

"Just some cops. Aren't you one of them?"

"Why would you say that?"

"You look like one of those ladies they put in the dancing parlors," he said, taking an exaggerated survey of me from head to toe. "Respectable-looking, and big enough to catch a girl if she ran. Hell, you'd catch me if I tried to run." He took the pipe out of his mouth and gave a raspy laugh, showing a gold tooth. Something about the man's convivial grin endeared him to me, even though he looked like a tramp, or like he was one week's rent away from becoming one.

"Aw, I'm sorry, miss," he said when I didn't answer. "I didn't mean to say that you were big, just that you're . . ."

"It's all right, Mr. . . ."

"Teddy Greene."

"Mr. Greene. The man who lived upstairs. Was he a shorter man, fair of complexion, German stock?"

"That's the one," he said. "Never did get a name. After Mrs. Reiniger passed away, he moved in. He's been quiet enough. Kept to himself. He left in an awful hurry. Must be in some kind of trouble, is that right?"

I glanced up the stairs. The final passageway was even narrower than the rest. Mr. Greene saw me looking up at it and said, "That one got added on. Used to be nothing but a tarpaper shack on the roof, but the landlord figured he could fix it up and charge rent for it. Go on up. You won't find nobody."

He was right. The topmost flat had been built as an afterthought. The steps leading up to it were made of rough wood that had once been painted black. At the top step was a scarred wooden door, and pinned to that was a note. I lifted it up and recognized Sheriff Heath's handwriting.

Dear Mr. von Matthesius,

I've sent my men to find you and to ask your help in searching for your brother, Herman Albert, who vanished earlier this evening from the Hackensack Hospital and may be in poor health and in need of a doctor's care. If you find this note before my men find you, I advise you to report to the Hackensack Jail immediately.

We await your assistance—

Yours very truly—
Sheriff Robert N. Heath

I reached out to smooth the folds of the letter. In the course of doing so, the door drifted open.

The room beyond was dim and still. I held my breath. Nothing moved. There wasn't a sound except the distant clamor of the street below.

It was only a small shabby flat with a sink and a hot plate

just inside the door. A pair of unwashed teacups sat alongside a jumble of saucers and spoons. If there was a window, it was heavily curtained. The rest of the room was too dark to make out from my vantage point.

I couldn't get over the feeling that someone was standing behind that door, waiting for me. I nudged it open another few inches with my foot and stepped inside.

The rooms—there were two of them, the one in which I stood and another beyond—had been built in the last ten years or so and were of simple construction, with odd-sized windows that didn't open and pieces of mismatched trim around the doors. It looked like the whole room had been made out of the broken and discarded remnants of other buildings. The walls were so thin that the sounds of the street drifted right through them: a train rattling past on its elevated tracks, a bell ringing on a pushcart, a newsboy calling an extra.

A heavy tapestry curtain hung in the doorway between the two rooms. I pushed it aside with my elbow—I was reluctant to touch anything for fear I'd leave with a case of fleas or pox —and found in the next room only a sagging mattress in the corner, an empty wardrobe, and a metal washtub. On a corner shelf was a bowl holding the kinds of things a man might pull out of his pockets at night: beer hall tokens, match-books, a stray button.

In the back was a small door with no knob and no lock, only an iron gate latch. I lifted the latch and gave the door a shove. It opened onto a wobbly tar and gravel roof. I stood looking at the uneven line of rooftops stretching along Ninth Avenue and down Sixty-First Street. I could've easily hopped from one to the next, dodging laundry lines and chimneys all the way to the end of the block.

A bucket on the roof seemed to answer for a toilet. I turned quickly away but couldn't help but see the alleyway below where, if I looked long enough, I would start to see rats scampering between the piles of ash and chicken bones and other filth thrown down from the roof. I squeezed back through the door and shut it behind me.

As I parted the curtain between the back room and the front, a voice said, "It's bigger than I thought it would be."

Teddy Greene was standing in the front room, huffing from the effort of climbing the stairs. He kept his pipe clenched in his teeth and grinned gleefully at me.

I started to explain what I was doing inside, but before I could, he said, "Don't worry about me, miss. No questions asked. I know you won't take nothing, a lady like you. Nothing here you'd want, unless he stole something. Is that it? Has he got some jewels hidden around here? 'Cause if he does, I'll help you look for 'em."

"Oh, no, Mr. Greene. In fact, I can't be sure he's done anything wrong at all. Another man is missing, a relative of his, and I—I mean, we—we need some help finding him."

"You and the sheriff?" he asked, with a gimlet-eyed look and that sharp, gold-toothed grin.

"That's right. You saw the note from the sheriff. Do you know anything at all about where Felix went or what he did? Had he any sort of employment?"

"He seemed to be some sort of peddler. Always carrying things upstairs and then hauling them down again to sell in one of the second-hand shops around here. I thought there might have been something under-handed about it. Selling other people's things."

"What things?"

"Paintings, mostly. Sometimes a rug."

"And you don't know how he came by them?"

"Never spoke to him."

"Well, he's in no trouble. We're only looking for a relation of his."

Teddy Greene took a step closer and peered up at me, pulling on his pipe and releasing a stream of smoke that had the peculiar odor of burnt oranges. "What'd he do? The one you're looking for."

"I shouldn't say."

"What's he look like?"

"Well, he's an elderly man, with silver hair and a mustache, although he's clean-shaven at the moment . . ." I trailed off, realizing von Matthesius had probably disguised himself already.

He coughed up another raspy laugh and pointed the stubby finger of his maimed hand at me. "You're hunting a fugitive, aren't you, miss?"

"I suppose you could say that."

"That's quite a job for a lady. Say, if you have a picture of the fellow, I'll show it around the neighborhood. Must be a reward out for him, right?"

Was there a reward? I didn't know and I wasn't sure it was within my authority to offer one, but then again, I wasn't acting under anyone's authority. "I haven't a picture, but I'll deliver a reward personally if you can help us find him. Just get word to the Hackensack jail if anyone turns up here. Can you do that?"

He nodded, puzzled. "Yes, miss, but don't they have a photographer at that jail in Hackensack? You're going to need a picture."

"The sheriff has one and I expect it will run in the papers."

"Then I'll look for it."

I paced around the room one more time to make sure there was nothing that might help me. Mr. Greene just pulled at his pipe and watched.

"Where are you going now?" he asked.

"Oh, there's quite a bit more to do," I said, but the truth was that I hadn't any idea where I might go next.

"Well. If I see that portrait in the papers, I'll take it around. Teddy Greene's your man."

At the mention of a portrait I knew all at once exactly where to go. I took my leave of Mr. Greene, rushed down the cramped stairs to the ground floor, and hurried across town to Henri LaMotte's studio.

❊ 9 ❊

PRISONER ESCAPES BY RUSE

Dr. von Matthesius Flees from Hospital
After Pleading Illness

HACKENSACK, NJ—Dr. Herman Albert von Matthesius, a prisoner in the Bergen County Jail, who said that he had been suffering from rheumatism ever since his arrest last January, and was sent to the Hackensack Hospital for treatment last Tuesday, escaped from that institution late last night. Sheriff Robert N. Heath of Bergen County formed a posse and searched the county all night, but did not find the fugitive, who, it was supposed, was carried away in an auto.

Von Matthesius was arrested in Rutherford on January 31 at his home, where, he said, he conducted a sanitarium. The complaint was made by three young men, Louis Burkhart and Alfonso Youngman of Brooklyn and Frederick Shipper, assistant engineer of the steamship George Washington. At his trial here on June 15 the prisoner testified that he was a graduate of the University of Berlin, had served as a missionary and missionary doctor in Mexico, and was an ordained minister. He said he was not a licensed physician in the United States, but had practiced medicine in the Panama Canal Zone. He also testified to having been connected with a nerve institution in California.

He has been visited weekly at the jail by his brother, Felix von Matthesius, whose address on the visitor's book at the jail is given as 110 W. 61st St., New York, but the man could not be found there by the Sheriff. Both County Physician Ogden and Doctor G. H. McFadden of the hospital staff have insisted that the doctor was feigning illness.

Henri LaMotte passed the paper to me after reading the story aloud. We were seated in his basement office, surrounded by the stacks of jute envelopes that held photographs he'd taken for detectives and lawyers all over the city. This was his version of a filing system: towers of envelopes so precarious that they slid over every table, chair, and windowsill in the place, giving the impression that anyone who sat still long enough might get buried under them, too.

Mr. LaMotte was not a photographer in the ordinary sense. He didn't run a portrait studio or take pictures for the papers. He earned his living by sending photographers out to get evidence for lawyers. Most of it involved following spouses accused of infidelity or trailing smugglers and embezzlers.

I'd stumbled across his studio the year before, when I was looking for another address in the neighborhood, and I did a small favor for him by going to a hotel for ladies just off Fifth Avenue to take pictures out a window.

Although Mr. LaMotte and I had only known each other a short while, we sat together as comfortably as old friends. He was a short, bald man who wore a preposterous wig that was always slightly askew, and he carried an expression of endless bemusement. He spoke with a faint French accent that betrayed his European roots, but when I addressed him in French he insisted that we speak the language of New Yorkers. "Go to Paris if you want to hear French," he would say airily, with a wave of his hand, as if that were a last resort that one shouldn't even consider.

I read the account in the paper a second time and wondered what Sheriff Heath made of it. He must have been infuriated to see that Dr. Ogden had spoken to reporters. It was entirely likely that the doctor had given reporters the story in the first place, and that he'd done it for the very reason Mrs. Heath feared the most, which was that it would publicly discredit the sheriff and bring about charges against him.

"They don't say a thing about you," Mr. LaMotte said. "Are you sure you're involved in this?"

"Of course I am. Only Dr. Ogden might not have known. The sheriff said he would try to keep my name out of it. It isn't widely known that the sheriff employs a ladies' matron."

"And if people did know, he'd be criticized for putting the ladies' matron on guard duty," Mr. LaMotte said.

"That's right."

"Then it's a good thing you came to me, Miss Kopp." He jumped to his feet and turned the sign in his shop window around from OPEN to CLOSED, then locked the door.

"I've nothing but black tea and soda crackers. Will that do?"

It wouldn't do—I hadn't eaten all day except for Norma's half sandwich at the train station—but I thanked him and said it would be just fine. He put a kettle on and in a few minutes we were sitting across from each other with cups and saucers perched on our knees. Just holding a hot drink in my hands calmed me a little.

"Now," said Mr. LaMotte, "have you a list of the places old von Matthesius might have gone?"

I blew on my tea and considered it. "The only address I knew about was his brother's, and nobody's been there."

"What do you know of his other associates? His friends or, for that matter, his enemies?"

"Nothing," I admitted. I must have seemed ridiculous for having run off in search of the man with so little in the way of information about him.

"And what exactly did he do to get himself locked up?"

That was the question I still couldn't answer. "There were charges of a serious nature brought by three boys."

"Yes, we read that much in the paper," he said, leaning back in his chair and lacing his fingers behind his head. He was clearly enjoying himself. "But you must know more about it than that."

I shook my head. "I wasn't part of the investigation or the trial. Once he was in jail, he started asking for me because I spoke German, but he never said a thing about his own past."

"Didn't the sheriff tell you anything?"

"He wouldn't, and he hadn't any reason to. I know everything about the female inmates but quite a bit less about the men. And the police down in Rutherford handled the case. Sheriff Heath might not have had all the particulars himself. He doesn't always."

"Oh, I'm sure he knows. He just isn't telling."

"Not necessarily. We've as many as a hundred inmates coming and going. We don't get them until after the arrest, and sometimes not until the conviction. We wouldn't have any reason to know about witnesses or associates or any of that. But he must be going back through the case now."

"Then we could telephone him."

"I can't. You don't understand what I've done. He was only just starting to hand me a bit of responsibility again, and I know he was prepared to give me a badge. Now I've gone and shown him that I can't do the job. If I'm so easily fooled by an old man, how can he trust me to do anything at all? If I'm to be of any help I must do it on my own, and quietly so as not to draw attention to myself."

Mr. LaMotte seemed impressed by my little speech. He waved a fist in the air and said, "That's good thinking. So you'll start at the beginning. Go and talk to those victims. Find out for yourself what he did. Get right into the thick of his old life, and you might just find him right there."

I had just taken the last cracker and nearly choked on it. "Talk to the victims? Do you mean to say that I should track down those poor boys and ask them outright?"

"What else would you do?"

I considered that. "I suppose it's better than lurking around a train station in the hope of spotting him. But . . ."

He waved his hand as if to bat away my objections. "Of course it is! Think about it. Do you suppose your Sheriff Heath will go interview those boys?"

"No. Why would he? Whatever happened, it took place almost a year ago, and I'm quite certain they haven't seen von Matthesius since."

"Exactly my point."

"I'm afraid I don't see your point." I ran my finger over the crumbs around the edge of the saucer, which only made me more hungry and irritable.

Mr. LaMotte set his teacup aside and leaned forward. "You went straight to the brother's flat, even though the sheriff had already sent his men over there. Why did you go?"

"It seemed like the best place to start."

"And where do you suppose the sheriff's heading next?"

Having no other place in his crowded office to put my cup and saucer, I set them on the floor. "He's going around to the train stations to talk to the station agents, and he'll get word out to the other police departments. He'll interview the doctors and nurses who were on duty at the hospital. He's sending someone around to the hotels and boarding-houses in case von Matthesius was too ill to go far and took a room nearby. Now that the story is out, he'll give a photograph to the newspapers."

"So you must do the opposite!" Mr. LaMotte exclaimed. "Don't go anywhere near train stations or police departments. Don't speak to witnesses at the hospital. If you want to be of help, go to the places your sheriff friend won't go. You must start with those poor boys."

I still wasn't convinced. "But—"

"Listen to me, Miss Kopp. The police can always be counted upon to do the same three or four things every time a crime is committed. They will speak to the neighbors and make inquiries at the man's place of business if he has one. They might stick their heads into a few saloons and flop-houses with the idea that if they can't find their criminal, they'll find another one, which is all the same to them. Then they'll go back to the station-house and write up their notes and be home in time for supper."

"But that's not true of Sheriff Heath," I protested. "He's been out all night hunting down von Matthesius. And he has to get him. Do you know that a sheriff can go to jail if he lets a man escape?"

"Yes, but until he does, he still has to manage the jail, and keep track of a hundred or so inmates, and think about winning an election in the fall if he's still a free man. And every day of the week brings another robbery or fire or missing girl, doesn't it? That's how it is for him. But not so for detectives. You have the opportunity to ask the questions no one else is asking. You can put yourself into the mind of the criminal and understand how he thinks. That's how you get your man. And if you don't, at least you won't have spent all your time turning up at the same places the sheriff has already been. There's no point in following behind him and doing all his work a second time. A detective does the work the police aren't doing or won't do."

"But I'm not a detective!"

He leaned forward and cocked his head to the side, which caused his wig to slip. He tipped it gently back into place and said, "You're not a deputy. You're not acting under the sheriff's orders. What do you call yourself?"

IT WAS DARK by the time I left his studio and bitterly cold. I was in desperate need of a hot meal and a good night's sleep. When Mr. LaMotte became aware that I had nowhere to go but home for the night, he telephoned the Mandarin, the hotel for ladies where he'd sent me to take the photographs last year. They'd hold a place for me if I came right over.

I took a large and comfortable room on the fourth floor with a fireplace and a reading chair, and a view down Fifth Avenue. It had been a year since I'd first visited the hotel, but I thought often about its quiet and civilized charms. There had been more than one night when I wished I could trade my bedroom in Wyckoff for a suite of rooms at the Mandarin.

I leaned against the window-sill and looked around with the uneasy satisfaction of a child who had succeeded in running away from home. Here was my bed, with its curved headboard that reminded me of a sun rising, and its coverlet of red Oriental silk. The fireplace was a modest tiled affair with a brass curtain and grate, and next to it sat a sturdy leather chair and footstool. Nowhere did I see the fussy floral chintz that one might expect in a room furnished just for women. Instead everything was simple and generously proportioned, as if the decorator knew that women might like a vacation from dainty straight-backed chairs and busy patterns of mignonettes and bluebells.

From the window I could look down along Fifth Avenue at the tops of carriages and automobiles forming a river of black below me, in endless motion from one end of the city to the other. Along the wide sidewalks, hats of every color and style bobbed along, from the brown tweed worn by newsboys to the black bowlers and silk top hats of men rushing home from the office and then back out again for the evening. They were accompanied by women's wide brims tied with ribbons in crimson, navy blue, and emerald green. It was a pageant that went on every day and night, but I wasn't accustomed to it and found it dazzling.

I sat down on the bed for just a minute, but I must've dozed off, because when I looked at the clock it was nearly eight and I was afraid I'd missed dinner. Downstairs, I found the dining room to be overly crowded with small round tables, each of them occupied. There was a lively chatter among the several dozen women in residence, and the pleasant ringing of glass and silverware, and a friendly glow from the brass lamps on the wall. At one end of the room was a row of tall windows that must have looked out over the street, but they were curtained against the cold. I could smell coffee and some kind of roast and warm sweet bread, a fragrance I could live on.

But there was no table for me. A girl rushed past with a tray of dishes and asked me to wait. Just then, three women at a table in the corner called out to me. "Make it a foursome," one of them said, waving me over. "We get so tired of hearing each other's stories. Come and tell us yours."

They all looked to be about my age, and were dressed in the plain and business-like attire of office girls. Two of them wore glasses, and all three kept their hair in the kind of simple knot that suggested they had better things to do than fuss over their appearances. I decided I wouldn't mind some company, although I wasn't so sure about telling my story.

"I'm Geraldine," said one as I thanked them and took my seat. She had black hair that shone like lacquer and gold-rimmed spectacles that sat easily on a rather prominent nose. "This is Ruth, and that was Carrie who called you over."

Ruth wore cherry-red lip-stick and a polka-dotted dress of navy blue and white. She gave me a wide smile and shook my hand, then Carrie took it and pumped it vigorously. "Nice to know you," she said. "Where are you in from?"

"I'm just down from Hackensack," I said. "I'm Constance."

"Well, Constance," Carrie said, "we're all here because we were lucky enough to be living on the third floor of a building that caught fire last week."

"And you escaped! Did everyone get out?"

"Sadly, no one was even singed," said Carrie with a sigh.

"It was the dullest fire in New York's history. There's smoke everywhere but no death or destruction."

"Carrie's a reporter," Ruth said. "She's been trying for years now to get off the social desk and do some crime reporting. I think she set the fire herself, just to have something to write about."

"I wish I had," Carrie said. "I would've done the job right."

"Are the two of you in newspapers?" I asked Ruth and Geraldine.

"I'm a lawyer," Geraldine said, "and Ruthie here does the filing at an accounting firm down the hall from my office. She's the one who found me the apartment. And now look at us! Living in a hotel while they clean up the mess."

"I hope someone else is paying for the rooms," I said.

Geraldine dropped her chin and looked at me over the top of her glasses. "Never rent an apartment to an attorney."

"Geraldine has us all fixed up," Carrie added. "And because of the high cost of our rooms here, ours will be the first apartments to be cleaned and made new again. We'll be back in a week."

"And she does mean new," said Ruth. "New curtains and carpets, and new electrical wires, done right this time."

"Oh, was that the problem?" I asked. I'd grown accustomed to thinking of fires as being set by arsonists and had forgotten that some of them were accidents of faulty wiring.

There was a menu card on the table. I picked it up and Geraldine said, "It's what you'd expect. It starts with radishes and celery, which we won't eat. Then there's tomato soup, salad, roast beef, and the usual cakes and pies. The apple is best, but have you ever had a bad apple pie?"

The merits of apple pies were debated around the table as the waitress set a dish of radishes and celery in front of us, along with a little bowl of mayonnaise. I waited to be sure that no one else was going to eat it, and then I did.

"You must be starving!" Geraldine said. "Aren't they awful?"

I shrugged. "That's what the mayonnaise is for."

"What have you been up to today, Miss Constance?" Ruth said, leaning forward. "You're to be our entertainment this evening, but we've yet to learn a thing about you except that you come from Hoboken."

"Hackensack."

"Aren't they the same?" Ruth said.

I hadn't planned to tell them anything about what had happened. But as soon as I sat down I became possessed of an inclination to be like them, to be one of those solitary women with interesting jobs and apartments that get only slightly soiled in a fire. I felt more than a little guilty about this urge to be alone, to leave Norma and Fleurette and our ramshackle home in the country in favor of a sparse little flat and a purse full of train tokens, but something about the Mandarin brought it on and I gave in to it. If an interesting story was the price of admission, I had one for them.

"I work for the sheriff of Bergen County," I said. "Or at least, I did. I'm hunting for a prisoner who escaped under my watch."

The soup arrived just then and no one noticed. There was a delighted, electric silence around the table. I smiled at them and picked up my spoon.

At last Carrie spoke. "Either you're telling the truth, or you are quite insane. I can't decide which I'd like better."

The soup was hot and salty and I only wished there were

more of it. "Oh, I'm telling the truth," I said as I scraped the bowl. "Just look at the *Times.*"

Ruth gave a little gasp and reached under Carrie's chair, but Carrie got there first. She rattled her copy of the newspaper. "Show us," she said, thrusting it at me.

I found the headline and folded the pages back. They read it as I finished my soup. The empty bowl was replaced with a scoop of cold creamed chicken on a pineapple ring. I looked around for some salt and, finding none, ate it anyway while the three of them passed the paper around.

"But they don't mention you anywhere!" Ruth said, turning to her dinner at last.

"The sheriff is trying to keep my name out of it. My sisters and I got into a bit of trouble last year and we'd rather not keep turning up in the crime pages. Besides, if the Board of Freeholders finds out that it was the lady deputy who let the prisoner escape, they might . . ."

"Might decide they don't care for lady deputies as a general matter," Geraldine said.

"Oh, I don't think anyone cares much for lady deputies," Carrie said. "We haven't even made up our minds about them in New York. I can't imagine what they must be thinking out in New Jersey."

"What kind of trouble did you get into last year?" Ruth asked.

"No, no," said Carrie. "I think we should hear about this fugitive first."

"I want to know how you got hired on as a deputy," Geraldine said.

"I'm not quite a deputy. I'm the ladies' matron at the jail —or I was. But the sheriff has been promising me a badge."

With that, I did become the evening's entertainment. I carried the conversation through the roast beef and the apple pie (which was good, but not extraordinary, and served to remind me that city-dwellers can make an awful fuss about simple food), past the coffee, and into the final clearing of the table. It was ten o'clock by the time we looked up. There was no one left in the dining room except a foursome playing bridge in the opposite corner.

"Well, Constance the Cop," said Carrie when I was finished, "I know one thing. You absolutely must let me write a profile of you for the Sunday papers."

"Carrie!" Geraldine said. "Haven't you heard a word? She doesn't want to be in the papers. Not everyone wants their name in print."

"But you'll be famous! And it's a corker of a story. We'll have an artist sketch the best scenes. I can just see a drawing of the three Kopp sisters with their revolvers." Carrie tapped on the table and looked off into the distance, picturing it. "'Lady Cop Makes Trouble.' That's our headline."

"Am I making trouble for the sheriff or the criminals?" I asked.

"Both, at the moment. You'll be famous either way."

"*You'll* be famous," Ruth said to Carrie. "You just want a big story about something other than club luncheons."

"Club luncheons are the very opposite of a story," Carrie returned, "unless they're interrupted by a charging elephant or an alligator in the fountain."

"An alligator?"

Carrie sighed. "It happened in Florida, and some other lucky reporter was there to tell about it. The luncheon was held at a hotel, and someone thought it would be charming to stock the fountain with baby alligators. They devoured all the goldfish and then waded out for a taste of the consommé. Every Daughter of the American Revolution jumped on her chair and shrieked. That never happens in New York."

"They might find a rat," Ruth offered.

"They're accustomed to rats. No, what I need is a girl sheriff with a gun."

"And someday I'll need a reporter," I said, pushing my chair back and rising to my feet. "You can be sure that you're the one I'll want. But I've got to get some sleep if I'm to catch my fugitive tomorrow."

Carrie begged to be allowed to follow me as I searched for von Matthesius, but the other two persuaded her to let me go about my business on my own.

I felt as though I'd traveled a thousand miles in one day. I said my good-byes to the three women and exchanged addresses. Ten minutes later I was back in my room and asleep in the terrible dress I'd been wearing all day and the pair of stockings with the hole at the ankle.

By two I was awake again and staring at the clock.

What was I doing, dozing in a comfortable hotel room while my fugitive was at large? Henri LaMotte's advice seemed misguided as I thought back on it. Why shouldn't I station myself at Felix's apartment and watch out for him? It was the only real lead I had, and I couldn't be so sure that a deputy was posted there for the night. How could I know where Sheriff Heath was sending his men?

I slipped out of bed in the half-darkness and went to the window. Fifth Avenue looked like a dream, with the fuzzy outlines of black taxicabs swimming through a purple mist and coming to a stop under the ochre lights of the street lamps. There were people out, but they, too, were cloaked in black and moved silently and furtively, as if they were somewhere they shouldn't have been. And who would be out at two o'clock in the morning, other than escaped prisoners and their accomplices?

Downstairs, I dodged a drowsy bellman charged with enforcing curfew and ran down the block, where I found a motor cab waiting in front of another hotel. I was soon rushing uptown and westward to Sixty-First Street.

"I can't let you out here, miss," the driver said, looking doubtfully down the street from Ninth Avenue. "There's all kinds out and about at this time of night."

"That's why I'm here." I handed him his fare and jumped out before he could argue with me.

I tied my scarf twice around my neck against the cold and pulled my sleeves down over my wrists. Steam escaped from boiler room vents. Even in those decrepit old apartments, the inhabitants were warmer than I was.

There were a few orange lights in windows upstairs along the block, but none at all in the building I had come to watch. The street was as quiet as a city street could be, which is to say that there was a constant rumble of engines and the clatter of wheels on stone, along with an occasional shriek of a cat and the cry of a baby that wasn't being attended to.

The door to Felix's building was locked. I circled the block and looked for the alleyway I'd seen from the roof. I even pulled on a few blind doors that looked like they led nowhere at all, which might have meant that they led right into the empty space I was looking for. But I found nothing.

The shop windows up and down the street were dark and

many had their shutters drawn down. I walked past a German bakery and a butcher with empty hooks in the window, and then a tiny shop no larger than a closet that sold knives, and next to it a druggist offering stick candy and relief from corns. In the half-light of a city that never went completely dark, the shops looked like set pieces in a theater, waiting silently behind the curtain for the lights to come up and the actors to step out in their costumes and take the parts of shopkeepers and pushcart drivers.

I rounded the corner and resigned myself to watching Felix's building for the rest of the night. Just as I settled onto a dark stoop across the street, Deputy English stepped out of a shadow and came walking toward me. I turned away and backed into the doorway.

He crossed the street before he saw me. I watched him walk back and forth and pause to rest on a stoop here and there. He was as inconspicuous as a sheriff's deputy could be on a night watch. He wore an ordinary coat without a badge, and he ducked off the street just often enough that he didn't appear to be pacing.

I wasn't needed if he was also on duty, and I knew he'd notice me eventually. A woman out at that time of night was bound to be stopped, even by a deputy outside his jurisdiction. There was no way for me to watch Felix's apartment if I had to hide from the man already assigned to do it.

The futility of it weighed on me. I was superfluous in a manhunt. The sheriff wouldn't have sent me to watch a building in a neighborhood like this all night. Of course, he wouldn't have sent me to New York at all, but there I was.

I stood in the shadows for a minute and watched Deputy

English lean in a doorway and make up a cigarette. The orange glow flickered and died and then came to life again. The sound of two men in a loud and drunken argument a block away distracted him. While he had his back turned, I dashed off my stoop and ducked around the corner to Ninth Avenue, and from there to the nearest hotel with a doorman willing to summon me a taxi.

✥ 10 ✥

THE NEXT MORNING I undertook a thorough review of the Mandarin's collection of New York and New Jersey directories. It required the better part of an hour to go through them in hopes of finding von Matthesius's accusers among the Burkharts and Shippers and Youngmans. Louis Burkhart was supposed to be living in Brooklyn, and to my relief I found just one listing by that name among all the Burkharts in the city. It seemed the easiest place to start.

I set off in a high spirit, having acquired my purse full of train tokens and a bracing sense of purpose along with it. There was something fine about having a man on the loose and a list of addresses to call upon about it. If word got out that I had let von Matthesius escape, New Jersey might indeed have its doubts about a lady deputy, but I was kindled up about it at the moment.

I boarded the train and soon found myself on Bedford, a wide avenue lined in brick apartment buildings that seemed to march right into the horizon and vanish. I had no difficulty in finding the Burkhart family—there was a shoe store bearing the name at precisely the address I had—but no one at the shop wanted to tell me where Louis could be found.

"Doesn't he live here?" I asked a man who introduced himself as Louis's uncle.

"Not anymore," he said, without taking his eyes off the sample book of shoe leathers in front of him.

"Would you have an address for him?"

He gave a little snort and shook his head.

"He's not in any trouble. Couldn't I leave a note?"

"I don't expect to see him around here, miss." The man shut his book and turned his back to me. He straightened a row of metal tins of polish and wax on a shelf. Over in the corner a girl who looked to be about fifteen watched me from behind a curtain of thin blond hair. I took her to be the man's daughter.

I went at it more urgently. "If I could only speak to him, he might be able to help with an important matter."

Finally the man turned and faced me. He wore an enormous beard and eyebrows larger than some men's mustaches. From behind all that wiry hair he glared at me and said in a low voice, meant for me but not for the girl in the corner, "I read the papers. I know why you're here. He doesn't want to talk to you people."

Once again he turned his back to me. If I'd had a badge, I might have persuaded him to answer a question, but as it stood I had no way to compel him. I lost the opportunity to press my case when four children ran into the store, followed by their weary mother. The man busied himself climbing up and down the rolling ladder behind the counter to retrieve shoeboxes for them. He very deliberately ignored me.

I stepped out to the street and wondered if I should go off in search of the next victim, Alfonso Youngman. Just then, a hand caught me on the elbow.

The girl from the shop had run out into the cold without hat or coat. I stepped under an awning a few doors down from the shoe store to get her out of the wind.

She kept her arms crossed in front of her and hopped up and down. "He isn't in any trouble, is he?"

"Not at all. I just want to ask him something."

She cocked her head and squinted up at me. "What do you want to ask?"

I wasn't entirely sure but didn't want to admit it. "I shouldn't say."

"But you're not with the police?"

"I'm helping the sheriff with a case."

The girl looked over her shoulder and then said, "As long as he doesn't get into trouble."

"He won't."

"Well, then, he's at the other shop."

"The other shop?"

"The other Burkhart Brothers Shoes. In Rutherford. It's closed now, but his mother still lives above the store."

"Do you know anything about these other boys? Alfonso Youngman and Frederick Shipper? Were they friends of his?"

She looked around nervously again and bit down on a strand of hair. "I'd better get inside. Ask Louis where to find Frederick. They went everywhere together. I don't know about the other one."

With that she turned and ran back into the store. Having no address for Frederick Shipper and an impossibly long list of A. Youngmans to chase down in Brooklyn, the only thing to do would be to go back to New Jersey and find Louis Burkhart. At the corner I took a newspaper and read it on the train, searching for news of von Matthesius and finding none.

ANOTHER RAINSTORM was working up to full strength as the train lurched into Rutherford. It hammered the shop awnings along Park, where women in their good hats gathered to wait it out. The crowds were such that I was forced to the curb and had to splash through the gutter to avoid the half-soaked shoppers. My boots sank into the mud but I pressed on, past the post office and the stationery shop and a tiny storefront where wooden trains for children rolled through a miniature version of the very street I was standing on. I recognized the red roof of the train station and would not have been surprised to see my very own figure, looking through the window of that very shop, carved in wood and carefully painted and dressed in a doll's tiny clothing.

The shoe store was closed, just as I'd been told, but the Burkhart Bros. sign still hung above it. Through the dusty windows I saw nothing but empty shelves and benches sitting in the darkness. A tarnished cash register stood shrouded in cobwebs.

I rang the bell at the door next to the shop. It took three or four attempts to get an answer, but at last a boy with disheveled brown hair appeared and looked at me through the glass. We eyed each other soberly for a minute, then he pushed the door open.

"Louis?" I said.

"No." It was more of a refusal of whatever I was going to ask next. He closed the door.

"Louis, there's nothing wrong," I said through the glass. "I've only come to ask you something."

He folded his arms in front of him and I saw a resemblance to the girl in Brooklyn, who must have been his cousin. He had the same wide-spaced eyes and long, narrow nose. There was something guileless and childlike about him, although he was almost a man.

We stared uncomfortably at each other and then I said, "I work for the sheriff."

"He got away." The boy spoke in a thin and nervous voice. His eyes flickered to the ground and his hands stayed tucked under his arms.

"We're doing everything we can to find him."

"Well, it's nothing to do with me," he said.

"I'd just like a word. If I could only come in for a minute."

"My mother's ill." We stood looking at each other in silence, and then he opened the door for me.

I followed him up the wide and creaky stairs. There was an odor of mildew on the landing and the residue of a lifetime's worth of cooking grease and oven smoke. Somebody had just discarded their fish bones and left the empty pail on the steps, where the stench lingered.

There was only one door on the second floor, so they must have had it all to themselves. The stairs continued up, probably to rented rooms on the floors above. I waited while Louis went inside and spoke to his mother. I could hear his low voice and a wretched cough in response. Then there was the sound of water being poured into a glass and more hacking and wheezing.

It was unexpectedly warm on the landing. I shook off my wet scarf. At last Louis opened the door and admitted me to a sitting room that was not prepared to receive visitors. An enormous pile of mending and washing covered the settee, and a wooden stand for ironing took up a place in the middle of the room where a table might have been. Along one wall ran a sink and an old black stove covered in pots and dishes. There was a drop-leaf table pushed against the wall and two wooden chairs next to it. I wasn't sure if I was meant to take one, so I didn't.

Louis had a wobbly chin and a nervous habit of pulling at his ear. He kept his lips pressed together in a tight white line. Most boys his age were full of swagger and ambition, but any trace of that had been robbed from him. It gave me a sick feeling to realize that he reminded me of the petty thieves and pickpockets who drifted through our jail. There was a sameness to them, a lifelessness, that I feared had already taken hold of this boy.

I began by saying, "Is that your father's shop downstairs?"

Without looking at me, he answered, "It was until he died. We haven't been able to manage it without him."

"I'm so sorry."

"All right." He kept his eyes on his feet.

I bent down in the hopes of getting him to look at me. "Louis, I'm trying to find out where Dr. von Matthesius might've gone. We're looking for any of his associates. Don't you remember anyone who might have visited him at the sanitarium, or the people he kept up a regular correspondence with? Any name at all might lead us in the right direction and tell us where he's hiding."

He shook his head and rubbed the back of his neck self-consciously. I waited, trying not to shift about too much even as my feet started to expand in their wet boots. I'd learned from my time at the jail that sometimes a witness will blurt out information just to fill an uncomfortable silence. That wasn't working on Louis.

I heard a cough from the other room and said, "Is your mother able to join us?"

"She's not fit for company. She's gone to bed."

"Has a doctor seen her?"

"Are you a nurse?"

"No, but I'd like to have a word with her if I could."

I wasn't sure I did want to have a word with his mother until I knew what was ailing her, but it seemed a mistake not to, after I'd come all this way. I let him lead me through a series of equally dirty and crowded rooms and into a small bedroom that looked over the alley behind Park. Mrs. Burkhart was propped up by a stack of thin pillows. She clutched a handkerchief and pulled the blankets up to her chest when she saw us. Gray hair fell around her shoulders and the skin hung loosely off her face.

"Mama, she wants to talk to you," Louis said. Mrs. Burkhart lifted a hand but said nothing. I attempted a smile.

"Go on back," I said to the boy.

He looked to his mother for confirmation and she nodded. After he was gone, she sat up and tried to say something but it brought on another coughing fit. There was a metal cup by her bed and I handed it to her, but she waved it away. Then I remembered that I had a sack of lemon candy in my pocketbook. She grinned and opened her hands when she saw it. We each took one and after a few minutes she could speak.

"Louis was just a boy," she croaked. "He's not to blame."

"Was it very hard on him?" I didn't want to admit how little I knew about what had happened.

She pulled a shawl over her shoulders and looked out the window. Her nose was red and grotesquely large. Hairs sprouted out of her nostrils like a bristle brush.

"His father wanted him to be a doctor," she said. "I thought this would start him off right. Let him work as an orderly, see what it was like. I'd no idea what that man was doing."

She gave me an accusatory look, as if it were my fault for not telling her. "I don't think anyone knew," I said lamely.

"He made Louis put the masks over their faces." There was something terrible in the way she said it.

"A mask . . . Do you mean ether? Or chloroform?"

She nodded. "Just enough to keep them in bed, so their families could be fooled into thinking they needed more treatment. And when they couldn't pay any longer, it was my little Louis and that boy Frederick who would have to go out and collect from the families. They took paintings and jewelry and even furniture. Grandmother's bureau, nice old things. Can you imagine my boy going around telling lies and taking from people?"

I couldn't imagine it. Louis was such a shy and slight boy. "When did you find out about it?"

"After it was too late to do a damn thing." She started wheezing and took a drink of water. "He thought he'd killed that girl. Thought he'd given her too much. He ran home and told me what he'd done and sat right there on the floor and cried like a little baby. It was the first I knew that anything was wrong."

Suddenly I could see it. A house full of women too drugged to leave, or even to understand what was being done to them.

And von Matthesius could have done anything he wanted with his patients, if they were in such a condition. How had this man been given only a year in jail?

"But he didn't kill her," I said, more hopeful than certain.

She shook her head. "She came out of it. And of course by that time it was all over. But you know about that." Something caught in her throat, and that brought on more coughing and another round of lemon candy for the two of us. I set the bag on the table next to her. She patted it gratefully and waved me off, dismissing me, but I wasn't ready to go.

"Mrs. Burkhart, has someone called a doctor for you? You don't look well. I know your boy depends on you."

"Nothing the doctor can do," she croaked. "Too many years at the tannery. Made my teeth come loose and now I got a fever all the time and these lumps on my neck." She pulled the shawl away and I was shocked to see a bulge the size of a pincushion under her ear.

A little potbellied stove kept the room exceptionally warm but she shivered in spite of it. I loosened my collar and wished for a little cool air. The rain fell in grimy rivulets down the window. I was suddenly eager to get back outside so it could wash me clean, too. The sickness and dust was stifling.

"Have you been to see Frederick?" she said, her breath coming out in a shallow rattle.

"I don't know where to find him. Do you?"

"I thought he was still at the glassworks."

"The one out on Orient?"

She waved me out again. "Go see him. Leave Louis alone. He's been through enough. And get that man." She looked at me with a kind of dead anger in her eyes.

My voice wouldn't hold steady. "The sheriff has all his men out searching."

"And you," she managed to say between coughs, giving me a rather terrifying toothless grin that nonetheless warmed me toward her a little. "You'll catch him."

Her pillow slipped and I pushed it back into place. "Get some rest."

THE GLASSWORKS SAT at the edge of the cemetery, just outside of town at the end of a gravel road. It was nothing but a hulking old warehouse of painted brick with a plume of smoke rising up from the back and dissipating in the drizzle. Men in blue overalls carried crates of glass panes out the front door and into a fleet of wagons.

A boy with a broom in his hand and a pail of broken glass tried to walk around me but I stepped in his way.

"I've got a message for Frederick Shipper. Can you send him over here, and be quiet about it?" I slipped a nickel in the boy's hand. It must have been enough, because he set his pail down and ran off.

In a few minutes Frederick strode out into the yard. He was a tall, broad-shouldered young man with thick wavy hair and the kind of inherent good looks that some working men carried around without realizing it: the square jaw, the expansive smile, the blue eyes fringed in black lashes. Half the actors on Broadway would've taken his looks over their own. But it would never occur to a man like Frederick that there was money to be made from the features of his face.

When he came close enough for a good look at me he stopped, his feet skidding in the gravel. A few of the other men turned to watch. Fearing that I was about to lose him, I stepped forward and called out, a little too loudly, "Mr. Shipper! I have good news."

He had little choice but to approach me. Before he could say a word, I leaned over and muttered, "Tell them I recovered a watch and some things that were stolen and just need you to make an identification."

Frederick groaned but turned back to the yard and said loudly, "Why, that is good news! I'll have a look, but then I've got to get back to work." Then he followed me across the road and we stood in a patch of wet grass. Behind me was the back of the cemetery, the old unused part that no one ever expected to fill with graves.

Once we were out of earshot, Frederick said, "You look like someone official. Am I in trouble?"

How did I become so easy to recognize? "I work with the sheriff. You know that Dr. von Matthesius escaped two days ago."

He kept his eyes on the glassworks. "I heard something about it."

"I'm just looking for names of associates, or friends, or anyone who might've come to visit him. Is there someone who might be helping to hide him now?"

Frederick shook his head. "I've been pretty busy trying to forget that place. But I never talked to nobody. I was just there to do a job. Help move the patients. Any kind of heavy lifting." He turned to go.

"What happened to Louis Burkhart?" I asked.

Frederick stopped and turned to me again. This time, he looked me over, starting with my boots and working up to my hat. "Who are you?"

"I told you. I work for the sheriff. Constance Kopp is my name."

He tilted his head from left to right and back again, calculating. "Lady detective," he said, stalling.

It wasn't an interesting line of conversation for me, so I didn't give an answer.

"Louis was just a boy. He shouldn't have seen some of those things. And the doctor—if that's what he was—he had Louis too scared to tell anybody. Said he'd have Louis committed to the boys' reformatory if he said a word about Beatrice. Louis thought he could do it, and maybe he was right. Poor kid had nightmares about that place. I bet he still does."

"Beatrice?"

"The girl. Beatrice Fuller."

"The one Louis thought he'd killed. He thought he'd given her too much chloroform."

He nodded. "She was the one the doctor was going to marry. Well, I guess he did marry her."

"I'm sorry, I don't . . ."

A man came outside and shouted for Frederick. He took a step away from me and said, "You don't know? I thought you worked for—"

"I do," I said hastily. "They just didn't give me all the particulars."

He made a little *tsk* sound and looked back at the factory. "You don't know nothing. Look, von Matthesius owed somebody a lot of money. He kept trying to figure out ways to get his patients to stay there longer so their families would pay more. He kept them sick, you understand?"

I nodded, a little sick myself at the idea of it.

"And this girl Beatrice—it looked like her parents had half

the money in New York. He had her father convinced that Beatrice was a very special girl, she was going to blossom under his care if only he could have more time, nonsense like that. One day he comes up with this idea to get Beatrice to marry him. She hardly knew her own name, he had her on so much dope. He called his old minister friend over and had a wedding right there in his living room. That's when Louis and I went to the police. We were too late to stop the wedding, but her parents had it annulled and he went to jail. That's all I know, miss."

"What about the other patients? What did he do to the others?"

He turned away, shaking his head. I called after him. "How do I find Alfonso Youngman?"

"Haven't seen him," he shouted over his shoulder. "Last I heard he was over at the Warren. It's a kind of a—you know, a stopping-over kind of place. In New York. Over on the East Side."

My fingers had gone numb in spite of the gloves and I rubbed my hands together the way one goes about starting a fire. Frederick Shipper had said all he was willing to, but it was enough. I'd begun the day with nothing, and now I had a flophouse on the East Side, a girl named Beatrice, and two boys with nothing but bad memories they wanted to put behind them. What did Sheriff Heath have?

⊰ 11 ⊱

I REALIZED AS I LEFT the glassworks that I would pass Carmita, the street where von Matthesius kept his sanitarium. I'd never seen the place but I had a dark and disagreeable feeling about it. There was no reason to think he'd be hiding there—it was too obvious and easy to search—but I approached it nervously, with a tight and breathless feeling. I'd never broken into an abandoned building before, but if I found it empty I knew I must try to get inside.

Carmita was a wide street lined with high and graceful trees that had shed their leaves, leaving a latticework of bare branches against a dismal low sky. The homes were comfortable but not luxurious, with deep front porches, second-story gables, and brightly painted shutters. On either side of the street the lawns sloped gently down to the sidewalks.

The sanitarium was no different from the other houses on the block. I stood looking at it and tried to imagine what had gone on inside: respectable families, cheated of their money, and nervous patients, too weak and drugged to know what was being done to them. Considering von Matthesius's cruelty and treachery, the house should have been one of those dark old ruins built of stone and rough wood, with a turret reached by a narrow unlit spiral staircase, a suspicious-looking trapdoor leading into a dank, forgotten basement, and iron bars across the windows to keep the patients from escaping.

But it was nothing like that. It was a stately home painted brick red with a row of white columns in front and a pair of doors outfitted in brass knockers. Hydrangeas held on to their papery blooms under the windows. Three brick chimneys rising from the roof suggested the possibility of companionable warmth within.

There was no sign identifying the place as a sanitarium, but that was probably the custom in neighborhoods like these. The patients would rather not be seen going in or out of a place that might house the infirm and insane. Well-to-do families liked to be assured of their privacy.

They would have been thoroughly deceived by such a genteel and discreet place. I would have, too.

The front door was padlocked and the windows curtained against curious eyes. I crossed the lawn and took a walk around the house. In the back, where the neighbors couldn't see, the windows did have bars across them. Those must have been the patients' rooms.

Through the shuttered first-floor windows in back I caught a glimpse of the cooling room and a large kitchen beyond it, outfitted with two stoves and two sinks as an institution of this nature might require. Under a rock on the back steps was a long-forgotten bill from the dairy, and a coffee can filled with the ends of old cigarettes, now swollen and swimming in rainwater.

Only one other window gave me a glimpse inside. A curtain had come loose and through one pane I could see into an empty room and another room beyond it. There were a few gold picture frames leaning against a wall, and a couple of odd chairs and tables scattered about, but it looked like the place had been emptied. Where were the lavish antiques and rugs I'd heard about?

I pushed at a few window frames and kicked at all the doors, but nothing would budge. There was no way in without breaking a window. I went around the house one more time, and then I saw a basement door at the back, painted the same color as the rest of the house and easily missed.

It didn't have a proper doorknob, only a metal latch rusted shut. I tried to force it open and couldn't. The only tool at hand was that old coffee can. I emptied it of rainwater and forced the lip of the can between the latch and the door jamb. I had to lean on the can hard enough to crush it, but it served its purpose and pried the latch open.

The door was still stuck. There must have been another lock inside. I gave it a good hard shake and nothing happened. Having no other way to gain entry, I stood back, lifted my skirts, and put everything I had into one hard kick. There came a splintering sound and I feared I'd taken it right off its hinges, but in fact I'd only torn the inside latch away from the door jamb. As I stepped down into the cellar, the rusted screws caught on my coat.

Fleurette had always been terrified of cellars, and of spiders and dust and small dark places of any kind, but they didn't bother me. I only found them uncomfortable because I had to stoop down so low to get through them. The cellar had a hard dirt floor and a few wooden shelves lined with empty glass jars. There was an old rocking chair in one corner and a broom with a broken handle, but nothing more. I turned around to look again at the door. The latch looked like it hadn't been touched in years. If anyone had been in the house recently, they hadn't come this way.

A short staircase led up to the kitchen, where I saw nothing that I hadn't already seen through the windows. The house had the stale musty odor of a place that hadn't been aired out in months. My boots made a hollow echo as I stepped into the dining room, empty except for a sideboard with a broken mirror, and into the parlors beyond. The only furnishings left behind had something wrong with them. There was a music cabinet missing a leg and knocked over on its side, and a faded rug with a burn mark in the center. Piles of papers sat around the corners of one room, but I found nothing worth keeping, only newspapers and medical journals and invoices from a grocer and a tailor.

I ducked low as I climbed the stairs so I wouldn't be seen going past a window. Every creak of the steps echoed around the empty rooms. I found myself wary of disturbing the stillness of the old house and treaded lightly.

Upstairs, the rooms were furnished in a dormitory style, with steel cots and old washstands. Darker spots on the wallpaper showed where pictures had been removed. In one room was a child's iron crib, with a pile of old pillows inside it, their ticking split and the feathers curling out from the seams. I found a fifty-cent alarm clock underneath the crib, its face smashed, and a tattered piece of lace that looked like it had been picked off the hem of a dress.

A room at the end of the hall held medical equipment: an old pair of crutches, an invalid chair whose reed seat had splintered, and a pile of yellowed contraptions made from elastic and webbing that I took to be hip supports, trusses, and those corrective braces meant to force the shoulders back. A brittle package of strengthening plasters sat on the window-sill.

Someone had taken everything of use out of the house. Whoever did it must have had a key, because I saw not a single window or door that looked like it had been forced. I paced around for another minute or two just to kick at loose floorboards and look into grates. It gave me an officious feeling to knock around the house and tap on things, but feeling officious was the easy part of the work and turning up something that might have been of use was quite another. Nothing I found meant a thing.

I left the way I came and latched the cellar door from the outside so it wouldn't look like it had been disturbed. Just as I walked away, the rain started again. I hurried back to the train station but slowed down in front of Louis Burkhart's shoe store. I hadn't noticed before that there was a sign for a doctor's office just up the street, perched on a slight rise that overlooked all of downtown Rutherford.

Some good had to come from this day. I ran over and rapped on the door.

A sign bolted to the house advertised the services of W. C. Williams, MD, with office hours from one to two and again from seven to eight-thirty in the evening. It was already the middle of the afternoon, but I persisted in knocking a second time and twisting the brass bell.

The door sailed open and I faced a man of about thirty with a fine thoughtful face and thinning hair that flew away from the top of his head. He looked impatient but not unkind.

"Office hours, miss," he said, pointing to the sign.

"I know, but I'm just on my way to the train station and hoped I could stop and—"

He interrupted and said, with a forced smile, "If you're well enough to catch a train, you probably don't need a doctor."

"It isn't for me." I had to put my hand on the door to keep him from closing it. He looked disgruntled about it and crossed his arms.

"It's Mrs. Burkhart, above the shoe store. Do you know her? She's right over there." I turned to point in the direction of the store, which was quite near. "Her son is Louis Burkhart. His father died a few years ago, and it's just the two of them now, only she's terribly ill and I don't see how she'll recover unless somebody goes and sees her."

He raised his eyebrows in a gesture of resignation and stepped out on the porch. "Burkhart Brothers? The shoe store?"

"That's right. You might have heard about what happened to that boy. He was one of the orderlies who brought a complaint against Dr. von Matthesius, who was running a sanitarium over on Carmita."

The doctor gave me a long and puzzled look. "Come inside."

I followed him into his parlor, where the morning's fire had been reduced to a few powdery coals in the grate. I nonetheless went to stand in front of it and pulled off my gloves. Although the parlor was situated in the front of the house, just off the entryway, it didn't seem to be set up to receive patients. There was a low divan of tufted green velvet and two chairs to match, and at the end of the room, near the fireplace, was a wide writing desk against a wall of bookshelves.

Next to a typewriter sat a stack of paper with an ashtray on top of it.

Dr. Williams saw me looking at the books and said, "Go ahead."

They were mostly novels, poetry collections, and paperbound journals. "These don't look like medical books," I said.

"Medical books are very dull, so I keep them by the bed if I have trouble sleeping. Do you read much poetry?"

I shook my head. "I see it in magazines sometimes."

"That's about all anyone does. Now, how are you involved in this? I heard the damn fools at the hospital let that lunatic get away."

I turned away from the books. "I work—well, I had been working for the sheriff, but I'm not here on sheriff's business. It's purely a personal call. I'd like to leave some money with you to look in on Mrs. Burkhart." I reached into my pocketbook and handed him ten dollars.

He took it but said, "I don't know what condition the woman is in or what treatment she might require."

"Won't that be enough?"

"It might be more than enough if I'm only to pay a visit. How would I get it back to you?"

"Don't send it back. She'll need all the help you can give her. You might have a look at that boy, too."

"What's the matter with the boy?" He was writing my payment down in a ledger book as he spoke to me.

I didn't know how to explain it, even to a doctor. "He suffers from a nervous condition. He had a terrible fright and he seems not to have recovered. He's very much afraid of being sent away on account of it. I don't think he has any sort of job or goes to school or does much of anything but look after his mother."

"I won't send him away if he's not making trouble for anybody."

"He isn't."

He picked up his bag and went back to the door. I followed him out.

"Dr. Williams, would you know any of Dr. von Matthesius's associates? Anyone who might be helping him to hide?"

"He's no doctor, I know that. And I've no idea about his associates. I only know what I read in the papers. It's a fine mess and I hope they catch him, but I don't suppose they will." He said good-bye and jogged down the porch steps ahead of me.

Any other detective would have gone directly back to New York to question Alfonso Youngman, but I was the sort of detective who was required to attend theater performances. Fleurette would never forgive me if I missed her stage debut. Von Matthesius might have been my responsibility, but so was Fleurette. There was a train leaving soon for the city, but I went the other way, back to Wyckoff, back home.

❧ 12 ❧

I FOUND OUR SITTING ROOM empty and the house silent. Already my own home looked foreign and unfamiliar. There was my mother's glass-fronted cabinet holding teacups and curios from her childhood, and across from it an old grand-father clock that had never quite worked right after getting knocked down last year. We'd been gradually lifting the lace doilies from the backs of the chairs and hiding them away. We were too attached to anything made by Mother's own hand to throw them out but too stifled by their pretensions at Old World gentility to want to look at them any longer.

Everything seemed to belong to the past, to some other era that existed before my prisoner ran away and before I left home to hunt him down. What I was doing would have been unimaginable to my mother. The traces of her, left behind in this room, sat in hushed reproach.

Fleurette was upstairs in my bedroom, in front of a large mirror, surrounded by face paints and powder puffs. When she turned to look up at me I jumped back in unrestrained horror.

"What have you done?"

She giggled and grinned, exposing teeth stained red with lip-stick. Her cheeks were a shocking cherry pink, her eyes smudged with black graphite, and the complexion above her neck line was of a chalky whiteness I'd never seen on a living human before.

"Do I look like a farm girl?" came Fleurette's voice from behind a marionette's face.

"You already were a farm girl. Now you look like the kind of girl they arrest in dance halls."

That only made her gaze more lovingly into my mirror. "I'm a farm girl who goes to the city and falls in with the wrong sort," she said dreamily.

"Is that in the script?"

"No. In the script I'm the daughter of a farmer who steals a potion that lets him grow the biggest pumpkins at the county fair."

"A farmer who cheats at the county fair? Is that the worst thing that happens in this play?"

Fleurette sighed and dabbed at her neck with the powder. "Mrs. Hansen had an overabundance of young students this year owing to the retirement of another teacher, so we had to find a play that was suitable for children. It's a dull role."

"At least you weren't cast as the pumpkin." I took out my handkerchief and scrubbed the color off her cheeks.

She wrinkled her nose and pulled away from me. "The part of the pumpkin will be shared by three boys whose talents are well-suited for it."

"And what happened to your gingham dress?" She was wearing a rest frock of heliotrope crêpe de Chine, cut with the sort of slouching low waist popular on Madison Avenue but rarely seen in New Jersey farmhouses. I used to look over her patterns and fabrics before she got under way, but she discovered that all she had to do was to talk at great length about hems, ribbons, buttons, and pleats, and I would grow bored and ask her to please proceed without my supervision. The result was that Fleurette was making herself into a Vogue sophisticate before our eyes.

"I'll change in a minute."

"I thought you might have dressed for the members of the pigeon club." Fleurette had invited everyone she knew to this performance, and several of Norma's club members would be attending.

She groaned. "If I ever come to you and ask to marry one of the men from Norma's pigeon club, promise me you will forbid it and lock me in a tower."

"Is that how it'll happen? You're going to come and ask my permission? What about our brother?"

"Francis would marry me off to the first man who had fifty dollars in his pocket, just to be done with it," she said. "But I think I should have my tour on the stage first, and be quite sure I've met all of my admirers before I marry one of them."

I found myself suddenly unable to breathe.

"What's the matter?" Fleurette said as I sputtered and loosened my collar.

"This is the first I've heard of the tour, and the admirers, and the marriage to follow."

"I've been making all sorts of plans. You haven't been at home to hear about them."

Oh, the sting this girl could inflict! "Would you like me to stay at home and await your every notion, or would you rather

I go and earn your music academy tuition? Either way, it all seems to be for you."

"Did you catch your man?"

"No."

"I wonder if it isn't too dangerous to have you chasing criminals around the city. Could you imagine what Mother would have thought? *Quel choc!*"

I yawned and pulled off my boots. "You shouldn't worry about that."

"Oh, I think I am worried," Fleurette said. "When you were at the jail, at least we knew what you were doing."

"Oh? What was that?" I dropped down to my bed and pulled off my damp and sticky stockings.

"Norma said you were just serving tea to the ladies and reading them stories."

"Norma's never been to see me at the jail, so she doesn't know anything about it."

"Norma doesn't have to see a thing to know about it."

"I can handle myself." I put a pillow behind my head and stretched my legs out.

She gathered up her things and went out of the room with them. I closed my eyes, but she was back just a few minutes later.

"Aren't you coming?" She tugged at my sleeve. "Norma wants you to eat something first."

I groaned and kicked away the blanket I'd become entangled in. She took up my hat and coat and held them out. "Hurry. Helen's father is driving us."

It was strange to hear Fleurette sound so authoritative. Usually I was the one ordering her out of bed and cajoling her with food.

"I'm coming," I said. "I'll be there."

I changed into a clean dress and packed a few things in an overnight bag. My hair was beyond hope but I managed to sweep it back and put a hat over it.

Norma was in the kitchen making beef and butter sandwiches. Fleurette had put on the Victrola and flung open the front door in anticipation of the Stewarts' arrival. I wouldn't have been surprised if she'd hung bunting in the foyer. Even the smallest occasions were getting more theatrical by the day around our house.

I dropped into a kitchen chair and Norma put a sandwich on a plate for me. She turned back to the sink and said, "I don't suppose you've found him yet."

I ate the sandwich and watched her shoulders work up and down as she wrapped two more in paper and tied a string around them. Norma always stood straight as a fence post and kept her chin at a very particular angle. I had a dim memory of a dancing teacher tapping a ruler under Norma's chin one time when we were girls and telling her that she would never miss a thing if she would only keep her head up.

"No. I'm making inquiries."

"There's been nothing much in the papers, which I take to mean that Sheriff Heath is going in circles." She turned around and held her bundle of sandwiches out to me in a strangely solemn manner, as if she wanted me to put my hands on them and make a vow. She raised one eyebrow and looked down at me with all the gravity she could muster. "You're certain to have made more progress than he has."

"I couldn't say." I was weak from overexcitement and still foggy from those few stolen minutes of sleep.

She sat down across from me. "Well, you must have been at some sort of business since yesterday morning."

I picked at a slice of roast that slipped away from the bread. "There's a man in New York I want to question, and the parents of a girl who was badly treated at the sanitarium. After that, I don't know what I'll do but stand on a street corner and hope he walks by."

Norma sat back and folded her arms across her chest. "I suppose that's all the sheriff is doing at this point."

"What do the papers say?"

"The *Hackensack Republican* is calling for his immediate dismissal."

"That's no different from any other day. What's been said about the case?"

"Only that everyone at the hospital has been questioned, and no one remembers him getting away."

"Except for me, because I'm the one who allowed it."

"No." Norma got busy sweeping the crumbs off the table. She couldn't sit still when she was working her way up to a declaration. "No, I won't let this be your fault. You're the only one bringing an air of respectability to the place. You and Mr. Morris."

Norma thought very highly of Deputy Morris, whom she regarded as an old-fashioned man who didn't entertain nonsense. He happened to agree with her that messenger pigeons were a superior form of communication in times of crisis—or, at least, he allowed her to believe that he agreed—and was always willing to take a pigeon home to Paterson and keep it for a day or two before sending it back to her with a cryptic, military-style report. He had a book of telegraph codes for police officers and loaned a second copy to her so that they could exchange notes in three-letter codes. "A thorough search should be made" was PVT, and "Prepare to go on a minute's notice" was JPM. Fleurette got hold of it and was soon slipping in warnings of a false mustache (MYP) and a female opium smoker (KBW), confusing matters between Norma and Deputy Morris for weeks until they found the culprit. ("She is guilty," JUM.)

From the other room, Fleurette shrieked and Helen joined in. It was time for a night of amateur theater, whether we wanted one or not. I gave Norma the address at the Mandarin, where I expected to stay the next few nights.

"Take the sandwiches," Norma said, pushing them toward me.

"They have sandwiches in New York." Fleurette was calling for us.

"Unfamiliar food disagrees with a body," she said. "It will put you off your work."

There was no refusing Norma. I took them and went to look for Helen's father, who turned out to be a man of about my age. He was standing in our foyer all alone, having been abandoned by the two girls.

"I'm so sorry, Mr. Stewart," I said when I found him examining a murky oil painting of my great-grandmother above our hall table. "You must think that no one in this house has any manners."

"Helen is the eldest of five children. I'm used to being forgotten." He had a round, freckled face fringed in hair a shade brighter than the pumpkin that was to be the subject of tonight's performance.

"I'm sure they never forget their father," I said. "Are they all redheads?"

"Every one of them."

"Then you might be in trouble after all. Won't Mrs. Stewart join us tonight?"

"I wish she could. We lost her in childbirth last year. The baby, too."

I couldn't help but gasp. "I had no idea. I'm so—"

"Sorry?" He gave me a defeated little smile. "Everyone is sorry. You needn't say it. Helen is so glad to have your sister for a singing partner. This school was the first thing I've been able to interest her in since her mother died."

I didn't know what to say, but he kept up the conversation for the both of us. "Since Fleurette has faced a similar tragedy, I believe it gave them something in common."

Our cold and austere Austrian mother, who had almost been too old to pass convincingly as Fleurette's mother, had to have been a world apart from the Scottish girl Mr. Stewart had wed. But I saw no point in disagreeing. I only wondered how it was that I knew so little about Fleurette's new friend.

We arrived at the theater an hour before the performance so the girls could get ready. The lobby was crowded with the other families who had done the same thing. Mr. Stewart seemed to know many of them and went around congratulating them on their child's stage debut and introducing the two of us. Norma and I were so rarely out in a social capacity that we both found it uncomfortable to manage the simple introductions and exchanges of pleasantries they required. At last a punch bowl was unveiled in the corner of the room and we pulled ourselves away, feigning a monstrous thirst.

"Are we doomed to become patrons of the theater?" Norma said with exhaustion in her voice.

"Some people like the theater," I said.

"Oh, I don't mind the theater."

"But you never want to go."

"I don't mind it on *principle*."

We were accosted by members of her pigeon club, all of whom had accepted Fleurette's invitation and appeared quite eager to enjoy a play about a farmer and his secret formula for growing enormous pumpkins. One of the men proposed that they write a play about messenger pigeons and train actual pigeons to perform roles in the production. They chatted gaily about this idea until the lights went down. Norma and I settled down near the front with Mr. Stewart.

"Have you heard them rehearsing their lines?" he asked before the curtain came up on the stage.

I shook my head. "We've been terribly busy at the jail. I've hardly been home."

"They don't have you out looking for that maniac, do they?"

A woman seated in front of us turned and gave me a pointed look. I dropped my voice to a whisper. "I'm sure they'll have him in custody soon. Don't let it worry you."

"Worried? Oh, no, I only wondered—I mean—it seems like an awfully dangerous job for you, being around all those criminals. I don't know how they keep a lady safe in a place like that."

A single light illuminated the stage, and from the orchestra pit came the first few notes of piano music. "I manage."

The play was boisterous and silly, but well-suited for the dozens of children who expected to have their turn on stage.

The farmer was played by a fourteen-year-old boy who was tall enough to be a man but too skinny, which meant that his shirt and trousers had to be stuffed with wool to make him look more substantial. He was convincing in his costume, and the children who played the part of the ever-expanding pumpkin did so with the kind of bravura rarely seen in a cucurbit. In the end, the farmer met his punishment for stealing the secret pumpkin-enlarging potion and redeemed himself by sharing the recipe with his fellow farmers so that they could all grow the most enormous pumpkins and bring fame to the dying and forgotten town. An ensemble musical number at the end celebrated their pumpkin-fueled rebirth.

The girls sang beautifully and had a better command over their lines than anyone else in the production. Fleurette delivered her part with the full-throated confidence of someone who was entirely at ease on the stage. She took full command of the space she had been given and filled it with her lively spirit.

Although Fleurette had always been attracted to the theater, I had assumed that she was mostly interested in theatrics and would not have the temperament to put in long hours at rehearsal and to memorize her lines. As the curtain dropped and we stood to applaud, I wondered if I'd underestimated her.

"Your mother must've had quite a time with her," Mr. Stewart said.

"We've all had quite a time with her. I don't know what we're going to do now that she's almost grown."

"Helen wants to go to Broadway. I'm looking into finishing schools."

When the curtain dropped and rose again, the little band

of performers were showered with cheers and whistles and orange paper petals that the ushers had sold us during intermission. A crowd of admirers rushed to the stage, and we soon lost sight of Fleurette and Helen.

We made our way to the lobby to wait, along with all the other families, for the performers to emerge from the stage door. The ceilings, painted in turquoise and gold, gleamed high above us, and from each corner a griffin or a joker grinned down on us. The cries of parents congratulating their children rang out and met in the air to create the kind of gentle roar that made it impossible to say a thing without shouting. I thought I saw Fleurette's dark hair bob above the crowd and disappear again. Norma and I stood in the corner and waited with Mr. Stewart.

"Have you heard anything about the Christmas production?" he shouted over the rumble of the crowd.

Norma groaned. "Is there to be a Christmas show?"

"Of course," he said cheerfully. "But don't worry. It's nothing but carols and candles. No auditions and no special costumes."

"Then Mrs. Hansen has some sense after all," she muttered.

It was too warm and close in the lobby, so I stepped outside. There I saw Fleurette leaning against a black auto, chatting with a man whose back was turned to me. Helen stood smiling nearby but said nothing. I squinted at the man's broad back and shoulders. He was half in shadow, so I couldn't tell if his hair was blond or light brown. I guessed that he was young, from the cut of his collar and Fleurette's lively laughter at whatever he was saying.

Mr. Stewart had followed me out. I jumped when I heard

him behind me. "I never know whether to break it up or just stand nearby and glare at the young man."

"You've more experience," I said, "but I'm inclined to do something more than glare." The boy leaned down to say something to Fleurette and she stood on her toes to hear. I was suddenly very aware of the revolver in my handbag.

"Helen gets all kinds of attention from boys at school," Mr. Stewart said. "But I understand that Fleurette was . . . privately schooled. So the boys are only just now finding her."

It had been my mother's decision to school Fleurette at home rather than subject the family to a schoolteacher's scrutiny. It wasn't until Fleurette was much older that she even remarked upon the fact that other children went to school. Mother just sniffed and said that the schools in Bergen County were not to her liking.

I wasn't accustomed to having to answer questions about it. I tried to summon up an answer for Mr. Stewart, but before I could, the boy disappeared down the street. Helen and Fleurette spotted us and came running, nearly knocking us over when they reached us. There was a damp sheen on both of them from the exertion and excitement, and, I feared, from their encounter with that young man. Ringlets of hair were plastered to their necks and their faces were flushed in an identical high blush. They were still shouting as if they'd forgotten they'd left the stage.

"How was I?" Helen asked her father, twirling around in front of him. "Did you see Fleurette step on my toes during our duet?"

"I did not," Fleurette protested. "You put your toes right under my feet. Keep them where they belong and they won't get stepped on."

She leaned against me and put an arm around my waist, looking up at me with the eagerness and longing of a girl seeking praise for what she already knew she'd done so well. Her dark eyes glittered behind the inky smudges around her lashes.

I was trying not to ask, but I couldn't help it. "Who was the boy?"

"Which one? The farmer?"

"Just now. Over there."

"Oh!" She squealed and turned to fling an arm around Helen. "Just an admirer of ours."

"We have too many to keep track of," Helen said, which her father answered with a weary half-smile.

"He said he'd bring his autograph book next time," Fleurette said.

"Doesn't he have a name?" I asked, but Fleurette just shrugged and the girls went back to chattering about the production. We granted them as many words of praise as their wild temperaments could handle, and I dared a swipe at Fleurette's painted lips with my handkerchief. She ducked and grinned at me, buoyant and beautiful.

⊰ 13 ⊱

NORMA AND FLEURETTE went home with Helen and Mr. Stewart. I walked by myself to the station and settled onto the train to New York with the weary resignation of a working man riding through the dark and chilly night to some distant factory, except that my factory was populated not by steam boilers and punch presses, but by flophouses and reluctant witnesses. The train raced across half-frozen marshes fringed in cattails that might have been pink by day, but stood black and solemn under the moonlight.

The following morning found me back in the Mandarin's dining room, where Geraldine and Ruth were finishing their coffee. Carrie had just rushed off to write a story about a parade.

"She hates parades," Ruth said, sliding a rack of toast across the table to me. "She's waiting for you to catch your man so she can put it on the front page."

"If there's to be a story, she can have it first," I said, and drained a cup of coffee.

"Haven't you learned anything yet?" Geraldine asked.

"I know von Matthesius owed someone money. It doesn't surprise me, as criminals are often on the run from their creditors. I know he gave sham treatments to his patients and abused them."

"That's the serious charge, I suppose," Ruth said.

"Oh, it's worse than that. He drugged a rich man's daughter and married her against her will."

"So he's a predator and a con man, too," Geraldine said.

"And arrogant, if he thought he'd get away with a scheme like that," I said. "There's a man to go see on the East Side this morning, and I'm going to try to speak to the girl he married, if I can find her."

"Ask Carrie about that business," Ruth said. "Newspapers have all kinds of ways of tracking people down."

Geraldine looked at the clock and stood up. "We're off to the office, and you have to go kicking down doors and poking through alleyways. I'm not sure I envy you, but I might."

This time I was much better equipped to be out on the streets, with a warmer pair of boots and a heavier wool coat and gloves. The doorman at the hotel put me in a cab. I didn't give the address of the Warren, thinking the driver would refuse to take me there. In fact, he didn't even want to let me off on Bowery as I requested, but I insisted that I was doing charity work and had gone there unaccompanied before.

The Warren sat on a narrow street populated by saloons and dingy dance halls. Most of the doors along the block stood open despite the cold. I resisted the urge to look into the gaping doorways as I hurried by.

A sign in the Warren's window advertised vacant rooms for men. I stepped into a small carpeted vestibule that accommodated only one person at a time. There was an odor of sulfur candles so strong that I had to bring my handkerchief to my nose. I took it to mean that bed bugs were being driven from the place and I hoped the effort had been successful. I stood a little taller to keep my hems from dragging on the ground.

Directly in front of me—for there was nowhere else to look—the reception window slid open to reveal an old man with an enormous red nose and an array of blue veins across his forehead. He pointed a polished wooden ear trumpet in my direction.

"I am here to see Alfonso Youngman," I said, speaking slowly and distinctly into the trumpet.

"Any young man?" the old man shouted. "We've got a few dozen of them. What are you after?"

"That's his name," I said, louder than before. "Youngman. First name Alfonso."

The old man dropped the horn. "Him? He went out feet first."

"Do you mean that he's dead?"

He didn't need his horn to understand the question. "Hung himself from the steam pipe. Made a damn mess."

"Can you tell me when it happened?"

The man shook his head and presented the horn again.

"When did Mr. Youngman die?"

"Just last month. Haven't been able to rent that room since. Nobody wants to go near it."

"Do you know why he did it?" I shouted into the horn.

"A girl. Name of Bea, something like that."

"May I see the room?"

The old man grinned, revealing a yellowed set of vulcanite teeth. "You can rent the room," he hollered, "as long as you're a man and you have two dollars."

I handed him four dollars and got a key.

Alfonso Youngman had lived at the end of the hall on the third floor in a room that looked out over the street. It was small and shabby, outfitted only with a metal bed, a wooden chair, and a small table and dresser. There was a tiny triangle-shaped sink wedged into the corner. The walls were papered in a faded pattern of brown acanthus and the floor was bare wood, although an accumulation of dust around the edges suggested that a carpet had been lifted up and hauled away. There was a fire insurance calendar from 1913 hanging on a nail, and two chipped plates on the table.

I slid open the drawers in the dresser, releasing the odor of moth balls, and closed them again. If Alfonso Youngman had any possessions, they had been taken away.

Finding nothing of any use, I stood in the corner and looked up at the bent steam pipe above me. There was a seam where it had been broken and welded back together.

CARRIE HAD JUST RETURNED from her parade when I got back to the hotel. As Ruth predicted, she was delighted to take up the search for Beatrice Fuller. We divided the city directories and sat in the telephone booths on our respective floors, ringing all the Fullers. One of her colleagues at the newspaper looked through the indexes and called any Fullers listed, the idea being that if the family was wealthy, they were also prominent enough to have been mentioned in the paper.

We took our supper together in Carrie's room. "Why don't you just ask the sheriff how to find Beatrice Fuller?" Carrie said as she blew on her soup.

"I—there's been some difficulty with the sheriff. I don't know where things stand with him at the moment."

She put her spoon down and dabbed at her lips. "There's more to the story of the sheriff and the escaped prisoner than you've let on. Why don't you tell me the rest of it?"

"Are you going to write about it in the paper if I do?"

"Of course. I'm a reporter. That's what we do. You ought to remember that, in your line of work. Everything you tell us will go in the paper."

"Then I'm going back to my calls."

It was the girl in the newsroom who finally hunted down Beatrice Fuller's parents and telephoned, at around eight o'clock, to tell us about it. The Fullers didn't want to see me, but the girl was apparently quite good on the telephone and made it sound as if they hadn't any choice in the matter.

"She said it was an official call and that you'd be right over," Carrie told me. "I only wish I had a sketch artist in my pocket."

"It isn't a night for sketching or for reporting," I said, although going out at night to question the Fullers did have a sense of occasion about it. I'd already taken off my boots and loosened my dress, but I put myself together, gave Carrie my thanks, and ran downstairs for a taxicab.

The Fullers lived across town in a building of peach-colored stone with a wide green awning over the door. There were lights blazing in all the windows and a bit of laughter and cigarette smoke drifting down from a half-open window next door.

A maid stood waiting for me just inside the door. When I gave my name she looked down at my hands, expecting me to present a card. I mumbled that I hadn't any but that I would give my particulars to the Fullers when I saw them. This must have sufficed, because she ushered me up a set of wide and elegant stairs, draped in a ribbon of carpet held in place with brass rods that looked like they were polished once a week. We arrived at a heavy oak door on the second floor. She held it open, announcing me as Miss Constance, and left me to make my way.

Inside was a little parlor, where Mr. and Mrs. Fuller were seated in deep stuffed chairs by the fire. They stood when they saw me and I was surprised to see that they were far older than I'd expected. Mrs. Fuller was one of those extraordinary women who aged much more beautifully than anyone else, so that even at the age of seventy or so, the young girl she'd once been was very much alive in her eyes and in her smile. Her hair was entirely white and as fine as corn silk, and she swept it into one of those smooth buns favored by European aristocrats. She wore a velvet evening dress that would have impressed Fleurette and seemed far too formal for a night at home.

Mr. Fuller was exactly her height—they were a charmingly compact couple, like one of those joined pairs of ceramic figurines—and he, too, was dressed for a night out, except that he'd exchanged his topcoat for an evening jacket as men of his class did at home. He wore a monocle and a silver mustache that curved up mischievously at the ends. I couldn't help but think that someone should paint their portrait and sell it on postcards.

"I'm sorry to disturb you at this hour. It's an urgent matter and I hope that you or Miss Beatrice might be of some help."

A look passed between the two of them and they invited me to sit down. I perched on the edge of the settee. They took the two chairs across from it.

"We weren't expecting a lady," Mrs. Fuller said. "You didn't come on your own, did you, dear?"

"Because there's a young girl involved, the sheriff thought I should make the inquiries."

"Sheriff? The girl from the newspaper wouldn't tell us what this was about," Mr. Fuller said, "but we don't wish to have our names mixed up in any trouble."

"You won't," I said hastily, and told them about von Matthesius's escape, which they'd read about in the papers, and how my search for him had led me to them.

"Well, we aren't hiding him here!" Mr. Fuller said with a nervous laugh.

"Of course not. I only wonder if you've any idea about his associates. Or could I speak to Beatrice? Is she at home?"

After another glance between them, Mrs. Fuller said, "Our granddaughter is under very good care in California. Her doctors hope to return her to us by summer. She isn't to speak of that time and she certainly shouldn't answer questions from the sheriff about it."

I could tell from her tone that she wouldn't tolerate many more questions. "Mrs. Fuller, we only want to see the man captured and put away again. If Beatrice mentioned any names to you, it might give us some idea of where he's gone."

"The only one she ever talked about was that Youngman fellow," Mr. Fuller blurted out, earning a sharp stare from his wife. "That's why we sent her out West. I was starting to think she was going to marry that boy."

I tried to proceed carefully, as I knew so little about what had happened. "From what I've heard, Alfonso Youngman tried to save Beatrice, and to put a stop to . . . to what was being done."

"And he's a very brave boy for that," Mrs. Fuller put in, "but it doesn't give him license to write letters and to keep trying to call on her. She's in a very delicate state and it was wrong of him to take advantage of the gratitude we all expressed at the time."

They didn't know he was dead. But how could they?

"Apparently Mr. Youngman was in a delicate state himself," I said, as gently as I could. "He was found dead in his room a month ago. I'm sorry to say that it was suicide."

Mrs. Fuller gasped and sat back in her chair. Mr. Fuller went and stood behind her. "If that's true, Miss Kopp, then it's another tragedy in a long string of them caused by this von Matthesius. I wish we'd never met him. I've still a mind to sue Dr. Rathburn. Someone's got to stop him."

"Rathburn?" I said.

Mr. Fuller helped his wife to her feet and it was clear that our visit was over. As we walked to the door he said, "It was Dr. Rathburn who was so insistent that we send our Beatrice to Rutherford for treatment. They were running this scheme together. My granddaughter meant so little to either of them that they were both trying to extort money from us over her care, and that's to say nothing of what must have happened to the girl when she was too drugged to remember. I hope she never remembers. You tell the sheriff to lock both of them up for good this time."

⊰ 14 ⊱

IT WAS BLUSTERY out on Fifth Avenue the next morning, with a bite in the air that hinted at snow. I pushed my way up-town past the hordes of shoppers and sightseers that always made this stretch of the avenue impassable. At several of the dress shops along the avenue the tailors had declared a strike and stood out on the sidewalk with placards. Their measuring tapes hung around their necks and tended to blow off in the wind. The young women employed as their assistants passed out leaflets and those, too, scattered in the street and flew in the faces of passers-by.

A blister worked at my heel, the consequence of being out in the rain and mud all week. Even my sturdiest pair of boots wasn't serving me particularly well. I gritted my teeth against the pain and forced myself not to limp as I turned down Fifty-Fifth Street and counted the addresses over to Dr. Milton Rathburn's office.

The Fullers had given me my last chance. If this doctor knew anything about von Matthesius, I might have another lead to follow. Without it, I had nothing. I could stay in New

York and wait around train stations and ferry docks hoping to catch sight of him, or I could go home and face whatever was to come. I didn't want to think what that might be. I couldn't imagine waking up every morning knowing that Sheriff Heath was behind bars. I bent my head down against the wind and told myself that I simply wouldn't leave without shaking something out of Dr. Rathburn.

He kept his medical practice on the third floor of a stone building that might have once been white, but looked now as though it had been scrubbed in charcoal. The door was unlocked and in the foyer I found a directory listing all the offices in the building, most of which belonged to doctors, dentists, and oculists. I climbed the stairs to the third floor and found Dr. Rathburn's door open. A serious-looking, dark-haired girl sat behind a desk. Her hands were folded in front of her as if she'd been waiting for me.

"I'm here to see Dr. Rathburn," I said. "I don't have an appointment but wish only to ask him a question."

"Oh, I'm sorry, ma'am." She flipped through an appointment book on her desk with the end of a pencil. "The doctor is very busy today. Let me arrange a time for you."

"I'm only here to ask a question," I repeated. "It's a private matter."

She looked up at me and raised two fine lines on an otherwise unlined forehead. "He isn't here."

"Then I suppose I'll wait."

"I don't know when he might be in."

"I haven't any other business today. I'll wait."

I read the newspaper in the little waiting room, then read it again, and picked up a magazine someone had left behind. The receptionist shuffled papers on her desk and tried to look busy. It was well after noon before Dr. Rathburn appeared. I'd grown so numb from sitting that I felt a little dizzy when I stood to speak to him.

He looked so absurdly the part of the mad doctor that I would have believed he was an actor playing the role. His black hair stood up in stiff clumps, pointing out at all angles like so many devil's horns. He wore thick tortoise-shell glasses and an expression of perpetual surprise that came from eyebrows shaped like mountain peaks. He carried with him a rumpled tweed overcoat, not the white smock of a modern doctor.

"I thought I didn't have anyone this morning," he mumbled, looking down at the appointment book.

"You don't," she said. "Only this lady wants to speak to you. She insisted on waiting."

"I'm here on behalf of my employer," I said quickly, "and he wishes to know more about your treatments. He's quite prominent and wants assurances of privacy."

The doctor sighed and ran a hand through his hair in an unsuccessful attempt to settle it down. "They're all prominent," he said, a bit wearily.

"If I could just have a moment."

He nodded and held open the door to his office. I followed him into a luxuriously appointed room, with tall windows, a grand electric chandelier suspended from the ceiling, leather chairs, and an enormous polished desk. It was a room intended to give people the expectation that they'd be parting with a great deal of money.

I'd prepared a simple story for Dr. Rathburn, thinking only that I should find out more about the sort of business he conducted before inquiring directly about von Matthesius.

"As I explained, my employer insists upon complete discretion. He learned about your services when his sister was treated at a sanitarium in New Jersey. I've forgotten the name of the doctor, but you must know him because he spoke so highly of you. It was a German name—how silly of me to have forgotten it."

"It doesn't matter." Dr. Rathburn drummed his fingers on the desk blotter. "I correspond with colleagues all over the country. Many of them have sent patients to me, and it's not uncommon for me to recommend a patient to any number of sanitariums outside the city where they may be treated with discretion. Please assure your employer that we offer the most modern treatments for any sort of nervous condition, and no one need ever know."

He pushed his chair back to suggest that the interview was over, then cocked his head and scrutinized me over the rim of his eyeglasses. "In what capacity are you employed with this man?"

"I started as his wife's social secretary, and now I oversee all of their engagements and manage the household staff. Sometimes I handle more delicate matters as well."

"And would your employer be satisfied with the arrangements?" He said it with fatigue in his voice. The rich must have been tedious for him, even as they paid him so handsomely.

I smiled brightly at him. "I'm sure he would. You'll be hearing from him."

He swept his arm toward the door and followed me back out to the front room, where the receptionist sat with her hands folded on her desk, just as she had been when I first arrived.

I thanked her for her help and tried to maintain the posture of the socialite's secretary. As I turned to go, I said to the doctor—casually, as if I'd only just thought of it—"You know, I think that sanitarium was in Rutherford. Are you sure you don't know a man up there? Von Matheson, a name like that?"

He might have flinched when I said it, or it could have been a speck of dust in his eye.

UNTIL I MET DR. RATHBURN, I'd been plagued by an uncomfortable suspicion that I should have never taken Henri LaMotte's advice. How would I ever find von Matthesius if I avoided the very places he was most likely to turn up—at his brother's apartment, at a train station, at any of the other places Sheriff Heath might have been watching at that very moment? Instead I'd been making inquiries of people who didn't want to talk to me. I'd turned up heartbreak and terrible secrets but they gave me no ideas about where von Matthesius might be hiding.

But there was something in the air at that office, something that told me I was getting close. It was the first time I had lied to anyone in the course of my investigation. It was the first time I hadn't stated plainly whom I was looking for and why I was looking for him. It was the first time I'd given into the electric thrill of my own instincts and followed where they led me.

And it was nothing but instinct that kept me in the hall after I left Dr. Rathburn's office.

His door had a frosted glass pane that let in a little light and let out quite a bit of sound. I stood next to it, pressed against the wall, and listened.

"Telephone over to Murray's and get Mr. Kyne on the line," he was saying to his receptionist.

I heard her ask the operator, and then there was a little tapping sound, as if someone were fidgeting with a pencil.

After a bit of a wait the receptionist said, "It's Dr. Rathburn for Mr. Kyne." There was another long pause in which I could hear them mumbling to one another but couldn't make out what they were saying. At last Dr. Rathburn's voice boomed into the telephone, "Pat? It's Milt. Has your cloakroom girl got anything for me? Yes, I'll hold the line."

The receptionist said something that I couldn't hear, and then the man came back on the line. "Are you quite certain, Pat?" he shouted. "It would've been a fellow named Felix von Matthesius. Same one as last time. He hasn't been by? All right, I'll send my girl over."

There was more murmuring between them and he told her to go. "Felix usually stops in after lunch. Hurry over before he gets there and leave this with the cloakroom girl."

She gave some muffled answer, and then I could hear keys rattling. I slipped around the corner and ran down the stairs ahead of her. From across the street I saw the receptionist leave and walk along Fifty-Fifth, never looking back at me. I followed from a half a block away and easily kept up with her. When she reached Murray's I stopped and waited outside. I didn't dare follow her for fear that she'd turn and walk out just as I was walking in.

Murray's occupied several floors of a fine brick building in the theater district. An elaborate series of stone columns, latticework, vines, and sculpture around the entrance gave the place the air of a Roman palace. It took only one inquiry at a newsstand on the corner to learn that it was a restaurant with a rather notorious cloakroom. One could check a coat or hat, or leave an envelope of money or some other dubious parcel for another party. Only a few days ago, the man told me, someone had left an urn holding the ashes of a famous musical actress. When the parcel was left unclaimed, the cloakroom girl opened it and believed the smooth metal surface to be the side of a bomb. The police were called, but a note inside explained the urn's contents and the package was returned to the funeral parlor to be reunited with its owner.

The receptionist was inside for only a minute. When she left, I dashed across the street and stepped inside.

I wasn't prepared for the decadent spectacle around me. At the end of the vast main dining hall stood a stage two stories high flanked by Roman columns and statues of nymphs and fantastical creatures. The ceiling was painted a deep ultramarine blue and hung with tiny lights that gave the effect of sitting out under the stars. Above the clamor of the luncheon crowd—and there must have been hundreds of people, all impeccably dressed for a matinee or afternoon shopping—above all of that, I could hear a good-size orchestra rehearsing tunes for the evening's dancing. There was even a barge fit for an emperor floating in a grand fountain, where I could imagine the dancers splashing and laughing under a glittering waterfall in the small hours after midnight.

This was a good place to be seen, but was it also a good place to hide? Could a man like Felix put on his best suit, slip into the crowd, and escape notice? If he did, I couldn't go in after him. I'd be too conspicuous in my plain street clothes and wide felt hat, towering as I did over all of the women and many of the men. I had to hope he was only going to stop into the cloakroom and not spend the afternoon there, dining on blue points and little neck clams.

I'd managed to push myself into a corner where the waiters rushed past and ignored me. I could see the cloakroom at the end of a narrow hall. There was a girl in a green dress collecting coats and handing out tickets. She would notice me eventually and wonder why I was watching her. The waiters who had been ignoring me thus far would want to put me at a table or send me on my way. There was nothing to do but wait outside and hope that I spotted Felix before he saw me.

I passed the next few hours engaged in the mundane and tedious work of waiting and watching. It may sound like a simple thing to stand outside a building and look at the people going in and out, but not everyone can do it. The job takes a particular kind of focus. One must look carefully at every hat and coat, asking the same question each time: Is he the right height? Has he the same hair color? What of his demeanor or his posture? Within a second, each man must be considered and dismissed. Although one wouldn't be aware of it, some amount of time is occupied in simply sorting the men from the women so that the mind knows which figures to follow. The work is dull and undemanding, but it requires a great deal of attention, for if the mind wanders for even a minute, the man in question could slip past.

It helped to move from one spot to another so as not to invite suspicion. I stood under an awning across the street, then moved to a row of shop windows, then crossed over Forty-Second to a busy street corner, and back again. My legs ached from spending so much time on the pavement. My feet were swollen, the blisters were screaming at me, and my nose was red and wet from the cold. All of these discomforts served their own purpose in keeping me alert and eager to catch my man and put an end to my suffering.

When Felix did appear, it was in the fading blue hours of early evening, and he was walking out of Murray's, not going in. How had I missed him? I caught only a glimpse of him in profile and doubted myself for a moment. But he would get away if I didn't move quickly.

He pulled his hat down and turned east toward Times Square, sliding into a crowd of overcoats and hats, where he would be easily lost. I was still across the street and had no choice but to risk my own limbs as I dodged motor cars to get to him. When I reached the other side, he'd gained quite a bit of distance and was moving fast. It was nearly impossible to keep an eye trained on his hat and shoulders, and not to lose it among all the others.

There was no avoiding notice now—I was running, pushing men in topcoats out of my way. I nearly knocked over a trio of young women walking arm in arm.

Already a man was putting his hand on my elbow to offer assistance. I was soon to be surrounded by a crowd of people eager to detain me and calm me down. I did the only thing I could think of, which was to shout, "Purse thief!" and tear myself away from them in pursuit.

It worked, for two young men took up the chase. There were so many people on the sidewalk that none of us could make much progress, but the two of them elbowed others out of the way and cleared a path. I pulled ahead and threw myself on him, panting, at the next intersection.

Felix was half a head shorter than me, and I managed to take him by the shoulder and throw an arm across his neck.

He coughed from the unexpected force of it. I pushed him to his knees and crouched behind him. He tried to elbow me but I took hold of his wrists and pushed him face-down on the sidewalk.

Judging from the size of the crowd gathered around us, it would appear that Felix and I were the most interesting people in New York City at that moment. There were so many onlookers that they spilled into the street, making one lane impassable. A man jumped right out of the coach he was riding while it was still moving to get a better look at us.

The two young men, each of them no older than twenty and looking like they'd just had the adventure of their lives, helped me up but kept Felix down on the ground. "Is this the man, miss? Is this the one who took your purse?"

Felix struggled to turn around but couldn't see me. "I didn't snatch a purse!"

I walked around in front of him and bent down. When he looked up and recognized me, he gave a sigh and slumped down again, his cheek on the icy pavement.

"I work for the sheriff of Bergen County," I said to the boys, "up in Hackensack. This man is wanted for harboring a dangerous fugitive." I looked around at the crowd of theatergoers, all in their fine dress, out for an afternoon's amusements. They looked as if they might start tossing coins at us in appreciation of our performance. "If someone could find the police, he'll be placed under arrest."

A few men went running off to summon an officer, but most people just stood and watched me with mild and bemused curiosity. Some of the onlookers were asking each other questions that I knew were soon to be posed to me:

Who was the dangerous fugitive? What had he done? Who was I, and in what capacity did I work for the sheriff?

But it was Felix who needed to answer questions. I knelt down and my skirts pooled on the sidewalk all around me. The boys pulled him to his knees and he had no choice but to face me. It was as close as I'd ever been to him.

Felix's face was a study in lines: narrow jaw, hollow cheekbones, pinched mouth, and vertical slits for eyes. He seemed leaden and angry, with none of his brother's highbrow pretensions.

"Where is he?" I demanded.

He coughed—his collar was chafing at his neck because of the way the boys were holding him—and said, "Who?"

I didn't like that sneaky little smile or the tea-stained teeth behind it. He had a small pinched face like a rat. His nose even twitched.

A whistle sounded from down the street. The police were on their way and I feared they would take him away before I learned anything. "Tell me now and it'll be easier for you."

He turned his head away. I felt a hand on my shoulder, and in an instant four policemen pulled us apart and arrested us both.

"You'll have a circular from the sheriff of Bergen County at the station," I shouted as I was being dragged off. "Telephone him if you don't. Robert Heath. Hackensack jail. The von Matthesius escape. This is Felix von Matthesius. It's been in the papers all week."

The officer who took Felix away paid no attention to my story. The jovial and red-faced Irishman who arrested me leaned over and whispered in my ear. "Not to worry, miss.

We'll have a nice long chat at the station. This gets us out of the cold for a good hour. It could be the rest of the night if we have to wait to speak to this sheriff of yours."

I didn't like the idea of spending the night in a New York City jail cell, but as long as Felix von Matthesius was locked up as well, I wouldn't complain.

They drove us to the squat brick precinct house on Fifty-First Street. Felix went to another room to be booked, but they kept me standing inside the front door with an officer on either arm. "We'll just have to hold you here for a few minutes, miss," the Irishman said. "We have to wait for a ladies' matron before we book you in."

"I *am* a ladies' matron." I was impatient with the idea of waiting for a woman to be summoned just so my name could be written in a ledger book. "Call the sheriff and ask him. Tell him Constance Kopp has made an arrest."

The Irishman laughed. "Kopp! That's a good one. You were meant for it, weren't you?"

I looked around at the small and sparsely appointed room, with its bare wooden chairs bolted to the floor and a wall covered with the *cartes de visite* of wanted men. I felt so terribly at home there that I said, "Yes. I was."

It occurred to me that if I'd lost my position at the jail, perhaps the New York police would have me, as long as they weren't bothered by a matron with an arrest record.

No woman could be summoned and I persuaded them to book me in themselves. The cell they found for me was larger and more comfortable than my own back in Hackensack. None of the officers could believe that I spent nights at the jail, living in the same conditions as the inmates.

"Don't you want to go home, miss? See your family?" the Irishman asked from the other side of the bars.

"I go home. They see me. Sometimes."

He left me alone and told me to rest as it would be some time before the sheriff could get into the city. I didn't want to, but my eyes drifted closed and I gave in to a heavy dark sleep.

The jingle of the jailer's keys startled me out of it, and all at once I was upright in my bunk with Sheriff Heath standing over me. His hat was down over his eyes and I couldn't make out his expression. I hadn't any idea if he was angry or pleased, or, for that matter, if he intended to take me back with him or let me serve out the night in jail. Nonetheless, a great wave of relief washed over me at the sight of him.

"You tackled him," he said.

"Well, I—"

"They told me you leapt across the sidewalk and threw him down."

"Give me a day and I'll have the bruises to prove it."

"You spotted him and chased after him without any regard for your own safety. There are men under my command who wouldn't have wrestled with a suspect the way you did."

"If you can show me an easier way, I'd like to know it."

We faced each other with the old familiarity that had developed between us. At last he said, "You're the only one who's brought me anything."

"I'm also the only one who let a prisoner escape."

He gave a tired half-smile. "Now that we have Felix, old von Matthesius will find it harder to stay hidden. If you've any other ideas, tell them to me. You were conducting a much more interesting investigation than we were. It was nothing but train stations and police departments for us."

The fact that I'd been the only one to make any progress gave me a little thrill that I tried to push away. I was disappointed to realize that Henri LaMotte was right. The sheriff had been doing the same three or four things anyone would do when a crime was committed. "If I hadn't found Felix today, it would've been train stations and police departments for me, too."

He shifted around inside his old tweed coat and said, "Then come back to the jail."

"It doesn't seem right."

"Miss Kopp, I have Morris guarding the female section and he's tired of it. There's a problem with Providencia Monafo's case and she won't speak to any of us."

"What's the matter?"

"Just come back to work. After we catch von Matthesius, I'll do something about that badge."

"After." I didn't have to ask what would happen if he wasn't caught.

He looked around the jail cell and I wondered if he was imagining himself living there. "What else are you going to do? I can't have you out here by yourself, without a partner, or a badge and gun and handcuffs . . ."

"I took my gun," I said.

He smiled and looked down at his feet. "That's right. The officer out there told me. He wasn't ready to believe your story until he found a Police Positive in your handbag. That's as good as a badge."

What else *would* I do? I stood up and shook out my dress. "There's another man involved, a doctor who was waiting for

Felix to deliver a package or to pick one up. The New York police wouldn't go after him on my word alone. He's probably run off, but someone should check."

"They've already sent a man."

"Felix isn't talking," I said. "He's a cagey little snake."

"Well, let's get him back to Hackensack. Miss Kopp, it's unseemly for me to beg. Come along."

⊰ 15 ⊱

"THIS IS YOUR CHANCE, FELIX," the sheriff said as we drove away from the station.

Felix jiggled the chains around his arms and legs. "Chance for what?"

"To set yourself free. What do you say about taking us to your brother? If you do, I'm prepared to let you go, right now, in the middle of the night. We'll take the handcuffs off you and put them on him."

From the back seat, I could only make out the outline of the sheriff's hat and collar. Felix was nothing but a dim shape next to him. He let out an aggrieved sigh.

"The way I see it," Sheriff Heath continued, "is that if we put the Baron back in jail and set you free, all of us would be exactly where we started. No one would be any better or worse off than they were a month ago. Your brother would be serving his jail time, I wouldn't have a fugitive on the loose, and you'd be at liberty to do as you please. Now, Felix, you tell me what's wrong with that line of thinking."

"I don't know where he is," Felix mumbled.

"Of course you do!" Sheriff Heath sounded almost cheerful about it. "You and Dr. Rathburn. Hasn't the doctor been helping to keep him? He's a good friend to the von Matthesius clan, isn't he?"

"I don't know any doctor."

"I'm under the impression that you two traded love notes over at Murray's cloakroom."

Felix only snorted and fidgeted again with his handcuffs.

"It's a shame the police didn't find a letter in your pockets tonight. How'd you manage to throw it out? Or did you eat it? You didn't eat it, did you?"

"I didn't eat it."

There was a police wagon up ahead and Felix started at the sight of it, in the manner of someone who is habitually fearful of arrest.

"You don't have to hide from the police anymore, Felix. Now, I will withdraw this offer when we get to the jail. Think on it. Bring us to your brother and away you'll go."

Felix made a dissatisfied little growl but stayed quiet. Sheriff Heath turned around to look at me.

"Has Felix ever seen the inside of our jail, Miss Kopp?"

"I don't believe he's made it past the visiting room, Sheriff," I said, leaning forward to put my head between them.

"That's fine. Sometimes a man doesn't want to be too well-known to law enforcement." Again Felix kept his head turned to the window.

"He might not be fond of all those doors and locks," I offered.

The sheriff turned and raised an eyebrow. "That could be. Steel bars can make a man uneasy."

We continued in this line all the way back to Hackensack,

the sheriff and I trying to tempt Felix into saying something that might be of use, and Felix refusing. I was glad to be back in Sheriff Heath's company. He had an easy way with criminals and always seemed unerringly sure of himself when he was working on a case. After a few days of running around New York on my own, with no real idea of what I might find, I was back on solid ground again.

"Here we are, Felix," the sheriff said when the jail's silhouette rose up before us. "I could turn around right now and we could go fetch your brother." Felix gave the smallest shake of his head. I could hardly even hear him breathing.

THE WOMEN OF THE FIFTH FLOOR were glad for my return. Mary Lisco, the pickpocket who had escaped from the Newark jail, had been sent back, and in her place we'd acquired yet another pickpocket, this one a girl of only eighteen who specialized in train stations, lifting coins out of purses and slipping brooches and stickpins right off the coats to which they were affixed. Our hosiery thief Martha Hicks was due to be released in a few days and had embarked upon a program of reform aimed at convincing the new girl to put thievery behind her and find respectable employment. She'd had little luck so far and hoped I would help persuade the girl.

Ida Higgins, the woman accused of setting fire to her brother's house, had originally been arrested on the strength of two cans of gasoline found in her bedroom. But it had been discovered that the fire was actually set by a friend of Ida's brother, over some feud between the two men. She'd just been cleared of the charges but remained in custody as a witness until the trial, which was scheduled for the next week.

Apparently Ida Higgins believed the man to be in love with

her and didn't want to admit that he had set the fire. But he never came to visit her in jail and seemed to have no idea that she had sacrificed her own freedom for his. After weeks of writing letters that went unanswered, she finally grew angry enough to tell the whole story to the prosecutor. She explained that she had seen the man sneak around with cans of gasoline and start the fire, and that she took the cans to hide what he'd done. Following her accusation and the testimony of another witness, the man, who had been jailed for arson before, had been arrested and now resided two floors below.

Because Ida remained in jail only as a witness, she was moved to a quieter cell near mine for the remainder of her detention, and she usually had a chop or a sausage with her dinner. We also allowed her to take a walk outside with a guard. She said she looked forward to taking her walks with me now that I'd returned.

"Are you more comfortable in your new cell?" I asked as I settled back into my own quarters.

"I'd be more comfortable at home," she said. "I told them it wasn't me. Why can't they let me go?"

"Because you're needed at the trial. You'll have to testify that you saw the man sneaking around your brother's place with the gasoline."

"What do I care about the trial? It's no business of mine. I don't want anything more to do with it."

"That's exactly why we're keeping you."

Then there was the trouble with Providencia Monafo. Sheriff Heath called John Courter over to explain it the day after I returned. The two of them sat in the sheriff's office looking about as unhappy to be with one another as two men ever have.

Detective Courter cleared his throat and glared at the sheriff. He had an egg-shaped head and wore a tight, stiff collar that made his neck bulge.

"Go ahead," Sheriff Heath said. "This is your case."

Detective Courter looked at the space between us for a minute, his lips pressed together. One leg bounced up and down impatiently. There was a kind of smothered anger about him.

Finally he said, "All right. Mrs. Monafo claimed that Saverio Salino went to her apartment in the morning to pay rent and they argued over his sister living there. Then he threatened her and she shot him. She was so frightened, she said, that she ran out of the house and boarded the streetcar. It's the same car she takes to work every morning, and the driver recognized her. After she rode a few stops, she thought better of it and got off and made her way back home—for reasons of her own that none of us entirely understand. By that time, Salino had dragged himself up the stairs and someone saw him. That's when we were called."

He seemed to be waiting for some kind of answer, so I said, "Yes, that's how I recall it. What's the problem?"

"The problem is that I have witnesses who heard the shot at eight o'clock in the morning, and Mrs. Monafo boarded that streetcar at seven-thirty."

I looked back and forth at them, puzzled. "But she confessed. Someone must have the time wrong."

Detective Courter shook his head. "The streetcar driver was on his first route of the morning and knows exactly what time he started. He has to get out and punch a card in Hackensack, and he punched it a few minutes before eight. Mrs.

Monafo was on board. And don't tell me he mistook her for someone else. You've seen her."

"But the witnesses who heard the shot could have been mistaken."

The detective paced around the room. "The man down the street sets his alarm clock for seven-thirty every morning and sits down in his kitchen just before eight to have breakfast. He heard the shot from the kitchen. There's absolutely no possibility that he was up an hour earlier than usual. His wife and children agreed that there had been no change to his morning routine. I have another witness who was walking nearby on his way to open his shop, and his stock boy also tells me that the shop definitely did not open early."

He walked up to a stack of ledger books on the table under the window and opened the top one, flipping through it casually, looking at the names of the inmates and the pictures we'd taken of each one of them. Sheriff Heath made a move to stop him, the records being none of Detective Courter's business, but then stayed quiet.

"But why would Mrs. Monafo confess if she didn't shoot him?" I asked.

Detective Courter looked pointedly at the sheriff, who said, "Miss Kopp has spent the most time with her. Let her try." Turning to me, he added, "Go and talk to her again about what happened. Find out what you can about her life. See if you can come up with another motive for the shooting. Ask her why she went back. Maybe someone else did it and she took responsibility."

The detective grumbled something unintelligible and dropped back into his chair.

"John, she can manage it," the sheriff said, glancing quickly at me.

"We need detectives talking to suspects," he said. "If this had happened six months ago, you would've sent me up to talk to her."

"And you wouldn't have gotten a confession," the sheriff said. "You know that. We've always had trouble with female suspects. That's why I hired a matron. Let Miss Kopp do her job, and if she doesn't make any headway, we'll call you right over."

He looked back and forth between the two of us for a minute and then pushed his chair away and walked out of the room, slamming the door a little too loudly.

Sheriff Heath jumped up to follow him out. "I don't like this," he said to me. "Go talk to her."

IT WAS THE dim, quiet hour just before dinner, when the older women were rousing themselves slowly from their naps. This was when I preferred to sit down with one or the other of them and try to win their confidence. The understanding that they were in jail—and therefore not obligated to cook dinner —dawned on them with a kind of muted relief. They were philosophical at that time and more willing to talk, unlike the younger girls, who preferred to come to me at midnight, when their fears and secrets kept them awake and aflame. The older women didn't let their lies and treachery deprive them of sleep. They took their secrets to bed like hot-water bottles and snored on top of them all night long.

I found Mrs. Monafo awake and sitting on the edge of her bunk, looking down at her feet. When she first came to us, there had been sores between her toes that looked like they hadn't healed in years. I'd been persistent with the petroleum oil and the delousing powder, and at last they had started to fade. She was looking down at them, twisting them back and forth to view from all sides, as if she was sizing them up and deciding to what use she might put them. She looked up and saw me standing outside her cell.

"They don't swell like they used to," she said.

"They look better."

"At the plant I'm on my feet ten, twelve hours. Here we do washing in the morning and that is all. My feet get a rest."

"Don't tell the sheriff you're enjoying a nice rest in his jail. He'll find another job for you."

"Oh, I don't say I enjoy it. But there is less to do. What my husband is doing without me —" She shrugged and gave a silent little laugh that turned into a cough.

"Will your husband pay you a visit?"

She pushed out her lower lip and gave the tiniest shake of her head. "He don't want to come. Don't like police."

"Then he should write you a letter."

"I never see him write."

She wouldn't look at me. I opened the door to her cell and sat down next to her. Still she kept her eyes on her feet.

"Why don't I go and see him?" I asked. "You've been here a week. He must wonder. I could let him know that you're being taken care of, at least."

"No," she said quickly. She eased herself off the edge of the bunk and went to the basin, but just stood over it, staring at the wall. Her shoulders slumped like a sack of potatoes. She had a way of shuffling around as if she had no legs at all, only a pair of feet attached to a shapeless form.

"We'll send him a letter when it comes time for your trial,"

I said. "He has a right to be there." Detective Courter hadn't mentioned her husband, and I wondered whether he'd been interviewed.

"Why have a trial, lady? I shoot the boy and I go to prison. What else is there to say?" Her mouth sagged into a defiant frown that she'd probably worn all her life.

"The prosecutor will have some questions for you, even if you do make a full confession. They always do."

She tilted her head and considered that. "What kind of question?"

I pretended to think about it for a minute. "He might wonder why a man would be shot over a single month's rent. It's a small amount of money for such a serious crime."

"I tell him pay that rent or else! He make threat to me."

"I'm sure he did. The prosecutor might also ask why you came back after you'd already run off. You were right there when the police arrived."

"Where would I go so they don't find me? I make it easy for them." She groaned and put a hand on her hip, and eased herself back down to the bunk.

She'd confided nothing so far and I didn't think she was going to. I had to tell her what I knew, or Detective Courter would, and he wouldn't be so kind about it. "Oh, you did make it easy," I said. "The only trouble is that the prosecutor has to go around and find witnesses to tell what they saw, too."

She had the small black eyes of a bird. She fixed them on me now. "Nobody saw."

"But someone heard."

She shook her head defiantly. "They don't hear nothing."

"Mrs. Monafo. Your neighbors heard the shot. We know

they did. Only they didn't hear it until after you boarded that streetcar."

Her fingers worked at the seam of her house dress and she crossed her ankles and then uncrossed them.

"This could be good news for you. If they think someone else shot Saverio Salino, they'll let you go. You can return home to your husband. Wouldn't you like that?"

She had worked a bit of thread loose and she was pulling on it. The seam was unraveling. I didn't bother to stop her. She would stitch it back together in the morning.

"You tell them," she said quietly. "You tell them I shoot Salino. He die?"

"Yes."

She pushed her chin out. "You tell them I kill him."

SHERIFF HEATH DID NOT find this to be a satisfactory answer and told me to keep after her. "I don't want to jail an innocent woman or let a murderer go free. We need an honest confession. It's one of the reasons I gave for hiring a matron, so see to it that I wasn't wrong."

I let her think it over and went to her again the next day. She had been excused from laundry duty over a stiff knee. After I took the other women downstairs to do their work, I went into her cell to talk.

"Lady!" she called when she saw me. "What he say?"

"What did who say?"

"The little detective. When you tell him I shoot Salino."

"Mrs. Monafo, I told you he wouldn't listen to anything but new evidence. There's nothing I can do unless you can tell us something else about that morning."

She nodded. "He tell me that."

"Detective Courter? When did you see him?"

"Just now," she said, looking a little surprised that I didn't know. "He just come here. I ask for you but he say you went home."

"I was only down in the laundry." I should have known that he would find a way to interrogate her when I was away. I tried to keep my face passive. "What did he say?"

She motioned for me to come closer. Even after she'd been subjected to the jail's rigorous grooming requirements, Providencia Monafo was not the kind of woman I wanted to get very close to. I always had the feeling that something would jump on me if I did: a louse, or a curse.

But as Sheriff Heath reminded me, it was my job to hear confessions, so I sat next to her on the bunk and waited.

"He keep asking about my husband," she said in a creaky voice barely above a whisper.

"And what has happened to Mr. Monafo?" I asked.

She put a hand to her chest and murmured a little prayer in Italian.

"You can speak to God all day, but you might help yourself by speaking to me right now," I said, as gently as I could. Already I was beginning to fear that I knew the truth, that it was her husband who shot Salino and she had taken the blame to protect him. Did I have an epidemic on my hands of women serving jail time for men's crimes?

Providencia's hands were like rough old claws. When she wrapped them around mine I didn't dare pull away for fear of getting scratched. "I tell you the truth. It was me who shoot Salino."

"Yes, but Detective Courter has witnesses—"

She leaned in and gripped me even more forcefully. "Listen, lady. I shoot him. But I don't aim for him."

All at once I understood. A prickly chill settled in around my shoulders. I hoped my expression didn't give me away, but Providencia squinted at me with those coal-black eyes of hers and sat back, satisfied.

"I aim for my husband. Salino come up behind him to pay rent but I don't see him in time. My husband jump and Salino get the bullet."

She released my hands with a great flurry of her fingers, the way a soothsayer delivers a spell. We each took a deep breath at the same time, exchanging old air for new and a lie for the truth.

Providencia leaned back against the wall and cast her eyes across her cell as if she were seeing a distant horizon. I followed suit and wondered how different her faraway vision must have looked from mine.

"So you see," she said, "I tell the truth. I stay in jail."

"But the witnesses," I said feebly. "Detective Courter is absolutely sure the shots couldn't have been fired when you said they were."

Without taking her eyes away from whatever she saw beyond her cell walls, she said, "I don't know about witness. I tell the truth."

"But he wants to set you free, and I don't see why . . ."

But then I did. Of course I did.

Providencia was terrified of her husband. I sat with my hands in my lap and my head cocked back against the wall and let her tell it to me. He was a drunkard and a gambler. He once held a job at the munitions plant but he'd been stealing gunpowder and selling it. When he got caught, they fired him, and Providencia went to beg the foreman to give him back his job. He refused, but he took pity on Providencia and let her work on the cleaning crew, which was so closely watched that no one had a chance to steal anything. Providencia worked ten hours a day at the factory and spent her nights keeping house and looking after the boarders, which, she said, exhausted her. (I'd seen no evidence of house-keeping or caretaking around her boarding-house but didn't say it.)

Lacking any sort of employment, Mr. Monafo took to spending all day in the saloons and became a violent and angry drunkard. He bellowed insults at Providencia over their reduced circumstances, caused mostly by his drinking and gambling, and once threw burning coals at her, nearly setting the place on fire. He frightened the boarders so much that two of them moved out. When Providencia told him that he would have to go and find a job to make up for the lost rent, he picked up a chair and swung it at her. She landed on her hip when she fell—which had to be why she shuffled around unevenly—and the chair shattered.

Providencia was tormented in this manner for months before another woman at the factory offered her a gun. It was intended as a preventative measure only, to give her some protection while she packed a few things and fled. The woman who brought it to her told her that if her husband saw her leaving, she had only to wave it at him and he would quiet down and let her go.

"She don't know my husband," Providencia concluded grimly. "Nothing will settle him down but a blow to the head."

"Or a bullet?"

She nodded. "He come for me and I shoot. What else can I do?"

"You could have called the police." I knew what a poor suggestion it was but felt obligated to make it nonetheless.

She didn't bother responding to that. She patted my knee and, groaning, pushed herself to her feet. "I stay here," she said, with a note of cheer in her voice as if that was all it took to settle the matter. "My husband"—and here she waved her arm triumphantly to indicate the world outside the jail—"he stay out there."

At last I understood why she had turned back toward home. She might have run out in a terror after shooting Salino, but once she sat down in that trolley car and had a moment to think, she realized that her husband was still alive, and that he'd seen her aim the gun at him. The plain truth was that she was safer in jail. If she tried to run, he would find her. She went directly back to the crime scene with the hope of being arrested.

Even in her rehabilitated state, there was a wildness about Providencia. She never pinned her hair up like the other women, and instead let it crowd around her shoulders like a thicket of briars. She tended to hunch her shoulders forward when she spoke as if everything she had to say was a secret. A black mole sat just above the corner of her mouth, and one cheek was fatter than the other, causing one eye to squint while the other gaped open. She had the air of a mystic or a witch.

"*Strega*," she said, standing over me and putting her hands on my shoulders.

"*Strega?*" I repeated.

"In Italy we say *strega* for witch."

How did she know what I was thinking?

"You look at me and think I look like witch," she said. "I know you."

I'd had a lot of strange conversations under this roof, but this had to be the strangest.

"I know you," she said again. "They put you in jail just like me. What did you do?"

She was staring at me so closely that I felt as if I were under some kind of spell. One eye squinted intently while the other opened even wider, calling for my response.

"What did you do, lady?"

I WENT DOWN to Sheriff Heath's office and was about to raise my hand to knock when I heard John Courter's voice inside.

"Because I got tired of waiting!" Courter was saying. I leaned against the door frame and listened. Sheriff Heath spoke in a quieter voice and I couldn't hear everything he was saying.

". . . if we release her now . . ." was the only phrase I caught from the sheriff.

"I don't see any other way." Courter was shouting. "Mrs. Monafo's either lying or covering up for somebody, and if she won't tell us who it is, she's not of any use to us. You aren't of much damn use either, between this mess and that fugitive you've got running around."

He said something else in a low voice I couldn't hear, and the sheriff replied, "I've got all my men out searching. What would you have us do?"

Next came a silence and the sound of something dropping

onto a desk or table. "Bob, it's been a week. We both know that von Matthesius is gone for good. The Freeholders have called in your bondsmen. I can speak for the rest of the prosecutor's office when I say that we won't wait much longer to start an inquest."

"We'll get him," the sheriff said quickly.

"Make plans for your family," Detective Courter said. "They can't stay here if you're in a jail cell upstairs—and you will be. Can't Cordelia go to her mother? You should start thinking about it."

Something else slammed down on the table and a chair slid across the floor. "Unless you've got business with this department, go on out of here. Have your papers drawn up if you want Mrs. Monafo released. I'm her jailer, and I don't let her go without an order."

They were coming for the door. I ducked around the corner, near the sheriff's residence, and waited until I heard Mr. Courter leave with a guard.

When I returned, Sheriff Heath was leaning against his office door, his head down and his shoulders slumped. He turned when he heard my footsteps. "You heard Courter."

"Some of it."

"It sounds like he tried a little funny business with Mrs. Monafo this morning. I told him to let you have another try, but he's not interested in my ideas on the running of my own jail."

"I just spoke to her," I said. "I believe her. I don't know what to say about Detective Courter's witnesses, but I think she's telling the truth."

⇥ 16 ⇤

THE MOOD AT THE JAIL WAS GRIM. All the deputies and most of the guards had been out searching for long hours at a stretch and ignoring all but the most pressing of their other duties. Everyone worried that von Matthesius had already slipped aboard a ship or taken a train out West, where we would never find him.

The New York City police officer sent out to look for Dr. Rathburn found no trace of him at his home or office. Even his receptionist was gone. Sheriff Heath went back the next day to question the manager and the cloakroom girl at Murray's, but learned nothing of significance.

The Rutherford police had very little in their files that could help us. A few names turned up in von Matthesius's correspondence, mostly other doctors in California and Texas where he had once lived. Sheriff Heath had already wired the police in those cities and asked them to make inquiries, but nothing came of it. While I was gone, the investigation had been running in circles: train stations, hotels, saloons, shipyards, and back to Felix's apartment and the shops in that neighborhood, all of it leading nowhere.

The deputies and guards were kinder to me than I'd expected them to be. They all knew that I was the one who let von Matthesius get away, thanks to Thomas English, who made it his business to tell. But I'd won their admiration by going out on my own and bringing Felix back. It was more than anyone else had done, English included. Fortunately, Sheriff Heath kept English out of the jailhouse and away from me. He was mostly assigned to watch train stations, a dull but essential post.

Still, there was unease among us. Deputy Morris confided in me that the men all feared for their jobs. If Sheriff Heath was jailed over the von Matthesius escape, a new sheriff would be appointed to serve until the next election, and it was becoming apparent that the Freeholders would put forth a man of the opposing political party.

"And you know who the Republicans want to see in the sheriff's office," Morris muttered. I shook my head. Norma kept up with politics, but I hadn't any idea.

"John Courter. He's next in line when the party hands out favors."

I couldn't imagine a petty, small-minded, vindictive man like Detective Courter serving as sheriff.

"There's talk of a trial already," Morris added, "and if the prosecutor wants to make it a public inquest, there's little Sheriff Heath could do to stop it."

"You mean that my name would be brought out. Everyone would know."

"I'm sorry, miss."

I could only imagine what my brother would say—both about the scandal and my failure to provide for us as I'd insisted I could. Finding another position would be impossible, once the truth was told in the papers. I wondered if I could find a post somewhere far away—Chicago, maybe, or Denver. Were we to flee again because I'd brought shame on my family? How often would I have to run to get away from my own mistakes?

Sheriff Heath had banned any talk of the recriminations that might come his way as a result of von Matthesius's escape. "If the sheriff's department was in need of a fortune-teller, I would go down to Palisades Park and hire one," he had taken to telling the men. "And if any of you have mystical gifts you've been concealing, kindly use them to tell me where our prisoner's been hiding."

But none of us knew, and Felix wasn't telling. He sat in his cell, mulishly silent, refusing to even lift his head and look at us. This was his revenge: if he had to be caught, he would say nothing, and make the fact of his arrest useless.

We put him in an interviewing room and worked on him for hours, but nothing came of it. In the detective stories in the Sunday papers, the witnesses are all too eager to give up what they know and point the police in the right direction. It appeared that our witness hadn't read the papers. His silence was of the brooding, snorting, red-faced, stormy variety, but he was silent nonetheless. He did ask at one point whether the sheriff had charged him with a crime. We reminded him that we didn't need to charge him. We could hold him as a witness until von Matthesius was found.

"Or you could tell us where he is," the sheriff said, "and we might let you go."

When he refused to answer or even look at us, the sheriff just shrugged and said that he hoped Felix enjoyed his time at the jail. "I've got an extra fifty cents a day to feed witnesses, so you'll get a little butter on your bread until we get around to filing formal charges for harboring a fugitive and make you an inmate of this institution."

He had nothing to say to that, so the sheriff added, "Usually I don't make the witnesses do any chores, but I think a little honest labor might clear your mind and help ease you into your jail sentence. We'll give you some floors to scrub. How does that sound?"

It must have sounded fine, because Felix didn't even raise his head to object.

Although he wouldn't talk, he couldn't stop us from having a picture made of him to send to police departments. The sheriff put a call out to all the reporters in town, inviting them to make their own pictures and to run them in the papers.

Deputy Morris brought Felix downstairs for the portrait session. Sheriff Heath asked me to come along in case the reporters had any questions about how Felix was caught. I didn't like the idea of stepping into a roomful of reporters and wasn't sure I should be credited with his capture. It would have been easy enough to say that a deputy made the arrest and leave it at that. But he insisted that his department had nothing to hide and that it would only be worse if we tried to conceal anything—so I went.

I did remember to keep my promise to Carrie. She received the same invitation the other reporters did. I had to put a hand over my mouth to keep from smiling when I walked in and saw her there, standing in the back, one smartly dressed lady reporter among two dozen cigar-smoking newspapermen.

The sheriff's office wasn't large—it was only big enough for his desk and a long oak table around which his deputies sometimes gathered—but the reporters crowded in congenially. Their presence had the odd effect of making the room seem bigger, not smaller. A haze of smoke hung over them and there was a convivial rumble of conversation, like men gathered at a saloon. The sheriff's desk had been pushed out of the way and a canvas curtain hung against the wall in imitation of a portrait studio. His camera was already situated atop its three-legged stand.

In the corner, Sheriff Heath was talking to a steely-haired man in a police uniform. The two of them turned at once when Morris and I arrived with Felix, and Sheriff Heath gave a sharp whistle that silenced the room.

"Gentlemen, and ladies, I'd like you to meet Felix von Matthesius, the brother of the fugitive and the man who we believe assisted in his escape from the hospital one week ago, on October 22. Miss Kopp is the one who made his capture, with the assistance of four fine officers of the New York Police Department."

"Is it Miss Kopp or Deputy Kopp?" called Carrie from the back, to a rumble of laughter from the men.

Sheriff Heath took it as a perfectly ordinary question. "Miss Kopp has been serving as matron here at the jail and has proven herself quite able in the field as well. This is her first arrest and it won't be her last. She'll get her badge, but the first business of the sheriff's office is to catch criminals and jail them. We ask your help in that today."

I turned away from the crowd, having been made uncomfortable by the attention, and saw Deputy English standing in the doorway with a guard. I hadn't seen him since that night in front of Felix's apartment. He and the guard were whispering at one another furiously. Any excitement I might have felt over the mention of a badge turned sick and sour at the sight of him.

Sheriff Heath didn't notice any of this. "Let's take our photographs. I remind you that the prisoner is answering no questions. I will explain what we're looking for, and he will remain silent—unless he'd like to tell us where he's hidden his brother."

Felix's wrists were chained behind his back, so he couldn't raise his hands to shield his face. He kept his chin tucked defiantly down on his chest and turned away from the cameras as Deputy Morris brought him to the front of the room.

Once his feet were planted on the marks the sheriff had made on the floor, the deputy shook him by the arm and told him to look up. He would not. Sheriff Heath handed Deputy Morris a yardstick and said, "Felix, you'll lift your chin up or we'll do it for you."

Deputy Morris put the yardstick under his chin and gave it a gentle tap. At last Felix raised his eyes to the room of reporters and gave them a squint-eyed glare that lasted just long enough for Sheriff Heath to make his picture. While he was winding the film, he invited the other reporters to come up. A few of them had cameras on stands waiting in the corners of the room. They brought them forward and a whole row of photographers took their pictures.

When it was over, the sheriff turned to the reporters and said, "Boys—ah, ladies and gentlemen—the police chief and I"—and here he gestured to the man next to him—"we're asking for the public's help in naming any lodgings or other places frequented by this man in the last month. If anyone has seen him going out of any boarding-house, saloon, dining hall, or other place of business, they should come forward and tell about it without delay. We believe he's been helping to conceal the fugitive, Herman Albert von Matthesius, whose portrait has already appeared in your papers. I remind you that he is a convicted criminal and considered dangerous."

He gave a description of the fugitive, which the reporters took down, and then Deputy Morris grabbed Felix by the elbow and led him out of the room. A tall, thin man with a sparse beard stood and asked, "Does the sheriff have any other leads in the case?"

"The sheriff always has other leads," came the answer, "but today we need your help with this one."

"Is it common practice for prisoners to fake an illness to get released to the hospital?" asked a jowly old man from the back of the room.

"Certainly not. I've spoken with doctors at the hospital and we now believe von Matthesius chewed the glass from a broken light bulb to make us think he was coughing blood, and probably swallowed soap and any manner of injurious liquids to make himself appear ill. It was a carefully calculated escape attempt, and one that would have failed had the Board of Freeholders allowed me a jail physician as I've requested."

A rotund man with a face the color of a boiled ham struggled to his feet and said, "If you fail to capture this fugitive, will you be sleeping in the same cell he once had, or have you chosen another for yourself?"

That brought a general grumble from the reporters, but Sheriff Heath raised his hands to silence them. "I appreciate the *Hackensack Republican*'s interest in my living quarters, but I'm perfectly comfortable in the sheriff's apartment and intend to remain there. Does anyone have a question about our hunt for the fugitive?"

"How was the capture made?" shouted Carrie from the back. Her mouth was painted carmine red and twisted in the most delighted grin.

Sheriff Heath looked over at me. "Miss Kopp spotted him coming out of Murray's Restaurant in New York City, where she had tracked him after several days of dogged detective duty. She tackled him herself and didn't hesitate to do it. It was quick work on her part and it is exactly this sort of thinking that we hope to encourage by putting word out to the public through your newspapers. Now go on, all of you, and get something in the morning edition."

❦ 17 ❦

LATER THAT NIGHT I went down to the kitchen for supper. The work crew had just gone upstairs and the floor was still damp and smelled of washing powder. The four enormous coffee urns that fueled the jail from dawn to dusk had been scrubbed and left on their sides to dry. The mop was draped over the sink. A pair of rubber gloves dangled from its handle.

A light bobbed inside the pantry and I could hear someone shifting around inside. I expected to find a guard, looking for whatever the cooks had left out for us, but it was Cordelia Heath in an apron, slumped down on a footstool in the corner. There was a flat little bottle in her hand and the unmistakable sweet and spoiled odor of brandy spirits.

She pushed the bottle under her apron when she saw me, but we both knew what I'd seen. Her nose was swollen and pink and the drink had dulled her eyes. She took hold of a shelf and pulled herself to her feet.

"Evening, Mrs. Heath," I said.

"Miss Kopp." She glanced at me and bent down over the

boxes of onions and potatoes in the pantry as if she were inspecting them. "You keep turning up."

She stumbled against the wall and kicked the stool out from under her feet. I saw her reach for her apron to make sure the bottle was secure, a gesture that looked habitual.

I hated to ask the question, but felt obligated to. "Are you ill? Is Mr. Heath at home? I could go—"

She turned and glared at me. "Where *is* Mr. Heath? You know more about my husband's whereabouts than I do."

"I haven't seen him tonight."

I thought about asking the guards if he could be summoned. I wasn't sure which was worse: leaving her alone in this state or calling attention to it by alerting the sheriff. Every family had its secrets, but the Heaths didn't get to hide away in the countryside like we did. They had no choice but to live here, where every member of the sheriff's department could watch their doings.

She shuffled the boxes around, searching for something. "I'm only looking for what's mine. We don't eat the prisoners' food."

"Of course you don't, ma'am," I answered, although I saw nothing wrong with the food from the jail kitchen.

"The grocer delivers my order now along with all the other provisions." She wiped a strand of hair from her forehead. "Because naturally I can't shop for myself anymore." At last she slid a crate off the shelf and balanced it on her hip, then jutted her chin up at me in the manner of a woman defending herself against an accusation.

She seemed to want some response, so I said, "It must be difficult to go out with the children so young. I'm sure Grayce is a help."

"Grayce!" Her voice hit a high and wobbly note as she laughed. "Grayce's brother made her quit after what happened. And do you think I can find any kind of cleaning girl at all, once it was in the papers that the inmates harass the maids?"

"Well, I . . ."

"Nor can I go to market myself, the way we're talked about in this town." She set the crate down and began rummaging through the boxes of sugar and flour on a high shelf. "If I even show my face out there, I face an inquisition from anyone who . . . Oh, here it is."

She put a box of cornstarch in her crate and turned back to me. "It hasn't been in the papers, but everyone knows it was you who let him escape."

"Everyone?" I hadn't realized it was all over town. I should have known.

"When my father served on the Board of Freeholders, there was a sheriff who wanted to bring in a lady guard. Daddy said he couldn't, on the grounds that a lady can't stop a crook from escaping, and isn't that a guard's responsibility?"

"We'll get him." I didn't bother to point out that I was the only one who had made an arrest in the case. She was in no mood to hear it.

A strand of hair had come loose and hung between her eyes. She squinted at me when she spoke, her voice shrill and tight. "It's the worst thing that can happen to a sheriff. I believe you know why. Some people resign in disgrace after a thing like that."

She hoisted her crate unsteadily and I backed out of the doorway.

"But you aren't concerned about what becomes of us, and why should you be? It's more important that you keep yourself amused, as unmarried women must do."

She made it sound dirty to be unmarried. "I'm not here to amuse myself."

"No? Why, you couldn't wait to get inside this jail and—" Then she waved her free hand at me in a pantomime of whatever it was she thought I did. "But I'm the one who has to live here, and I'm the one about to get turned out if that old man isn't caught."

There was no arguing with her in this state, so I said, "I'm sorry, ma'am. We'll all be turned out if he isn't found."

My effort at sympathy seemed only to harden her. "But you'll be fine, won't you?" There was a cruelty in the way she said it.

She stumbled out with her box. The door swung shut behind her and I stood alone in the kitchen, a little sick and unsteady myself.

"I don't know," I said to an empty room.

It didn't seem to me that anyone would be fine if Sheriff Heath went to jail.

THE ODOR OF A WOMAN awash in brandy is impossible to forget. When I was ten, my aunt Adele came to live with us and brought that particular fragrance with her. She was my mother's older sister, nearly forty, recently widowed, and stricken by an illness nobody would name.

At the time our father was working for a small and unscrupulous wine importer. The goods were cheap and usually adulterated. Port wine might be diluted with the juice of

sloes or elderberries, then blended with cheap brandy and un-
filtered juice and soaked in wood chips. Wine was mixed with
filbert husks or strychnine (useful, in small doses, for adding
a bitter flavor), and what passed for champagne was nothing
more than Jersey cider mixed with cochineal and gooseber-
ries. When they needed a sweetener they reached for sugar
of lead. As long as it was red or gold in color and intoxicating,
Messrs. Bonham & Koch would offer it for sale, often in bottles they collected from hotel kitchens and affixed their own
labels to.

One of the proprietors—I believe it was Mr. Koch—was
arrested after a restaurant in Brooklyn complained about a
delivery of murky, foul-smelling wine that stained the teeth
of patrons, as if ink had been added, or coal-tar dye. Com-
pounding the trouble was the fact that no import taxes had
been paid on the wine, which raised the question of whether
it had been smuggled into the country.

Mr. Koch was taken off to jail and my father with him. Although he only spent a few nights there, his employer having paid the right man to secure his release, my father didn't
come home for months after his arrest. Mother told Francis that he was too ashamed to show himself to us. (She was
ashamed, too, and never told her daughters any of this. It was
only because Francis swept the wine shop after school that
he knew about it, and Norma, domineering even at the age of
six, insisted that he tell us.)

Aunt Adele was in our house the very minute our father
was out of it. Norma and I expected to have to move into
Mother's bed so that Adele could have ours, but instead our
aunt chose for herself a closet under the stairs just big enough

for, as she put it, "a cot and a candle." I couldn't understand why anyone would want to crawl into such a cramped and windowless space at night when an ordinary bed could be had, and Mother went silent and tight-lipped when I asked her about it. I found out the truth one day when Adele was in the parlor being attended by the doctor and I snuck into her cubbyhole to have a look around.

There it was: the peculiar odor of sweet gas and rotten fruit. She kept a brandy bottle under her pillow and hid a few empty ones inside the boots she never wore, because she never went out. Next to them was a stack of clean rags stained brown with old blood and stuck all over with pins. I didn't know what the two had to do with one another, the stench and the sickness, but to my mind they were the same, and since then I have always associated liquor with secrecy and disease.

When Adele grew weaker she had no choice but to come out into the light, and to submit to Mother's nursing and my help. That's when I saw what had sent her into the closet: a surgical wound under her arm that had never closed, the result of an attempt to excise a lump the size of a nutmeg. A bigger one grew back in its place and I feared I could see it, wrinkled and brown as a baby's fist, when we peeled away the bandage and washed the ulcer with weak but nonetheless intolerable carbolic acid. Adele screamed when we did it, and bit into a rag soaked in brandy.

"She has to have it," Mother would say. "It's unbearable otherwise." I would watch her overturn the bottle into the rag and wet it freely, so that Adele could suck furiously at it while we worked. Somehow the rag made it more like medicine.

When Adele went back to bed and Mother thought I wasn't looking, she tucked the bottle under Adele's good arm the way one presses a doll against a sleeping child.

Now Cordelia was locking herself in a closet with a bottle and a wound of her own. But unlike Aunt Adele, who came to us willingly, even eagerly, Mrs. Heath snarled at me like an animal caught in a trap when I found her. I couldn't get near enough to help and hardly dared interfere with the brandy habit of the boss's wife. I knew of only one way to cure her pain, and it was to find our fugitive.

AT MIDNIGHT THE HIGH, domed window above the fifth floor rattled and creaked in the wind, and when the hail came, the sharp hammering against the glass lulled me in and out of sleep.

I awoke to Sheriff Heath's voice. "I'm sorry, Miss Kopp," he was saying.

There was a light coming through the bars of my cell. It receded and I heard his footsteps walking away.

"Sheriff?"

The lantern in his hand stopped swaying and he turned.

"What is it?" I whispered.

He came back. The lantern hung down at his knees and cast a pool of yellow light on the ground. His face took on the greenish-white pallor of the lime-washed walls.

We peered at each other through the bars until it occurred to me that he wouldn't come in unless I invited him. I pushed open the door and he paced around, looking at my lamp, my comb, and the book I'd been reading.

Finally he said, "You were asleep."

"It's all right." I wore a corduroy dress at night that was no different from what I wore during the day, in case I was called back to duty. It wasn't as if he were seeing me in my night-clothes. I sat on the edge of the bunk. "You can sit down."

He sighed and dropped down next to me, leaning his head against the wall.

I'd been torturing myself over Mrs. Heath all night. "I don't deserve to be here," I said. "Not while he's out there. It isn't right."

He snorted and said, "Miss Kopp. Do you know how many crooks go their whole lives without once ever being arrested?"

I stared at him and thought about it. "Almost all of them."

"That's right. The ones we do catch manage to commit ten crimes before we lock them up for one. You know that's true."

I nodded. Prisoners loved to boast about the schemes and cons they got away with before they were caught.

He turned and waved at the windows at the end of my cell block. Beyond them rose the first few buildings at the edge of Main Street, their backs turned to us. In the daylight we could have seen the entire town unfurled below us. The jail stood at the edge of Hackensack, along the river, next to everything else the townspeople didn't want to look at: a coal yard, a yarn mill, and a cemetery.

"They're like fish out there, swimming through a net," he said. "We catch a few of them. We slow them down. But we don't ever stop them. There will always be more criminals than cops. We don't win in the end. You know that, don't you?"

"Of course I know that," I said stiffly. But maybe I didn't. It hadn't occurred to me that I wouldn't defeat them some-how. In some way, I'd been thinking that the sheriff and I would rid Bergen County of crime if we just kept at it long enough.

"So we lost one. Now we're going to get him back. But, Miss Kopp—"

I folded my arms across my chest and tried to tuck my chin down in that formidable way Norma had.

He smiled a little and continued. "Every day some sneak or thief gets away with something. Every day someone calls for help and we don't get there in time. There's always a fistfight or a gunshot or a fire set deliberately or a girl gone missing."

"Yes, but—"

He wouldn't let me finish. "Yes, but we go back to work."

I dropped my arms and all the air went out of me. Those were three very powerful words.

"Back to work," I repeated, trying it out.

"That's right," he said with a smile that pushed against the corners of his eyes. "The work of this department goes on. We're conducting a manhunt, and we will get him."

"But if we don't—If you don't—"

"We will," he returned sharply. "And in the meantime, I have a jail to run. We've eighty-five other prisoners in here. We can't forget about them."

I thought again of Cordelia. "But Mrs. Heath doesn't want me here, after all the trouble I've made for you."

He took a breath and said, so quietly that I had to strain to hear him, "Mrs. Heath cares a great deal about appearances and reputations and titles and honorifics. When I signed on as undersheriff, she saw it as a stepladder to sheriff and then to mayor and then to senator. She wants to sit in a parlor in

Washington, D.C., and pour tea out of a silver pot. How does that sound to you, Miss Kopp?"

"Horrible. I'd rather chase old von Matthesius through the gutters."

He grinned and something broke open between us. "So would I. Cordelia doesn't understand that. She never will."

"Well." I swallowed, almost unable to speak. "Poor Cordelia." I regretted it immediately. I shouldn't have poked fun at her.

"I've given Cordelia everything a wife wants—children and a nice home," he said, and then it was my turn to laugh.

"It's not a nice home."

He kicked his shoes against the ground and shook his head. "All right. It isn't the home she wants. But this is the sheriff's residence, and she's the sheriff's wife. I decide who to employ, not Cordelia. What the newspapers say doesn't matter. I'm going to run this department as I see fit, and if Cordelia didn't know that before, she knows it now."

He spoke about his wife with a quiet authority that was familiar to me. It was the same way he spoke to his deputies. It was the same way he ran the jail. For the first time I understood that what was admirable in a sheriff might be less than admirable in a husband.

"Where were you tonight?" I asked.

"Out on a search party. A man came in and told us about an old place in the woods where he thought someone had been hiding and we hoped it was our fugitive. But it was just a tramp."

"Mrs. Heath wondered where you'd gone."

"And she asked you?"

"It was . . . less civil than that." I couldn't bring myself to tell what I'd seen. "She appears to be under a great deal of strain."

He rubbed his forehead with the palm of his hand. "I told her not to worry about it."

"I don't know how she can help it. She said people are talking. Someone bothered her on the street."

"It's nothing. She was out with her mother and heard an unkind remark."

He pushed himself off the bunk and put a hand over his mouth to cover a yawn. "I tried to tell her that if an unkind remark is the worst thing to ever happen to the wife of the sheriff, we've done all right. She didn't take to that."

"She'd have to be awfully tough not to be bothered by strangers gossiping about her family and the prospect of her husband in jail."

"Mmmm." He turned to leave and closed the cell door behind him. "That's just how a sheriff's wife has to be. Tough."

We stood in the dark with the white bars between us.

"You don't have to stay here so much," he said at last. "You have a home to go to and people who are waiting for you."

"So do you," I said.

⪫ 18 ⪪

I HADN'T BEEN HOME since I caught Felix. What if they found von Matthesius and required a translator again? What if Felix confessed? I didn't want to be miles away in the countryside, with no telephone and no auto, if I could be of use.

But since the opening night of Fleurette's play, I'd been worried about that man I saw speaking to her at the theater. Her play, as childish as it was, put her in front of men who had only one idea about girls on the stage. She loved any sort of attention—I'd seen that already—and thought it old-fashioned to be suspicious of a strange man paying her compliments.

But I knew what could happen. I knew how easily a girl could get trapped. I thought about Lettie, answering Mr. Meeker's advertisement for a housekeeper, and about all the girls like her I'd seen in just a few months of working for Sheriff Heath. I didn't like to tell Fleurette those stories, but perhaps I'd sheltered her too much. She was incautious and not at all vigilant about the way men might try to take advantage of her. I hadn't been cautious enough myself, at that age.

Norma would have admonished her about it already, but she never took Norma seriously. She knew that Norma hadn't the first idea about what to do with a handsome man offering compliments. I wasn't sure I knew what to do about it either, but it fell to me to try, so I went home the next day to speak to her.

Fleurette's bedroom was starting to look like a dressmaker's shop. Three mannequins stood near the window like guests at a party, their costumes pinned carefully together. Bolts of fabric were stacked in the corner according to color, from a deep purple wool, to a turquoise silk, to a pale lilac chiffon. Her wardrobe doors were flung open and festooned with dresses on hangers, many of which she had made for herself but had not yet worn.

Her taste ran to the fashionable and outlandish, which I had always attributed to an overactive imagination and an allowance for sewing goods that permitted her to be a bit impractical. But as I walked in the room and looked around, I saw that she'd been making herself a wardrobe for a very particular kind of life, and it was not a life that could be lived out here on the farm with me and Norma. She wanted the theater, and dinners in restaurants, and parties at the homes of witty and sophisticated people in New York. She wanted champagne and pearls, and her picture on the front of the playbill, and a string of admirers.

In short, she wanted nothing that I had on offer. I thought suddenly of my own mother, and how it must have been to see me reaching for a life that she couldn't fathom. I would send off for a correspondence course and she would burn the papers. I thought it monstrous at the time. Now I could only smile a little at how bold she'd been. She was only trying to keep me in her world, when I wanted out so desperately. And now Fleurette wanted out of my world.

She was propped up in bed against three enormous pillows—all the best pillows in our house seemed to find their way to Fleurette's room and never return—wearing an ivory kimono and her hair in loose curls around her shoulders. I could imagine her, quite suddenly, as somebody's wife, paging through a volume of Vogue patterns in bed while her husband shaved in the mirror. The thought of it made a tendon in my knee give way and I had to catch myself before I stumbled.

"The farmer's wife is ill and I'm to take her role tomorrow night," she said, without looking up from her book.

"You'll do just fine." I eased down on the edge of her bed. Then, as casually as I could, I said, "I wish you'd tell me about that young man outside the theater."

"Why should I?" Her breath came faster, working in and out of her little turned-up nose, but she kept her eyes fixed on the page. Already I'd annoyed her.

"It's my responsibility to keep up with your friends." I ducked down to catch her eye, but she shook a wave of dark hair over her face. Between the locks I feared I saw the stain of a lip-stick. "Don't you think I see the kind of trouble girls get into?"

In a small voice she said, "It was nothing."

"Then you won't mind telling me."

She put her pattern book down at last. "I can't possibly recite every word I speak to another person all day long."

"I just—"

"I'm not like you and Norma. I won't live on this old farm

forever. I'm going to meet people, and talk to them, and go places, like anyone else does. And I won't answer to you about it."

"Of course you will." I tried not to sound too frantic, but this talk of leaving the farm made me uneasy. "You're no different from any other girl. You might not have a mother or father to tell you where you can go and who you can see, but you have me and Norma. And it's our business to look after you."

"All right." Fleurette pushed her book aside and sat up straighter in bed. "On what grounds will you decide who's suitable for me and who isn't? Neither of you have had a single male visitor for as long as I can remember, unless you count the sheriff and his deputies, which I do not. Apparently you never found a man who was agreeable to either of you. So how will you decide whether one is right for me?"

There was a hot defiant look in her eyes. For once, she was not begging or whining. She was issuing a direct challenge, and I hadn't any idea how to answer. It had never occurred to me to imagine a suitable man for Fleurette.

"I never said you couldn't talk to anyone. I only ask to know about your acquaintances."

"You haven't any right to."

"But I do. If it's such a secret that you can't tell us, then you're not being properly supervised and we'll take you out of Mrs. Hansen's."

"You can't do that!" If a girl could stamp her foot while lying in bed, Fleurette would have.

"Of course I can. I pay for your lessons and your costumes."

"Then I'll pay my own tuition. Some of the girls at the

academy have already said they'd like me to do their spring dresses."

Before I could say anything about that, she added, "And don't you dare tell me that a seamstress is a poor occupation for a sister of yours. It's far more respectable than police work. If Mother were alive, she'd be happy to see me sewing and horrified to see you down at that dirty old jail."

I reached out to put my hand over her ankles but she pulled them away. I tried to speak kindly to her anyway. "I just can't watch you put yourself in danger. Not after what we went through last year. It was you they were threatening to kidnap. Everything we did was to keep you safe."

She picked up her book again and flipped through it rapidly, blinking back tears.

"What's his name?"

"I don't know."

"Have you seen him again?"

"Not yet."

I tried very hard to sound calm. "What does that mean?"

She wrapped a strand of hair around her finger and looked up at me. "He promised to take me and Helen to a show on Broadway when he had the money."

"You can't possibly go to New York with a man. Nor can Helen. Girls your age go on a train with a man and—well. I won't have it. I'll speak to Mr. Stewart about it."

She sniffed.

"You know we wouldn't have allowed it. I'll take you to a show myself if you want to go."

"It's dull to go places with you!"

"Then we'll bring Norma along too."

She smiled to herself and I hoped we'd understood each

other. She put her book down and looked up at me as I turned to leave.

"Haven't you caught that man yet?"

"No. But we will, and then I'll be home more. Although Sheriff Heath has promised to make me a deputy. I don't know what things will be like after that."

Fleurette brightened at the possibility. "Does that mean you'll be out chasing after criminals at all hours? Won't that be awfully dangerous?"

"It's dangerous for the criminals," I said. Fleurette giggled and I made my exit while a fragile peace still hung in the air between us.

THE LIGHT WAS ON IN NORMA'S ROOM. She'd taken recently to wearing Mother's old spectacles when she read, claiming farsightedness, but I suspected she mostly wore them so that she could regard me suspiciously over the rims. When she looked up at me, they slipped so far down her nose that she had to reach her hand out to catch them.

"You could get your own pair," I said. "We could have them fitted to you."

"I like these fine." She was reading an article in *Popular Science* about a German druggist who filled prescriptions by carrier pigeon before the war. He'd devised a means to attach a camera to his pigeons so that they might fly over enemy camps and take pictures. There was a photograph of a pigeon with a contraption strapped to its breast by means of elastic bands. Next to it was one of the pictures claimed to have been taken by the bird from a vantage point high above a river. We studied the pictures together for a minute.

"I don't see how it could manage the weight," Norma said, "but this leaves us no choice but to carry out a trial."

"Or risk the Germans gaining the advantage for its pigeon fleet?"

She nodded grimly and I thought she really did believe it was a matter of military superiority. "It isn't correct to call pigeons a fleet," she said as she studied the pictures. "Although a flock sounds too frivolous. I think we'll call them squadrons."

She took up a pencil and made a note of that in the margin, then put the magazine away and turned her attention to me. "I heard you talking to Fleurette."

"I just want her to be careful."

Norma passed a pillow to me so that I could lean against the bedpost. "She doesn't want to be careful. She wants to be on her own. She's been talking about getting a furnished room with Helen."

I groaned and loosened the buttons around my collar. "And who does she think is going to pay her rent?"

"She'll take in sewing. You know that. What else do you expect her to do?"

"I haven't any idea," I admitted. "I've been happily avoiding that question for years."

"Well, we can't let her move into town and do as she pleases. She'll fall for the first traveling salesman who knocks on her door."

"Norma!" It was unlike her to bring up my past, but she was right—I had been Fleurette's age when I gave in to the attentions of a traveling salesman.

Norma deployed her spectacles in her most dramatic fashion. "Back when we were girls, I don't remember you ever even mentioning a boy before one turned up in our parlor. Imagine how it would be for Miss Girl About Town, who would throw open the window and invite them up."

"I'd rather not."

"I suppose that man you arrested didn't have von Matthesius in his pocket, or I would've read about it by now."

"He won't talk. We can only hope that he was helping to keep von Matthesius in hiding, and that without anyone to help he will slip up."

"Well, you'd better do something more than hope."

I reached down to unlace my boots. "I don't know what else to do. It's been almost two weeks. The sheriff has his men out looking every day, and we've spoken with everyone who was involved with the case."

"Why was he arrested in the first place?" It infuriated Norma when the newspapers resorted to euphemisms like "serious charges" and "sensational testimony" in the name of propriety and didn't tell her what she really wanted to know.

I described what I'd learned about the sham treatments offered as nervous cures, and patients being drugged and made to appear sicker than they were so that their families would pay for a longer stay, and about von Matthesius taking payment in the form of paintings and heirlooms when the families' money ran out. I told her about Beatrice Fuller and his shameful attempts to force a marriage upon her, and the bravery of the boys who went to the police to stop it.

"Then you haven't been to see everyone," Norma said.

"Who else is left? Alfonso Youngman is dead, and Beatrice Fuller is in California. The sheriff has said he can't force her grandparents to tell where she is."

Norma tapped the end of her pencil on my knee impatiently. "You don't need them. You need the minister."

"What minister?"

"The old man he called in to perform the wedding when that poor girl was too drugged to stand. He's the only other criminal in this mess. I don't know why you haven't spoken to him."

⇥ 19 ⇤

THE GERMAN REFORMED CHURCH was a small white-washed building of a style that was common a hundred and fifty years ago. It was clad in clapboard that ran from the earth to the heavens, and from its roof arose a spire topped with old copper streaked in verdigris. Around the sides were the kind of tall, skinny Gothic windows that encouraged those inside to look inward, not out onto the world. The church sat proudly atop a plain carpet of lawn, with not so much as a shrub or flower box to suggest that there were pleasures to be had in this life. The only advantage to the secluded upbringing my mother imposed upon us was that we had managed to avoid spending our Sundays in such strict, austere places as the German churches of Brooklyn and northern New Jersey.

It had taken us a few days just to find Reverend Weber. He hadn't testified during the trial due to an illness. The sham marriage he performed had been witnessed by several people, and the certificate signed properly, which meant that there was little doubt or controversy over his role in the matter. Because of this, his name did not appear in any records of the trial, and it took quite a bit of digging through the prosecutor's notes to find it. As soon as we did, we went directly there.

Sheriff Heath pushed open the heavy front doors of the church. We leaned in and squinted at the dark and oiled pews only long enough to see that there was no one inside. A footpath led around back to the rectory, where my knock was answered by a frail old man so bent over by rheumatism that he had to contort himself to look up at me.

"Guten Tag," he said in a raspy voice.

"Einen guten Tag auch Ihnen," I answered. *"Mein Name ist Constance Kopp, und mein Begleiter ist Herr Heath.* May we come in? I'm here about a member of your congregation."

That must have been enough German to satisfy him, because he nodded and opened the door.

We stepped into a small, shabby sitting room meant more for the accommodation of visitors than for the comfort of the rectory's inhabitant. There was no wide and cushioned settee, no lamp for reading, and in fact no books or pictures or personal effects of any kind. A collection of mismatched straight-backed wooden chairs were placed in a precise semicircle, in anticipation of a serious conversation among several uncomfortable visitors. Only one of the chairs was equipped with arms and a withered old cushion. I took this to be the reverend's. On the wall hung a single cross and a devotional calendar printed by the church.

Reverend Weber settled into his chair, and Sheriff Heath and I sat down across from him. Because he was so badly stooped over, we found ourselves staring at a few strands of white hair combed over a scalp as bare and fragile as a baby's, with blue veins running underneath skin that was at once pink and red and a strange chalky white. He had to turn himself sideways to look at us. His lips trembled and his eyes were pale and watery.

"We're looking for a man you might know," Sheriff Heath said. "He's gone missing and we very much hope you can help us find him."

"Oh, dear," the old man said. "Missing?"

"It's more that he's in hiding. He escaped while under guard at the hospital two weeks ago. I'm speaking of Dr. von Matthesius."

His mouth dropped open and his chin wavered. I could tell he was working on a response and I didn't want to give him too much time to think.

"Reverend, it's dangerous for all of us if an escaped prisoner is on the loose," I said. "The sheriff has deputies out looking every day. They're armed and ready to shoot if they have to. Someone could get hurt—someone who has nothing to do with it. You don't want that to happen, do you?"

He looked down at his swollen and twisted knuckles. He shook his head and said quietly, "I'm afraid I couldn't help you."

"You'd be helping Dr. von Matthesius," the sheriff said. "We've already arrested his brother, who we believe was helping to keep him. Now he has nowhere to turn."

"Felix is in jail?" Reverend Weber said, leaning forward as if he hadn't heard it right. "Is someone going to take his things?"

Sheriff Heath and I glanced at each other, puzzled, and then he said, "Yes, we've come in my wagon and we can take his things this afternoon."

The old man waved in the direction of a door just behind him. The sheriff and I stood up and went over together, both of us trying to act as if nothing were out of the ordinary. The door opened into a little dark and windowless room, too small to be a bedroom, filled to the ceiling with small pieces of furniture, wooden crates, a few trunks and suitcases, and paintings in heavy carved frames.

Reverend Weber hadn't risen from his chair, but he twisted himself around and watched us. "He said he'd have most of it sold by now. It's taken too long. People don't want those old things."

Sheriff Heath rubbed the back of his neck and took a long breath. "This must have come out of the sanitarium. I suppose Felix was raising money for his brother."

"What's that?" the reverend called.

Sheriff Heath went back to the little circle of chairs and knelt down in front of the old man so he wouldn't have to strain his neck to look up. "Reverend Weber. These things don't belong to Felix. Some of them could have been stolen or taken from people under fraudulent pretenses. If we find that Felix has broken any laws by selling them—and I think we will—you could be charged for helping him. Do you understand?"

The sheriff sat back on his heels while Reverend Weber whispered to himself. His lips worked furiously but no sound came out. He had a cane in his hand, and it wobbled under his grip.

I sat down next to him and took his other hand in mine. *"Haben Sie eine Ahnung wo er sich versteckt?"*

He shook his head. *"Nein."*

Sheriff Heath looked up at me. "He says he has no idea where he's hiding," I said.

The sheriff looked back and forth between the two of us for a minute, his arms folded across his chest. Then he stood and wiped the dust briskly off his trousers. When he spoke, it was in the voice he used to read the riot act to strikers or to give orders to a room full of deputies.

"Reverend, here's what you're going to do for us. Write a letter by way of general delivery addressed to Dr. von Matthesius and tell him that the rest of his things have been sold and that you have the money for him. That's all you have to do. For your willingness to help us capture a dangerous fugitive, we'll make sure that no charges are brought against you."

Reverend Weber craned his neck up at us, then shrugged with the helpless air of a man who'd been outmaneuvered. "I don't see any harm in writing a letter, but I can't say that it will get to him."

"We'll take care of that." The sheriff looked around the room for writing paper.

"Over there." The old man pointed a shaky finger to a desk in the corner. I didn't think he'd be able to manage a pen and paper, but he wrote in a surprisingly bold and clear hand and before long we had three letters to send.

"Good work, Reverend." Sheriff Heath shook his hand and spent a few minutes running back and forth, carting von Matthesius's things to his auto. "I'll send a deputy for the rest," he called, and we rode off.

I couldn't remember the last time I'd seen him so exhilarated. "What makes you think he'll inquire about general delivery?" I asked.

"Oh, every kind of clandestine correspondence is sent that way now," Sheriff Heath said cheerfully. "You can pick up more criminals at a general delivery window than you can at a ten-cent flophouse. We'll get him."

. . .

WE DROVE DIRECTLY to the post office in Hackensack, where Sheriff Heath and I walked past the lines of people standing at the windows and down a little hall off to the side. At the end was the postmaster's office. The sheriff walked in without knocking. We were greeted by the soles of a man's shoes propped up on a desk, the rest of him concealed behind a newspaper. A mess of curly black hair appeared above the paper, followed by intelligent gray eyes and a shout of "Bob! What have you got for me?"

"May I first introduce you to Miss Kopp," the sheriff said, as the postmaster scrambled to his feet. "She's the jail matron, and she's working on a case with me."

"You are!" He looked me over with genuine interest. "How'd you manage a job like that?"

"She earned it," Sheriff Heath said mildly, then he turned to me. "This is Mr. Fulton."

"How do you do?" I said.

He dropped his newspaper and shook my hand. "Better all the time."

"Mr. Fulton is the father of four very troublesome girls," the sheriff said with only the slightest trace of a smile.

"I'm sure they'd be shocked to hear themselves described that way by the sheriff," I said.

"Oh, they know they're troublesome, but no one's bothered to tell them that they're girls," Mr. Fulton said. "Our eldest goes out hunting with her uncle, and the twins want to play baseball, and the youngest is convinced that she'll be a doctor and spends all her time bandaging the others. We had to stop her before she turned the kitchen into a surgery and strapped her sister to the table. Not one of them is going to marry if they don't settle down." He made a face of mock horror that he couldn't sustain. Already I liked Mr. Fulton very much.

"I don't know about that. They might surprise you," I said.

"They surprise me every day! Last year the four of them took it in their heads to run away together. They must have thought their mother and I wouldn't notice that they'd been studying the train tables all week. When they tiptoed off with their little rucksacks, I called your friend Robert Heath here and had him run over to the station and pick them up. They spent a night in jail under a charge of waywardness and vagrancy."

"You didn't!" I gasped.

Sheriff Heath nodded briskly. "It taught them a lesson."

"It did no such thing," Mr. Fulton said. "They had the time of their lives. Didn't even want to go home the next morning. Nothing rattles those girls. I've always said that they'll either be cops or outlaws, and now, Miss Kopp, I've got some hope that one or two of them might take the legitimate path."

Sheriff Heath gave a polite little cough. Mr. Fulton said, "I'm sorry, you've got business, Sheriff. What is it?"

We showed him the letters, which were already sealed and addressed by Reverend Weber's hand. Sheriff Heath told him very little about the case, only that we were trying to catch a man and needed the clerks at the windows to watch for him.

Mr. Fulton nodded and turned the letters over in his hands. "One for us, one for Paterson, one for Manhattan. I'll get them out today."

"You've done this before?" I asked. "Tried to trap a man like this?" I hadn't any idea that general delivery was used so often by criminals and fugitives.

Mr. Fulton's eyes widened. "Oh, you wouldn't believe what people get up to by mail. The Postal Service almost put an end to the general delivery plan a few years ago. We kept hearing complaints from the clerks at the windows that they had an unusually high number of young women coming to claim letters. Both married and unmarried."

"What's wrong with that?" I asked.

"Well, some of our clerks came to believe that the mails were being used to carry on clandestine correspondence. They raised a big fuss over it in Chicago and wanted the whole program shut down."

"Over a few love letters?"

"That's not what they called it," Mr. Fulton said. "The papers accused us of supplying 'a bit of the machinery by which young girls are led into the devious paths of sin,' or something along those lines. I was more concerned about gangsters and Black Handers, but it was the idea of girls and sin that got everyone talking. Now they ask for identification and keep lists of everyone who picks up their mail at the general delivery window."

"I suppose that's reasonable," I said, although I wasn't sure it was.

"Well, we do what we can. And we keep a sharp eye out for anyone the sheriff is looking for and hold them if we have to."

"That's fine," Sheriff Heath said. "We've got to catch this one."

Mr. Fulton looked at the envelopes again. "Is this the fellow who ran out on you at the hospital?"

"That's him," the sheriff said.

"Who's the damn fool who let him get away?"

Sheriff Heath paused. "The only thing that matters is getting him back."

"IF YOU CAN be bothered to think about your other duties, Miss Kopp," the sheriff said as we drove back to the jail, "then I wonder if you would turn your attention to Mrs. Monafo."

"As long as the female inmates are locked up, I don't see how they take priority over von Matthesius." I was wound up over those letters and couldn't think about anything else.

"Providencia Monafo won't be locked up much longer," Sheriff Heath said. "Detective Courter is working on an order for her release. If it weren't for the carelessness and ineptitude of the court clerks, he'd have it by now."

"But I'm sure she's telling the truth. Of course she was aiming at her husband. It makes perfect sense. Is he going to charge someone else with the crime?"

"He's working on it. The husband's a likely candidate, as are just about any of the boarders who can't account for their whereabouts at the time of the shooting."

"I wouldn't mind seeing that husband of hers in jail," I said.

"But not for a crime he didn't commit."

We had to slow down for a line of schoolchildren crossing the street hand in hand, all in identical mackinaw coats. Sheriff Heath drummed on the steering wheel while we waited.

"I've had plenty of inmates plead their innocence and beg for their release, but this is the first one who wants to be found guilty. Still, Mr. Courter can't ignore those witnesses. They could go to the papers and claim he disregarded their testimony. He knows that."

The children crossed the road and we drove on. It was

clear to me that Sheriff Heath hadn't any idea what to do about Mrs. Monafo. I also couldn't trust Detective Courter to run any sort of competent investigation into the question of why her account was so at odds with that of the witnesses.

Henri LaMotte would tell me to start over at the beginning. "We're not far from the boarding-house," I said. "Let's have another look."

In a few minutes we were back in Garfield. We parked on Malcolm across the street from the house and, finding the door unlocked, slipped inside and crept down the stairs to the Monafos' basement apartment. No answer came to the sheriff's knock, so he gave the door a push with his shoulder and it fell open.

The flat was, if anything, more squalid than the last time we'd seen it. I would not have believed that Mrs. Monafo exerted any sort of beautifying influence over her surroundings, but in her absence the place had disintegrated such that it had more in common with a lean-to under a bridge occupied by hoboes than a landlady's flat. There was a stench even more appalling than what I'd remembered from my last visit, and it appeared that no effort at all had been made to scrub away the blood stain that was Saverio Salino's last mark on the world.

"At least we know her husband's gone," I said. "No one would live in this filth."

"I've seen people living in worse."

We heard—or rather felt—footsteps on the stairs above us and froze.

"I'll go see who it is," the sheriff said. "I don't know who's been interviewed in this building. Look around and see if you can find anything Courter might've missed. Letters or . . ."

He mumbled the rest as he ran up the stairs. I examined every corner of the apartment but found no letters and no places where a letter would be kept even if one were to arrive. There was no desk, no bookshelf, and no place for pen or paper. They hadn't a lamp to read by nor a chair to sit on. There were only piles of filthy clothes beyond mending, soiled dishes beyond washing, and furnishings too broken and moth-eaten to use. There was not, in fact, anything in the whole place that shouldn't have been taken outside and burned.

I saw nothing that contradicted what we knew so far. What evidence could I possibly be expected to find that would prove that Providencia had shot the man? The plain fact of her standing over a pool of blood with a recently discharged pistol seemed evidence enough to me.

Footsteps struck back down the stairs and Sheriff Heath's face appeared in the doorway. "Didn't you hear me?" he called out impatiently.

"No. When?"

"I yelled down twice for you to come up and help me with these fellows. They only spoke Italian and I wanted to question them before they drove off."

"I was right here. But I don't speak Italian anyway," I said, making my way back to the door.

"Can't you get by with French, or pick up a few words?"

I followed him up the stairs. "Are you asking me to learn a fourth language so I might be of better service to the sheriff's department?"

"That'd be fine, Miss Kopp."

⇥ 20 ⇤

THERE WAS NOTHING TO DO but wait for a response to Reverend Weber's letter. Every day I awoke with a weight on my chest. I was starting to grind my teeth together and my jaw ached from it. I begged the sheriff to send me out on patrol with the other deputies, but he refused.

"There's not much point in having them out marching around to train stations and hotels," he said. "Von Matthesius doesn't want to be seen. We're not just going to stumble across him on the street. It's a waste of their time and it would be a waste of yours, but we haven't any other leads so I keep them at it."

What he didn't say was that he had to keep up the appearance of a vigorous investigation because he was being investigated himself. The patrols were nothing but a bit of theater and a way to stall for time.

I wouldn't have known that the inquest had begun, except that I happened to walk past the sheriff's office one afternoon in the middle of November and heard a familiar voice. It was John Ward, the attorney who had, for a short time, represented Henry Kaufman when he threatened us a year ago. The door was slightly ajar, but I didn't dare get too close once I understood what they were discussing.

"The justices in this county don't know the law! I've seen you go around and instruct them as to their own duties," Mr. Ward was saying. "It's no wonder they've no idea what to do with you. Why, you could just tell them that no such law exists, and then sit back and wait ten or twenty years while they try to look it up for themselves. You'll be retired before they get around to bringing charges against you."

"The county prosecutor has put the matter before them quite plainly," Sheriff Heath said. "It's apparent to me—and to Mrs. Heath—that they have their sights on putting me in jail. It's been three weeks and they're ready to start the inquest. I'm going to need you in the courtroom with me every day, and that's not all. My bondsmen want to know how I intend to hold on to this office and it's time to give them an answer. You and I will sit down with them tomorrow."

"I'd still like to speak to the guard who let this von Matthesius slip out," Mr. Ward said. "If we could make a complaint of drunkenness against him or find evidence that a bribe was paid, we might have—"

Cordelia's voice interrupted. "My husband is protecting one particular individual in his employ at the expense of his family's safety and reputation, not to mention his own personal liberty. I believe that it would be quite possible to put up a good defense on the grounds that the guard was ill-equipped and incompetent."

"Well, that describes half the prison guards in New Jersey," John Ward said. "We need something more uncommon than shiftlessness."

"What about—"

Now it was Sheriff Heath's turn to interrupt his wife. "I won't allow it. The sheriff has full charge of the jail and its inmates. Whatever happens is my responsibility. I won't put it off on a guard. I've heard what you have to say on the matter, Cordelia, and I've made my decision."

But Cordelia wouldn't be quieted. "How do you think it's going to look when they find out that the ladies' matron was put on guard duty, for which she was naturally incapable? If you can't show good judgment about a simple matter of posting a guard, you'll never be elected to another office in this county."

"Did you say—" Mr. Ward put in, but the sheriff ignored him.

"The ladies' matron has been the only one to make an arrest in this case," he said quietly, "making her far more competent than anyone else in my employ, and you would know that if you would just listen to the facts."

"I know all I need to know," she said. "You've stood by her and the rest of us be damned. I won't tolerate the idea of a husband of mine going so willingly to a jail cell over that woman."

There was a scuffling of chairs. Cordelia was about to run out of the room. I backed down the hall as she yelled, "I hope she's—" and the last word was lost as she slammed the door and ran back to the sheriff's apartment, little sobs burbling out of her throat as she went.

Around the corner, out of sight, I leaned against the wall and slid down to the floor, my knees against my chin. The corridor smelled of ammonia and camphor from the soft soap we used to wash the floors. Behind it was the lingering odor of sassafras that reminded me of candy stores. We used it in the summer to cover the stench of a poorly ventilated prison, but the scent hung around all year, faintly green and now intimately familiar to me. If I lost my job, I would even miss that smell.

Surely there was nothing special about the way Sheriff Heath was defending me. He would do the same for any of his men, no matter the consequences. He had a way of championing a noble cause even when it worked against him. I'd seen him do it when he argued for a jail physician, and when he had to defend the cost of a gold tooth for an inmate whose gums were so rotten that ordinary rubber teeth wouldn't hold. He insisted on uniforms for prisoners when he saw how shabby their clothes were, and started holding church services on Sunday and organizing a jail library. All of it required a fight with the Board of Freeholders, and he took up those fights eagerly, with little regard for gossip and newspapers. This was no different.

But Cordelia didn't see it that way. She was too terrified to think straight. The poor woman probably got a case of nerves the day she moved into the jail and never shook it off. She had no neighbors, nor friends that I knew about, and I'd never seen her husband show her much sympathy. With no one in her corner, it had all become too much for her.

I knew what she would do behind that door. As long as her husband stayed away—and he would, after that performance—she'd crawl into a closet like Aunt Adele did and take to her bottle.

She'd like nothing more than to see me disappear. For just a minute I considered it. I could have left and never returned.

But that wouldn't make up for what I'd done. Nothing would, but bringing von Matthesius back.

THE INQUEST WENT FORWARD, but I knew little about it. Sheriff Heath persuaded a judge to hold the proceedings behind closed doors so that the newspapers couldn't print anything that might endanger our search for von Matthesius. He was at the courthouse most days, for a few hours at least, but never spoke about it.

I kept myself busy at the jail. Martha Hicks had served her time and been released. She made a teary and wide-eyed promise to me that she would not resume her thieving ways. I had my doubts—she'd been running a long-standing and profitable scheme wherein she stole hosiery and sold it in her sister's dress shop—but I wished her well. Ida Higgins had also been turned loose after the man confessed to setting the fire and her testimony against him was no longer required.

A new girl, Frieda Burkel, had been arrested for assaulting a visitor to her home, but it looked like the charges were to be reversed and the visitor charged with assaulting her. Apparently a former beau walked right into her house without knocking and tried to kiss her after three years away in the navy. She broke a milk bottle over his head, having failed to recognize him or to remember that he had been her beau. The man stumbled and pulled her to the ground with him. When the police arrived, they were covered in the blood issuing forth from his fairly shallow and harmless head wound. Still, they'd both been delivered to us. I worked on getting her released on the grounds that a virtuous woman was practically obligated to break something over a man's head if he came in uninvited and stole a kiss.

It seemed to me that the police were getting more eager to arrest young girls now that they knew the jail had a matron. They hadn't any idea what to do with wayward females, but we couldn't do much for them, either. We were an institution of correction, not a charity house. Once we had von Matthesius in hand again, I would speak to the sheriff about it.

Calls kept coming in from police officers on the lookout for our fugitive. We wasted a great deal of time running to and from New York to have a look. An officer on street patrol said he spotted him in Long Island but couldn't catch him. We spent a full day canvassing the street where he'd been seen, but turned up empty. A report came in from Brooklyn that someone matching von Matthesius's description had been going in and out of an apartment building. The police kept the building under watch for two days and then, despairing of ever finding him again, decided to just round up every man of his age and general build in the vicinity. We rushed to the station to have a look at them, but none were von Matthesius.

After nearly two weeks of this, an Officer Weisenreider telephoned from the East Twenty-Second Street station to say that he had our man and we needed only to come and get him. It was after midnight when he called, but the sheriff and I rode out together, each of us agreeing that we wouldn't be able to sleep until we had him in hand. When we arrived we were presented with a Polish man of about seventy-five who spoke no English but, for reasons we never understood, nodded vigorously every time someone said the name von Matthesius to him. A translator had to be called in to make sure he didn't know anything about our fugitive or his relatives. He did not.

"Are you sure you don't want him?" the officer asked, as if an elderly Polish man might be of some use to us.

"That's generous, but no," the sheriff said. We rode back to Hackensack in disappointed silence.

Finally, one morning around the first of December, the postmaster appeared unannounced at the jail. Sheriff Heath called me down to his office so we could both hear what he had to say.

Mr. Fulton was waiting in front of the fireplace, bouncing on the balls of his feet with the air of the cat who had swallowed the canary. Sheriff Heath came down the hall from his living quarters, looking grimmer than I'd ever seen him. I didn't dare ask what was bothering him.

As soon as the sheriff was settled behind his desk, Mr. Fulton said, "The New York police keep a man assigned to the general delivery window as a matter of practice. On any day of the week, they have a list of a dozen or so fugitives and con men who might be expecting a letter. What a city, eh?"

"It is quite a city," the sheriff said wearily.

"Well, the way it works," Mr. Fulton continued, obviously enjoying himself, "is that the police put an officer in view of the postal clerks at the window. They've rigged up a hand signal to let the officer know if any suspicious letter is being claimed. And today, someone came in for your letter!"

He clasped his hands together in satisfaction. We waited in silence for the rest. When it didn't come, I said, "You mustn't leave us in suspense, Mr. Fulton. Has our man been arrested?"

"What? Oh, no. That's what I came to tell you. He sent a messenger to get the letter. He knew better than to turn up himself. The officer chased the messenger across the street and into a subway station, but would you believe the train doors closed just as he was about to leap into the car and nab him?"

Sheriff Heath sighed and shut his eyes against the image. "I do believe it." He spoke in a distracted manner that was entirely unlike him, and I wondered what could have been disturbing him more than the matter at hand.

"The officer wouldn't really have grabbed him on the street like that, would he?" I asked. "Surely he intended to follow the messenger and find out where he was taking the letter. He could have gone straight to von Matthesius."

"Oh!" said Mr. Fulton, even more delighted with this version of the story. "I suppose you're right."

"Did the messenger know he was being chased, or did he just happen to slip into the subway station ahead of the police officer?" I asked.

"I didn't think to ask," Mr. Fulton said, a note of wonder in his voice at all the possibilities. "I only just heard from the postmaster in New York and rushed right over. Here, I have the name of the officer. You can speak to him yourself."

He handed the sheriff a slip of paper. Sheriff Heath stared blankly at it for a minute. His head seemed to clear and he said, "When did this happen?"

"About half an hour ago."

"I wish you'd just telephoned. We should have had someone at the church with Reverend Weber by now."

Mr. Fulton's mouth dropped open. "Sheriff, it took no more than—"

Sheriff Heath held up a hand to silence him and turned to me. "Bring Deputy English down. We'll put him at the church. The letter promised money, so we have to hope someone will turn up to collect it. "

"Couldn't I go?" I asked.

"No."

"But—"

He jumped to his feet and said sharply, "Miss Kopp. I thought we agreed that you'd stay here and do your job."

"But he's my—"

"It's December, and I'll have him waiting outside on a twelve-hour shift. It's guaranteed to be cold, damp, and pointless."

"That's fine. I don't mind."

"You will mind, once you've been there all day," Sheriff Heath snapped. Mr. Fulton shrank back into a corner, shocked. "He's been on the run for six weeks and we all want him caught. That doesn't mean we all have to wait in the bushes in the freezing cold for a messenger who might not come for days, if he shows at all. He must know it's a trick. Go and get English."

When I didn't move, he said, with his eyes down and his hands knotted together, "Please do not be insensible to the fact that I am answering some rather difficult questions at the courthouse right now. English is the man for this job."

I didn't have to guess at his meaning. This was too important a post to assign to me. I ran out of the room, my face burning. When I found Deputy English, I could barely get the words out.

At some point in the middle of the afternoon Sheriff Heath left suddenly, telling no one where he was going. A few minutes later I knew at last what had been worrying him. From the fifth-floor window I saw Cordelia Heath and the children leave the residence and walk over to the courthouse, where they stood with suitcases and hatboxes until an auto came to the curb and took them all away.

⇥ 21 ⇤

IF I'D BEEN TOLD, only a month or two earlier, that I would be responsible for an escaped prisoner, criminal charges being filed against the sheriff, the dissolution of his marriage, and several guards and deputies at risk of losing their places, I might never have left the house again. In one careless moment I had set into motion a carnival of disasters, each more spectacular than the last.

I couldn't bear it. I wondered how any of our inmates managed the weight of their own regrets. Some of them regretted nothing, or claimed not to, but surely a few of them sat in their cells and let their misdeeds gnaw away at them as mine did.

But unlike our inmates, I was free and at liberty to do something about my troubles. All day I paced and fretted over that letter. Sheriff Heath had put his worst man on the case and seemed not to know it. I'd had misgivings about English all along, and not just because of his treatment of me. He was arrogant and careless and dismissive of the sheriff's ideas. I didn't trust him to do the job, and I knew that if the messenger got away, we wouldn't have another chance. The fact that I had already failed at guard duty—catastrophically so—didn't enter into my way of thinking about it. If there was a man to be caught, I would catch him. I had no doubt of it.

I also knew that if I'd done as Sheriff Heath asked and stayed in my place, I never would have captured Felix. It occurred to me that listening to Sheriff Heath might not be the way to capture this man.

That night, after supper and lights-out, I told the guards I was going home. Instead I marched right through downtown and over to Reverend Weber's church. I found Deputy English crouching between two overgrown shrubs behind the rectory. When he saw me he jumped and raised a finger to his lips.

"I'm taking your place," I whispered.

Deputy English squinted at me, his face nothing but a long dark shadow. "You couldn't possibly. Go on away from here before you frighten the messenger boy."

I looked around and saw no other place to hide. He'd taken the only available shrub. How was I to make him leave? I said the only thing that came to me.

"Sheriff Heath sent me to take the night shift. You're to go home."

"You're lying."

I was lying, but I took offense at the accusation anyway. "I'm to relieve you, and if you won't let me, I'll have no choice but to go back to the jail and return with the sheriff, who has better things to do than explain his decisions to you."

In the dark I could make out a row of white teeth. Deputy English had a mean-spirited grin that was always more of a threat than a smile.

"Even Sheriff Heath isn't so boneheaded as to put you in charge of this. Someone might have to make an arrest tonight. Are you expecting the old minister to do it?"

"Have you forgotten that I made the only arrest in this case?" I showed him the revolver in my pocket and the handcuffs looped to my skirt, just under my coat.

The deputy snorted and leaned around the corner of the rectory to get a look at the street. Finally he emerged from behind the shrub, brushing away leaves and spider webs, and stood right in front of me, toe to toe, so close that his nose nearly touched mine. His face brought to mind some small rodent I disliked: a hard-toothed beaver or a greedy little squirrel.

"I don't know why the sheriff hired you, and I don't know why he kept you on after you let an inmate walk right out of the hospital. But plenty of us have ideas about it."

I held my breath. I wasn't about to answer to that kind of accusation. I'd never stood so still.

"So you can stay here and wait for the messenger, Miss Kopp. The sheriff sent me in a motor car, but there's no reason to leave that for you, is there?"

He knew I couldn't drive. I'd assumed the messenger would arrive by train, but with a sinking feeling it came to me that he could, of course, come in an auto, and I'd have no way of following him.

"And I'll stop in at the jail on my way home to let the sheriff know how good it was of him to send a replacement for the night. How does that sound?"

That didn't sound very good to me. It wouldn't take English any time at all to get back to the jail. Sheriff Heath could be here within the hour. I'd let myself be propelled by rage and frustration and hadn't thought about what would happen if the sheriff found out I was here before the messenger arrived. But I saw nothing to do but stand my ground.

"Go and tell him. It doesn't matter."

He paused for just a second longer, so close that I could feel his breath on me, and then he turned abruptly and walked away, his hands in his pockets, whistling a little melody. A few minutes later I heard his engine fire and rumble down the street.

I stood listening to a train whistle off in the distance, and to the shuffling of leaves in the trees in the little graveyard behind the church. After just a few minutes my fingers were numb and I was fighting the urge to stamp my feet against the cold. In the solitary dark my sense of outrage dissipated and I wondered if Sheriff Heath had been right. This siege could go on for days. How long did I think I'd last?

I couldn't stay outside all night, I knew that. I tapped quietly on the rectory door and Reverend Weber opened it just wide enough to look at me.

"I'll be inside the church," I said. "Is there a door to the rectory in there?"

He nodded.

"Keep it unlocked."

He twisted himself around to meet my eyes. His arm wobbled atop his cane in such a way that his whole body shook. *"Gute Nacht,"* he said, his voice raspy and faint, and closed the door gently in my face.

The poor man had agreed only to write a letter. He never agreed to this.

Inside the church, I pulled a chair over to the rectory door. I opened it to check that it was unlocked and peeked through a small passageway to the sitting room where the reverend sat alone. Then I removed my hat so I could lean against the wall and listen for any sound on the other side of the door. After a few minutes I opened it just once more and reminded the reverend to speak clearly, but not so loudly that it would raise suspicion. He waved his hand at me, wearily.

Over the next few hours there was no sound but the faint tick of my watch and the sighs and moans issuing forth from the old man as he shifted in his chair on the other side of the door and tried to stay awake. He kept a light on. I heard him shuffling the pages of a newspaper. Outside, the branches of an elm tree creaked when the wind picked up. Twice I heard a man whistle as he walked by. To keep myself alert I paced the length of the church and stood at the high and narrow window looking out at the darkened neighborhood. The warm lights in the houses grew dim one after another, the neighbors either falling into untroubled sleep, or sitting up with their predicaments as I was.

Deputy English would have spoken to Sheriff Heath by now. I sat in the dark and looked down the long empty rows of pews and wondered at my own arrogance. The sheriff was fond of saying that Cordelia hadn't been elected to any public office and had no say in the running of his department. The same was true of me. I had no right to send his deputy away. English could have stood his ground, but he couldn't resist leaving me here, where I wasn't supposed to be, and going to tell Sheriff Heath what I'd done. At least I knew that I'd been right about him. He didn't care about catching von Matthesius and was too easily persuaded to abandon his post.

Still the sheriff didn't come. He might have gone after Cordelia. He could have been standing on her mother's porch, begging her to come home. There was nothing for me to do but to wonder about it, and to sit like a condemned woman awaiting my fate.

It was nearly midnight when I heard the scrape of the church door and jumped to my feet. Sheriff Heath walked noiselessly up to me, took me roughly by the elbow, and pulled me through the pews to the other side of the room, as far from the rectory door as we could be.

"I won't tolerate this." He wouldn't even look at me.

"He was my prisoner. I should be the one to bring him in." I said it even though I no longer quite believed it myself.

"Damnit! You don't even figure into it." His eyes were fixed on some point over my shoulder. When he did look at me, it was the blank stare of a stranger. "My wife is at her mother's over this. I've got a lawyer trying to keep me out of jail."

He did blame me. Of course he did. I had the sensation of falling to the floor, but somehow I was still standing, frozen, mute.

"Bergen County won't see another lady deputy for years because of this mess. And they probably won't see a Democratic sheriff again, either. Try to think about someone other than yourself, Miss Kopp. And don't ever tell one of my deputies what to do."

He would have sent me home at that moment—or he would have tried—but through the rectory door we heard the reverend call out.

"I'm coming!" the old man shouted, in exactly the sort of desperate and overly loud voice I'd warned him against. We both rushed to the door to listen.

I caught a glimpse of a dark figure through the window. From his shape I could tell it wasn't von Matthesius. He was shorter, and rounder, and he had the voice of a Brooklyn-born boy.

"You got a package for me?" he said when the reverend opened the door.

"Yes, please come in." He persisted in using a booming, theatrical voice, which must have been the way he delivered his sermons. I cringed and held my breath. Sheriff Heath had his hand on the door. "Are you a friend of Dr. von Matthesius?"

"Sure," the boy said.

"And your name is?"

"The messenger boy."

"I didn't catch that." The reverend's voice floated even higher.

Something was knocked over or kicked around and the boy said, "Where is it?"

"What's that?" Reverend Weber hollered.

"The package! The envelope. The bag. Whatever you have. Go and get it."

The reverend mumbled his answer and shuffled around the room. Something slid across the floor and there came the sound of a club striking the wall.

"Why'd you do that?" the reverend said.

"To get you moving! You're the one who sent for me. Now, where the devil is the money?"

I had the uncomfortable impression that the reverend was stalling on my account. He was supposed to hand the envelope over and let the man go. Keeping him there was of no help to us. The sheriff pulled his revolver and held it down at his side. I did the same.

"Why, it's just a small envelope and I thought I put it

right here, but let me look, Mr.—what did you say your name was?"

Now the club landed somewhere else and something—a lamp, a mirror—shattered. If the reverend didn't stop this nonsense, we'd have to run in and ruin the whole operation.

"Here you are! Here you are! Now just go!" There were tears behind his voice.

The club thundered again and then came the sound I'd been dreading: a strong and solid fist landing a punch on the old man. He must have fallen and knocked over a chair, because there was a clatter and a moan, and the boy ran out the door and down the street.

"Stay with him," Sheriff Heath told me, and went in chase of the messenger. It took everything in me not to run after him.

Inside the rectory, the reverend was in a heap on the floor and bleeding from a cut on his forehead, but he was alive and already struggling to stand. I pressed my handkerchief against his head and helped him into a chair.

"Gehen Sie!" It meant, "Go on!"

I told him I had to stay with him. He waved me out.

The door stood open, a gaping black hole that led away from the church, away from Hackensack, away to wherever von Matthesius was hiding. A wind picked up and rattled the door a little, and a few orange leaves flew inside.

It was impossible to resist. I slammed the door behind me and ran down the street after Sheriff Heath.

⇥ 22 ⇤

THE BOY WAS BOARDING a train for New York by the time I stumbled, wheezing and red-faced, into the station. Sheriff Heath stood in the doorway to the ticket office with his back to me, talking in a low voice to the station agent, the two of them framed in the orange light of a single lantern. The messenger seemed not to have noticed him. I stayed out of the way and watched the sheriff step into the car after the boy had boarded.

When the whistle sounded I climbed to the platform and hopped aboard the following car just before the train started to move. There were only a few sleepy travelers on board. If I stood at the front, I could just see through the window into the car beyond, where Sheriff Heath and the messenger had their backs turned. In this way I watched the two of them, unnoticed, as the train rattled into the city.

In New York I got off behind them and trailed them out of the station and onto Seventh Avenue. Even at this late hour there were people about, and hacks looking for fares, and porters carrying trunks. The weak light of a few lampposts was all we had to see by. It would be easy to lose the boy. There were plenty more like him, solitary figures in dark coats rushing away from the station.

When I came up alongside Sheriff Heath, he didn't turn to look at me but spoke quietly, out of the side of his mouth. "Deputies generally do what the sheriff tells them, or they find themselves in another line of work."

"If I can't catch him, I don't deserve any line of work."

He snorted at that and broke into a run to keep up with the boy. I matched his pace. We slowed when we were about half a block behind him.

"If you'd like to try following a sheriff's orders just once," he said under the cover of a sudden clatter of horses' hooves as several old wagons rolled past us, "then you may go back to the station, and send a police officer to help me. I could have used English, if you hadn't sent him away."

Before I could answer, the boy paused to look into a shop window and we skidded to a stop ourselves. I realized with a start that it was soon to be Christmas. Each window down the block showed a winter scene: a fairy-tale castle nestled in a cloud of cotton batting, miniature carolers carved of wood and holding out wrapped presents instead of songbooks, and a little porcelain doll sitting in front of a fire clutching a kitten with a bow around its neck.

Sheriff Heath was panting in the thin winter air. There was something frantic about the way he was adjusting his hat, fidgeting with his pockets, fingering the button beneath his collar. He turned to speak, undoubtedly about to order me away again, but the boy started walking and we had to hurry to catch up.

He took the most indirect and meandering route through

the city he could've possibly contrived, sticking to narrow streets where the shops had all been shuttered for hours, where wide faceless buildings held box factories and printing presses by day but looked entirely abandoned by night. He never again stopped or slowed down. More than once he crossed in the middle of an avenue without any regard for the drivers of motor cars and carriages who couldn't see ten feet in front of them, forcing us to chase after him and risk our own limbs. It was too hurried a pace for conversation, but the sheriff kept trying to wave me away and I kept ignoring him. It was too late for me to abandon the chase. He needed me, not a New York officer who didn't know what we were after.

The boy stopped again and bent down, perhaps to tie a shoe, and we backed up into a stack of crates outside a grocery.

The sheriff started again on his harangue but I said, "You wouldn't go home. If you'd been the one who let him get away, you wouldn't ever go home."

He took his hat off and I thought for a minute he would smack me with it. But he slicked his hair back and shoved the hat down on his head and said, "I'd do what the sheriff told me to do. I was a deputy for four years, and do you think—"

Then the boy was off again, walking much faster this time, crossing Fifth Avenue and making his way into the slums on the East Side of town. There were young men huddled in tight knots on the corners, rubbing their hands together over the meager spark of an ashcan, and girls in moth-eaten coats shivering in doorways. The sidewalks were so uneven and riddled with broken and half-open cellar doors that I had to lift my skirts to see where I was stepping.

At last the boy stopped in a doorway down on Second Avenue and felt around in his pockets for a key. Sheriff Heath pulled me into the darkened window of a Polish bakery a few doors away. He kept me so close that I could feel his mustache against my ear. "It's your fault if he runs. Catch him no matter what."

"Of course," I said, but he looked desperate and uncertain as he let go of me and ran noiselessly across the street.

The boy fumbled with his keys and finally pushed one into the lock. The sheriff stole up behind him, took hold of the door, and pushed in after him. I couldn't see the boy's reaction, but I heard a scuffle and crept closer.

Sheriff Heath mumbled something I couldn't hear, and the boy yelled, and one of them hit the other. I ran up to the door, which had drifted closed but not caught, and opened it in time to see the sheriff pulling the boy's hands behind his back and putting handcuffs on him. They were both on their knees in the narrow hallway. Sheriff Heath staggered to his feet and pulled the boy up with him.

The sheriff looked over at me and jerked his head for me to step inside and close the door. "Not a word," he said to the boy in a low voice. "Just nod yes or no. Any sound and I'll make it worse for you."

The boy nodded. He was turned away from me. I had a feeling that Sheriff Heath didn't want him to see me. Maybe the boy would be more frightened if he thought there were no witnesses.

He stood behind the boy, keeping hold of the handcuffs, and spoke quietly in his ear. "Is Dr. von Matthesius upstairs?"

The boy shook his head no.

"Has he been staying here?"

He nodded yes.

"Then who are we going to see? Just say it real quiet. Don't wake anybody up."

"Rudy Schilga."

"Rudy? Rudolph?"

"I guess so."

"Apartment?"

"What?" The boy tried to turn around again and Sheriff Heath gave him a little shove forward.

"What apartment? Where are we going?"

"Oh. 3R."

With that they began to climb the stairs, the boy in front and the sheriff right behind him, still holding him by the cuffs. At the top of the first flight, the sheriff leaned down from the landing and waved me up. I climbed as quietly as I could and stayed out of sight.

On the third floor, they stopped in front of 3R. The boy didn't say a word. He kept his head down and panted from the exertion of the climb.

"Key?" Sheriff Heath whispered.

"In my coat."

The sheriff reached around and pulled it out of his pocket. He turned the key and pushed the boy inside.

I stepped in behind them and closed the door. The place was empty. It was an ordinary tenement flat, with a bathtub in the kitchen and two bare iron beds against the walls. There was a shelf holding cups and saucers and a battered tin pan. Apart from these few furnishings, there was no sign that anyone lived there. It smelled of dust and grime.

At the sound of the door closing, the boy turned sharply and jumped when he saw me. "Who is she?"

"Keep your voice down," Sheriff Heath said. "This is Miss Kopp. What's your name, son?"

"Reinhold Dietz."

It was a German name I wouldn't have any trouble remembering. Reinhold kept his eyes on me. He had a round, doughy face and blank, nickel-blue eyes. "I got followed, didn't I?" he said, sounding resigned about it. "Rudy told me to watch for police, but he didn't say nothing about a lady."

Sheriff Heath yanked his handcuffs and turned him away from me. "What's the plan, son?"

"Am I going to jail?"

The sheriff paused and looked down at him, taking in his navy coat with holes at the elbows, and a pair of old shoes that were starting to split at the soles and leak newspaper stuffing.

"That depends upon you."

In the room next door a man succumbed to a tubercular coughing fit. His steps fell heavily across the floor and there was the sound of water being poured from a pitcher. We waited in silence until he settled down and then the sheriff said, "Reinhold, I'll let you go the minute I get von Matthesius. When I put the cuffs on him, I'll take them off you. It'll be just like that."

Reinhold kept his head down. "Rudy said if he wasn't here to go meet the Baron at the ferry building."

"What ferry?"

"East River. Twenty-Third Street."

"When?"

Reinhold twisted his neck around, glancing first at me and then at the sheriff. "Now! I should be there by now."

That was all the urging Sheriff Heath required. He told

Reinhold again to be quiet and the three of us shuffled out of the apartment.

"Is anybody coming back here tonight?" the sheriff whispered on the stairs.

"Nobody's lived here since they moved the Baron out. It's just a meeting place."

Outside, the sheriff looked back up at the building and over to me.

"I can stay here in case someone comes," I said.

"Except you won't stay."

"I will if I say I will."

"I see. But not if I tell you to. You only take orders from yourself."

Reinhold Dietz looked back and forth between us like we were two parents arguing over a child.

"I can't leave you on Second Avenue in the middle of the night," he said.

"You left me in Hackensack."

"At a church!" The sheriff shook his head and groaned. "Let's get going. As long as we have Reinhold, we'll get the Baron. Won't we, son?"

Reinhold gave a discouraged moan but went along without a fight. This time we took a more direct route up to Twenty-Third Street and over to the ferry building. If it was unusual for a man and a woman to lead a boy along in handcuffs in the quiet hours after midnight, I wouldn't have known it. No one who passed us gave us a second look.

The streets of New York's East Side at that hour were far livelier than those of Hackensack or Paterson had ever been. There were lights on in every building—not all of them, but enough to let me know that for every dozen people asleep, there were one or two awake and doing whatever a body does at two o'clock in the morning. Silhouetted against one window was a woman walking a fretful baby, and in another a man leaned over a fire escape with his cigarette. Even some of the shops were occupied. I saw a boy pounding dough in the kind of nondescript bakery that turns out nothing but brown rolls and dark bread. At a laundry two women bent over sewing machines, each illuminated by a single gas lantern. At the corner of Nineteenth Street, two men appeared to be emptying the contents of an apartment onto the curb, and a horde of rag pickers had already found it and started to carry the mess away.

Reinhold panted noisily as we walked, with great puffs of steam coming from his mouth in the cold. The handcuffs seemed to throw him off balance and he kept stumbling against us. I thought about telling the sheriff that we should unchain him, but I knew that he was in no mood to make things comfortable for Reinhold, so we stomped along, heading east on Twenty-Third until the ferry building came into sight under the ruddy glow of the street lamps.

As we approached, Sheriff Heath said to Reinhold, "Does von Matthesius know you? Does he know what you look like?"

"He knows me."

"Well, he knows us, too. Here's what I'm going to do. I'll find a nice comfortable bench and chain you to it. Miss Kopp and I will be nearby even if you don't see us. If you call out any kind of warning to him, you're coming back to Hackensack for a nice long stay in my jail. As soon as we get him, I let you go. Agreed?"

Reinhold coughed and nodded. "Suppose so."

We stood across the street from the ferry building and Sheriff Heath looked it over. It was a long, low-slung building in the shape of an L, with wide bays for boarding carriages and motor cars. There were plenty of spaces to hide. We could have used five or six more men.

"Why does he meet you here? Where is he coming from?" Sheriff Heath asked.

"I don't know. I never know."

Sheriff Heath gave his handcuffs a little tug, the way you might pull a horse up short. "Where would you wait for him?"

Reinhold nodded toward a row of benches where the two sides of the building came together. "Over there, maybe."

"That's fine. Miss Kopp, go take a walk. See if he's here. Try to stay in sight of us. After I get our friend settled, I'll come find you."

I ran off without a word. There was a walkway of wooden planks around the edge of the ferry building, and when the heel of my boot struck a loose board, the sound rang out like a gunshot. I dashed under a canvas awning near the ticket window, in a deep shadow, hoping that von Matthesius hadn't spotted me.

But there was no sign of him, or any other man expecting a rendezvous. There were only the men hauling buckets of water out of the river and washing down the docks, coiling enormous ropes around their posts, and cinching gang-planks into place. A few of them looked up at me but didn't say anything.

Across the way, Sheriff Heath had Reinhold on a bench and was kneeling in front of him, locking him to it. I saw him take Reinhold's face in his hands and speak to him. Reinhold nodded vigorously and Sheriff Heath stepped away. The boy arranged himself so that it looked like he was just sitting casually and not chained to the bench.

The sheriff joined me at the far end of the building. "Nothing?"

"Just a few dock workers."

"All right. I'll go talk to them. You keep watch around this side. Stay in plain sight and do not lose sight of that boy. If von Matthesius does turn up, he's likely to go straight for him."

He disappeared behind the ferry building. I stayed at my post at the far end, where I had a clear view of Reinhold and would see if anyone approached him from the street side. It wasn't until I was standing still that I began to feel the biting cold that blew in off the river. In spite of my gloves, the blood had drained from my fingers and I had to rub them together to get the feeling back. My feet were just as frozen but I didn't dare stomp around and make too much noise. Behind me, along First Avenue, came a steady rumble of motor cars, and from farther away, across the whole of the island, there was the general din of horns squawking and engines misfiring and boilers hissing that made up the incessant, spectral roar of the city.

Reinhold Dietz sat perfectly still on the bench with his chin down against his chest. He might have fallen asleep, although I couldn't tell from this distance. I worried about leaving him for too long in the cold. I paced back and forth simply as a matter of survival and couldn't believe that Reinhold could tolerate sitting still for much longer in his thin coat.

Every few minutes I caught a glimpse of Sheriff Heath moving along the docks on the other side of the building.

Men's voices rose and fell, drifting around the way they do so close to the water.

Finally he emerged at the opposite end of the ferry building and stood out in a little pool of light cast by a lone street lamp. He raised his palms up to show that he'd found nothing and I did the same. Reinhold Dietz lifted his head long enough to look at each of us and dropped it again.

We both stayed at our posts a while longer, but no one approached except a few dockworkers coming and going. When the clock tower read three o'clock, the sheriff crossed the trolley tracks and sat down next to Reinhold. They spoke for a few minutes and then he released the boy from the bench, locked his arms once again behind his back, and the two of them walked over to me. Even in the darkness I could see that the boy's face was red and puffy. He'd either been crying or he was frostbitten, or possibly both.

"We're going back to the apartment," the sheriff said. "Reinhold says that von Matthesius is never late. If he hasn't shown by now, he isn't going to. There's no point in waiting around in the cold anymore."

I hated to leave the only place our fugitive might be expected to turn up. "I'll stay here," I said. "You two go back."

Sheriff Heath squinted at me. "Is that your punishment? You're going to stand out all night in the cold?"

"Would that take care of it?"

He rolled his eyes. "There's another meeting set up for tomorrow at the subway station. We'll get him there. This way, Miss Kopp." He had Reinhold Dietz by one elbow and took me by the other.

"Why don't you call her deputy if she works for you?" Reinhold asked as we hurried back to the flat.

"Deputies follow the orders given to them by the sheriff. That is the sole purpose of a deputy. People who don't follow the sheriff's orders are more commonly referred to as . . ." He paused here as we navigated a tricky intersection along Twenty-Third, and Reinhold offered a suggestion.

"Outlaws?"

Sheriff Heath fought back a smile as he pulled us down the street. "Thank you, Mr. Dietz. Outlaw is exactly right."

⚜ 23 ⚜

WE SAT IN THE DARKENED APARTMENT, Sheriff Heath and Reinhold on one bed and me on the other. Sheriff Heath watched the boy uneasily. Reinhold didn't seem clever enough to fabricate much of a lie, but we had every reason to wonder if we were being misled.

"Can't you think of any other way to get word to him?" the sheriff asked.

Reinhold shook his head. "I only talk to Rudy. If Rudy has a job for me, he comes here or he leaves word at a restaurant over by Times Square."

"Murray's?"

Reinhold lifted his chin and looked Sheriff Heath in the eye, impressed. "How'd you find out about Murray's?"

"She did." Sheriff Heath jerked his head toward me.

"Her? Say, I didn't know they had lady detectives."

"It's a new idea. I haven't made up my mind about it myself."

I didn't like the way this conversation was going, so I said, "How does Rudy know von Matthesius?"

"Rudy? Rudy knows everybody. He used to run errands for a doctor uptown. What was his name—something about a rat?"

"Dr. Rathburn?" I put in.

"That sounds right. Dr. Rathburn wanted Rudy to find places for the Baron to hide. Rudy knows all kinds of places."

"And Dr. Rathburn's paying to keep the Baron hidden?" I asked.

Reinhold shrugged. "Somebody pays. They leave the money at Murray's. Or they were for a while. Something went wrong. There hasn't been any money for a few weeks."

"What happened?" I asked, although I already knew.

"All of a sudden the doctor was just gone, and another fellow who used to leave money for Rudy stopped turning up too. Rudy's been stuck with the Baron. We don't know what to do with him. We were supposed to keep him hidden and move him every few days, but nobody's paying us. It was Rudy's idea to ask at the general delivery window."

"Why didn't the Baron just leave town?" the sheriff asked, trying to sound casual about it. "If I were running from the law, I'd get on a train."

Reinhold leaned back against the wall and rolled his neck around. "The doctor said not to let him get too far. Said the Baron owed him money. He wanted to keep him close."

"And Rudy has no idea where Dr. Rathburn went?" the sheriff asked.

Reinhold was slipping away. He slumped over to one side and mumbled, "Nobody tells me."

We watched his eyes roll shut and his head drop. After a few minutes he commenced a quiet snore. There was nothing in the room to look at but each other and the broken plaster on the wall. I looked at the wall.

After a long stretch of each of us studying the cracks above the other's head, Sheriff Heath said, "I might have suggested it was selfish of you to go after von Matthesius on your own. I didn't mean to put it that way."

"Of course you did. And it was."

"You felt a sense of duty and you acted upon it. I wish more of my deputies would."

I unpinned my hat and sat it down next to me. "It doesn't matter why I did anything. I've made a mess of your affairs and all you ever did was to try to help me."

"I wasn't interested in trying to help you, Miss Kopp. I hired you to do a job."

"And look at what happened."

Reinhold gave an enormous snort and we feared we'd awakened him, but he settled back into a dull snore.

"It's been difficult for you, too," he said.

"Don't bother yourself about me," I said, stifling a yawn. "You have your family to think about. Go and buy some roses for Mrs. Heath and persuade her to come home."

"Mrs. Heath will be back tomorrow," he said. "Her father will tell her she never should have married me, and her mother will tell her she has a duty to her husband, and she'll be so tired of it that she'll come back just to get away from them."

"You should ask her to come home," I said. "A wife wants to be asked back."

"I don't have to. She knows where she lives."

It wasn't my place to lecture him about Cordelia, so I didn't.

"Get some sleep while you can," he said.

"I'm not going to sleep on the job." But I unlaced my boots and tucked my feet under my coat. It was almost as cold inside the apartment as it had been outside. There was a rusted iron radiator under the window, but it served no purpose other than to attract soot.

"You sleep on the job almost every night," Sheriff Heath said. "You're there so much we should charge you rent. Most people want to leave their jobs in the evening."

In the darkness I couldn't see his eyes, just the two shadows across them. We faced each other over a long silence.

"I don't want to leave my job."

The next time I looked up, the meager light of early morning had crept into the room. Reinhold Dietz was still asleep, having fallen over to one side, his feet still on the floor. Sheriff Heath was looking straight ahead with the impassive air of a lawman who was accustomed to waiting alone for long stretches of time.

I sat up quickly, my hair down in my face and my skirt tangled around my knees. Reinhold heard me shifting around and he yawned and tried to stretch, but was hindered by his handcuffs. He pushed himself up and looked around the room, blinking at us in surprise.

"I must have dreamt it," he said. "I dreamt you let me go."

"I let you go to *sleep*," the sheriff offered.

He bent his neck from side to side, groaning. "Did you tie me in a knot first?"

"You'll be all right." The sheriff stood and shook out his coat. "It just so happens that witnesses in the custody of the sheriff are entitled to a decent breakfast. Get yourselves washed up, both of you, and we'll go."

There was a water closet in the hall. Sheriff Heath took Reinhold there while I washed my face in the rusty water from the bathtub. When we were as clean as we could make ourselves, we stepped out into the cold and quiet street at the one hour when it was truly empty, when even the pickpockets were asleep. The street lamps were still lit, faintly amber in the bluish light around dawn. Not a single shop was open.

Sheriff Heath allowed Reinhold to walk with his hands cuffed in front of him, concealed in the folds of his coat. He kept hold of the boy's elbow on one side and I took the other. We must have looked like an odd trio, this boy who was just a little younger than Fleurette walking arm in arm with a woman of thirty-six and a man of about the same age. We could have been mistaken for his parents, if only he resembled either one of us.

It was just before seven in the morning. Von Matthesius was expected at the Borough Hall subway station at ten. I was eager to get there and didn't want to linger over breakfast. Reinhold, however, claimed to be faint from hunger and the sheriff insisted that we stop.

Near Astor Place was a lunchroom that opened early to feed truckmen and hack drivers. We took our seats at the counter and were quickly furnished with eggs and rolls. Reinhold asked for corned beef hash and the sheriff indulged him and even ordered a corned beef sandwich to be wrapped up and put in his pocket. As we blew on our coffee, Reinhold looked back and forth between us.

"Do you always take a lady along to chase after people?" he asked the sheriff. "Wouldn't you rather have another fellow? What if I'd been hard to catch?"

"Oh, you don't want Miss Kopp chasing after you," Sheriff Heath said. "She nearly choked a man in Times Square recently."

"He deserved it," I said.

Reinhold sopped up the rest of his hash with a roll and chewed it thoughtfully, looking me over. "Doesn't your husband want you home at night?"

"I haven't got one," I said, "and I can't imagine a husband who would approve of overnight trips to East Side flats with the two of you."

"Then you won't ever marry, or else you'd have to give this up."

I drank the last of my coffee and said, "I might be giving it up anyway, depending on how the day goes."

"The sheriff must not be married either," he said as Sheriff Heath paid the bill and led us out into a bright, windy morning, "because I know a wife wouldn't stand for the two of you running around together all night."

"That's enough, Mr. Dietz," the sheriff said, pushing him against the wall of the lunchroom to handcuff him again.

"Ow!" the boy cried. The sheriff might have been a little rough.

"He didn't mean anything by it," I muttered as we turned toward the subway station.

"Course he did," the sheriff said, without looking at me. He bought two newspapers and we took them on the train.

"Don't I get a paper?" Reinhold asked.

"It's just something to hide behind if we need it." The sheriff passed a paper to me and rattled his to signal that he didn't want to be disturbed. Reinhold looked around, restless as a little boy, and rubbed his wrists against his knees.

"Couldn't you take these off while we're on the train?" he

said with a child's whine in his voice. "You know I'm not going anywhere."

"I don't know anything about you, Reinhold," the sheriff said mildly, not looking up from his newspaper. "You fell asleep during our interrogation last night. I didn't find out anything I wanted to know."

"That was an interrogation?" He tried to maneuver the sandwich out of his pocket. "I thought you and me were just talking."

"I'll give you a little advice, son. When a sheriff's asking you questions, you're never just talking."

I pretended to study my newspaper, but there was nothing on my mind but my fugitive. The train swayed and shook on its tracks, and when we went under the river the pressure in my ears was so fierce that I couldn't hear anything for a minute. I felt like I was in a trance, the world suddenly hushed, this enormous piece of machinery carrying men in their good suits and women in their fur collars alongside the three of us, three people who'd slept in our street clothes and waited all night for another chance at catching our man.

I became suddenly aware that I had no idea what we'd do if von Matthesius wasn't there. I bent down to Reinhold and said quietly, "Where's tomorrow's meeting place?"

Sheriff Heath glanced at me over Reinhold's bowed head. I could tell he already knew the answer.

"Nobody's told me nothing about tomorrow," the boy mumbled. "This is the end of the line."

⤝ 24 ⤞

THE TRAIN LURCHED into the Borough Hall station. Sheriff Heath took Reinhold's arm and I followed them onto the platform. Before we went up the stairs, he pulled me aside but kept Reinhold as far away as possible without letting go of him. He spoke right into my ear in a low voice.

"Reinhold doesn't know which entrance von Matthesius prefers. We've got plenty of time, so let's walk around the station and decide which one we'll each take. I'm going to keep Reinhold with me. If you spot von Matthesius first, you're just going to have to chase him down. I don't want you pulling out your revolver with all of these people around."

I nodded. "Couldn't we call in the police and have a few officers nearby?"

"Not now. I'm afraid they'll scare him off. He's probably already suspicious about Reinhold not making the meeting last night. Besides, the police won't recognize him like we will and I don't want them grabbing the wrong man. You and I are going to have to do this ourselves."

We climbed the stairs and emerged into the frigid wind

that had whipped up in front of Borough Hall. A steady stream of black motor cars raced past on Court Street. We were just a few blocks from Atlantic Avenue, in that part of Brooklyn where the streets made unexpected turns and dissolved into a mess of oddly arranged intersections and sidewalks that didn't lead where you expected them to. All three of us stood for a minute and tried to get our bearings.

"Oh!" I said, once I'd picked out a few landmarks around me. "I used to take dancing lessons around the corner."

"Dancing! You?" Reinhold Dietz said in surprise, earning him a sharp poke in the back from Sheriff Heath.

"Everyone took dancing," I said. "It was just down Court, on the other side of Atlantic. My uncle worked there. He played the piano." I hadn't had much reason to be in Brooklyn since I was a girl. It was a strange feeling to be standing on a street I'd passed almost every day twenty years ago. What would that girl think if she could see me?

There were two entrances to the station in front of Borough Hall, one facing Court and the other Boerum. The sheriff took us over to the other entrance, and from there we circled the block to make sure we weren't missing another way out.

We had to be standing on the busiest street corner in Brooklyn. The trolley rattled in its tracks, mothers walked small herds of children to school, and peddlers pushed their carts of apples, hot buns, and the best of whatever they'd picked up on the street the night before—battered pots and pans, strips of fabric, dirty glass bottles and jars, and fat tallow candles, all half-burned. A girl of about eleven pulled a wagon filled with potted red geraniums. From some window high above us, a child dutifully practiced at the organ. There were bells clanging and engines growling and the chatter of a thousand people all around us, in every direction, block after block. At home in Wyckoff we could see straight to the horizon without a single person in our line of vision, but here there was no horizon, just more of Brooklyn, and more beyond that, until it dropped straight off into the water.

Somehow, in the middle of all of it, we were to find and capture a fugitive.

"All right," the sheriff said when we'd circled the block and come back to where we'd started. "We'll stay here on the Court Street side, and you go to the other entrance. Don't cross the street, but keep your eye on the corner and look around the side of Borough Hall as well. We don't know whether he'll be coming in or out of the station, so just stay close. Mr. Dietz doesn't seem to think he'll be early. Roam around for a while so you don't attract too much attention, but by nine-thirty you should be at your post and stay there."

Reinhold was fidgeting in his cuffs. "Say, Sheriff, they're a little tight this morning. Couldn't you just loosen them?"

"Not now, son," the sheriff said. He took me by the arm and leaned closer so Reinhold couldn't hear. "Are you ready for this?"

In truth, my heart was racing, a vein in my forehead was pounding, and I was sweating under my collar in spite of the cold. I might have been starting to see spots. A woman who faints would have gone looking for a bench right about then.

But I wasn't the type to faint. "I'm the one who took Felix, remember? We'll get him."

He held my elbow for just a second longer and looked closely at me.

"I'm fine," I said.

"Be careful," he said, although he couldn't possibly have meant it. We didn't catch crooks by being careful.

"I certainly will not." Reinhold heard that and smiled.

"You'll be free before lunch," I told the boy, and went to stand at my post.

No hour ever passed so slowly. I would've never guessed that a life in law enforcement was mostly spent waiting, that catching criminals requires not just clever thinking and a quick step, but a willingness to stand still while the rest of the world moves about, and that what was required was not strength or grit but the ability to get into place and stay there, and to ignore the desperate rising certainty that something more urgent might be happening, somewhere, and that if only one could leave one's post and tear down the street in pursuit, some kind of prey would surely leap up and allow itself to be caught.

For an hour I had to fight the urge to grab hold of something, to wrestle anyone down to the ground. A policeman at his post could be a very dangerous creature. If I'd so much as seen a pickpocket lifting a handkerchief, I would've torn him apart. So far the criminals were leaving this block of Brooklyn alone. It was well for them that they did.

Sheriff Heath asked me to move around, so I shifted my position from the top of the stairs at the entrance to the subway, to the hack stand at the corner, to the doorway of a little printing shop that seemed mostly to print announcements and proclamations issued by Borough Hall. If I stood at a particular point near the hack stand, and if Sheriff Heath happened to be walking toward Court Street at the same time, I could see him pacing as well, his hand on Reinhold's elbow.

I wondered what they talked about in their hour together.

Sheriff Heath would undoubtedly be attempting to set the boy straight and convince him to stay away from Rudy and to take a legitimate job or enroll in some kind of course. He would have admonished him for hitting Reverend Weber. Whenever I had a glimpse of Reinhold, his head was down and he was nodding slightly as if he was listening. I had my doubts as to whether an hour-long sermon from the sheriff of Bergen County would turn his life around.

At last the hands of my watch reached nine-thirty and I took my post at the top of the stairs. Every man, woman, and child who walked in and out of the station got my full scrutiny, as did everyone passing by on the sidewalk and anyone I could see getting in or out of a motor car. I reminded myself that von Matthesius would have made himself as unremarkable as he possibly could. He would wear an ordinary suit and a plain hat. He would make himself hard to spot.

It wasn't easy to watch every face. Men had the maddening habit of walking in groups of three or four, clustering together and hiding behind one another so that I couldn't get a good look at each of them. They wrapped scarves around their necks. They pulled their hats down over their heads. They looked away at exactly the wrong moment.

Half a dozen looked enough like von Matthesius to make me want to run over and knock them to the ground. Every time, I saw that I had the wrong man only a moment before I jumped.

Then I turned and saw him coming up from the dark, climbing the stairs out of the station, in a gray overcoat too big for him and a hat down over his eyes.

I'd been picturing that man's face every day for six weeks

and I knew it in an instant. As soon as he stepped foot on the pavement I slipped in behind him, twisting one of his arms behind his back and kicking the back of his knee to throw him down. He fought harder and faster than I was prepared for. When he spun around, his elbow hit me directly in the face and knocked me back. More people were coming out of the subway station all around us and we were both about to lose our footing.

I only had hold of his coat and feared he would shake himself loose and run. "You're under arrest!" I shouted, hoping to attract Sheriff Heath's attention or at least get some help from the men around me.

Von Matthesius's eyes connected with mine for only a second before he looked over my shoulder, at the brick-lined stairway descending into the subway station, and threw his weight against me. I lost my footing and fell, but I took him with me, and the two of us rolled halfway down the staircase. We would have tumbled all the way to the bottom if not for the train passengers climbing up at the same time.

I hit the stairs first and he landed on top of me. A blinding white pain in my ribs made me lose my grip on him and he struggled to his knees, looking around for a way out. His feet found their purchase and he was about to run when I grabbed his pants leg and pulled him down again. His face hit the sharp edge of the stairs and he let out a high shriek.

I was dimly aware of the shoes and trouser cuffs gathered around us, but no one reached down to stop me—or to help me. I climbed over his backside in what had to be the most undignified position a woman had ever been seen in on the streets of Brooklyn. One of his hands was pinned underneath me and the other flailed around and tried to grab me. I wanted to reach under my coat to free my handcuffs, but I couldn't get to them.

"Sheriff! Clear the way!" came a voice above me, and Sheriff Heath was on the stairs. His foot landed heavily on von Matthesius's shoulder, eliciting another groan. I rolled off him and sat on the step, panting, fumbling for my handcuffs. One of the Baron's hands was still groping around to get hold of me when I locked the cuffs on it. Sheriff Heath pulled his other arm around. Once we had him chained, we dragged him to the top of the stairs and pulled him to his feet.

The Baron's head was turned away from us, but the crowd of onlookers took a good look at him and gasped. Blood was running freely from his mouth, the result of a hard fall on an unyielding staircase that split his lip and knocked out a tooth.

He spit the tooth out along with a small and viscous pool of blood, stared down at it, and mumbled, *"Ich möchte ihn behalten."*

I turned to the sheriff, who was staring at me with a kind of fierce and terrible wonder. There passed between us a feeling that no one can understand who hasn't hunted and captured a criminal. No matter what else had happened between us, we were one person at that instant. We'd done something together that few people ever do. I didn't want to say anything that would pull us out of that moment, but time hadn't stopped and the crowd was pressing in on us.

"He wants to keep the tooth," I said.

The sheriff laughed and shook his head. The spell was broken. "There's no harm in it. Go ahead."

I picked it up with a handkerchief and pocketed it. With great effort the three of us started walking, the Baron and I each groaning over our own injuries. The crowd around us had grown so large that I couldn't see past it. We each held on to the old man, but neither one of us could stand to look at him. He was a dirty and deceitful creature and now that we'd caught him, we were both disgusted with him, and disgusted with everything he'd cost us—our time, our reputations, possibly even our livelihoods. He was a trophy we didn't want. It was like winning a raffle only to find that the prize was something monstrous and disgusting—a catch of rotten fish, a pig dead of scours.

Sheriff Heath looked around and said, in a voice loud enough for all of them to hear, "Herman Albert von Matthesius, you are under arrest by the Sheriff of Bergen County, New Jersey." By then we'd attracted the attention of a few police officers, who ran over to offer their help in getting us all back to Hackensack.

I would've expected Reinhold Dietz to disappear, still in his handcuffs, the minute Sheriff Heath let go of him. But he stood by, just behind the crowd gathered around us, and waited with a kind of trusting patience. The sheriff handed me his keys and I released the boy, smiling down on him as I did.

"You did a fine job," I told him as he rubbed his wrists. "You helped us catch a dangerous criminal. You'd make a good cop if you'd set yourself to it."

"That's what the sheriff told me," he said, and tipped his cap at me. He was across the street and out of sight before I could say another word to him.

⚜ 25 ⚜

GIRL DEPUTY SHERIFF "PINCHES"
A MINISTER

Jersey Woman Wrestles with Husky Prisoner
in Front of Brooklyn Borough Hall

BROOKLYN—Miss Constance Kopp, who once hid behind a tree near her home in Wyckoff, N.J., for five hours waiting to get a shot at a gang of Black Handers who had annoyed her, is now Deputy Sheriff of Bergen County, N.J., and a terror to evildoers.

Armed with a pistol, handcuffs and other accessories, she came over to Brooklyn yesterday and made an arrest in a manner at once neat and thorough. She stepped up to a husky, well-dressed man in front of Borough Hall and tapped him on the shoulder.

Norma put the newspaper down. "You didn't get all those bruises from tapping a man on the shoulder."

I groaned and shifted the pack of ice under my arm. "Of course not. It was nothing like that."

"I also don't believe that you said, brusquely, as they put it, 'Come along. I want you. You're pinched!'"

I started to laugh, but it hurt so much that I had to press my hands against my ribs to keep still.

Fleurette was sitting on the arm of Norma's chair, reading over her shoulder. "'The man was the Reverend Dr. Herman Albert von Matthesius, who had escaped . . .' Oh, we know all that. Here we go. 'He gazed at the young woman in astonishment.'"

"He didn't gaze at me," I said. "He was face-down on the stairs with a split lip."

Norma cleared her throat and started over. "'He gazed at the young woman in astonishment. 'My dear Madam!' he exclaimed, 'you are a total stranger to me, I assure you. I don't know what you're talking about!'"

I yawned and pulled the blanket over my knees. "Correct that to read, 'He spit out a tooth and muttered about it in German.'"

Fleurette jumped down onto the ground as if she were crouching over the prisoner. She was wearing a silk dress of the most astonishing peacock blue with a white fur collar trimmed in velvet. Now that she was making costumes for the theater, she managed to put all sorts of their scraps to use in her own wardrobe. We were seeing quite a bit more feathers and fur than we'd like. "If there's going to be a motion picture made of you, I'll take the role. I'll make a very convincing girl detective."

"I'm afraid you'd never be cast," Norma said mildly, without taking her eyes off the newspaper. "It says here that Deputy Kopp has an athletic build and weighs a hundred and eighty pounds."

"What?" Fleurette cried out.

"They printed that?" I said.

"Well, you do, don't you?" Norma said.

"At least that. But I didn't think they'd put it in the paper. They kept asking Sheriff Heath if I was fit for duty as a deputy, and for some reason they demanded to know my height and weight, but I never supposed—"

"Always suppose," Norma said archly. "You'd better learn how to talk to these reporters if they're going to keep writing you up like this."

"I talk to them just fine."

"At least he's calling you a deputy now," Fleurette said.

"The reporters did it first, but Sheriff Heath says it's for the best. There's to be no more tiptoeing around the subject now that it's in the papers. He promises to get my badge after Christmas, and says the Freeholders wouldn't dare to block my appointment after I've caught a fugitive."

"Oh, I wouldn't presume to know what the Freeholders will do," Norma said, and went back to her article. "Did you grab him by the coattails and stick out a neatly shod foot?"

That sent Fleurette into a fit of giggles. "She was wearing those monstrous boots!"

From behind her newspaper, Norma said, "Did you open your handbag with your teeth to get out your handcuffs?"

"What nonsense!" I said. "Read another one. Don't we have Carrie's story?"

Norma shuffled through the stack of papers beside her chair. "This must be hers. Where did you meet this girl?"

"Just read it."

Fleurette settled back on the arm of Norma's chair and looked over her shoulder. "Oh, this is much better. It says that you were determined to hang on to him, no matter how rough he might be, and that none of the men nearby offered assistance."

"That's exactly right," I said. "Men seem disinclined to come to my aid."

Norma looked at me over the top of the paper, impressed. "'Having the advantage in weight, he started to hurl her down the subway stairs, but she hung on.' She says that by the time Sheriff Heath found you, von Matthesius was 'still writhing in the clasp of his determined captor.' I do prefer her version."

She folded the paper and set it aside. "But why is it that the only man who ever seems to come to your rescue is Sheriff Heath?"

I struggled to sit up and defend myself, but the cracked rib bit sharply and sent me back down again. "We were working together!" I stuffed a pillow behind my head so I could get a better look at her. "It was his job to help me get the prisoner. If he'd been the one to catch him, I would've rushed to his assistance. What else were we to do?"

"I just wonder what Mrs. Heath has to say about her husband being out all night with a girl deputy," she said. Fleurette watched the two of us in uncharacteristic silence.

I gave up my struggle with the pillows and tossed them on the floor, lying flat on my back and staring up at the ceiling where three divergent cracks in the plaster had found their way to each other, forming an irregular triangle that was threatening to work loose and fall on us. Could the ceiling really collapse? Was anyone paying attention to the upkeep of our house but me?

Norma's and Fleurette's eyes were still on me, so at last I said, "If Mrs. Heath had any idea how dirty and disagreeable our work has been, she wouldn't be bothered by it in the least."

"Does she?" Fleurette asked. "Have any idea?"

IN FACT, MRS. HEATH knew exactly how dirty and disagreeable our work had been, because she was called upon to get me polished up in advance of my session with photographers and reporters. I didn't want anyone to make a picture of me, and Sheriff Heath might not have, either, but the reporters in Brooklyn had hold of the story within hours of von Matthesius's capture and insisted. Sheriff Heath decided to make the best of it, believing that if reporters had a good picture and a headline about a lady deputy wrestling a man to the ground, every paper in three states would run the story and it might turn the public in his favor. "There's no point in hiding from the reporters if they're going to write about us anyway," he said. "And if they're talking about us in New York and Pennsylvania, the *Hackensack Republican* will have to see us in a different light."

I didn't think there was any chance of that and told him so.

"Thank you for your ideas," he answered, "but it's your obligation to sit for the photographer, and a condition of your continued employment in this department."

In other words, I was at last to pay my penance for letting von Matthesius escape.

While Deputy Morris took von Matthesius off to be registered, showered, and deloused, the sheriff went straight to the telephone to start ringing newspapers. Along the way he deposited me in his sitting room. Mrs. Heath had returned home just as the sheriff said she would, and sat furiously embroidering a pinecone and a pair of acorns onto a dishtowel.

"Find her something to wear," was all he said by way of greeting to his wife. "She's going to be in the papers, and she's a mess."

I couldn't have been more ashamed of myself. There was Cordelia Heath, smelling not at all of brandy, but only of bath powder and rose water, wearing a perfectly pressed afternoon dress the color of fresh butter, her children napping obediently in their own tidy beds, her sitting room an ever more extraordinary tribute to the powers of persistent stitchery. She had completed the tablecloth since I'd seen her last, and on it a trio of nightingales flew about the corners and came to land on a set of dogwood branches in bloom. Around the edges, where anyone else would stitch a border of lace or piping and be done with it, she had taken up her crochet hook and manufactured a few dozen orange butterflies, each affixed to the edge of the tablecloth by a proboscis of purple silk.

With von Matthesius captured and her husband safe, Cordelia had stitched herself back together. It was the best I could hope for her.

But now she had me to contend with yet again. I stood before her in a corduroy dress with the following smeared or spilled upon it: mud, ashes, dust, horse manure, puddle water, dried egg, coffee, sweat, and the blood and other unnamed discharge of an escaped convict.

She attempted a smile. I couldn't bring myself to return it.

"Well," she said briskly, "the sheriff seems to have made up his mind without consulting either one of us. I suppose you are to become quite famous and have all sorts of newspaper stories written about you, which will no doubt give my husband quite a bit more to explain to the Freeholders every week."

"I don't think . . ."

"Unless, of course, you refuse to do it. I don't believe anyone could stop you from walking out the door right now and going home."

There followed a forced smile that she must have hoped would look friendly but only had the effect of frightening me a little. Cordelia Heath surrounded herself with soft and beautiful things, but there was something altogether rigid and metallic inside her.

"Thank you, but I'll stay," was the best I could manage.

"Of course you will." She looked me up and down again with the air of a woman surveying a muddy and flea-ridden dog. Then she sniffed the air around me delicately. "I just know you would give anything for a bath, but we haven't the time. Go and get yourself cleaned up any way you can, and I'll see what I have that might . . ."

Her voice trailed away as she stood up. Even with her hair piled up in one of those fashionable top-knots, she was a good half a head shorter than me. Nothing she owned would fit me.

She waved me nonetheless in the direction of the tiny powder room the family shared. I stripped off my outer garments, leaving only my petticoat and corset cover, which had a lower neckline than I would allow myself to be seen in, but was otherwise fairly substantial for an undergarment. I washed my face and smoothed my hair in a little oval mirror, then applied to my neck a single dusting of Cordelia's fragrant powder, which sat on the washbasin next to a cake of shaving soap and a tin of tooth powder. I looked no better than I did before, but I felt a half-measure more civilized.

Cordelia returned with her arms full of garments I couldn't possibly wear. She piled them all on an armchair and started flinging them at me. There was no mirror in the sitting room so I just stood helplessly and let her have her way. She held up first one dress and then another, but I didn't even bother to look down at them because I knew there was no hope and in fact suspected she was only trying to embarrass me. Then she pulled out a selection of shirtwaists, all beautifully tailored for her slender rib cage. The delicate lines in her brow grew a little deeper with each successive failed attempt, but she kept at it, tossing bits of silk and poplin and tweed at me until she'd exhausted most of the pile.

"You are frightfully large," she mumbled. Some people would apologize after a remark like that, but she just walked in a circle around me the way one might survey a tree before chopping it down and then said, "They don't have to photograph all of you, do they?"

"Are you suggesting they take my right half or my left?"

"No, a seated portrait. Just head and shoulders. You see those in the paper."

"I suppose so." I didn't like to imagine where this might be leading. "But wouldn't they expect a deputy to be standing?"

"Let's not worry about what they expect," Cordelia said. "We'll just insist on it."

She ran back to her bedroom and returned with a new bundle of clothing. I had no idea a sheriff's salary could buy so many nice things.

"These come from my mother," she said, as if she could read my expression. "Now, if it's only a seated portrait, we don't have to actually dress you. We can just"—she paused and twirled her arms around me to demonstrate—"wrap you."

She took a wide shawl the color of copper and draped it over my shoulders, tucking it into the hem of my skirt. Then she produced an enormous silk bow, wider than my head and almost as tall, and pinned it right to the front of the shawl.

"What is that?" I cried, horrified. It looked like the sort of thing Fleurette would have worn when she was twelve. It was a piercing emerald color, and matched nothing else Cordelia had brought out with her.

"The color won't matter for the picture. And when you're seated, it'll look like you're just wearing a dress with a bow at the neckline."

I looked ridiculous. The plain, dirty sleeves of my corset cover were only half-hidden by the shawl and the bow. Those three garments had never been put together in such a fashion before, and in a just world they never would again.

I was already scheming to get out of Cordelia's sitting room and back to my own jail cell. I would have worn one of the prisoner's uniforms rather than be photographed in the get-up in which I'd just been swaddled. In fact, it was starting to dawn on me that we had at the jail plenty of serviceable dresses for women, and all I had to do was to go downstairs to the laundry and choose one.

A knock came at the door and Sheriff Heath's voice called, "The fellows just got here. Is she ready?"

How could they have come so fast? Had they nothing else to do? He must have walked over to the courthouse and fetched them.

"Almost!" Cordelia called out. She was enjoying herself now. I was becoming more miserable by the second. I couldn't allow myself to be photographed like this.

Cordelia turned her back to me and rummaged through her things. "Here it is!" She settled a mink wrap around my shoulders, slowly and ceremoniously, with the air of someone placing a wreath upon a grave. It was lined in unbearably soft brown velvet.

"I can't wear a fur! I'm a sheriff's deputy, not an opera singer."

She seemed not to have heard me. "There's a hat to match." She produced an enormous velvet hat, also trimmed in a wide bow, and settled it on my poor condemned head.

Sheriff Heath knocked again at the door. "You can come in now, Bob!" Cordelia called out, before I could stop her.

He rushed in and looked me over without really seeing me. He was like any other man in that he had no opinion on women's clothing and considered all fashion equally ridiculous. "Fine. They're coming to my office. We'll take the picture there, and then you'll answer some questions."

"It has to be a seated portrait, dear," Cordelia said, but the sheriff had already turned to go back to his office.

"Never mind," she whispered to me. "I'll go with you and see to it that it's done properly."

My humiliation was complete. Having lost the last possible opportunity to slip down to the jail laundry for a house dress, I allowed Cordelia to lead me to the sheriff's office, where I sat for my first and most preposterous portrait for the newspapers.

NORMA STUDIED THAT PICTURE with a look of dark consternation. Fleurette took it from her and slapped me on the head with it.

"Why didn't you let me dress you? I would've found something smart and suited to the occasion, not this—what is this supposed to be? It looks like a big silk bow right on the front of your blouse."

"I think it's supposed to be a big silk bow." I handed my ice-bag back to Norma, who took it to the kitchen.

"Well, that does it," Fleurette said. "If you're going to be a deputy sheriff and have your picture in the papers, I'm going to make you a proper uniform. No, I'll make you two. No, three. One to keep here, one to keep at the jail, and one to wear. And something lighter in the summer. What would a lady sheriff wear in the summertime?"

"Don't make it too light," I said. "It's rough work."

"I'll have to do them soon. Did Norma tell you Mrs. Hansen has offered me a job sewing for the academy? I'll be there two days a week, and you won't have to pay for my lessons anymore. I'll get a salary and free classes."

I opened my mouth to tell her why she couldn't do it, but then recognized that I was only acting out of habit and that there was no good reason to stop her. She'd gone out and found useful work for herself. What reason had I to complain?

"That's just fine," I said. "Mrs. Hansen sees your talent. I'm not surprised."

She smiled and returned to her pattern books. I dozed on the divan for the rest of the afternoon. After keeping me in his office all evening so that reporters arriving from Newark and Trenton and New York City could have their turns with me, Sheriff Heath ordered me to take three full days of rest and to see a doctor about my ribs if they weren't better by the end of it. I was not at all pleased about being sent home, but it was true that I had most likely cracked or dislodged a rib, wrenched my knee, bruised my hip, and given myself any number of other sores and scrapes.

When I awoke on the second day, I hurt worse than when

I'd fallen asleep. The third day was even more painful. I could hardly dress myself and shuffled around like an invalid. Norma delivered my meals on a tray but otherwise left me to look after myself. Fleurette fussed around with pillows and bandages, made a bouquet of some silk flowers she must have taken off all the hats in the house, and brought me frivolous magazines that I had no interest in reading.

By the fourth day, the pain had truly settled in and I was beginning to believe that I'd been saddled with a weak knee, a bad hip, and an unreliable rib for the rest of my life. Having accepted that, I decided to go back to work—in a manner of speaking. I wanted to check on something that had been bothering me.

"You aren't going out!" Fleurette said, jumping up from her sewing machine when she saw me in my coat and hat. It was a frigid and gusty day. The roads were covered in dirty, slushy snow that had hardened to slick ice overnight. There was a kind of swirling wind that seemed to come from nowhere at all and blow snowflakes in every direction. It was impossible to tell whether the snow would drift off as capriciously as it had arrived, or whether we were in for a blanket of white before Christmas.

"I'll be back tonight," I said. "I'll have to take the buggy. I can't possibly walk."

Norma was outside in her pigeon loft, repairing a torn screen with baling wire. The pigeons slid as far down their roost as they could go when I approached.

"I don't know what I've done to offend them."

"Go back to bed."

"I'm tired of being in bed. I need to go into town. Help me harness Dolley."

With some reluctance she went with me into the barn. "I don't like you taking the buggy. You can barely raise your arm."

"I just need to go see about something," I said. "It isn't strenuous. If I can sit around the house, I can ride in the buggy."

"It isn't the riding that bothers me. It's whatever else you'll get up to. I have the worst feeling that you just remembered about another criminal you left standing at the top of a staircase somewhere, and have decided to rush off and get yourself tossed down again."

"If you're so worried about it, why don't you come with me?"

She looked up at me, surprised. "What would I do?"

"You can drive the buggy, to start. You're the one who said it. I can hardly raise my arm."

"Where are you going?"

"Over to Garfield to have another look at the room where a man was shot. In fact, it would help to have you along. I'd like to try something, and it would take two people to do it properly."

She opened her mouth to say something and then closed it again. Dolley tossed her head around but eventually took the bit from Norma and allowed herself to be led outside. "Well . . . I shouldn't leave. The pigeon loft needs a patch before it snows again."

"Those pigeons already have better accommodations than we do. No, come with me and do a little detective work."

Norma's frown had become so deeply etched in her face over the years that it took a great deal of effort to reverse its direction, but I thought I saw some change come over her. There was a hint of interest in her eyes. She looked down at her barn coat, which was covered in bits of straw and muck.

"I'll have to change," she said.

"Don't bother yourself too much over it. No one will see us."

She turned and ran to the house. It took me three attempts, but I managed to heave myself into the carriage under the force of one good knee.

⊰ 26 ⊱

ON THE WAY TO GARFIELD, I told Norma everything I knew about Providencia Monafo and the death of Saverio Salino. She'd read about the case in the papers, but nothing had been printed about the discrepancy between her story and that of her neighbors, or about Detective Courter's efforts to get her released and to charge someone else with the crime.

Norma took the matter very seriously and puzzled over it all the way into town. She was deeply interested in other people's private affairs. This was exactly the sort of mix-up that she liked to spend hours ruminating over.

"Mrs. Monafo herself admits to shooting the man," she said.

"Gladly. She's terrified of her husband and eager to take the blame and stay in jail where he can't get to her."

"The streetcar conductor is quite certain that she boarded at seven-thirty."

"That's what we've been told."

"But the witnesses heard the shot at eight o'clock in the morning, and they couldn't possibly be wrong about the time."

"That's what the detective says, yes."

We rode along in silence while she thought it over. "Do you not agree with me that John Courter is the most untrustworthy man in public service in Bergen County?"

"We haven't met them all, but he's certainly the worst of the lot I've had dealings with."

"Then I don't like it that we have to rely upon his witnesses," Norma said, "and I don't understand why he's so eager to let this lady out of jail."

"The witnesses could say something to the papers, and then it would look bad if he'd locked up some poor old woman and left the real killer on the loose. Besides, if he truly believes that Mrs. Monafo couldn't have done it, he's no doubt expecting her to say so one of these days."

"Then he's in a fix, isn't he?"

We came to a stop behind a long line of black motor cars that had stalled for no reason that we could see. Dolley hated to be crowded so close to the machines. She tossed her head and stamped her hooves to let us know it.

Norma stood up and tried to get a better look. She sighed and sat back down. "One of them is broken down at the intersection, and now we must all sit and wait. It used to be that you could just make the road a little wider."

She was right. We used to just veer off into the fields if something was in the road, or else we'd take the lane opposite without worrying about an automobile running into us. Two horse-drawn carriages approaching one another were not much of a threat. But automobiles were driven by people who cared for nothing but going as fast as they could and pushing everyone else out of their way.

After a tiresome delay a constable arrived at the intersection and started directing traffic around the overheated motor car. "Do you know that Fleurette wants one of these, and thinks that she can learn to run it herself?" Norma said.

"No!" The thought of Fleurette in control of a machine on the open road gave me a pain at the back of my neck, which was one of the few places that wasn't already hurt.

"She thinks she's going to talk you into buying her a motor car on the grounds that she'll carry you back and forth to work."

"Fleurette wants to be my chauffeur?"

"And in exchange, she expects to roam freely about New Jersey and New York, enjoying—"

"Stop," I said. "I don't want to know what she hopes to enjoy. I don't trust her with a telephone, much less a motor car."

"Oh, she wants a telephone, too, but they'll never bring the wires down our road, and I'm glad of it. I can't abide a bell ringing in our house at all hours."

We arrived at Mrs. Monafo's boarding-house before I had to hear any more about it. I asked Norma to bring Dolley to a halt across the street and down a few doors. She stood squinting at the brick building, which had only grown more squalid in its landlady's absence. Now two windows had boards across them. A piece of gutter had broken away from the roof, probably under the force of wind and snow. It hung across the upper floors, looking as if it might drop to the ground at any moment. The walk hadn't been shoveled, and an overturned garbage can had been rifled through by the neighborhood cats.

"I don't like to leave Dolley here," Norma said. "Shouldn't we have taken her over to the stables?"

I pitched myself awkwardly out of the carriage, landing on my good leg but almost losing my balance as I did so. The ice was starting to melt, but there were still a few frozen patches, and navigating around them wasn't easy in my condition.

"You can stay here," I said. "I just wanted to check something."

"But doesn't this require the both of us?" Norma asked.

She had the most eager expression I'd seen on her in a long time. I noticed that she'd actually dressed the part of a detective, in a smart tweed suit, leather gloves, and a wool riding cap. She looked more like a woman in law enforcement than I did.

"Then come on inside," I said. "Dolley will be fine for a minute. There's no one around."

She followed me in. The front door was unlocked as it had always been before. I showed her down the back stairs into the Monafos' basement apartment, where, once again, no one was at home. Norma walked in as boldly as if she owned the place, then took a step back when the stench hit her.

"I'd say that she's been keeping animals in here, but a barn doesn't smell this bad." She folded her arms across her chest as she looked over the dusty and increasingly moldy furnishings and the rubbish that had continued to accumulate since Mrs. Monafo's arrest. Her husband must have been living there, because empty liquor bottles were adding a note of stale barley malt to the miasma.

Norma was already starting back up the stairs. "If this is how people live, it's no wonder they go to such lengths to get locked up in that nice clean jail of yours."

"Go and wait upstairs with Dolley, then. I'll only be a minute."

For once, Norma agreed with me. "Shake out your skirts before you get back in the carriage. I suspect they've got bugs."

"I guarantee they do." That was enough to get Norma up the stairs and across the street.

Once she was gone, it took only a moment for me to do what I'd come to do. I made sure the door to the apartment was open as it would have been the morning Salino was shot, assuming he'd just come in and not had time to close it behind him. Then I cleared a pile of old papers out of one corner of the room, exposing the brick foundation. I took from my pocket a pinch of wool batting, which I stuffed into each ear.

Then I pulled out my revolver and fired a shot into the corner.

The explosion rang around the room and nearly deafened me in spite of the wool. A haze of smoke settled around me. The crisp blackened odor of the gunpowder momentarily improved the air.

The bullet went into the mortar between the bricks and lodged there. I put the newspapers back where they'd been, pulled the wool out of my ears, and climbed the stairs. Down the street, Norma was feeding an apple to Dolley.

"Did you hear that?" I asked.

She turned to look at me, puzzled. "Did I hear what?"

"BUT YOU MUST'VE HEARD IT," Sheriff Heath said. "It was a gunshot. It would have gone all over the neighborhood." He leaned back in his chair and looked at me impatiently. Norma was standing in front of the small fire he kept going in his office.

"It's a basement apartment," I said. "It's in the back of the house, and what windows they have are mostly covered in rubbish. Even with the door open, Norma didn't hear it. Or if she did, it was so faint that she didn't notice it. I hadn't told her to expect it, so she wasn't listening closely. But the neighbors wouldn't have been listening closely, either."

The sheriff went over to stand next to Norma in front of the fireplace. "What do you make of this, Miss Kopp?"

Norma never missed an opportunity to say exactly what she made of a thing, but coming inside the jail had put her off and she'd been unusually quiet. "It's exactly as Constance told it," she said, keeping her eyes on the fire. "It shouldn't matter what I make of it. You don't need me to tell you how to do your job."

"All this time I thought I did," the sheriff said with a smile. He insisted on liking Norma. I used to think he was only being polite to her on my account, but I'd come to see that, with very few exceptions, he treated everyone with the same mild courtesy—even the criminals under his watch.

Norma surrendered her place in front of the fire and walked over to the window, which looked out onto the dull and tenebrous Hackensack River. "I will say that I didn't like leaving Constance alone in that horrible little flat, so if I had heard anything at all unusual, I certainly would've run back to check on her. You and Detective Courter could go and try the same thing yourselves if you don't believe us. You'd have the same result."

Sheriff Heath rattled the coins in his pocket and thought about it.

"Do you remember when we went there together," I said,

"and you called down to me from upstairs and I couldn't hear you? I'd forgotten it myself, but I've had three days to do nothing but lie around and think about things, and that came back to me all at once. It occurred to me that I should at least try an experiment."

"But what about our witnesses who heard the shot at eight?"

"I'm not saying they didn't hear a shot. They might well have. I just don't think it was the shot that killed Saverio Salino. It could've been an engine firing, or someone shooting at a target, or maybe it was another murder no one has bothered to do anything about."

"Mmmm." The sheriff picked up his poker and went to work on the fire, shifting the embers around and dropping another log on top. He watched until the bark started to burn and then said, "Well. I'm sure Detective Courter hasn't gone over to the Monafos' apartment and fired off a round. I don't think he'll be happy to find out that you did."

"He should thank me for getting rid of a worthless piece of evidence," I said.

"I doubt he will. But I suppose Mrs. Monafo is ours to keep."

"I don't know how you'll bear it, if she's half as appalling as that room of hers," Norma said.

THE STORY OF HOW I'd turned Providencia's case around pleased her immensely. She walked back and forth cackling to herself and telling it to me in bits and pieces.

"You shoot your gun in my house." She grinned broadly and shook her finger at me.

"I hope you don't mind."

"And you keep another lady upstairs to listen!" She screeched delightedly at that. "But she don't hear nothing."

"That's right. And it appears to have worked, although you might have to speak to a judge. I suggest you tell the whole story, exactly as it happened. It's your best chance. A man was killed, and you must understand how serious that is."

I could never be sure if Providencia did understand the gravity of the matter. She'd expressed no remorse for killing Mr. Salino. She seemed to regard the fact of his death as a mere outgrowth of everything that had happened to her, rather than a singular tragic event of its own. The poor man appeared to have no family in this country—the sister who'd been staying with him was, as I suspected, not actually a sister—and as far as I knew, there was no one to visit, no one to question, no one to whom Mrs. Monafo might consider making amends, if such a thing occurred to her, and I don't think it ever did.

In fact, the news that she was to stay locked up put her in such good spirits that she found herself quite active and restless, and volunteered for kitchen duty. Sheriff Heath refused, unable to reconcile his memories of her living conditions with anything he'd like to see happening in his kitchen. He told her that he'd just put a new crew on dinner duty, and that they were all rough-edged men greatly in need of the morally restorative effects that only the slicing of onions and peeling of potatoes could bring about. Providencia accepted this but took every opportunity to remind him that she could make a better dinner from the pigeons roosting on the courthouse roof than the men downstairs did with a leg of mutton.

"That'd be just fine, Mrs. Monafo," the sheriff would call back cheerfully. "We've a nice crop of river rats this year too, if you think you can do something with those."

That made her clap her hands gleefully. She was enjoying her sentence more than either of us would have liked. Then again, we'd always take a cheerful inmate over a bad-tempered one or, worse, a con artist whose next move we couldn't guess.

❧ 27 ❧

I TRIED TO STAY AWAY from von Matthesius's cell but I couldn't. A strange dreamlike air hung about the jail now that we had him back. It seemed that he'd been gone for an eternity, that I'd spent my whole life hunting him, and that at any moment he might vanish again, drifting away from the bars of his cell like a curl of smoke escaping from a pipe. I wanted to forget about him, but no matter where I went in the jail, his presence exerted a terrible pull on me. At times I thought I could hear him pacing and scheming like a trapped animal in a zoo.

I finally went to him late at night, about a week after his capture. He was once again at the end of a cell block, isolated from the others. We kept Felix on a separate floor and promised the severest of punishments to anyone who helped to pass messages between them.

The Baron was sitting up on the edge of his bunk as if he'd been expecting me. *"La Mademoiselle Kopp formidable,"* he said in a perfect Parisian accent. He gestured for me to join him in his cell but I didn't. I tested the gate to make sure it was locked.

"We never knew you spoke French," I said through the bars.

"Only for you."

There was something plain and common about him now. The jail uniform had a way of shrinking him down to size. Someone had shaved his head and his beard, and taken away his monocle. All of his pretenses were gone. His face sagged like crumpled tissue.

"We haven't found Dr. Rathburn," I said.

He looked up quickly at the sound of the man's name, then slumped over. "It's better for the von Matthesius clan if you don't. He believes I owe him a great debt, and he was only keeping me until it could be paid."

"You had a house with so many nice things. What happened to the paintings and the rugs?"

He made a *tsk* sound as if spitting the idea away. "People don't appreciate fine things."

"Couldn't Felix get a good price for them?"

But he wouldn't answer, so I said, "You should have stayed in jail. You only had nine months left. It was far less than you deserved. You'll have much more time in prison now."

He gave that dismissive little shrug the French do. "You didn't have to go looking for me. It would've been no trouble at all to simply forget all about the old Baron."

"You know we can't do that."

"No. You do your job, and I do mine."

"And what is your job, Mr. Baron Reverend Doctor?"

"Not to sit in a jail cell and wait to die." He coughed and went to the basin to splash a little water in his mouth. We didn't let him have a cup, not even a tin cup he couldn't break.

When he finished he walked right up to the bars and said, "You have me. Why don't you let my brother go free?"

I shook my head. "There's no leniency after a jailbreak. He had a chance to cooperate and he refused."

He took a long and noisy breath in. "You would never tolerate your sister going to jail for your crimes."

That was bait and I knew not to rise to it. "I wouldn't involve my family in my wrongdoings. And of course I wouldn't break the law."

His eyes were locked on mine. "Maybe you didn't break the law. But you're guilty, aren't you, *Fräulein?* You're guilty of making it so easy for me to escape. How are they going to punish you?"

The man was poison. I stepped away, quickly, not daring to even breathe the air around him.

Our prisoners came to us with all their horrors in tow: their dyspepsia and weak livers, their gout and catarrh, their boils and fevers, their scabies and lice. Some of it could be scrubbed away or banished with pills. An infected tooth could be pulled, a scrape bandaged. But when they brought in their lies, their devilish intentions, their wickedness and treachery —nothing could scrub that away. It gave me a diseased feeling to be too near it. As soon as I was out of sight of him I scratched at my neck and brushed down my skirts to banish the sensation that the old man's wrongdoing had taken bodily form and leapt through the bars at me.

After that, I vowed to stay away from him. Sheriff Heath wanted the strictest possible jail sentence for the old man, which meant that we'd have him for a good long while. I couldn't stand to be under the same roof with him and only hoped he would never be afforded my services as a translator again.

Felix would come up for trial soon for harboring a fugitive, and the Baron would receive a longer sentence for his escape. The Baron had managed to secure an attorney to defend both of them. The attorney made liberal use of the jail's visiting hours, speaking to each von Matthesius in turn and undoubtedly helping to pass information between them. This caused Sheriff Heath no end of vexation, but there was little we could do about it.

I couldn't understand why Felix remained so stubbornly silent. The Baron was not a man anyone should defend. He was a fraud and a con artist. He'd taken in sick people under false pretenses, failed to treat them, abused them, and made them sicker. Beatrice Fuller could have died from an overdose of ether. She'd have to start her life over again, if she ever got well.

Why would Felix help a man like that? It was a complicated job, rigging together a system of notes and packages and envelopes of money to hide his brother all over the city. For his loyalty he would get nothing but a jail sentence. He should have turned his brother over to us when he still had a chance at freedom.

The two of them sat resolutely behind bars, having decided, apparently, that they would trade their liberty for familial solidarity. Sometimes a family was like a swamp, everyone mired in the same mud.

AS SOON AS I had an afternoon free, I took the train to Rutherford and knocked on Dr. Williams's door. I arrived just five minutes before the conclusion of his midday office hours. The door opened immediately—he was on his way out, in his coat and hat—and he nodded when he saw me, as if he'd been expecting me.

"It's our lady cop," he said, with a shy and sudden smile. "I saw you in the papers."

"I've only come to ask after Mrs. Burkhart," I said.

"Well, since you paid the bill, you have every right to. I'm afraid the news is not encouraging." Dr. Williams had a friendly and open face, and lively eyes that seemed to take everything in, but he delivered his opinions in that flat, matter-of-fact way that doctors had. "She suffers from a cancer that has struck her liver and, I suspect, the other major organs. There are further difficulties that come from all the years she worked at that tannery."

"Can she be made comfortable?"

"Morphine will make anyone comfortable if they'll take it. I left her with a good supply and instructions to call the druggist if she needed more."

"I wonder what her son's going to do."

"He's an anxious and fearful boy. If he were mine, I'd get him work on board a ship, or send him out West. He could use a little adventure, and he isn't getting it in Rutherford. I suppose the war might be just the thing for him if we go, and if he can manage to stay alive over there."

I didn't want to think about motherless, fatherless Louis Burkhart at the Belgian front, but it was the way we were starting to see all young men: soon to disappear, the minute President Wilson decided to send them. "He has an uncle in Brooklyn. They run another shoe store."

"Then he'll go there."

"There is one other matter, if you have the time," I said.

He nodded, but didn't invite me in. We stood on the porch, our hands in our pockets.

"I learned some things about Dr. von Matthesius after I spoke to you," I said. "It has to do with a physician in New York, and I wonder if you've heard of him. Dr. Milton Rathburn."

The wind lifted Dr. Williams's hat and he pushed it down. "Rathburn. Caters to nervous millionaires, is that right?"

"That's the one. Have you ever spoken to him?"

"No, the way I'd put it is that he spoke to me. He was making calls to doctors up here, looking for a business arrangement. He wanted to set up a home offering rest cures and take a share in the profits."

"And you wouldn't agree to it, but Dr. von Matthesius did," I said.

"Is that what von Matthesius was up to? He went into business with Rathburn?"

"How do you suppose the two of them met?"

"I can't imagine. Von Matthesius wasn't practicing medicine in Rutherford, as far as I know. They could have met in a bar-room and worked up the whole scheme right over there." He nodded toward the saloons off Park Street.

"Whatever happened, it caused an awful lot of trouble," I said. "He must have treated a hundred patients—if you can call it treatment—and I only learned what happened to one of them."

"Is that the girl? The one he tried to marry?"

"Yes. I can't help but wonder how many more there were, and how such a thing could be allowed to happen right here in Rutherford. Isn't there anything to stop a man like von

Matthesius from opening his house to patients and doing as he pleases?"

Dr. Williams buttoned his collar against the wind. "Putting him in jail is a good way to stop him, but I take it you see that as a temporary situation. There's a great deal more to be done, Miss Kopp. I've long argued that we need medical inspectors in each town, and wouldn't you know that they've gone and put me in charge here in Rutherford. I'll be going around to check on the other doctors, as well as the hospitals and sanitariums, which is sure to make me popular among my colleagues. I can keep him out of Rutherford, but I can't do much about the rest of the state or the country. I don't suppose anyone can. Now, I hope you don't mind, but I have patients to see."

"I just can't bear the idea of him winning his release and going right back to his old ways."

Dr. Williams looked at me with a regretful half-smile. "Isn't that what they all do? The bank robbers and the arsonists and the sham doctors? Won't they all get out and do it again? Did you ever think they wouldn't?"

Having no answer to that, I offered him another five dollars for Mrs. Burkhart. He refused.

"I'll look after her," he said.

I kept holding out the money. "I want to do some good for someone."

But he waved it off and left me standing alone on his porch, where a brisk wind was being overtaken by a flurry of ice pellets. The ice blew down the street, and someone heard it rattling against a window and lit a fire, sending the bitter dry smoke from a bundle of newsprint into the air, where it stood in defiance against the inevitability of winter.

⊰ 28 ⊱

THE NEW YORK POLICE made no progress in finding Dr. Rathburn or Rudy Schilga, the man from whom Reinhold Dietz took his orders. Even if the men could have been found, Sheriff Heath wasn't sure what charges could be laid against them. The fact that Dr. Rathburn proposed a questionable scheme to Dr. Williams didn't amount to a crime. Only the charge of aiding an escaped fugitive would put Rathburn in jail, and we needed the testimony of the von Matthesius brothers for that. When asked if they might like to tell the truth about Dr. Rathburn in exchange for their own release, they both decided to plead guilty to whatever charges we might bring against them and be done with it. We could only assume that they were sufficiently afraid of Dr. Rathburn to refuse to testify against him. There would, in the end, be no trial, only a few minutes in front of a judge for each of them.

"The Baron keeps demanding that we release Felix," Sheriff Heath said on the morning of the hearing. "I suspect he has a piece of business he wants him to attend to. If we let him go he might lead us straight to Rathburn, but the prosecutor doesn't want to take the risk of releasing him and having him disappear. Neither do I."

"They're a strange family," I said.

"I don't suppose I've ever had two brothers in jail at once before. If we ever run across another von Matthesius, we ought to arrest him on general principle and keep the whole clan locked up."

The sheriff persuaded a friendly judge to hold the hearing on Christmas Eve in the hopes that reporters would be too distracted by the holiday to make an appearance at the courthouse. He had no idea what they might say in court and didn't want every word repeated in the papers. His idea was a good one, save for the fact that it failed entirely. Nothing of consequence was happening on Christmas Eve, and every reporter in three counties turned up.

It was a clear and bright day, terrifically cold but free of ice. The reporters stood around on the courthouse steps, their hands tucked under their arms, arguing the particulars of the case while great clouds of steam drifted from their lips.

We brought the prisoners in together and installed them along a bench in the front of the courtroom. The doors opened and within minutes the room was filled.

Judge Seufert, a frail and elderly man who suffered from near-deafness but was nonetheless a sharp jurist and friendly to Sheriff Heath's ideas, took his place at the front of the room and called the proceedings to order.

"As I understand it, pleas have already been entered and this is to be a simple hearing. Mr. von Matthesius, please rise." Both men stood at once, and a ripple of laughter went around the courtroom. The judge pounded his gavel. "Not a sound or I clear you all out. I haven't the patience today. Mrs.

Seufert is home roasting a goose and I'd rather be in my arm-chair attending to that business than sitting here with all of you. Not another warning."

The reporters grew perfectly silent. There was not so much as the sound of a pencil scratching on paper.

"Now," he said, addressing the inmates. "Felix von Mat-thesius. We'll start with you. May the stenographer indicate in the record that I shall address each defendant by his full name to stop them from popping up and down like a troupe of puppets."

A wiry, gray-haired woman in the corner nodded and made her notes. The Baron sat down.

"Felix von Matthesius, you are charged with assisting Her-man Albert von Matthesius, an inmate of the Bergen County jail and your brother, with his escape from the Hackensack Hospital, where he had been sent for medical care during the time of his incarceration at the jail, and of harboring said prisoner. How do you answer?"

I could only see Felix from the back. His shoulders slumped and his head hung down. The jail had laid him low.

"Guilty, Your Honor," Felix said.

"He's not guilty!" the Baron shouted, jumping to his feet. "Release him! He's done nothing!"

The Baron's attorney leaned forward to clasp him on the shoulder, but it was too late. The judge pounded his gavel again. "Is Herman Albert von Matthesius to be called as a wit-ness on his behalf?" he asked the attorney.

The attorney stood and said, "No, Your Honor. Felix von Matthesius has admitted his guilt and begs the court to im-pose a sentence and allow him to serve it."

"That's fine," the judge said. "Herman Albert von Matthesius will keep quiet or be taken out of this courtroom."

"Yes, Your Honor," the attorney said.

The judge leaned over to get a look at Sheriff Heath, Detective Courter, and Courter's boss, Prosecutor Wright. "Does the prosecutor wish to make a statement?"

Mr. Wright rose and read from a paper in his hand. "The Office of the Prosecutor of Bergen County begs the court to impose the strictest possible sentence upon anyone who assists in a dangerous criminal's escape from jail."

Judge Seufert nodded. "The court imposes a sentence of one year, to be carried out at the Bergen County jail commencing immediately."

The judge looked out over the courtroom with an expression of satisfaction. "This is moving right along. Mrs. Seufert thanks you." He ordered the Baron to rise.

"You are charged with escaping from the Hackensack Hospital while serving a sentence at the Bergen County jail that was imposed upon you by this court. How do you plead?"

"Herman Albert von Matthesius is not guilty by reason of insanity," said his attorney, "and the defendant respectfully requests that this court release him to the Morris Plains Insane Asylum for care."

A roar went up in the courtroom. Prosecutor Wright turned and whispered to Detective Courter, who slid out of his seat and ran out of the room. Sheriff Heath just shook his head.

The judge banged his gavel again, and shouted as loudly as his weak and trembling voice would allow. "Silence!"

It took a few more rounds with the gavel to quiet the

room. The judge nearly sent all the reporters out, which Sheriff Heath would have very much preferred. In the end, everyone settled back into their seats and the judge continued.

"Prosecutor, how do you respond?" the judge asked.

"I've sent one of my men to round up the county physician, whom we will call to lend his expert opinion to these proceedings," the prosecutor said.

"There's no need for that," the Baron's attorney said. "I have a medical report completed by a respected physician in Trenton who has examined the Baron's record and declared him to be insane and unfit for incarceration in the county jail. He recommends immediate transfer to Morris Plains."

The attorney handed a letter to the bailiff, who passed it to the judge. He waved the letter away without looking at it. "We don't ask physicians in Trenton for their opinions on our prisoners," he told the attorney. "Our county physician decides who goes to Morris Plains, and it does not appear that you've consulted with him."

The rear door to the courtroom opened and Detective Courter reappeared. The prosecutor whispered to him and then stood to say, "Dr. Ogden was reached at the hospital and can be here within the hour."

The judge sighed and looked at his watch. "All right. I don't see how we can finish this today, but bring him in and let's hear the prosecutor's version of events. The court will go into recess until—"

There was a crash in the front of the room and everyone jumped to their feet to see what had happened. Only Sheriff Heath remained sitting, his head in his hands. I slid off the bench and ran around to the side of the room to see Baron von Matthesius rolling around on the floor, kicking at his overturned chair, quaking all over like an epileptic. His hand-cuffs rattled as he shook and struggled. His eyes were turned up in his head and he had cut his scalp when he fell, leaving a jagged trail of blood behind him as he slithered and rolled around. His convulsions were accompanied by a strange, high-pitched whine that soon gave way to a sputtering cough.

"He's choking," his attorney shouted, kneeling down and reaching for him. "Help me hold him."

The bailiff knelt down and attempted to take the Baron by his shoulders, which only caused him to roll over into the bailiff's lap and disgorge the ammoniac contents of his innards. The bailiff gave a shout and let go of the Baron, shaking his coat sleeves and letting loose with a string of expletives of the sort not usually heard inside a courtroom. The judge turned his head away and looked as though he wanted to run out himself. The reporters all rushed over to get a better look, and I'm sorry to say that one of them had a camera and was attempting to make a picture of the scene.

Finally Sheriff Heath's men pulled everyone away from the prisoner, and someone was sent to find a janitor. The Baron lay twisted and unresponsive amid the streaks of blood that he had managed to kick, in a painterly fashion, all around him, laced with all the unmentionable matter that had issued forth from his gut. No one would go near him but his attorney, who, I noticed, had managed to slip on a pair of gloves before reaching in to take hold of him.

The judge ordered all of us out of the courtroom while it was cleaned. Someone found a wheelchair and the Baron was placed in it, limp as a dead cat, and rolled back to the jail to await Dr. Ogden.

The reporters filed out and headed to the courthouse steps

to resume their customary duties of cigarette smoking and gossip. The deputies and guards stood around outside the courtroom, awaiting their next order. The Baron's attorney insisted upon staying with his client, and no one objected as we were all relieved to have him out of the way.

Once the courtroom was nearly empty and blessedly quiet, and the janitors covered the stench of vomit with that of wintergreen, Sheriff Heath approached the judge, who was slumped over in his seat, looking defeated.

"Don't even try it, Bob," the judge said. "There's nothing to do but wait for Doc Ogden to come down and sort this mess out."

"But you know he's play-acting, don't you? It's all a trick."

"Well, it's some trick," the judge said. "I've never seen anything like it in my courtroom. I don't know how a man fakes an epileptic fit, and I think the janitors will tell you that he didn't fake the rest of it."

"But he did it deliberately, can't you see that?"

I was sitting behind the sheriff and couldn't see his expression, but I could tell from his voice that he knew he was losing this one.

The judge leaned down and spoke in a hushed, conspiratorial manner. "Have you ever done a thing like that, Bob? Deliberately, I mean? If I ordered you, right now, under penalty of imprisonment in your own jail, would you be able to do a trick like that on command? The sickness, the gash on the head, all of it?" The judge wore an expression of wide-eyed wonderment. He seemed genuinely impressed that a man could do such a thing.

"I suppose I could if I practiced," Sheriff Heath said, "and Dr. von Matthesius has had plenty of practice. He must have swallowed something—mustard powder, or laundry soap, or some such. Why, he tried it on us and fooled us into taking him off to the hospital. He only wants to go to Morris Plains because it'll be easier to escape."

Now it was my turn to put my head in my hands. The sheriff had gone too far. Judge Seufert sat back in his chair and crossed his arms in front of him.

"Are you suggesting that the Morris Plains asylum is incapable of holding on to the lunatics we send over there? Because if that's the case, I'll turn down every request you send me from here on and let you keep them in that nice new jail of yours. And I'll be sure to let the state authorities know that the sheriff of Bergen County has misgivings about the security at the asylum. They can send you up to Morris Plains to tell them exactly where they're going wrong. Would you like that, Bob?"

Sheriff Heath sighed. "No, Your Honor. I think they do a fine job up there. It's just that this is an unusual case."

"Thank you for telling me, Sheriff. I hadn't noticed."

⇥ 29 ⇤

DR. OGDEN WAS DELAYED in getting to the courthouse because a boy had been kicked by a goat and it looked as though he might lose an eye. It took another hour to calm the boy and do something about the eye. Once he arrived, there was yet another delay as Baron von Matthesius pretended to be comatose and could not be roused. It took a bucket of ice water, brought in under absolute silence so as not to alert the inmate and give him time to brace himself against shock, to bring him, shrieking, to his feet.

By the time he was alert and delivered back into the courtroom, I was supposed to have left for Fleurette's Christmas pageant. I had been conscripted into pouring punch in the lobby before the show.

"All the other girls have mothers," she'd pleaded, looking up at me with enormous liquid eyes. "They've all made tarts and cookies to raise money for next year's costumes. I don't have anyone to make tarts for me."

"You poor creature." I lowered myself to the divan and stroked her hair. "Was Bessie truly too busy to bake anything at all for you?" Our brother's wife was the only member of the family to be trusted with a pie.

She giggled and punched me in the ribs, which hadn't entirely healed. "All you have to do is pour the punch! You don't even have to make the punch. Just stand there and put it into cups. Do you think you can do that?"

"I suppose I could," I said, still trying to think of a reason why I couldn't.

"And don't tell me you'll be needed at the jail. I'll speak to Sheriff Heath myself. He'll force you to go. You know he does anything I ask him to do."

"Sheriff Heath is not as charmed by you as you might believe. He's cordial to everyone, even to girls who make unreasonable demands."

In the end, though, I agreed to be there. Fleurette also invited Sheriff and Mrs. Heath, and Deputy and Mrs. Morris. It was because of this invitation that Sheriff Heath sent me out of the courtroom just as von Matthesius was being brought in.

"Go and attend to your punch bowl," he whispered as the proceedings were about to begin.

"Now? I couldn't possibly."

"We all have our duties."

"Won't you need me to testify?"

"I'll be the only one called to speak. It won't make a difference anyway. The judge was impressed by his performance, and you know as well as I do that von Matthesius will pull one trick after another in this courtroom until he gets what he wants. Go on before you get us both into trouble with Miss Fleurette. I'll be there when I can."

I had no choice but to slip out of the courtroom just as

Baron von Matthesius was being wheeled in by his attorney, with a dour-faced Dr. Ogden following behind.

"THERE YOU ARE!" Fleurette shrieked, and ran across the lobby to meet me. I'd been instructed to arrive an hour before the first ticket holders would be admitted. The lobby was empty save for a few women setting out trays on a table. Fleurette wore a red velvet dress with the sheer sleeves she favored in winter and summer.

"We don't have much time," she said, skidding to a stop in front of me. "Let's get you dressed."

"I'm already dressed." Even as I said it I knew that I'd been trapped.

She took my hand and led me down the stark narrow hallway past the backstage entrance, where the younger children were already gathering behind the curtain and practicing their dance steps. She backed into a dressing room, tugging at both of my hands, bouncing up and down on her toes in that gleeful manner of hers.

"Give me your hat," she demanded, and I surrendered. What choice did I have?

Fleurette had managed to get hold of a length of Chinese pongee silk dyed a deep wine red, and had sewn a walking suit and duster set with a wide and handsome collar, fabric-covered buttons, a perfectly tailored cummerbund, and embroidered cuffs. There was a single pleat down the front and a piece of braid joining several pleats in the back. The duster slid over it and buttoned off to the side, which Fleurette assured me was very much in style.

It was, I had to admit, an extraordinary piece of work. No

dress had ever fitted me so well. "I left out the bone stays," she said as she buttoned the bodice around me. "You can breathe in it."

I took a deep breath and the dress expanded to precisely the girth of my rib cage. "It really is fine. Although I'm not sure I would've chosen red . . ."

"Don't be ridiculous! You can't go around in gray and tweed all the time. Just look at yourself."

I turned to the mirror propped up on the dressing table. The red brought color into my cheeks and turned my eyes almost green, and the precise tailoring made me look—not slimmer, exactly, but better proportioned. The silk rustled agreeably when I moved.

Fleurette put her arm around my waist and leaned against me. We made a comical sight in the mirror, a tall and matronly woman in a handsome tailored suit alongside a young girl in greasepaint.

I had no choice but to submit to her hairstyling efforts as well, so I was wearing an elaborate top-knot with a ribbon woven through it that hardly felt like it would hold. I would have to pour punch with my chin held very still for fear that it would all come tumbling down at once.

THE LINE FOR PUNCH was surprisingly orderly. The mothers of the other girls had done this sort of thing before and knew that the crowd should be made to pass by a long string of tables, each laden with sponge cakes and jelly rolls, almond creams and stuffed dates, Scottish fancies and marguerites. The time it took to choose from among them slowed them considerably, and they arrived at my punch table in measured doses so that I could handle them on my own. I had assumed that Norma would also work at the punch bowl, but she announced that she would arrive at her leisure and take a seat, which was exactly what she did.

"Look at you!" a familiar voice called as I was bent down behind my table to pick up another tray of cups. It was Bessie, with an arm around each of her children. The three of them looked me up and down in shock.

"What happened to you?" little Frankie asked.

"Are you going to be in the show?" Lorraine asked.

Bessie gave them each a shove. "Hush! You've just never seen your aunt Constance dressed for the theater before." She grinned at me and stepped to the side so I could keep pouring punch for the crowd. "Did Fleurette make it?" she whispered. "She must have. She did your hair, too."

"She did."

"It's perfect for you," Bessie said. "Only I don't know how she talked you into it."

"I wasn't talked into anything. It was forced upon me."

"Well, it suits you."

We were called to the theater just as my punch bowl emptied. My brother ran in at the last minute, having come directly from work. I filed in with the rest of the crowd and took my seat next to him and Bessie and the children. Norma sat next to me and on the other side we had places reserved for the Heaths and Morrises, but by the time the lights dimmed they still hadn't arrived.

"Is something wrong at the jail?" Norma whispered.

I shook my head. "Just more nonsense with von Matthesius."

The curtain parted and revealed a stage decorated to resemble a medieval castle, with stonework painted on a backdrop and tapestries draped from the walls. The lady and lord of the castle—as portrayed by Helen Stewart and an older boy I didn't know—sat in high-backed chairs as the rest of their court filed in. There were ladies-in-waiting arranged around Helen like a chorus, Fleurette among them. The boys, dressed in tunics and tights, marched in carrying drums, zithers, bells, and trumpets.

"It's going to be a noisy evening," Norma whispered.

And it was, with a dogged pianist driving the raucous young musicians through performances of "Over the Hills of Bethlehem" and "When from the East the Wise Men Came." Each song was accompanied by the arrival of still more members of the troupe, first bearing a yule log, then a boar's head (which was made of some sort of pink leather and, thanks to Fleurette's efforts, appallingly lifelike), then, at last, a wassail bowl and the entrance of Father Christmas.

I was still suffering from the aftermath of my wrestling match with von Matthesius. I shifted in my chair and tried to stretch my legs to ease the pain in my knee. All of this twisting and sighing annoyed Norma so much that she elbowed me in the ribs, which resurrected another ache and made it even more difficult to sit still.

I was about to give up and go stand in the back of the theater when Sheriff Heath slid into the seat next to me. He was still in his everyday worsted suit, which suggested he hadn't had time to go home and change for the evening. Mrs. Heath and the children must have been waiting for him, wondering when their Christmas Eve would begin. I started to tell him that he should have left me waiting and gone home to them, but it was impossible to think of anything but von Matthesius.

"What happened?" I asked, even though the answer was already sinking like a stone inside of me.

He watched the children perform an awkward little dance that involved holding hands and doing something like a waltz in a circle. The older ones had practiced and did their parts with a kind of wooden precision, but the younger children abandoned any attempt at following the steps and just hopped up and down, grinning broadly at the audience. Laughter and applause went around the room, and while it did, Sheriff Heath leaned over and said, "Judge Seufert ordered the Baron to Morris Plains. I sent him there straight away. I don't want to see him again."

"Surely he didn't give credence to a criminal over Dr. Ogden and the rest of us?"

Norma kicked me and leaned over to glare pointedly at Sheriff Heath. We sat quietly until the trumpets burst into a chorus and then he said, "He babbled like an idiot when they brought him back in, and then he stripped off almost every stitch of clothing right in front of the judge. We all stood up and said it was an act, but how do you prove that a man is sane when he's acting insane?"

There was an enthusiastic round of applause following the trumpets. I couldn't bring myself to join in.

"He'll break out within a week," I said.

"I know. But it'll be their fault if he runs this time, and their job to bring him back."

I shut my eyes against the image of the nurse or orderly or guard who would be the next to take the blame for von Matthesius's escape. I'd been trying to absolve myself of responsibility, but in fact I was only passing it on. If he succeeded again—and I had no doubt that he would—the failings and missteps that allowed him to get away would belong to someone else and would haunt them the way I was haunted.

"And what are we to do?" I whispered to the sheriff.

He gave me the smallest smile and nudged my arm with his. "We go back to work, Deputy."

The lights came down on the stage and a little girl of about ten stepped into the spotlight to sing the first lines of "It Came upon the Midnight Clear." The other girls gathered in a semicircle and hummed behind her. She was a perfect angel of a child, her hair smoothed into black ringlets and topped with a red velvet bow. She reminded me of Fleurette at that age. Norma must've been thinking the same thing, because she glanced over at me and smiled a little.

Beatrice Fuller could have stood among those girls only a few years ago. Even Providencia Monafo had been this young once, and she might have sung with the other girls at Christmastime just like this. All the women under my care—the pickpockets, the arsonists, the runaways—each one of them had been these girls, or some version of them.

Every girl stepped up to take her part. Helen sang the third verse.

> Yet with the woes of sin and strife
> The world has suffered long;
> Beneath the angel-strain have rolled
> Two thousand years of wrong.

Then Fleurette stood next to her and took the rest of the verse. She sang clearly and confidently, with a quiet humility

I hadn't often seen in her. The first line came with such tenderness that it seemed as if it was meant for each one of us. Sheriff Heath sighed and sank deeper into his chair.

> *And man, at war with man, hears not*
> *The love-song which they bring.*

I closed my eyes and pictured Baron von Matthesius settling in for his first night of sleep in one of the long, cold dormitories at the Morris Plains asylum. He would've already taken note of the windows and the doors, and he would be awake now, listening to the footfalls of the nurses, memorizing their routes on the night watch.

But Fleurette's voice banished the criminals and lunatics from my mind, if only for one night.

> *O hush the noise, ye men of strife,*
> *And hear the angels sing.*

MISS CONSTANCE KOPP

Constance Kopp, 1915. This photograph accompanied newspaper stories
about the von Matthesius case.

Ithaca Daily News, December 22, 1915,
evening edition

Historical Notes, Sources,
and Acknowledgments

AS WITH THE FIRST BOOK in the series, *Girl Waits with Gun,* this novel is based on actual events and people, but it is a work of fiction, populated by fictional characters inspired by their real-life counterparts. This time, the title does not come from a real-life headline about Constance, but is inspired by several real-life headlines from the era about women in law enforcement.

According to newspaper reports, Constance Kopp was asked by Sheriff Heath to help find the escaped prisoner Dr. von Matthesius, but she was not actually responsible for his escape. At the time, she was not yet a deputy. I don't know exactly why she hadn't been hired on officially. It really was true that New Jersey had only just recently passed a law allowing women to serve as police officers, and the law did not mention deputy sheriffs. It's also true that the sheriff of New York County tried to hire women deputies in 1912, but was prevented from doing so because the law required that deputies be eligible to vote. That law remained in place and became irrelevant when women in New York won the right to vote in 1917.

Regardless, Constance did prove herself to Sheriff Heath through her work on the von Matthesius case. She really did arrest Felix, although I don't know the exact details of the arrest. In real life, Felix's son Hans was also arrested in connection with the case. All of the troubles Sheriff Heath faced —the dentistry bills for inmates, the possibility of serving jail time for the escape—were reported in the newspapers as I have described them.

The police in New York did call the sheriff several times, believing they had captured the fugitive when in fact they had the wrong man. And Sheriff Heath and Constance really did work with Reverend Weber to send a letter via general delivery. Reinhold Dietz and Rudy Schilga were real people who played more or less the same roles described here. The last night of the hunt and the capture of von Matthesius happened almost exactly as described. Von Matthesius was, in fact, sentenced to the Morris Plains Insane Asylum (later called Greystone), but in real life his sentencing did not happen until April 1916.

I never have discovered the exact nature of von Matthesius's crimes. Beatrice Fuller and Dr. Rathburn are fictional characters, but the three boys who reported him actually were named Louis Burkhart, Frederick Shipper, and Alfonso Youngman. I know nothing more about their real lives, so everything but their names is fiction.

The character of Henri LaMotte is fictional, although there really were photographers who specialized in collecting evidence. Also fictional are the women Constance met in New York: Geraldine, Carrie, and Ruth. The Mandarin Hotel is based on many similar hotels for women that existed in New York at the time. (If Constance had stayed in a hotel that also served men, she would have gone in through a separate women's entrance, aimed at protecting women against even the suspicion of impropriety.)

Providencia Monafo really did shoot her boarder Saverio Salino, but the bit about aiming for her husband, and wanting to stay in jail for protection from him, is fiction. Also, in real life, her crime occurred a few months earlier than it does in this novel.

Many other small details are true to actual events, as you'll see from the list of citations that follow. Grayce van Horn really was Sheriff Heath's maid and was frightened by a prisoner, although that prisoner was not von Matthesius. Murray's was a fantastic and highly theatrical restaurant near Times Square, where packages of a very interesting nature were sometimes exchanged in the cloakroom. The general delivery plan really was almost canceled by the post office because women were using it to send illicit correspondence to their lovers. Ida Higgins's fictional story illustrates a forgotten fact about those days: witnesses were often held in jail just like the criminals they were expected to testify against. For more on this topic, I highly recommend Carolyn B. Ramsey's excellent article "In the Sweat Box: A Historical Perspective on the Detention of Material Witnesses," *Ohio State Journal of Criminal Law* 6, no. 2 (2009): 681.

And poetry lovers may recognize Dr. Williams. William Carlos Williams lived in Rutherford in those days and practiced medicine from his house overlooking Park Avenue. He was involved in all sorts of public health issues at the time. One of the great joys of reading through newspapers on microfilm from those days is to come across a letter to the editor from Dr. W. C. Williams, advocating for some improvement to local health care. I have no reason to believe that he knew Dr. von Matthesius or Constance Kopp, but it's at least possible that he did. I urge you to read his book *The Doctor Stories* if you'd like to know more about what his medical practice might have been like.

I don't know what, exactly, Norma and Fleurette were doing during the months covered in this narrative, but Fleurette really did sing a soprano solo at a concert with a girl named Helen Stewart and entered singing competitions in Paterson. Norma's interest in pigeons is, as always, entirely fictional.

Belle Headison's appointment as Paterson's first policewoman was described in the *New York Times* on July 21, 1915 ("Name First Policewoman"). She did, in fact, serve without pay. Many of her opinions about the role of a woman in a police force (p. 3–4) came from newspaper articles describing commonly held beliefs about policewomen at the time, as well as accounts of conferences and congressional testimony on the subject. *The Policewoman: Her Service and Ideals,* by Mary E. Hamilton (Frederick A. Stokes Company, 1924), is a particularly good source. See pp. 4–7 of that book for a more extended version of the argument Belle Headison lays out about the proper role of policewomen.

The story of Lettie and Mr. Meeker (pp. 5–8) is drawn from similar accounts in Gloria Myers's excellent book *A Municipal Mother: Portland's Lola Greene Baldwin, America's First Policewoman* (OSU Press, 1995).

Providencia Monafo's shooting of Saverio Salino (p. 26) was described in the *New York Times* on July 14, 1915, in the article "Woman Shoots Boarder."

"Prisoner Escapes by Ruse" (p. 82) ran in the *New York Times* on November 8, 1915.

"Alligators Terrify Diners" was the headline of the actual February 16, 1916, *Jacksonville Dispatch* newspaper article about the ill-fated Daughters of the American Revolution dinner that was ruined by a crocodile invasion (p. 94).

One of my most prized possessions is *The Peace Officer's Telegraph Code: An Economical and Secret Telegraph Code for the Exclusive Use of All Peace Officers of the English-Speaking World,* by H. M. Van Alstine, published by the Peace Officer's Telegraphic Code Co. in 1911 and used by Norma on p. 126.

There really were a series of tailors' strikes on Fifth Avenue in the fall of 1915 (p. 141). See the *New York Times'* "Row in Tailors' Strike," September 25, 1915, and "150,000 Tailors May Strike," November 26, 1915.

The incident over the ashes left in the cloakroom at Murray's on p. 147 was described in a *New York Times* article on November 29, 1915, titled "'Bomb' in Murray's Is Mabel Hite's Urn."

The article on German pigeons flying around with cameras strapped to them, which so captivated Norma on p. 196, was found on p. 30 of the January 1916 edition of *Popular Science.*

The controversy over dentistry bills on p. 214 was described in the *Trenton Evening Times* on November

5, 1915, in an article called "Fancy Dentistry Jail
   Attraction."
Frieda Burkel's story (p. 215) was described in the *Daily
   Star* on December 8, 1915, under the unforgettable
   headline "Tar Tries to Kill Old Playmate: Biff!"
"Girl Deputy Sheriff 'Pinches' a Minister" (p. 256) ran
   in the *New York Press* on December 20, 1915. Other
   accounts quoted come from the *New York Herald*'s
   story on December 20, 1915, "Girl Detective Seizes
   Fugitive in Subway" and the *New York Tribune*'s "Girl
   Captures Fugitive Parson, Who Fights Her" on the
   same date.

Thanks to the volunteers and staff at the Bergen County and
Passaic County historical societies, and to the librarians at
the Johnson Public Library, Paterson Free Public Library, and
Ridgewood Public Library, where I've spent more hours than
I want to count reading microfilm, and to Billy Neumann
for giving me the insider's tour of Rutherford. Thanks also
to the O'Dell and Birgel families, who have been so kind to
share their memories of the real-life people who inspire my
fictional characters. I'm endlessly grateful to Masie Cochran,
my agent, Michelle Tessler, my editor, Jenna Johnson, and
everyone else at Houghton Mifflin Harcourt. Finally, all my
love and appreciation to my husband, Scott Brown, who has
been living with the Kopp sisters as long as I have.

Keep reading for a sample from the next Kopp Sisters novel,
from *New York Times* best-selling author Amy Stewart

MISS KOPP'S MIDNIGHT CONFESSIONS

Out in September 2017

Don't miss a Kopp Sisters adventure!

ON THE MORNING of her arrest, Edna Heustis awoke early and put her room in order. She occupied the smallest of Mrs. Turnbull's furnished rooms, nothing more than an alcove under the eaves, with just enough space for a bed and a wash-stand. A row of iron hooks on the wall held the entirety of her wardrobe: two work uniforms, a Sunday dress, and a winter coat. The only decoration was a picture of a sailboat, furnished by Mrs. Turnbull, and for reading material her landlady had issued her a history of the Italian lakes, a guide to Egyptian art, and a general's wife's account of Army life on the western plains. Those sat on a hang-shelf, alongside an oil lamp—although Edna preferred to do her reading in the parlor, under the single electrical light offered for that purpose.

Absent from her possessions were any portraits of her family or mementos of home. She'd left in such a hurry that she hadn't thought to bring any. She'd been inquiring at factories for weeks, and when the women's superintendent at the

DuPont powder works in Pompton Lakes agreed to hire her on, she dashed home, gathered up only that which she could carry, then slipped out the back door while her mother was occupied in the kitchen.

Edna might have been a quiet and serious girl, but she'd been raised among boys and had a fine sense of adventure about her. The war in Europe had reached its boiling point, and every American boy was eager to join the fight. If there was work to be done for the war, and women were allowed to do it, Edna was impatient to begin. She left the briefest of notes on the day she left: "Gone to work for France in Pompton Lakes. I have a place in a good house and you needn't worry."

It was true about the good house. Mrs. Turnbull only rented to girls from the powder works and maintained a strict policy about curfews and church attendance on Sundays. She was in many ways a tougher task-master than Edna's mother had been, but Edna didn't mind about that. She believed the regimen of living in a boarding-house to be similar to that of the Army, and liked to imagine that the daily making up of her room (tucking in the sheets, folding down the coverlet, stowing her bed-slippers and nightgown, arranging her brush and comb in an even row alongside the basin) might resemble, in some way, the orderliness of military camp life, of which her brothers were so eager to partake.

But France seemed very far away that morning as Edna stepped into her work dress, washed her face in the basin, and ran down the stairs for breakfast. In the cramped butler's pantry that served as a dining room, Mrs. Turnbull had put out porridge and stewed apples. Edna sat, as she did every morning, in comfortable silence among the five other girls who roomed there: Delia, Winifred, Irma, Fannie, and Pearl. Their conversation ran along familiar lines:

First Delia said, "There's a ladder in my stocking so far beyond mending that I might as well go bare."

Then Fannie said, "Albert's good for another pair."

To which Irma replied, "Then it's a shame she threw off Albert and went with those men from the Navy, who don't need to supply a girl with stockings before she'll go to a dance hall with them."

Then Pearl said, "Delia, you didn't go with all of them, did you?"

And Delia retorted, "You couldn't expect me to choose one!"

This kind of talk had embarrassed Edna terribly the first time she heard it. Before she left home, she'd allowed a friend of her brother's to pay a little attention to her, but she could never imagine stolid and steadfast Dewey Barnes buying her a pair of stockings or taking her to a crowded and noisy dance hall and then letting her stumble home, as the girls at the boarding-house did, dazed by liquor and cigarettes, with a sort of swollen and bruised look about the lips that they wore like a badge until it faded.

It wasn't that Edna disapproved of their feminine vanity, or their wild ways. She just couldn't do what they did. She didn't know how to make herself up and put herself on display. Dancing was a foreign language to her: she felt foolish trying to work out the Kangaroo Hop or the Peabody, and never could master Delia's trick of kicking her heel back when she turned to make her skirt fly up. She practiced with them because they insisted, but more often than not she took the man's part, maneuvering woodenly while the other girls practiced their flourishes.

Only once did she allow herself to be dragged along to a dance hall with them, and there she found herself entirely outmatched. Over the whirl of laughter and music, the other girls chatted gaily with any man who came into their orbit. They had a knack for making the sort of easy, meaningless chatter that would lead to a turn on the dance floor, then a sip from a bottle secreted away in a man's pocket, a taste of his cigarette, and a kiss just outside the door, sheltered under a dark and discreet night sky.

But Edna hadn't any idea where to begin, and wasn't sure she wanted to. Every dance step, every smile, every laughing word exchanged with a man was like a piece of machinery that she didn't know how to operate. Instead she held her friends' purses, and went home at midnight with all of their keys, rattling them in every doorknob so that Mrs. Turnbull might hear the sound of all six girls returning home at once.

The others didn't mind that Edna stayed home from the dances after that, and for her part, she'd grown accustomed to their ways. She was sitting placidly among them that morning, listening with some amusement but relieved, as always, that they didn't expect her to join in.

"You remember Frank, don't you? From the train station?" Delia whispered.

Pearl leaned in and said, "The one with the walking stick filled with whiskey?"

"Yes," Delia said gleefully. "That one. He asked me to Atlantic City for the weekend. How am I going to get away? I'm all out of sisters with birthdays."

"What about an elderly aunt in a state of decline?" Fannie offered.

"What about inviting me?" Irma complained.

"Oh, Frank would like that, but he's to register us as man and wife, and who would you be?"

"I'll be the sister with the birthday! Or the elderly aunt. Just take me along."

They were all laughing at that when heavy footsteps stormed the porch and someone pounded the brass knocker hard enough to rattle their saucers. Every girl leapt up at once, flushed and guilty, as if they had, improbably, been overheard and caught. Mrs. Turnbull, having just come up from her lodgings in the basement, bustled past and admonished them to finish quickly and wash their own bowls.

But not a single girl moved, and not a single spoon clanked against a dish, as the door swung open and a policeman's brusque voice demanded to see a Miss Edna Heustis, who was to be put under arrest on a charge of waywardness and taken without delay to the Hackensack jail.

Adventures featuring the forgotten but fabulous Kopp sisters.

Made in the USA
Coppell, TX
24 September 2021

62965371R00198

HOW TO RUN AN
INTERNET
BUSINESS
NOW

Aligning Modern Academic Principles with Professional Best Practices Post Pandemic

DR. CHAS FOX

Fundamentals by AG Fox 2017

FIRST EDITION

ISBN: 978-1-946466-74-7

Library of Congress Control Number: 2021908834

Published by

3741 Linden Avenue SE | Grand Rapids, MI 49548

Printed in the United States

Table of Contents

List of Tables

List of Figures

Introduction

How to Run a Business Now is a guide for current business managers and owners, people considering starting a business, and students of business management. Business was changing rapidly before the COVID-19 pandemic. We were dealing with new taxes, tariffs, increased government regulations, changes in digital marketing, reductions in brick-and-mortar stores, and much more. Then the pandemic hit. Many businesses had to close their doors. Everyone had to rethink space and how to work.

I run an e-commerce company called Micro-Mark, which sells precision tools worldwide to high-end craftspeople. I have run several e-commerce companies over the years but the changes we have seen recently were more than ever before. At Micro-Mark we had converted to systems that allowed many of our workers to work from home prior to the pandemic. After some adjustments, we became even more efficient than we were before the pandemic. Many of these workers will continue working from home after this virus crisis is gone.

We also saw a jump in our e-commerce sales like several other Internet companies. This book is written for people who want to know more about how to run a business in today's online business environment and hits many critical aspects of running your business. You may prefer to jump around from section to section based on your interest. We also attempt to provide the history of the topic we are examining along with current peer-reviewed academic research. Finally I provide personal stories on these topics based on my experiences.

We start by discussing why businesses fail. Then, if you are determined, we discuss how to develop a business plan. Modern academic tools are examined that can be used to help you derive your businesses' competitive advantage. The book provides choices about organizational structures, including options for legal structures. We also examine your options for organizational management structures.

The important subject of customer guarantees is examined and options for types of guarantees are offered. We examine how to put together the business plan in a format that is professional and standardized. This is an important piece of the puzzle because you will need to secure funding and make financial projections. We provide a full discussion about sources of funding for the business. A discussion of how to develop financial statements, including the income statement, the balance sheet, and the statement of cash flow is provided. A detailed 13-week cash flow projection is also provided and discussed.

We discuss the many changes that have disrupted online marketing in the business environment. We discuss best practices for—
- Websites
- Organic and paid searches
- Email marketing
- Short message service (SMS)
- Social media
- Influencers
- Catalog production
- Print advertising
- Trade shows
- Brick and mortar businesses

The book examines other areas of digital marketing, including Amazon. We provide some strategies to consider navigating Amazon. Other marketplace channels, including Walmart.com, HomeDepot.com, eBay, Etsy, and Alibaba are detailed. We discuss the many changes happening in freight, including USPS, UPS, and FedEx. We even examine Amazon shipping.

We have a chapter dedicated to how to find employees and how to manage organizational culture. We highlight the fact that many companies use a strategy of giving back to the community to build the organizational culture. The inevitable employee resistance to change and the mitigation of resistance to align your employees are presented.

The book emphasizes product development and innovation as the key to gaining a sustained competitive advantage for your business. We discuss the five methods of product development and delve into brand and brand management. We also discuss the world of franchising today and some the opportunities there, plus identifying the most critical topic to survive and thrive in today's business environment, which is to continually learn. The world is changing quickly, and to keep up you have to make continuous learning and innovation an everyday habit.

I base that thought on my own experience in sports, business, and academia. I have the unusual experience of having played in the NFL, running multiple companies, turning failing companies around, and creating rapid growth. I also have a deep academic background as a doctor of business administration and adjunct professor at Seton Hall University's Stillman School of Business. I understand the modern business tools that academia provides and I show how to apply them to your business. With that introduction, I hope you enjoy the book.

Dr. Chas Fox, CEO of Micro-Mark

1

Do You Really Want to Be an Entrepreneur?

"No more romanticizing about how cool it is to be an entrepreneur. It's a struggle to save your company's life— and your own skin—every day of the week."
—Spencer Fry, co-founder of CarbonMade

Understanding what starting a business will mean to your life and your lifestyle is the first critical question to be answered in this venture. It is a life commitment that includes the risk of money, time, and spirit. Many people are just not cut out to be business owners. That's okay; people should not try to be something they are not. Business owners risk everything, and the odds are low that they will succeed. Starting a new company will mean that you will be the last one to get paid. In starting up, many times you will not be able to pay yourself.

The United States Bureau of Statistics (2020) says that 20% of businesses fail during the first two years of operation. Forty-five percent will fail within the first five years, and 65% will collapse within ten years (U.S. Bureau of Statistics, 2020). Only 25% make it to 15 years. This means that 75% of businesses fail. Failing means lost investment, time, and other opportunities. It can be devastating.

A business that just barely survives can be worse than closing the business doors. In today's market only 40% of small businesses make a profit (SmallBizGenius, 2020). Sixty percent are somehow surviving but not making a profit. Why are so many businesses failing? Here are seven reasons:

1. Not Investigating the Market

Many businesses open without the owners understanding the market they have entered. Understand that once you enter a market, you are in competition with other businesses that are all trying to attract the limited number of customers in that market. It is indeed a competition. Just as in sports, you have to understand the strengths and weaknesses of your competition to find your competitive advantage. Market research is key to finding your competitive advantage. We will discuss more about competitive advantage in later chapters.

2. A Poor Business Plan

A business plan is the foundation of your business. Most loans and investments require some form of a business plan, which requires you to think through your business. In a later section we will detail the key elements of a good business plan. Many new businesses owners do not create a well-developed business plan and therefore have not thoroughly thought through the details of the business. An effective plan will detail weekly financial projections, including expected revenue and expenses.

3. Under-Financed

Determining how much capital is a critical element to the success or failure of the business. Sixty-four percent of businesses start with less than $10,000 in capital, and 25% of businesses start with no capital

(SmallBizGenious, 2020). Small Business Funding (2020) says that undercapitalization is the number-one reason small businesses fail.

This fact highlights the need for business owners to plan and create financial projections. If you are borrowing the money, you must ensure that you have enough to run the business as outlined in the business plan. If you get the projections wrong and you fail to borrow enough, it is very difficult to go back for more money. The lender loses confidence in your plan. However, you don't want to borrow more than you need because you'll be paying interest on the loan.

4. Bad Location, Website, and Marketing

If you get everything right but have a bad physical location or website, you'll fail. The best business cannot survive in a bad location. Also, most business owners are not experts in real estate. Determining an optimal business location is a science and a specialized field in real estate.

Bad websites are also common in businesses. Internet customers have come to demand specific components of a website. A bad website will have virtually no traffic and no business. Also, Google has specific requirements that have been getting tighter and tighter. If your site does not meet those requirements, which include product feed, image requirements, link requirements, and other specific components, Google will suspend your site, and your website will not show up in Google. In other words, you'll be invisible.

Additionally, marketing has changed considerably. The Yellow Pages of telephone directories used to be a good channel to get new customers but now provide virtually no customers. Digital marketing has become the best method to reach customers. However, digital marketing is getting harder and harder to effectively get a return on investment.

5. Not Tracking Performance and Making Adjustments

"Anything that is measured and watched improves," writes Bob Parsons, founder of GoDaddy. Even if you have a good business plan and have developed projections, you must track those projections to the actual results on a weekly basis. The data has to be collected and compared against the projection and/or last year's performance. If the projection is off track, identifying the reason or reasons is critical. Then, based on the assessment, adjustments to the strategy need to be made or the business will continue getting off track quickly.

6. Scaling Too Fast

Even if things go well at first, expanding too quickly can cause failure. Expanding the reach of the business requires new market research. Expanding the scope, like new products, also requires new research. You cannot assume that the scaled business will operate efficiently.

7. Owning a Business May Not Be for You

Owning a business is a big commitment, as discussed before, and if you do not have the personality, endless determination, energy, aptitude for risk, and discipline, you should not open a business. Understand that you have to develop products or services, do accounting, be good with customers, effectively manage employees and merchandise, lead marketing campaigns, file taxes, abide by government regulations, and much more. The responsibility for these tasks is not something that appeals to everyone. However, most people considering starting a business do not have anyone telling them the challenges and difficulties. Starting a business is romanticized in our culture.

However, if after considering these details you are still interested in running your business, the next sections will provide guidelines for best practices in many areas. These best practices come from current business school academic teachings and experienced professional management. Business schools and professional needs do not always align. But used together, they can be very powerful.

Business schools provide tools and principles that if properly implemented can improve business performance. The academic principles discussed here are those that will work in real-world businesses today. We will discuss the business plan, tools for competitive advantage analysis, the organizational structure, financial tools, marketing, finding and managing people, product and services development, franchising, and continuous learning and innovation.

2

Getting Started

"Ideas are a commodity. Execution of them is not."
—Michael Dell, chairman and CEO of Dell

Whether you are currently running a business and need to reconsider your approach or you're planning to run a business, there are two main considerations. The first is the product or service. The second is who is your customer?

How Will You Produce Your Product?

Product is a pretty broad term, but if you have an idea for a product that you think customers would want, then you have to take small steps to starting a business. Obviously that product needs to be designed and manufactured somewhere. If you do not already have a manufacturing company, you could consider starting one. It is doable. Mike Lindell in his book *What Are the Odds? From Crack Addict to CEO* (2019) says he started My Pillow in 2004, and the company has grown to be one of the largest manufacturers in Minnesota. He started in his garage sewing his patented pillows himself.

Those stories are rare but real. Most people don't have the wherewithal and access to capital to do what Mike Lindell achieved. If you can take that path, then I recommend that you do. Many products can be made at your residence or in your garage. If you bootstrap the business, working at night or weekends while working full time, you'll have less debt and will know more about your product than anyone else.

Some products and ideas need protection. Many times, people consider a patent. In some cases it can make sense. However, it can be expensive and difficult to defend. I've been the inventor of several products and processes patented, and in most cases the time and money were not worth the result. Some products can be protected with a secret formula that is not fully disclosed. Other products are protected by the sheer cost of the tooling required to make them.

If you cannot start a manufacturing company, you need to collaborate with a manufacturer. You will also need an engineer to design the product. Several companies can provide soup-to-nuts solutions for manufacturing. These services come at a cost. Many consumers appreciate companies that can manufacture in the United States. Sometimes customers will pay a little more for items made in the USA. If you cannot manufacture at an efficient price in the United States, you'll need to look internationally.

Many countries specialize in certain products. Almost all do some form of textile and clothing manufacturing. China and Japan are heavy into power tools, electronics, and other complicated production items. India is heavy into fabricated metal items without motors. Vietnam has a growing manufacturing sector. I have just named a few, but manufacturing is carried out in virtually every country of the world.

Trade shows are a good source to find a manufacturer. Also, if you know a country that has a reputation for manufacturing your type of product, you could contact that country's consulate in New York City or Washington, D.C. Another source for connecting with manufacturers is Alibaba.com. Alibaba has a process to connect people and companies that need specific design   and manufacturing.

In addition to product manufacturing, you must consider packaging.

If your product will be sold in retail stores, you'll need packaging with attractive marketing that will stand out against the many other items. The packaging should present the key features to highlight the value of the product. If your product will not be in a retail environment, packaging design should consider protection and consolidation. Products need adequate protection to survive shipping. Also, most shipping carriers will charge based on weight and the dimensions of the package.

The product, service, and packaging discussion have many elements that are specific to the idea. Many resources are available to your specific product. Next, we will discuss your customer.

Who is Your Customer?

The design of the product should be in concert with the needs of your customer. These two elements are inseparable to achieve a good value proposition. Well-designed products were conceived with the customers' needs and desires in mind. In most cases your ultimate customer will be the consumer. Even if you sell to other businesses, your product will likely end up in the hands of the consumer.

B2C

Business-to-consumer (B2C) is selling directly to the consumer. This can be done through a brick-and-mortar store or online. Brick-and-mortar stores have been the traditional channel to sell products to consumers. Retail stores will continue to be the primary form of sales to consumers post pandemic. However, even before the pandemic of 2020–2021, retail sales were slowing in the brick-and-mortar channel while online sales were growing rapidly.

Digital marketing is growing faster than any other segment in retail, and retail managers are failing to adjust to the new market (Bonsu and Kuofie, 2019; Fulgoni, 2018). These managers are failing to adjust to the differences in the digital channel from traditional retail (Bonsu and

Kuofie, 2019). A major problem in the retail market is the problem of the failure of retailers to compete successfully in the digital marketplace, resulting in financial losses and record closures (Bonsu and Kuofie, 2019; Fulgoni, 2018). Digital commerce is growing four times faster than other sales channels, and retailers have struggled to resolve the shift to digital as retailers closed at a rate of 229% more in 2017 than in 2016 (Fulgoni, 2018). Based on articles I have read, these are the companies that filed for bankruptcy in 2020 because they could not figure out how to effectively navigate the digital marketplace as B2C companies: JCPenney, Neiman Marcus, Pier 1 Imports, Brooks Brothers, Dean & Deluca, and Modell's. We will address online marketing later in this book.

The benefit of B2C is that the product profit margins are traditionally higher than by selling to a business. In most cases the average order value (AOV) is lower per order. Also, the cost of marketing is higher than with business-to-business (B2B) transactions.

One word of caution if you are a B2C structure. Make sure you price your product to allow B2B sales later. If you price too low, there will not be room in the B2B space for the other business to make a profit.

B2B

A company can also sell business-to-business. The product could be something that the business uses either consumed or included as a component in manufacturing. Business customers are easier to locate through trade organizations and other listings. Generally, the orders are larger than B2C. These sales do not generally occur with cold calling but are commonly managed by a sales team who focus on a geographic area or product category. Profit margins are lower than B2C sales, but the AOV is much higher. Also, B2B sales tend to have reoccurring orders that make transactions flow easier.

Ideally you are selling to multiple B2B customers who are reselling to consumers. In order to reduce the chances of a price war for your product, you should create a manufacturer's suggested retail price (MSRP). This price is the lowest price a reseller can go. If the reseller goes below the MSRP, other resellers will complain. Resellers that do not comply should not be allowed to buy again.

Both B2C and B2B

Many of the companies I have led have sales in both B2C and B2B. At Geo Park Seed Company, we had Park Seed (B2C), Wayside Gardens (B2C), and Park Wholesale (B2B). At Jackson & Perkins we had J&P (B2C) and JP Wholesale (B2B). These five companies were run as independent units sharing a campus and not much else. Each unit had its own profit-and-loss (P&L) statements, executives, and employees. The product lines were completely different. Additionally, both Park Wholesale and JP Wholesale sold to big box stores, including Home Depot, Lowe's, Whole Foods, Costco, and more. These products ended in the hands of consumers.

The largest B2B program that I have been involved with is with Costco. Costco has a membership format that requires $100 per year to be able to purchase their products and services. They have just under 100 million members worldwide (Coppola, 2020). Costco obtains these members by providing value for the customer. They do not just have low prices—they have high-quality products. Costco also packages products in larger bundles. Many of the customers are other businesses. Local restaurants buy some of the food they serve in Costco stores. Many businesses go to Costco for office supplies.

While I was running JP Wholesale, we had a $20 million packaged bareroot rose program with Costco that was only in stores for about four weeks. Costco operates on low margins but high volumes. The rose program with Costco was the larges ornamental rose program in the world at the time. We leveraged the J&P name to create a JP Bulb program that was similar in size to the rose program. Because the roses and bulbs were sensitive to cold weather, we would introduce the programs depending on the area of the country. We would be in southern California and Florida first and then move north to groups of stores based on the temperature increases. We found that as we opened in the Costco stores in southern California and Florida, we would see increased web traffic to our Jackson & Perkins (B2C) website. And each area as we moved north would result in increased web traffic from those areas. The B2B program was creating sales and customers for our B2C business.

The company I currently run, Micro-Mark, sells to both consumers and businesses. We run these transactions through the same P&L and use the same staff. The product lines are the same. The only difference is the prices. We price the products to sell B2B to allow the business customer to resell the products to consumers. Both structures work very well.

If you are primarily a B2B structure, you should consider selling B2C in some way. Direct feedback from B2C sales is critical. You will hear directly what the consumer thinks of your product. Also, this data will help your B2B sales. More information is critical to survival and success.

Marketing: How You Reach Your Customer

How you reach your customer is critical to your future. Dr. Yoham Jerry Wind is the Lauder Professor Emeritus of Marketing at Wharton Business School of the University of Pennsylvania. His research is compelling in regard to how businesses market themselves and the value or valuation of businesses. I heard him speak in Princeton, New Jersey, and was taken by his research. He said that companies that sell a product have a multiple markup of earnings before interest and taxes of 1x. Companies that provide a service have a multiple of 2x. Companies that have an intellectual property element have a markup of 3.4x. However, companies that market through networking have an 8x mark up. Dr. Wind cited Airbnb and Uber as companies that utilized networks to obtain increased valuations. Dr. Wind has several books in publication, and I recommend his book *The Network Imperative* (2016).

Figure 1: Valuation Model from Jerry Wind

IP 3.4x	Network 8x
Product 1x	Service 2x

Summary of Chapter Two

This section provided some considerations for products and customers. Getting the product designed, manufactured, and shipped to you at a price that you can resell for a profit is critical. Packaging can be critical to both in-store sales and protection for efficient shipping.

You should be an expert on your customer, and the product should bring value to the customer's needs and desires. The product should be designed around the targeted customer. Your customers can come from B2C, B2B, and both types of transactions. The advantage of B2C is the potential for higher profit margins. B2B transactions have lower profit margins but are generally higher AOV and can experience reoccurring orders.

3

The Business Plan

"By failing to prepare you are preparing to fail."
—Benjamin Franklin

Whether you are starting a business or currently running a business, you need a detailed business plan. Ideally this plan should be updated annually. I write a brief at the end of each year highlighting the results of the performance, what worked and did not work, and what corrective action should be taken in the next year with key performance measurements (KPMs). This develops into an ongoing business plan.

A business plan takes some time to develop. But your business deserves the time to plan and hone your strategies. If you cannot take the time to write a business plan, you probably should not be in business. The reasons to write a business plan are many. Here is a partial list of what you should include:

- Identify the resources needed to execute the plan.
- Identify the key goals of the company.
- Identify key steps with timelines to achieve those goals.
- Identify potential risks and how to mitigate the risks.
- Identify key metrics to track company progress.

- Disclose to investors, potential investors, and/or bank managers the company path to success.

I hope you see that a business plan is necessary. Let's discuss the critical components of good business plan. Each of these components is discussed in the next section.

Executive Summary

The executive summary is the eye-catcher of the document. This section should be written last. Some people will read only the executive summary. Before you write this section, you should have thought through the entire document. The executive summary should highlight the business and provide a realistic perspective. Understand that if the executive summary is not compelling, the reader might not continue the business plan. Many high-level investors read the executive summary only to determine if the firm will carry out the due diligence to consider investing.

The executive summary should contain the company mission statement, a brief description of the marketplace you plan to enter, a summary of the products or services, and a brief description of the funds needs and projected return on the investment. A good executive summary is intriguing. A description of the functions of the company is needed. For example, if you plan to do most functions yourself, you need a brief description of the product development, operations, creative functions for marketing, and administrative functions. If you are outsourcing some of these functions, the summary should provide a brief discussion.

Your plan should include a brief history of your team's experience in relation to the business. Finally, the executive summary should provide the "ask." If you are using the plan to raise capital, the summary should explain. The plan could be used to organize your staff and align priorities. End the summary with the goal of the company.

Company Description

The company description section should summarize the solutions your company will provide to customers. It should describe the specific type of customer you will target. Understanding your customers is key to success. This section should leave the reader with reasons that customers would want to buy from your company.

Competitive Analysis and Competitive Advantage

The competitive analysis or market analysis section should detail the target market and the overall condition of your market. It should highlight your competition in the market and list the strengths of those companies. Provide a description of the strategies these competitors are currently undertaking. Demonstrate your knowledge of this market and list the current trends. Also, the description should discuss some of the strengths of your company, including experts on your team, a new innovation, or a secured ideal location.

Based on the competitive analysis framework, list your specific competitive advantage. The next chapter will go into detail from the current academic perspective and the professional business perspective. The competitive advantage is key because it discloses why customers will prefer your company over the competition. The competitive advantage highlights the reason you will succeed.

Products and Services Description

The products and services description should identify the specific products and services your company will provide. It should provide details about how you will manufacture your product, the supply chain and logistics, and the time necessary to produce or receive your produce. Key to this section is highlighting the reasons that customers will prefer these products. I prefer to list the reasons as bullet points.

This section should provide information about packaging and any advantages to your particular package design. A discussion of how you will ship your products to your customers should be included. Also, if your product has patent protection or some intellectual property component, a description should be included in this section. Included should be details about your product's tooling cost if required in the manufacturing process. All investments to get your product to the production mode, including design and engineering costs, should be discussed.

Details about total product costs should be provided in this section, including manufacturing cost, freight to you (freight in), and expected returns. These costs total to calculate your **product cost (PC)**. Next you should include a discussion of what you expect to charge your customer. This could include the cost of expected discounts or promotions. This calculation will provide the **sales revenue (SR)**. Use this calculation to obtain your **product profit margin (PPM)**.

$$PPM = 1 - (PC/SR)$$

The calculation is represented as a percentage. For example, if the cost of producing your product, or PC, is \$60, and you will sell it for \$100, your product profit margin is:

$$PPM = 1 - (\$60/\$100) \text{ or } 1- 60\% = PPM \text{ at } 40\%$$

This is just one component of your costs. You will have the cost of shipping to the customer. In some cases you will be able to charge for shipping to the customer. Customers are less willing to pay for shipping. But the cost of shipping using United Parcel Service (UPS), Federal Express, or the United States Postal Service (USPS) is not incidental. You must calculate this cost as part of your expenses. If you are able to charge for freight, the calculation for **Net Freight** is the Freight Revenue less the Freight Expense.

$$Net \ Freight = Freight \ Revenue - Freight \ Expense$$

If you are able to charge $9 for shipping for the $100 item and the Freight Expense is $10, the Net Freight is -$1. If you cannot charge for shipping, the Net Freight is -$10.

Marketing and Sales Plan

Every business will need a marketing and sales plan. You must detail how you will get your products and services noticed by customers. The marketing plan could include advertisements, flyers, trade show exhibits, and digital marketing. These marketing channels will be discussed in detail in chapter seven.

The business plan could also include a sales plan. Sales can be inbound, like a call center or a website. The plan should provide the details of either or both of these methods. The sales plan should be included, plus the related cost. The sales plan could consist of an outbound strategy that would include sales representatives who would connect with potential target customers. Also, some companies have a combination of inbound and outbound sales strategies. These efforts should work in concert in ideal conditions.

The marketing and sales plans should include a budget for the execution of the plans. This budget should tie back to the sale as the **cost of the sale (COS).** The COS is usually represented as a percentage of the sale. Going back to our example of the $100 sale, if the cost to market and obtain the sale is $20 on average, the calculation is represented by the following:

$$COS = \$20/\$100 = 20\%$$

In this example, with a product cost of $60, COS at $20, we are left with $20 to pay for operations, rent, and hopefully some profit.

Organizational Structure

The organizational structure of the business plan should include the corporate structure of the company and the organizational management structure. The corporate structure could be a C Corporation (C Corp), a Limited Liability Company (LLC), a Limited Liability Partnership (LLP), an S Corporation (S Corp), a Benefit Corporation (B Corp), or a 501(c)(3) Organization (Nonprofit). We will discuss these in chapter five.

This section should also include an organizational chart depicting the management responsibilities and chain of command. The organizational chart also displays how information flows within the company and decision-making responsibilities. Chapter five will also review organizational management structure options.

Financial Projections and Resources Needed

In a later chapter this book will provide a deeper dive into the financial requirements to properly operate a company today. For the business plan, if the company is in current operations, a summary of the financial performance of a historical income statement and cash flow by quarter is needed, along with an ending balance sheet of the company. These documents can be in the Supporting Documents section as an exhibit. Similar documents for financial projections and cash flow going forward for five years should be included. I like to use a 13-week projection for the quarters, breaking down the months in four-four-five week increments. The first two years of the projection should be the 13-week quarters, and the last three years of the projection can be shown quarterly.

If the business plan is also used to obtain a loan or investment money, the projections should show the cash infusion and the expected timing. Whether the projections are used to obtain a loan or investment or not, the projections should be tracked weekly to the actual performance of the company. This projection and the weekly tracking of performance can be used with your management team at weekly meetings to engage your team and to make adjustments.

Finally, if you're seeking outside money, you should organize a use-of-funds document. This is a general summary of what categories and amounts of the money that will be used. These types of categories include payroll, inventory, purchase of a production machine, and more. Lending organizations and investors do not want to be surprised about how you used the money. If you're seeking outside investment, the financial section should end with the ask of the amount of the investment needed or the increments of an investment. This section should also provide the timing of the needed funds.

Supporting Documents

The last section is made up of the supporting documents for the business plan. The financial projections section will have a summary of the projection. The supporting documents section would have more detail projections with detail for expenses and revenue. The supporting documents section could have a listing of intellectual property, including patents or patents pending. This section provides the reader with more detailed information and is displayed as exhibits. If you're raising a significant amount of money through investors, you should not do so without an attorney. This type of investment has many state laws that govern disclosures and who can even see your business plan. This type of plan then becomes a private placement memorandum (PPM). In most cases you will still write the plan, but there will be requirements that your attorney will provide that you must include in the PPM.

4

Your Competitive Advantage

"Always deliver more than expected."
— Larry Page, co-founder of Google

*"If you're going up against me, you'd better be willing to
give up your life—I'm giving up mine."*
—Tom Brady

Your competitive advantage is what distinguishes you from your competition. Managers select a strategy that was designed to create a competitive advantage based on the available resources of the organization (Gamble, Peteraf, & Thompson, 2019). The competitive advantage can be based on cost, differentiation, or focus (Gamble et al., 2019). A firm that outperforms competitors in the same business or industry has a competitive advantage (Rothaermel, 2017).

If you currently run a business or you plan to start a business, finding and managing your competitive advantage is your main job. First you have to identify your competitive advantage; then you have to use your time and resources to manage and capitalize on your competitive advantage. Business schools have developed several tools that have proven to help professionals identify a company's competitive advantage. These tools help you to focus on the advantage that you perceive to be the reason customers will come to you. The tools we will discuss are attributes of value, rarity, cost to imitate, and the organization's ability to capture value (VRIO); Porter's Five Forces; Porter's Generic Strategy; strengths, weaknesses, opportunities, and threats (SWOT); and the balanced scorecard (BSC). This section will discuss these tools and show you how to apply them to your business.

VRIO

The resource-based analysis used the attributes of VRIO framework (Rothaermel, 2017). A company can get to a sustainable competitive advantage only if it has the resources, capabilities, and competency organized to obtain or capture the value (Rothaermel, 2017). The VRIO decision tree examines the resource for the attributes of valuable, rare, costly to imitate, and then asks if the company is organized to capture the value (Rothaermel, 2017). The decision tree asks the question moving from left to right, and only if the answer to each of the questions is affirmative does the company have a competitive advantage. Any *no* answer negates a competitive advantage for the company.

Figure 2: VRIO Decision Tree

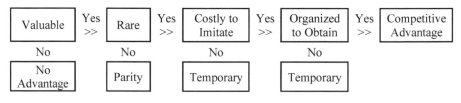

Rothaermel (2017, p. 113)

Look at the key products or services that attract customers and move through the decision tree to look for a competitive advantage. If you do not see that your product or service has a competitive advantage, then you have a problem. I see this decision tree as a way to find what you can do uniquely around a product or service. How can you stand out? If you cannot answer that question, you need to rethink your business.

Porter's Five Forces

Some think that Porter's Five Forces is the top theory used for the study of business strategy (Arslan & Wang, 2015). This model displays the impact of pressures from the buyer bargaining power, the pressures of substitute products, the supplier bargaining power, the pressures of new entrants into the market, and the rivalry among competing sellers (Gamble, Peteraf, & Thompson, 2019).

The competitive advantage is higher if the answers to the pressure are low. Porter also defined the quest for competitive advantage as either low-cost, broad differentiation, focused low-cost, focused differentiation, and best cost (Gamble et al., 2019). Porter also said that the competitive advantage should be based on cost, differentiation, or focus and that a blended or stuck-in-the-middle strategy would be a disadvantage (Gamble et al., 2019).

Table 1: Porter's Five Forces

Porter's Five Forces	Rating
1. The impact of pressures from the buyer bargaining power	Low/High
2. The pressures of substitute products	Low/High
3. The supplier bargaining power	Low/High
4. The pressures of new entrants into the market	Low/High
5. The rivalry among competing sellers	Low/High

Porter's Generic Strategy

Porter's Generic Strategic approaches define four different strategies, as shown in figure 3. The strategy to provide low cost to a broad market is strategy one in the diagram. The strategy to provide higher cost with differentiation is strategy two. The strategy to provide low cost to a narrow target market is strategy three A, and the strategy to provide differentiated products to a narrow market at a high cost is strategy three B. Porter suggested that an organization must select one of these strategies or else the strategy will be "stuck in the middle" and underperform (Porter, 1996, p. 68).

You do not want to be stuck in the middle, according to Porter. My favorite market is the broad market with a product of high cost and high margins with a differentiation. This market gives the best of all worlds in terms of potential customers, unique products, and high-profit margins. The number 2 is the best competitive advantage.

Figure 3: Porter's Generic Strategy

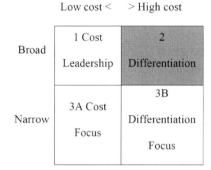

SWOT Analysis

Another important tool with which to examine the strategy of a company and the competitive advantage is that of the strengths, weaknesses, opportunities, and threats (SWOT). This tool was invented by the Harvard Business School in the 1960s (Al-Araki, 2013). In *Strategic Thinking for Decision Making*, Gamble, Peteraf, and Thompson (2019) said that managers should use SWOT analysis to examine the internal and external environments and develop new strategies to give a company a competitive advantage.

The SWOT analysis can help ascertain the company's current situation and develop a plan to capitalize on the strengths and opportunities (Gamble et al., 2019). Some say that SWOT is the best analysis tool to examine business strategy, and once implemented properly, the right directions emerge (Karatop, Kubat, & Uygun, 2018). These researchers said the SWOT model required the determination of the weights of criteria and sub-criteria from managers and stakeholders and that the weights become part of the decision-making process about strategy (Karatop et al., 2018).

Table 2: Example-Weighted SWOT Analysis

Internal Strengths	Impact	Probability	Score
Long-term profitability	0.15	1	0.15
No debt	0.1	2	0.2
Loyal customers	0.2	2	**0.4**
Operational competencies	0.1	2	0.2
Vender relationships	0.05	2	0.1
Internal Weaknesses			
Shrinking revenues	0.25	2	**0.5**
Company morale	0.15	3	**0.45**
Poor website	0.1	3	0.3
Customer base shrinking	0.1	2	0.2
External Opportunities			
New online customers	0.1	2	0.2
New products	0.15	3	**0.45**
Trade shows	0.05	2	0.1
Affiliate program	0.05	1	0.05
Amazon	0.25	3	**0.75**
External Threats			
Mature market	0.05	1	0.05
Online competition	0.1	2	0.2
Technology changes	0.05	3	**0.15**
Increasing cost of labor	0.05	2	0.1
Increasing cost of advertisement	0.05	2	0.1
Increasing cost of paper and mailing	0.1	2	0.2

The weighted SWOT provides estimates on the probability of the issue happening and the rating of the potential impact. The higher the number the more likely the event will happen and will have a greater impact on the organization and should receive a higher focus than lower numbers. To create a weighed SWOT, first create four categories that include Internal Strengths, Internal Weaknesses, External Opportunities, and External Threats. Think of the two Internal categories as together and the two External categories together. After creating the categories, list out areas that apply. In this case the Internal Strengths are long-term profitability, no debt, loyal customers, operational competencies, and vendor relations. Then list out the Internal Weaknesses. Next create an Impact rating for each line listed. This is the importance of the issues to the company. The total of each line of both the Internal Strengths and Internal Weakness should come to 1.

The next task is to rank the probability of this line to happen, with 3 being more likely than 1. List a probability rating for each line. The score of the line is the Impact Rating x Probability. The higher the score the more the employees and resources should focus attention. This attention should be spread proportionally for each line. Then repeat for External Opportunities and Threats.

There's only so much time in the day. Business owners do not have time to do everything, yet everything needs to be done. Moreover, the employees' time is a valuable resource for the company. This tool allows you to see and align activities and resources with your priorities. It allows your team to know your priorities and align their time and efforts accordingly.

Balanced Scorecard

Robert Kaplan and David Norton introduced the balanced scorecard (BSC) in 1992 in an article in the *Harvard Business Review*. The concept was designed to align employee activities and company resources with the company-designated business strategies (Kaplan & Norton, 1992). The BSC is great for managing employees' activities. However, the tool is also excellent for measuring competitive advantage.

The BSC is a widely used tool today to analyze a company's strategic and financial goals, to measure performance, and provide an overall organizational performance (Gamble et al., 2019). It is used to measure financial performance, customer engagement, internal organizational processes, and the capacity of the organization's learning and growth tendencies (Meredith & Scott, 2016).

Many think that the BSC as a strategic management tool connects the mission and organization's strategy while communicating it to develop the company into a learning organization (Quesado, Guzmán, & Rodrigues, 2018). We will discuss later the need to create a learning culture in your organization. Upon the implementation of the BSC, a company can more easily align actions and next steps of employees with the strategy to have actionable objectives to achieve the strategy (Quesado et al., 2018). Others see that the BSC is critical in evaluating the performance of the strategies in an uncertain environment and allowing companies to improve learning capabilities (Rasolofo & Distler, 2018).

The BSC is a widely used tool to analyze a company's strategic and financial goals, measure performance, and provide an overall organizational performance (Gamble et al., 2019). It is used to measure financial performance, customer engagement, internal organizational processes, and the capacity of the organization's learning and growth tendencies (Meredith & Scott, 2016). It also helps to align individual priorities with organizational goals, align strategy to resources, and is a continuous measurement of organizational and individual performance (Meredith & Scott, 2016).

To develop a BSC for your company, list the four Critical Success Factors (see table 3), which include the Financial Perspective, Customer Perspective, Internal Capabilities, and Learning and Growth. Then list the areas and issues that will help your company the most in these areas. List at least three per category. The in order to track these initiatives, list out the Measures for the goals to be achieved. The more numerical or specific the Measure the easier the Measure is to track. These initiatives are specific to your company and are a list of what you want to achieve and measure. Take the time to develop these initiatives and know that developing Key Performance Measurements (KPIs) will drive your employees' activities. Derive success measurements that you can track weekly, quarterly, and annually to compare against previous periods.

Table 3: Example of a Balanced Scorecard

Critical Success Factors		Measures
Financial Perspective		
Increase sales		Increase revenue by 10%
Keep product margin		Reduce margin by <2%
Inventory		**Improve Inv T/O ratio to 6**
Increase profit		**Increase EBIT to 9%**
Customer Perspective		
New products		Introduce 200 new products
Cosplay		**Build the Cosplay Customer Segment**
New market channels		**Amazon 2x each year, grow Walmart and HD**
Internal Capabilities		
New product Development		Resolve pandemic disruption
Time to receive process		**Reduce the time to receive to 1 day, FBA**
Website		Update new platform
Learning and Growth		
Manufacturing		Increase in-house manufacturing 10%
Employee skills		Increase cross-training
ERP skills		Continual improvement

Summary of Chapter Four

We discussed five tools that can help examine your company's competitive advantage. These tools should be tailored to your company's profile and goals. They include VRIO, Porter's Five Forces, Porter's Generic Strategy, weighted SWOT analysis, and BSC. Use these tools to identify your competitive advantage, set priorities, and align your employees' activities and the company's resources to your strategy.

5

Organizational Structure

"Hire character. Train skill."

—Peter Schutz

"We are what we repeatedly do. Excellence then is not an act but a habit."

—Aristotle

We will now examine the options for your company's legal structure and the organizational management structure. The company structure involves options for the legal structure of the organization. There are many options, including a sole proprietorship, a limited liability company (LLC), a limited partnership (LLP), an S subchapter Corporation (S Corp), a C Corporation (C Corp), a benefit company (B Corp), an employee stock ownership plan (ESOP), and a 501(c)(3) company (nonprofit).

This chapter will also discuss organizational management structures and the options for organizational charts. These management structures include the simple form, functional form, multi-divisional, and the matrix structure. Each of these structures will be discussed in this chapter.

Company Legal Structure

"Mission defines strategy; strategy defines structure."

—Peter Drucker

I am not a lawyer or an accountant, and this section is not to replace or to advise which legal structure you should create. Also, the state laws that govern these legal structures are different, and you should meet with an attorney and accountant in your state to get sound advice. That said, many entrepreneurs create a legal entity without consulting an attorney. Most legal structures are started by obtaining the proper forms from the IRS at www.irs.gov. The types of structures you can create under the IRS are sole prior proprietorships, partnerships, corporations, S corporations, and LLCs.

After registering with the IRS, then register within the state in which you choose to incorporate. Many companies incorporate in the state of Delaware because their state laws are favorable to corporate activities. Some incorporate within the state of the primary business or headquarters. Either way, you must pay state sales tax for the states in which those transactions take place. The next section examines several options for legal structures with the benefits and challenges of each.

Sole Proprietorship

According to the IRS (irs.gov, 2020), the sole proprietorship is the most common legal structure. A sole proprietor reports net income or loss from a business on the personal income tax return for both federal and state taxes. Sole proprietorships do not have employees. The company is unincorporated, and you are the sole owner of the company. There is no cost to create a sole proprietorship (irs.gov, 2020).

The downside is that a sole proprietorship does not provide liability protection. If your sole proprietorship is sued, you are personally liable in a case for damages, and your personal assets might be used to resolve it. If you chose the sole proprietorship route, you should create a "doing business as" (DBA) with your county clerk's office. This DBA prevents others from doing business under your DBA name in the county. Just as important, a DBA allows you to open bank accounts, apply for credit cards, open a PayPal account, obtain small business loans, and take advantage of other vital business services under your DBA name.

LLC

The limited liability company (LLC) is a separate business entity owned by investors who are designated as members. The entity is managed by the members or by hired managers. The LLC structure is a hybrid of a partnership and corporate structure that provides liability protection of the company over the actual investment of each member. Therefore, members are not personally liable for the debts of an LLC. Income is taxed directly to the members and is disclosed on the members' 1040 tax returns using IRS Form 1065 (irs.gov, 2020) and related state returns.

S Corp and C Corp

The S Corporation and C Corporation can be viewed together for comparison. Forming either, shareholders can receive capital stock for the investment of money, property, or both. Both entities must file taxes by submitting IRS Form 1120 (irs.gov, 2020). A C Corp is recognized as a separate taxpaying entity for tax purposes. A corporation conducts business, realizes net income or loss, pays taxes, and distributes profits to shareholders. The shareholders of a C Corp are in essence double taxed. The C Corp is taxed at the corporate rate, and the shareholders are taxed for returns at their individual rates. In opposition, shareholders in an S Corp are taxed only at the individual rate.

This is juxtaposed against some of the restrictions of an S Corp. An S Corp can have only 100 shareholders who are U.S citizens, and it is more difficult to transfer. An S Corp has only one kind of stock. Also, S Corps have more federal and state paperwork to remain compliant and seem to be more scrutinized by the IRS. C Corps have no restrictions to stock ownership and have an unlimited number of shareholders. So, if you're thinking big or want to sell your company in the future, a C Corp is the right vehicle. The double taxation is the biggest negative of a C Corp.

B Corp

"King Author Flour became a B Corp after 200 years of operations to thrive for the next 200 years."

—King Author's CEO

The B Corporation came out of the collision of hip-hop music, YouTube videos, and the retail demand for sports apparel. The company And1 was created by Jay Coen Gilbert and Bart Houlahan and their friend Andrew Kassoy, a Wall Street private equity investor (Honeyman & Jana, 2019). And1 used "street balling" videos to promote their products. The videos showed lightning-quick basketball handling with dunking to attract customers. You can see the videos today on YouTube by searching And1. What was also unique about And1 was that the company was socially responsible, using organic materials in the shoes, recycled tires, and great perks for the employees (Honeyman & Jana, 2019). And1 also gave five percent of its profits to local charities. Finally, And1 worked with overseas factories to improve the conditions and provide safety and fair wages (Honeyman & Jana, 2019). The company used novel techniques to attract customers and soon grew into the number-two United States basketball shoe brand by 2001, behind Nike (Honeyman & Jana, 2019).

Nike took notice, putting And1 in their crosshairs, and the company suffered. And1 was sold quickly, and the social impact was quickly stripped from the residual company. However, after considering several options, the same three founders of And1 created B Labs. B Labs would certify organizations to become certified B corporations based on certain criteria (Honeyman & Jana, 2019). B Corp certification is a thorough, third-party, sustainable business certification offered by B Lab, which is a global nonprofit business headquartered in southeastern Pennsylvania (www.bcorporation.net) (Ivanova, Maher, Marco, & Reinbold, 2018).

The crux of the B Corp definition is that the company is for-profit, has some benefit for the community, and some benefit for the environment. To execute this "triple bottom net," you would track profit, you would track some metrics to show measurement to improve the community, and you would track some metrics to improve the environment. Tracking profit is straightforward. Tracking improvement to the community could be hiring some number of ex-offenders who are transitioning. The improvement to the environment could be tracked by increasing some level of recycling that is tracked against the previous year. For a certified B Lab company, this tracked data is made public through the B Lab website to provide transparency.

Virtually any type of company can be certified by B Lab, including manufacturing firms, retail stores, consumer products, law firms, and marketing operations (Ivanova et al., 2018). The entire process takes about two years to complete certification, and the fees are based on the size of the company (Ivanova et al., 2018). Also, academic research shows that consumers are willing to pay a premium for products and services provided by B Corp (Ivanova et al., 2018).

You do not have to go through B Labs to be a B Corp today, although it is a good way to make sure you are operating properly and a great way to obtain transparency. Each state is slightly different. The steps are straightforward in New Jersey, however. Just go to www.benefit corp.net to get the forms you need to become a B Corp. Depending on your state, there are several tax benefits in a B Corp. Other reasons for becoming a B Corp include the ability to recruit talented people, giving back to the community, and retaining employees (Honeyman & Jana, 2019).

Table 4: Sampling of B Corps

Method	Kickstarter
Ben & Jerry's	Rhino Foods
Patagonia	Spotlight: Girls
Seventh Generation	Lunapads
New Belgium Brewing Co.	Fairphone
Beneficial State Bank	Divine Chocolate
BluPlanet	North Coast Brewing Co.
King Author Baking	DOMI Earth

While the B Corp movement started in the United States, this list in table 4 is of companies all over the world. They also represent many diverse types of businesses. Finally, the CEOs of these companies are from diverse races and cultures.

Columbia, Harvard, New York University, and Yale business schools offer loan forgiveness to MBA graduates who go to work for a Certified B Corporation or benefit corporation (Honeyman & Jana, 2019). You will be able to recruit top talent. Also, many high-wealth investors have moved to the B Corp because they can obtain a profit and do well.

ESOP

"Meanwhile, what about the workers in those state monopolies that are being put up for sale? I am reminded of a technique for employee ownership that has worked well for many U.S. companies. It goes by various names, but the best known is an ESOP."

—Ronald Reagan

The employee stock ownership plan (ESOP) is a plan that allows employees to buy stock in the company that the owner is selling (Hall,

2019). The most common scenario is a business transaction in which the business owner sees that selling the company to the employees is the best method to preserve the company's legacy, reward employees, and obtain tax benefits for succession purposes (Rosen & Rodrick, 2020)

An ESOP allows the company's contributions to pay for the buyout in an ESOP tax-deductible transaction (Hall, 2019). The contribution to the owner is pre-tax for the company, and the owner is not taxed if the contribution is reinvested in stocks or other similar investments. The tax advantage is to both the company, or the employees, and the seller/owner. The best part of the ESOP is that it offers an effective benefit plan for companies that wish to attract, motivate, and retain employees with ownership in the company.

The first ESOP was created by Louis O. Kelso, a San Francisco attorney and economist, in 1956 for Peninsula Newspapers Incorporated to allow the two aging owners to pass the company on to the employees (The Menke Group, n.d.). The Internal Revenue Service had for many years allow qualified ESOPs as a tool for business succession (The Menke Group, n.d.). Since Kelso's novel approach, many companies have become successful ESOPs. Chrysler Corporation and United Airlines became ESOPs over time (The Menke Group, n.d.).

Companies of different sizes have been successful ESOPs: Publix Super Markets, with 200,000 employees; Amsted Industries, with 18,000 employees; W. L. Gore and Associates, the maker of Gore-Tex, with 10,720 employees; and Davey Tree Expert Company, with 10,500 employees (National Center for Employee Ownership, n. d.). Many resources exist to help you consider and plan for an ESOP.

New Community Corporation (NCC), in Newark, New Jersey, is a Community Development Corporation (CDC) and a 501(c)(3) or nonprofit. NCC has an annual budget of $67 million and employs 600 local residents. The CDC manages 2,000 housing units, has roughly $500 million in assets, and owns businesses whose proceeds go toward underwriting such social programs as daycare and medical support for seniors. One of the elements that NCC focuses on is the community development of ESOPs in the Newark area.

According to NCC (Employee Stock, n.d.), ESOPs play a critical role in building community wealth for several key reasons. ESOPs help to stabilize the economic base of local communities with ownership of the company by employees who live in the community, and the firm is less likely to relocate. The structure also provides a mechanism for local owners to retire and liquidate the ownership while ensuring the business remains financially viable and rooted locally. ESOP companies are less likely to lay off workers and provide an opportunity for employees to accumulate wealth through stock ownership (Employee Stock, n.d.).

The ESOP structure is great for the local communities and provides a legacy for your ownership. It is a more complicated structure and requires legal advice and generally a trustee to manage.

Nonprofit

"What we have done for ourselves alone dies
with us; what we have done for others and the
world remains and is immortal."

—Albert Pike, American author

Depending upon your goals, a nonprofit structure is an option. You could receive a salary in a nonprofit while supporting a cause that could be religious, community-oriented, supportive of a historical issue, or some other cause. To be a nonprofit, you would need to register federally as a 501(c)(3) with the IRS at https://www.irs.gov/charities-non-profits/application-for-recognition-of-exemption. Once approved, you have to register at the state level. Usually, you have to state your mission. Once you have a federal and state 501(c)(3) identification, you can operate.

The benefit of a 501(c)(3) is that your company is exempt from taxes. The company does not have to pay federal income, state income, or state sales tax. Any donations to your company are tax-deductible by the donor. Any product your company sells does not include sales tax. However, you must disclose how much of your income is spent directly on the direct cause you support. Most donors want to see a significant amount of your nonprofit revenue go toward the cause. The nonprofit, if you can balance the revenue to cause promotion, might be a consideration for your structure.

I was hired by a nonprofit as a consultant to examine alternative revenue sources for the future. The company was the Pennsylvania Horticultural Society (PHS), a company with a long history. The society started in 1827 with a mission to promote the appreciation, science, and distribution of information about plants. The society had a multi-million-dollar annual budget and a large staff. The main fundraiser was the annual flower show in Philadelphia. The show's performance had declined each year and the donors were giving less each year, not unlike the experience of many other nonprofits nowadays.

My task was to examine the PHS resources and design a path to alternative sources of revenue. The PHS staff were intelligent but lacked business acumen. In fact, the discussion of how to make money was not a priority. However, all nonprofits need to acquire the resources to operate in order to survive.

I found out by searching in the PHS library that the foundation of the society had a lot to do with apple production in the Philadelphia area and apples were a part of the flower show for many of the early years. PHS even previously held the flower show in in the fall during apple harvesting season. Also, the archives showed recipes for making hard cider. I make cider, so I tried the recipe and found that the cider was less sweet than the traditional ciders on the market. I also found a nearby cider maker to make the recipe, and we designed a label for it.

The idea was for PHS to make a percentage on each cider sale and to promote that cider and all the PHS events, which were numerous. Also, PHS could promote the history of the cider throughout the year and get earned press for the media content. The cider manufacturer would profit from the cider, and the PHS cider would pull the other lines of products offered.

We went into production and introduced it at the 2015 flower Show with great fanfare and widespread publicity. Stores and bars started requesting the PHS cider. Unfortunately, PHS did not do much promoting after the flower show. The culture of the nonprofit did not recognize that this cider was a year-round revenue stream. The PHS organizational culture required event-oriented processes. Good idea, bad execution.

PHS Horticultural Cider

The truth is that nonprofits have to think about how they will acquire resources in a sustainable manner. This may be unnatural to someone who wants to work for a good cause. Capitalism might appear to be unseemly. I immediately connected with Rev. Dr. Sidney S. Williams Jr.'s book *Fishing Differently* (2018). Rev. Dr. Williams's background with a Wharton MBA and Wall Street experience combined with his experience as a minister has created a novel approach for the many ministries that are suffering financially today. He brings some much-needed old-fashioned community network together and some entrepreneurial premises to the nonprofits.

I serve on Rev. Dr. Williams's community development corporation in New Jersey called Spring Street CDC, found at https://springstreetcdc. org. I see firsthand the practice of his teachings with the assembly of a diverse and talented board of directors engaged with the concerns of those in need and those who serve. Rev. Dr. Williams also founded Crossing Capital, a consulting company that helps judicatories, seminaries, and established congregations to access multiple sources of capital through capital stewardship training and coaching experiences. You can see his services at https://crossingcapitalgroup.com.

This section covered the options for your legal structure. This is an early decision that you make in a startup but can also be reconsidered as you grow; you may find that a different structure is needed, and you can change to a new legal structure.

Organizational Management Structures

The reason we need to discuss organizational management structure options is that the right structure will help to align the organization's strategy and employee activities. Organizational structures are critical to the success and execution of a company's strategy. The decision about a company's organizational structure should consider information flow through the company to reduce uncertainty in decision-making and the coordination of integration (Duncan, 1979, p. 60). You should consider the state of the business, including internal and external influences, before determining the proper structure. The selection of the proper structure will greatly enhance the chances of your success, while the wrong selection will result in failure. Moreover, because of the importance of the structure strategy relationship, new structures are constantly being created because of new influences (Miles, Snow, Fjeldstad, Miles, & Lettl, 2010). A firm can consider different structure based on the goals and the organization's complexity. Some think that the organizational structures should change as the organization matures, going from simple to functional to multi-divisional, as represented below (Rothaermel, 2017).

Figure 4: Organizational Structure Evolution

| Simple | >>> | Functional | >>> | Multi-Divisional |

We will examine each of these three structures in figure 4 and also discuss another form that I believe is not related to the maturity of the company, the matrix structure.

Simple Structure

A simple structure is used in the early stages of a company's life cycle. Decisions are made by the founders, and the structure is less formal and departments are not specialized (Rothaermel, 2017). In my experience in founding two companies, the structure of the company is not given much consideration in a startup, but the decision to transition to an improved structure is critical as the company matures. However, many founders cannot give up decision-making control, and the company is unable to grow due to the structure. The simple structure is limited by the small group of decision-makers and is not scalable.

An example of a simple structure was the beginning of Amazon, when Jeff Bezos set up the business in his garage in Belleview, Washington. Other companies that started in a garage with simple structures before maturing to more complicated structures include Google, Apple, Mattel, and The Walt Disney Company. Mark Zuckerberg started Facebook in his dorm room.

Functional Structure

A natural progression as a company matures and becomes more complex is to move to a functional structure. A functional structure divides the employees into functional departments based on expertise (Rothaermel, 2017). The functional organizational structure, or U-form (unitary), first appeared at the beginning of the 19th century with the growth of the steel industry and consists of segmented departments based on the function of each department (Miles, Snow, Fjeldstad, Miles, and Lettl, 2010). These groups typically include accounting, human resources, operations, product development, and more. Each department reports to the CEO, who coordinates the work overlap.

The goal of the functional organizational structure is efficiency. Frederick Winslow Taylor pioneered scientific management, which stated that a focus on narrow tasks would provide efficiencies and produce more output with less input (Daft, 2016). The concept provided improvements in output in the railroad and steel industry initially and quickly spread into most forms of business organization.

Scientific management and functional organizational structure were used by Henry Ford's auto manufacturing company (Miles et al., 2010). Ford's assembly line was a classic functional design with labors performing repetitive jobs to each automobile traversing down the assembly line. The success of Ford highlights the value of a functional organization historically.

At Microsoft, chief executive officer (CEO) Steve Ballmer decided to reorganize from a divisionally structured organization to a functionally structured organization (Dhillon & Gupta, 2015). Microsoft named this new functional structure "One Microsoft" and planned to improve performance and deliver growth with a single strategy as one company and not a collection of divisional strategies (Dhillon & Gupta, 2015).

Figure 5: Functional Structure Organizational Chart

The strength of the functional structure is that the departments can benefit from specialization because employees focus on specific departmental functions to obtain economies of scale. But in a rapidly changing business environment, communication and information do not typically flow well between departments (Rothaermel, 2017). A functional organization structure is slow to react to internal and external influences or changes. The structure is less innovative because information flow between departments is slow and there is little feedback.

Multi-Divisional Structure

The multi-divisional structure, or M-form, was introduced by Alfred Sloan, the CEO of General Motors (GM), after the purchase of a new division in the 1920s (Miles, Snow, Fjeldstad, Miles, & Lettl, 2010). The concept was that each division of GM focused on the production and needs of the division while sharing market and technological information across divisions. This was to enable information flow and provide feedback to maximize innovation in the organization. Divisional managers were allowed to make decisions and were more autonomous.

The multi-divisional organization has the ability to respond rapidly to an unstable business environment, puts customer satisfaction as a focus, and allows divisions to change based on customer needs (Daft, 2016). The downside is that the divisions have duplication of functions, and therefore the organization loses economies of scale, and the depth of knowledge of departments makes it less attractive for a low-cost strategy.

Figure 6: M-Form Organizational Chart

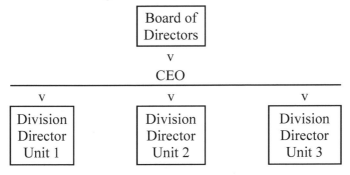

While the divisional organizational structure has lasted for many decades, companies are newly adopting the structure today. One example is Sony. Sony lost the digital music player business to Apple (Daft, 2016). Because the company was trailing behind the financial performance of Google and Apple, Sony recently restructured to a collaborative divisional structure and defined three core businesses as digital imaging, games, and mobile (Dhillon & Gupta, 2015). The key to the success of the divisional structure is the collaborative nature of the divisions.

As shown in the chart in figure 6, the CEO has unique business units. One unit might be selling to resellers and another to consumers. Each business unit would have a different marketing team, sales team, and accounting staff. I had this structure while at J&P and Park Seed as shown in the below figure.

Figure 7: J&P and Park Seed Organizational Chart

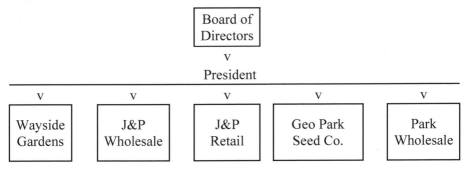

The benefit of this structure is that each division can focus on a specific customer and brand. Each brand is different, and each customer base is different. The downside of this structure is the overlap of accounting, marketing, and purchasing for each unit. It does not allow for economies of scale.

Many years ago, I was hired as the president of Geo Park Seed Company to financially turn around a company that had lost money for 15 years. The company had flourished as a direct-to-consumer catalog company during the 1980s but started losing money in 1990. The culture was a family-run business, or simple structure, with all decisions running through the owner. This structure worked well during times that the owner was competent but failed under the third-generation owners.

Also, the catalog industry had changed with the advent of the Internet, and the company had not adjusted to the new marketing channel. The process for new product development, creative development, and photography were driven by the catalog process, which was slow and inadequate for the fast pace of Internet marketing. The culture was a family environment with groupthink and little creativity. The values were to follow the processes of the past and to keep quiet since other managers were fired for speaking out in the past. Portraits of previous presidents of the company hung on the walls and were the artifacts of the company. The common saying "We've always done it that way" was practically adhered to.

The managers were not informed of the financial crisis in the company as information was not shared within the organization. Consequently, managers did not talk to each other and held on to information as a source of power. Rumors and distrust were rampant, and cliques of managers made employees chose sides. The company was paralyzed by culture and strategy, and consequently the organization lost the competitive advantage and market share. Moreover, with over 500 employees the company was on the verge of collapse, and yet the culture resisted any change.

We were able to set new values, goals, and norms and change the culture while moving to a strategy to keep the catalog customers while converting the majority of the marketing to the Internet channel. The strategy required improved and more rapid information flow that coordinated marketing and new product development to introduce new products and launch new marketing initiatives in a much more rapid manner. The structure moved to a matrix structure and the success of the change in strategy and culture created acceptance by managers and the company finally saw financial success. Moving from an M-Form organizational structure to a matrix structure was part of the improvement.

Matrix Structure

In the 1960s John Mea argued that functional organizational structures might not be suitable for companies that pursue multiple projects, and managers could report to two supervisors and a matrix structure might be a better fit (Pitts & Daniels, 1984). Sometimes an organization has multiple areas that need to be emphasized. These areas could be product-oriented, combined with functional or geographical influences. The matrix structure supports multiple project focus with horizontal and vertical linkages and reporting (Daft, 2016). Matrix organizations are complex by nature, and a balance between emphases creates a dual hierarchy for employees to balance.

Matrix organization structures have several decades of existence with mixed results. By 1979 Citibank and Boeing were two companies that had implemented the matrix structure (Duncan, 1979). Also, in the late 1970s Texas Instruments moved to a matrix structure to capitalize on fast-changing technologies to deliver new products and services while still utilizing upstream capabilities. The company combined multiple departments to utilize the fast-developing research and development

(R&D) using the benefits of the function structure and the benefits of the divisional structure (Miles et al., 2010).

A company that changed to a matrix structure recently is Bayer CropSciences (BCS) in their Global Public and Governmental Affairs (GPGA) department. In 2013 BCS hired Lisa Cohen to run their GPGA, which was organized geographically but had poor communication. The company also had poorly aligned goals, priorities, strategies, and roles. Cohen created matrix structures that allow information flow to go in multiple directions as opposed to the downward flow of information (Townsend, Coen, & Watson, 2017). The company moved from a hierarchal formal functional structure to a network and collaborative environment, and the performance improved considerably through listening to key stakeholders and using networking tools.

The matrix structure combines the functional structure with the M-form structure to get the benefits of each, including responsiveness, decentralization, domain expertise, economies of scale, and improved information sharing (Rothaermel, 2017). The matrix structure is good for a quickly changing environment, using R&D discoveries quickly, product development, and nimble or smaller companies. Information is shared horizontally and vertically across departments.

The strength of the matrix structure is that it is good for a company with multiple goals and scarce resources. However, employees must report to a product manager (horizontal) and a functional manager (vertical) (Daft, 2016). Employees can be conflicted between managers' requests, and managers can feel slighted if the employee does not prioritize directives. Therefore, managers and employees must be made aware of the company's priorities.

Figure 8: Matrix Organizational Chart

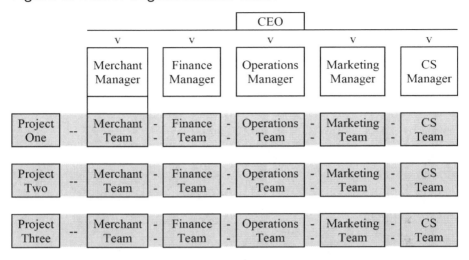

The matrix organization organizes members from needed departments to work within projects or tasks. Some team members can be on multiple projects. The goal is to put teams together that give the best chance of success. The department managers and project managers must coordinate because team members answer to both managers. Communication and consideration are critical components to allow the matrix organizational structure to work effectively and efficiently.

Jeff Bezos uses a form of the matrix organization. Amazon teams are no larger than what two pizzas can feed, or around six employees, to keep the teams nimble and able to make quick decisions (Galetti et al., 2019; Bezos, 2018). This structure provides rapid improved innovation for Amazon.

Virtual Networks and Outsourcing

Outsourcing is contracting with outside companies to perform a task or function. Virtually any task or process can be outsourced. It allows a company to reduce employee headcount and the related risk of labor and pass the expense and risk to a third party. The cost of outsourcing can be higher or lower, depending on the function. The cost can be lower if the third party is specialized and more efficient. The cost can be higher because of a third party's need for profit. Third parties can manage the functions of an organization with minimal oversight and can be outcome-based. Therefore, managers can focus on narrow and core issues.

Virtual network structures are managed by a small unit or headquarters that contracts all functions that were traditionally performed internally via outsourcing (Ontiveros, 2017). All the functions are connected electronically, and the outsourced units communicate from remote locations. Outsourced contractors can come and go based on need, and new contractors can be hired to address new issues or problems rapidly.

The modular nature of virtual networks creates increased flexibility that enables the headquarters to manipulate components quickly and efficiently (Schilling & Steensma, 2001). These networks allow a company to meet unstable demand spikes without a commitment to long-term contracts. Virtual network structures can scale and downsize quickly in reaction to the market.

Summary of Organizational Management Structures

Organizations can have numerous strategies depending upon the core competencies and external business environment. Some research suggested that companies fail because of the requisite organizational theory, which states that nearly all organizations fail due to selecting the wrong organizational structure and not due to actions of the employees (White & Ivanov, 2017). Therefore, selecting the organizational structure to align with the organization's strategy is critical. I don't know if I buy into that theory wholly because good people can overcome difficult situations. However, I do believe that the type of organizational structure can create walls to slow communication and ideas.

In the early years of development or startup, the use of a simple structure can make sense. If your company's strategy is cost leadership, differentiation, or the combination of the two, a functional strategy is adequate to capitalize on economies of scale and/or product innovation (Rothaermel, 2017). If your strategy is to offer numerous unrelated products, you could select the M-Form structures to allow decentralized decision-making and competition among business units. If you offer numerous related products, the firm could also operate as an M-Form with centralized decision-making and cooperation among business units (Rothaermel, 2017). If you are small, have limited resources, and are in a rapidly changing business environment, a matrix structure is a good selection.

If you plan to do business internationally, you should consider your organizational structure options. If you have a global strategy, the selection should be functional. For multi-domestic, you *should* consider the M-Form. For global standardization you should use the M-form. For transnational you should consider the matrix structure (Rothaermel, 2017). Ultimately, you should look at the structure options, including the benefits and disadvantages. Then look at your market, team, and strategy. Your organizational structure selection should best fit your organization's profile. The pros and cons are laid out in the graph below.

Table 5: Pros & Cons of Organizational Management Structures

	Pros	Cons
Functional	traditional specialization economies of scale	not the best for innovation many different outputs
Multi-Divisional	good for customer satisfaction good for numerous products	duplication of tasks for large companies
Matrix	meets multiple needs economies of scale good for new product development	dual hierarchy employee time wasted
Virtual Network & Outsourcing	scalable flexible fewer employee issues	loss of control can be expensive

Summary of Organizational Structures

In this chapter we covered organizational structure options, including company legal structure options and organizational management structure options. The legal structure should include how you want the ownership of the company to be distributed, the liability protection, taxes, and the number of shareholders.

The organizational management structure is how the company is organized in an organizational flow chart. The simple structure is commonly used when a company is in a startup with few employees and most decisions made by the boss or CEO. The next step up is a functional structure, which is divided by departments that handle particular company functions that answer to the CEO. The multi-divisional organizational structure has independent functional business units that can operate separately and answer to the CEO. The matrix organizational structure assembles teams of individuals from different departments to focus on a particular project or task.

6

The Guarantee

"The U.S. Constitution does not guarantee happiness, only the pursuit of it. You have to catch up with it yourself."
—Benjamin Franklin

The guarantee is a critical decision. In a start up company, the customers do not know you or your product. They have concerns about the risk of purchase. The guarantee is a disclosed settlement of the risk and allows the customer to be more comfortable with the risk. However, some customers unfortunately will take advantage of you with an unlimited blanket guarantee. Sometimes an existing company has to reconsider the guarantee. The guarantee should consider the areas listed below.

Table 6: Guarantee Considerations

1. Build trust with the customer.
2. Improve the customer experience.
3. Be competitive with your competition.
4. Consider the type of product.

We will discuss several options to consider for your guarantee, including the refund guarantee, the replacement guarantee, the best-price guarantee, the lifetime guarantee, and the free-trial guarantee. Each of these has benefits and costs and will hit your profit and loss statement differently.

Refund Guarantee and Replacement Guarantee

You can use a refund guarantee or a replacement guarantee or both. If you use both, you should let the customer decide if he or she prefers a refund or a replacement. Also, this type of guarantee usually comes with a time limit of 30 to 90 days. More expensive products might have a longer time limit because the customer risk consideration is greater. Below is my company's guarantee, which is posted on our website and in our catalog:

> *Micro-Mark's Guarantee: Satisfaction Guaranteed. We hope you will be completely satisfied with your order. But if an item does not meet your expectations, you may return it in as-new condition within 30 days of delivery for a replacement, exchange, or refund of the purchase price.*

Micro-Mark is not a new company, and the mother company, Scientific Models, has operated for 93 years. Micro-Mark's experience with returns or refunds is low by industry standards. One reason is that the products we sell are of higher quality than some others sold in the industry. Our customers can find less expensive tools and supplies but at a lower quality level.

If a customer wants a refund, this transaction should show as a reduction to revenue. If the customer wants a replacement, the cost of the replacement should increase your cost of goods. The cost of shipping the replacement to the customer should increase your shipping cost and reduce your net freight summary.

Best-Price Guarantee

Another type of guarantee is the best-price guarantee. Priceline.com provides customers who book trips this guarantee:

WE GUARANTEE THE LOWEST PRICE

See a better deal? We'll refund the difference if you find a lower price within twenty-four hours of booking. ***(Priceline. com, 2020)***

Expedia.com, one of Priceline.com's competitors, provides this guarantee:

1. *See if your booking qualifies Not all bookings qualify. See below for details.*
2. *Tell us about the lower price We'll need a screenshot and the URL of the page.*
3. *We refund you the difference It's that easy. If your claim is eligible, you'll receive a refund. (Expedia.com, 2020)*

The two competing companies have slightly different guarantees. Both provide a quick refund with exceptions. Priceline.com asks that you disclose where the better price is located online, and they will confirm before refunding. Expedia.com requires a screenshot of the better price.

Some research indicates that only very large companies can offer the low-price guarantee (Mamadehussene, 2019). A business with this offer sends a strong signal of confidence to consumers, and many of the customers do not conduct a post-purchase price search (Mamadehussene, 2019). One note of caution about this type of guarantee is that you cannot control how your competition will price similar products. The price wars can inflict damage, especially to small businesses.

Lifetime Guarantee

Some companies provide a lifetime guarantee. Patagonia provides what is essentially a lifetime guarantee without calling it that:

Patagonia's Ironclad Guarantee

*We guarantee everything we make. If you are not satisfied with one of our products at the time you receive it, or if one of our products does not perform to your satisfaction, return it to the store you bought it from or to Patagonia for a repair, replacement, or refund. Damage due to wear and tear will be repaired at a reasonable charge. **(Patagonia.com, 2020)***

L.L. Bean once had a lifetime guarantee. Many customers were returning L.L.Bean's products that were decades old, and the company had to end its lifetime guarantee and changed it in 2018 to a one-year guarantee. The lifetime guarantee is an accounting nightmare. A lifetime guarantee must book some liability pending based on the amount of product still under warranty. This booked amount is based on the return experience, which might change over time.

Free-Trial Guarantee

The free-trial guarantee allows customers to experience the product or service for some time before committing and paying. These companies usually provide a service at a lost cost. Match.com is a company that allows the user to have free access to the site for three days by providing a valid credit card. The trial converts to a subscription unless the customer cancels the subscription.

We have reviewed some of the options for the guarantee. The goal is to reduce the perceived customer's risk at a reasonable cost. You also have to keep your competition in mind. Internet fashionwear companies know that many customers will return at higher rates than other business types. Amazon's guarantee is one-sided to the consumer. Amazon has set the bar low for customers who want a refund. In some cases, these customers are taking advantage of third-party sellers. Amazon return rates will be higher than those of other market channels for your company.

Find a guarantee the works for you. Track the returns and refunds to examine the costs. Look at your competition's guarantee and return policies. Tweak your guarantee to provide trust for your customer without giving away too much to make a profit.

---7---

Financing Options

"Stay self-funded as long as possible."
—Garrett Camp, founder of Expa, Uber, and StumbleUpon

"Don't worry about funding if you don't need it.
Today it's cheaper to start a business than ever."
—Noah Everett, founder of Twitpic

This chapter will discuss funding sourcing and financial performance tracking. Let's put the cart before the horse before estimating how much money you might need and discuss the options you have for funding. After we discuss those options, we will discuss how to prepare financial reports, projections, and implement tracking. The projections will provide the basis for the funds needed and the timing of the funds needed. Finally, we will show you how to track your 13-week cash flow.

Sources of Funding

There are many sources of funding you can consider depending upon the funds needed. These include bootstrapping, crowdfunding, loans, friends and family, angel investment, and venture capital.

Bootstrapping. Scraping together enough funds through your savings or other sources is called bootstrapping. You can do this by working full time or parttime and using some of the money to start your operation. You do not have to start big. Starting small is not bad. No matter how much you know about the business you will enter, you will learn a lot from bootstrapping. You might even learn more. Moreover, you will not waste as much money while learning.

It's really hard to take enough money out of the business for you to make a living. If you do, you will need more money. And that money will be expensive because it will come from a loan or from stock. The stock seems fine when you start, but if you somehow become successful, you will wish you had that stock. Money that is invested in a startup usually comes at a great cost because of the risk to the investor.

Many companies have successfully started by bootstrapping. Some examples include Dell Computers, Facebook, Apple, Oracle, and eBay. Many people do not want to bootstrap because they want it now. If you can force yourself to work through the hard times of bootstrapping, you'll learn what you do not know and will save yourself a lot of money.

Crowdfunding. Crowdfunding has proven to be a good method to get funding. There are many success stories of companies that have used Kickstarter, Indiegogo, Crowdfunder, and many more crowdfunding websites to connect with like-mined consumers to buy your product. A couple of things to consider: You can obtain small amounts of donations or investments in your company in exchange for your future product. You do not get the money unless you are fully funded. Also, if you cannot come through with the product you promised, you might face legal issues.

The key to success with crowdfunding is to have a great story and to convey that story. A compelling story about your product is key. It should be told well on your website and through digital public relations. If you have a good story, the crowdfunding solution is good because you can see the popularity of your product to individuals interested in it.

Some companies that were successful in crowdfunding include Glowforge, a company selling a laser-cutting machine that raised over $27 million in crowdsourcing. Tile, the company with the square that attaches to your keys or other items to locate them, raised $200,000 in 24 hours on Kickstarter. BauBau, the company with a versatile travel jacket, raised $9.2 million on Kickstarter and followed with $2.3 million from Indiegogo.

Loans. If you have some history of business, you could apply for a loan through the Small Business Association (SBA) or a local bank. To do so, you would need to show two years of financial statements that include a profit-and-loss statement, balance sheet, cash flow statement, and supporting bank statements. Your personal credit would also be checked, and you would need a score of at least 640 or more. If you turn in everything correctly in an SBA loan or a local bank loan, it should take about 60 days to close on the loan. Also, you would have to personally guarantee the loan. That means that you would still be liable for the loan regardless of the legal structure of your organization.

Friends and Family. The friends-and-family option might not be available to everyone. Also, this option has caused much tribulation within families. These arrangements are not unusual, but they usually do not memorialize the arrangement, and if it goes bad, each party has their own version of the story.

Friends and family can be a loan or an investment in stock, or both. How to evaluate the value of the stock can be hard in the early stages of the company. At the very basic level, you should have a term sheet the clarifies the investment or loan and the expected return, plus the timing. There should be contingencies if the loan cannot be paid back on time. While this form of funding might seem favorable, please note that combining friends and family with business can end in separation and disruption.

Angel Investors. Another source of investing is angel investment capital. This option has legal constriction that must be adhered to. For example, angel investors must show to be sophisticated investors with a net worth exceeding $1 million or annual income over $200,000. To obtain angel investment, you should create a private placement memorandum (PPM). This document should be review by an investment attorney to be compliant. A PPM is an inclusive document that takes some time to develop. You can find angel investors in several places, including your local chamber of commerce, your economic development association, and the Angel Capital Association (https://www.angelcapitalassociation. org), who connect investors interested in particular segments with like companies.

Venture Capital. Venture capital (VC) consists of full-time investors in particular market segments. They are sophisticated investors who can provide insight into the market segment and competition. They expect a significant return on investment and will likely be involved in the operations of the company. Also, VCs will have terms that can be onerous to you, and you will lose authority and control. However, if you can obtain a VC investment, you are likely on to something pretty good. Also, their expertise will help you along the way.

Summary of Funding Sources

We have discussed several sources of funding and all of them have pros and cons. Some of this decision is a lifestyle choice. If you want to do things your way, then just bootstrap. Obviously as we move from bootstrapping to VC you lose more and more control. The light at the end of the tunnel is that if you are successful, you have the best chance of more control.

Many companies use multiple methods as they evolve. They start out with bootstrapping and then obtaining a loan after experiencing the learning curve. They could later obtain angel investors before receiving VC investments. Each of these levels of investments requires an incrementally higher level of your expertise to get the loan or investment. Also, not obtaining loans that add risk to your business or investments that dilute your ownership is a good way to go if you can. Using your profits to invest back into the business will lower the business risk and maintain your equity in the company. In the next section we will discuss financial documents and how to use them to manage your business.

Financial Statements

Anything that is measured and watched improves.

— Bob Parsons, founder of GoDaddy

The founder of modern accounting was Luca Pacioli, an Italian monk who wrote the 615-page mathematical compendium *Summa de Arithmetica Geometria Proportioni et Proportionalita*, published in 1494, and provided the foundation of accounting today (Sangster & Scataglinibelghitar, 2010). Pacioli is also known for his friendship with Leonardo de Vinci (Sangster & Scataglinibelghitar, 2010). The key invention that Pacioli provided was the double entry in the accounting ledger (Sangster & Scataglinibelghitar, 2010). This novel entry method to the common ledger is the basis of our accounting today. In the double-entry method, every transaction has a debit and credit that is entered for the account.

Table 7: Double-Entry Register Example

A	Inventory	$100.00	
	Cash		$100.00
B	Inventory		$100.00
	COG	$100.00	
	Acct Receivable	$150.00	
	Revenue		$150.00

Transaction A is the purchase of inventory for $100.00. Inventory is debited $100.00, and you paid $100.00, so your cash account is credited. Then transaction B happens, and you sell the inventory item for $150.00. The inventory account is credited, and the cost of goods (COG) account is debited. Additionally, the accounts receivable is debited and the revenue account is credited. The inventory item is no longer in your possession, so you relieve the inventory and add to the COG, which is the account that tracks the cost of the inventory sold. You also record the sale by crediting the revenue account and debit the accounts receivable account until you get paid. The double-entry method, with debit and credit accounts that fall into different categories, is the backbone of the financial statements, which are the balance sheet, the income statement, or profit and loss (P&L), and the statement of cash flows. Today in the United States, businesses are governed by generally accepted accounting practices (GAAP), which is the standard that the U.S. Securities and Exchange Commission (SEC) uses. We will discuss these three statements and how they work together to help you manage your business.

Accounting Period

The decision of the timing of the financial statements is called the accounting period. You have to decide the period. One option is the calendar month, starting on the first and ending on the last day of the month. You could start January 1 and the first quarter would end March 31, and the year would end December 31. This is simple and easy to remember. However, these dates start and end on different days of the year each year, which can cause some inconsistencies with year-on-year comparisons.

Another option is to start the weeks on Sunday and end them on Saturday. Then keep the quarters at four weeks the first and second months with the last month of the quarter as five weeks. This is called the 4-4-5, making four 13-week quarters for the year. The benefit of this type of accounting period is that the week-on-week comparisons to the previous year are more consistent. To some this accounting period is strange because sometimes you start or end an accounting period year in a different actual calendar year.

You can also start your annual accounting period at the beginning of any quarter. Some companies start their accounting periods at the beginning of July because of the seasonality of their businesses. With any of these options you should stay consistent once you chose. However, the IRS will allow you to change accounting periods if you want to, but it is a big hassle. The accounting periods set the base for the time periods to be examined in the balance sheet, the income statement, and the statement of cash flow.

Balance Sheet

The balance sheet is a statement at a specific time of the assets and liabilities. The assets are divided between current assets and non-current assets. Current assets are those that can quickly be used like cash, accounts receivable that will be paid within one year, and inventory. Non-current assets are property, vehicles, and other assets that you will not convert to cash anytime soon.

Liabilities are also divided between current and non-current.

Current liabilities are liabilities that are due within one year, like accounts payable, loan payments that are due within a year. Non-current liabilities are those that are not due within a year. The equity section of the balance sheet tracks the investment and the value of the shareholders' stock balanced to the difference of the assets to the liabilities. To get U.S. GAAP information on the balance sheet, go to https://financialaccountingreview. com/us-gaap-far/2120-balance-sheet.htm. An example of a balance sheet is found in table 8.

The simple math on a balance sheet is Assets – Liabilities = Equity. The sheets show that balance between the assets, and the liabilities and the difference are the shareholders' or owners' equity. This representation is shown below in table 8. The current assets less the current liabilities show the liquidity of the company. In other words, if the company hit hard times, could it survive on the difference between the current assets and the current liabilities?

In the example balance sheet in table 8, the total assets less the total liabilities equal the shareholder equity. The balance sheet can be used to examine several things. One is the liquidity of the company using current assets less the current liabilities. In other words, as noted in the previous paragraph, if the company hit hard times, could it survive on the difference between the current assets and the current liabilities? Several different equations can be used to examine your liquidity.

Table 8: Balance Sheet Example

Assets		
Current Assets		
	Cash	$20,000
	Accounts receivable	$10,000
	Inventory	$10,000
Fixed Assets		
	Office property	$100,000
	Vehicles	$20,000
Total Assets		**$160,000**
Liabilities		
Current Liabilities		
	Accounts payable	$10,000
	Short-term loan payments	$20,000
Long-Term Liabilities		
	Mortgage payments	$60,000
	Vehicle loans	$5,000
Total Liabilities		**$90,000**
Equity		
Shareholder Equity		**$70,000**

Here are some of the formulas that banks and investors use to examine your liquidity:

Current Ratio = *Current Assets/Current Liabilities = $40,000/$30,000 or 1.33; the greater number the better the liquidity.*

Quick Ratio = *(Current Assets – Inventory)/Current Liabilities = $30,000/$30,000 or 1.0; the greater number the better the liquidity.*

Debt to Equity = *Long-Term Liabilities/Shareholder Equity* = *$90,000/$70,000* = *1.29; the lower the number the better.*

Debt to Assets = *Long-Term Liabilities/Total Assets* = *$90,000/$160,000* = *.56; the lower the number the better.*

Each of the numbers generated summarizes the corresponding account at the given point in time. Cash, inventory, and other assets are tallied from the double-entry register to make up the current assets. The double-entry register can be kept on paper; however, most businesses keep the register in accounting software. QuickBooks is common accounting software that can calculate financial statements, including the balance sheet. You have to keep up with transactions. Another common software used is the enterprise resource program (ERP). The most common ERP in the United States today is a licensed software called NetSuite, a product from Oracle Systems Corporation.

Income Statement

The income statement or the P&L (profit and loss) is a statement of the financial performance of the company over a time period. It can be any period, but normally the P&L is run over a month or a quarter of a year and annually based on your selected accounting period. The income statement is the summary of the revenue and expenses in a period. To review GAAP recommendations for the income statement, go to https://financialaccountingreview.com/us-gaap-far/2130-income-statement.htm.

To me the income statement is like your report card in school. In the example we provide in table 9, the revenue is reported and then some of the key metrics are as a percentage against the revenue. For example, the cost of goods in the example is $25,100, which divided by the revenue is 50%. In this case the product profit margin is 50%. But there are more expenses in the business, mainly the operating expenses. In this case the operating expenses are the administrative cost, the fulfillment costs, and the marketing costs. These are also juxtaposed against the revenue as a percentage.

Table 9: Income Statement Example

2020 Fourth-Quarter Income Statement		
Revenue		
Sales	$50,000	
Cost of Sales		
Cost of items sold	$25,000	
Returns	$100	
Cost of Goods	$25,100	50%
Gross Profit	$24,900	50%
Operational Expenses		
Administrative labor	$2,500	
Administrative expenses	$100	
Administrative costs	$2,600	5%
Fulfillment labor	$2,500	
Fulfillment expenses	$200	
Total fulfillment	$2,700	5%
Marketing Expenses		
Catalog expenses	$2,000	
Digital marketing expenses	$8,300	
Total marketing expenses	$10,300	21%
Total Operational Costs	$15,600	31%
Net Income	$9,300	19%

The final number that is important is the net revenue, which is also aligned as a percentage of revenue. Also, for every dollar the company brings in, $0.16 is collected as profit. Different businesses operate at different net profit levels. Amazon operates at razor-thin profits, usually less than two percent. Other industries operate at higher profit levels. The level of risk for investors requires a higher profit margin to justify the investment. In the example income statement in table 10, the net sales are $50,000 and the gross profit margin is 50%. Each major expense is examined as a percentage of net sales.

The administrative costs and fulfillment costs are at five percent of net sales. The total marketing cost is 21% of net sales. Another way to view this is to say that for every $1 in net sales, the company had to spend $.21 in marketing. Some companies separate the operational expenses and break out the marketing expense separately. The total net income is $9,300, or 19% of net sales. In this business the product profit margin is $24,500 (50%), less the operational costs of $15,600 (31%) to obtain $9,300 in profit. This profit is also called earnings before interest and taxes (EBIT). You can also compare the actual income statement to the projected income statement or previous income statements. In this example we are comparing the fourth quarters of 2020 to 2019.

The comparison shows an improvement from 2019 to 2020 of gross profit margin going from 47% of net sales to 50% of net sales. Also, the operational cost was reduced by six percent as a percentage of sales, going from 37% down to 31%. Finally, the net income as a percentage of sales improved from 11% to 19%. This company looks to be moving in the right direction.

In summary, the ratios that are important to derive from the income statement are as follow:

Gross Profit Margin = 1-(COG/Sales)
Profit Margin = Net Income/Sales

Table 10: Example of Income Statement Comparison

Diff	2020 4th Quarter Income Statement			2019 4th Quarter Income Statement		
	Revenue			**Revenue**		
$10,000	Sales	$50,000		Sales	$40,000	
	Cost of Sales			**Cost of Sale**		
	Cost of items sold	$25,000		Cost of items sold	$21,000	
	Returns	$100		Returns	$100	
$4,000	**Cost of Goods (COG)**	$25,100	50%	**Cost of Goods (GOG)**	$21,100	53%
$6,000	**Gross Profit**	$24,900	50%	**Gross Profit**	$18,900	47%
	Operational Expenses			**Operational Expenses**		
	Administrative labor	$2,500		Administrative labor	$2,500	
	Administrative expenses	$100		Administrative expenses	$100	
	Administrative costs	$2,600	5%	Administrative costs	$2,600	7%
	Fulfillment labor	$2,500		Fulfillment labor	$2,000	
	Fulfillment expenses	$200		Fulfillment Expenses	$200	
	Total fulfillment	$2,700	5%	Total fulfillment	$2,200	6%
	Marketing Expenses			Marketing Expenses		
	Catalog expenses	$2,000		Catalog expenses	$1,800	
	Digital marketing	$8,300		Digital marketing	$8,000	
	Total marketing costs	$10,300	21%	Total marketing costs	$9,800	25%
$1,000	**Total Operational Costs**	##	31%	**Total Operational Costs**	$14,600	37%
$5,000	**Net Income**	$9,300	19%	**Net Income**	$4,300	11%

In larger companies, we would also look at the Price-Earnings Ratio, or P/E ratio. If this company were publicly traded and there were 1,000 shares on the market and the stock price was $100 per share, the P/E ratio = $100/($9300/1000) or $10.75. As a representation of percentage return per share, it is 10.75%. The PE ratio is usually used in comparison with other companies within a market segment.

Statement of Cash Flow

The statement of cash flow tracks the cash from operations, investments, and financing to calculate the difference in cash for the accounting period. The statement of cash flow is created quarterly and annually. The balance sheet and income statement are used to calculate some of the items on the statement of cash flow.

Table 11: Statement of Cash Flow—Example

Cash Flow from Operations	
Net earnings	$9,300
Other Changes	
Accounts received increase	$5,000
Accounts payable decrease	$5,000
Depreciation	$1,000
Taxes payable	$1,000
Changes to Cash	
Inventory increase	($6,000)
Net Cash from Operations	$15,300
Cash Flow from Investments	
Equipment	($3,000)
Cash Flow from Financing	
Notes payable	$1,000
Cash Flow for Fourth Quarter	$13,300

The net earnings on the income statement should match the net earnings on the statement of cash flow. The net cash flow difference between the balance sheet from the previous period and the ending balances should equal the increase or decrease in cash for the period.

The statement of cash flow is a recent addition to standardized financial statements. In 1987 the Financial Accounting Standards Board made the statement of cash flows a requirement for financial reporting, and since then organizations have included the statement of cash flows in quarterly and annual reporting (Arnold, Ellis, & Krishnan, 2018). The use of the statement of cash flow arose out of the accounting debacles of Adelphia, Dynegy, Qwest, Tyco, WorldCom, and other financial disasters (Broome, 2004). The statement of cash flows allowed investors to see how the cash was used (Broome, 2004). To see more information about GAAP statement of cash flow standards, go to the following website: https://financialaccountingreview.com/us-gaap-far/2140-statement-cash-flows.htm

The occurrence of these disasters fell after more companies in the 1980s moved to accrual accounting systems and recognized the revenue transaction before the cash was received. This caused challenges with disclosures to investors, depending on the form of statement of cash flow using direct or indirect cash flow methods. Indirect cash flow removes the revenue from the income statement on the statement of cash flow because it is an accrual accounting and not true cash. The statement of cash flow provided a more transparent view of the cash. The statement does this by connecting the activities on the income statement to the categories of assets and liabilities on the balance sheet.

The three financial statements at the end of each period are compared to those of previous similar periods and to the projected financial statements for assessment. The assessment should examine what happened and why. If on the income statement the product profit margin dropped from one period to the next, you should find out why.

Did the cost go up? Was the product sold at a discount? What happened? If the balance sheet shows less cash, what is the reason? Did inventory go up, and is your cash tied up in inventory? The statements will tell you the story of what happened for the period, and you should be able to take corrective action based on what happened.

The ratios that we need to examine in the statement of cash flow are the following:

Current Liability Coverage Ratio = *Net Cash from Operating Activities ÷ Average Current Liabilities. The average current liabilities are derived from the balance sheet.*

Price-to-Cash-Flow Ratio = *Share Price/(Net Cash from Operating Activities/Share Price. In this cash assuming the share price is $100, the Price to Cash Flow = $100/ ($15,300/$100) = 65%.*

Cash Flow Margin Ratio = *Net Cash from Operating Activities/Sales. To calculate, we have to get the sales from the income statement of $50,000 to show $15,300/$50,000 or 31%. I like to see this ratio, and of course, the higher the better. Next we will discuss projections and the 13-week cash flow model.*

13-Week Cash Flow

Table 12: 13-Week Cash Flow—Example

VERSION A	January				February				March				
	Week 1	Week 2	Week 3	Week 4	Week 1	Week 2	Week 3	Week 4	Week 1	Week 2	Week 3	Week 4	Week 5
Revenue:	1	2	3	4	5	6	7	8	9	10	11	12	13
Core Bus	$193,273	$185,921	$176,968	$167,640	$249,449	$209,543	$182,184	$186,101	$167,977	$184,525	$171,966	$156,968	$201,128
Amazon rev		$40,000		$45,000		$50,000		$55,000		$60,000		$65,000	
Freight	$28,777	$28,777	$28,777	$28,777	$28,777	$28,777	$28,777	$28,777	$23,022	$23,022	$23,022	$23,022	$23,022
	$222,050	$254,698	$205,745	$241,417	$278,226	$288,320	$210,961	$269,878	$190,999	$267,547	$194,988	$244,990	$224,150
Expenses:													
Payroll	$50,925	$27,470	$27,470	$27,470	$50,925	$27,470	$27,470	$27,470	$51,162	$26,492	$26,492	$26,492	$26,492
Admin Exp	$2,874	$2,874	$2,874	$2,874	$3,060	$3,060	$3,060	$3,060	$2,340	$2,340	$2,340	$2,340	$2,340
Rent	$8,200			$8,823	$8,200				$8,200				
Am Exp 1		$152,332				$99,398				$94,861			
Am Exp 2		$24,478				$22,360				$21,650			
Advertising	$1,341	$1,341	$1,341	$1,341	$4,112	$4,112	$4,112	$4,112	$1,848	$1,848	$1,848	$1,848	$1,848
Catalog	$0	$2,734	$77,424	$21,893	$5,392	$15,146	$0	$4,116	$1,500	$0	$49,569	$0	$2,250
Emp Benefits				$22,184				$11,842					$28,361
erp								$8,225					
Bank Fees	$6,905	$6,905	$6,905	$6,905	$5,578	$5,578	$5,578	$5,578	$3,961	$3,961	$3,961	$3,961	$3,961
r & d	$1,200	$1,200	$1,200	$1,200	$1,200	$1,200	$1,200	$1,200	$960	$960	$960	$960	$960
shipping mat	$2,909	$2,909	$2,909	$2,909	$1,578	$1,578	$1,578	$1,578	$494	$494	$494	$494	$494
misc	$3,149	$3,149	$3,149	$3,149	$3,260	$3,260	$3,260	$3,260	$3,054	$3,054	$3,054	$3,054	$3,054
	$77,503	$225,392	$123,272	$98,748	$83,305	$183,162	$46,258	$70,441	$73,519	$155,660	$88,718	$39,149	$69,760
	$144,547	($51,360)	$82,474	$142,670	$194,921	$105,158	$164,703	$199,437	$117,480	$111,887	$106,270	$205,841	$154,390
Purchases:													
Domestic	$45,993	$68,556	$60,721	$63,152	$61,635	$79,615	$72,487	$58,430	$101,456	$72,613	$52,567	$63,419	$43,410
Foreign	$16,751	$12,110	$9,238	$1,405	$3,722	$6,176	$5,466	$117,553	$0	$78,482	$53,927	$46,981	$12,697
	$62,744	$80,666	$69,959	$64,556	$65,357	$85,791	$77,953	$175,983	$101,456	$151,095	$106,494	$110,400	$56,107
	$81,803	($51,360)	$12,514	$78,113	$129,564	$19,368	$86,749	$23,454	$16,024	($39,208)	($224)	$95,441	$98,283

The 13-week cash flow is a tool to examine your cash needs in your business. If you are on a 4-4-5 accounting period, it is a 13-week quarter, and 13 weeks times four quarters is 52 weeks, which make up the year.

The 13-week cash flow displays each week of projected or expected revenue and expenses. The revenue is shown as sources of revenue categories by week. The expenses are itemized expenses by category. As you create this document, some of the expenses will be known. Others will have to be estimated.

The purchases section is the product you plan to buy. The week that is entered is not the week when you place the order or receive the material—it is the week when you pay, as this document should represent only receipts and payments. From this document we can see that we are short funds in Week 2, Week 10, and Week 11. The most is Week 2, at over $51,000. This document indicates that we need some source of outside revenue to operate in Week 2 from a cash basis. Either a small line of credit or an available credit card is necessary to get through these weeks.

This document shows 13 weeks or one quarter but you should extend the cash flow projections to four 13-week projections, or one year. Also, some of the rows are estimates. You should create at least three cases of projections—a low-ball, middle, and high-ball—that can provide some different perspectives on your cash needs and when you have those cash needs. Finally, you should track your projected 13-week cash flow to the actual performance to see how well you track and to identify any future problems that your projections did not identify.

8

The Current State of Marketing

"Stopping advertising to save money is
like stopping your watch to save time."

—Henry Ford

In getting my doctor of business administration (DBA) and my master of business administration (MBA), I was not required to take a lot of courses in marketing. I suspect the reason is that marketing is changing so rapidly. Best practices in marketing have certainly changed in my multi-decade career, but they have changed faster in the last four years than ever before. This section will discuss the recent disruptions in the marketplace that have impacted marketing. We will also discuss tracking your performance and attribution. Chapter nine will dive into marketing in today's economy.

Disruptions

Managers should continuously examine internal and external opportunities and threats to determine the best path to customer value and profit (Gamble et al., 2019). Academic researchers agree and say that business leaders must make decisions about how to operate in rapidly changing environments and about what quality strategy to employ, plus how to properly allocate resources (Jeong-Eun, & Morgan, 2017). The impact of managers' response to rapid change environments is more critical than ever (Bohórquez Arévalo, 2016; Patè-Cornell, 2015). Other research shows that business is changing more rapidly than ever before, so managers must use all of an organization's tools and techniques to evolve and adapt to the external changes (Esposito & Tse, 2018). Managers must respond to rapid change across technology, government regulations, customer demand, and external trends in order to innovate faster than the competition (Galetti, Golden, & Brozovich, 2019).

E-commerce Sales Tax. The perspective that business is changing rapidly was pervasive before the pandemic hit. In the few months before the pandemic, marketing faced many new obstacles. In June 2018 the United States Supreme Court agreed with South Dakota in *South Dakota vs. Wayfair Incorporated,* which initiated the collection of sales taxes in states that collect retail sales tax and eventually local tax. This put the burden on the company to somehow collect the exact amount of sales tax for each location. To put this in perspective, my company, Micro-Mark, had to collect sales taxes in the shopping cart, live on our website, for each of these areas.

Map of Sales Tax Rates

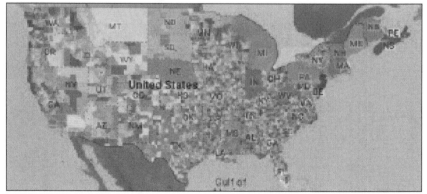

Avalara.com

Each color on the map above represents a different rate area. Sometimes the rates are different in the same town from one side of the street to the other. We were able to solve this problem by using Avalara tax solutions to collect the sales tax when needed in the website shopping cart and help file returns to each state and relevant county. Several other solutions are available, like Sovos, Vertex, and TaxJar. Of course, e-commerce customers did not like the new taxes, which caused them to pay more for the same product. Getting a solution took time, but some states forced companies to pay sales taxes going back to the date of the decision, knowing that the companies could not have been able to collect sales taxes.

Proposition 65. More significant than the sales tax issue was California's Proposition 65 extension. Increased regulations in Proposition 65 went into effect in August 2018, which created wide-sweeping labeling warnings under the "right to know" requirements (Bergeson, 2017). This required manufacturers and retailers to re-label thousands of product packages. The regulations were confusing and difficult for companies to comply with, but non-compliance could result in a $2,500 fine per day per violation.

My company does significant business in California, and we had to spend countless hours figuring out what labels were required for what products and then undertake re-labeling. Additionally, California has predatory attorneys who find unsuspecting companies. The example label seen below went on a brass clamp that could have had brass that could have been made with lead.

Proposition 65 Warning Label

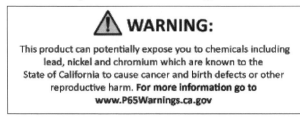

⚠ WARNING:

This product can potentially expose you to chemicals including lead, nickel and chromium which are known to the State of California to cause cancer and birth defects or other reproductive harm. **For more information go to www.P65Warnings.ca.gov**

Tariffs. Another challenge that retailers faced recently was the additional tariffs that the Trump administration applied to particular products or components manufactured in China. Our company purchases some unique power tools from a Chinese manufacturer that we collaborated with on the design. These tools received a 25% additional tax, which was impossible to pass on to the customer. Many companies have suffered from these tariffs.

Google's Changes. To add to the issues, Google has tightened the product feed requirements in several areas. Primarily, the changes include text descriptions and images. If the company does not fix the issues, Google will suppress the product from the Google feed. Google does not want any promotional copy on the image. Consequently, this product image on our Micro-Mark website was suspended.

Suspended Product Google Feed

The reason the product was suspended was the Micro-Mark logo and the name of the product. While this may seem unreasonable, the review is done by Google's artificial intelligence (AI). After many appeals to Google, we were able to get this product restored. However, some companies might not be as nimble with the Google Merchant Center to recover.

Free Shipping. Finally, the increased customer resistance to paying for shipping has caused disruptions. Amazon Prime has set a precedent for free shipping despite the fact that Amazon loses millions of dollars on it. An example is below with one of my company's best-selling items.

	MicroLux Mini Tilt Arbor Saw #80463	
	Method 1	Method 2
Price	$349.95	$372.49
Shipping	$22.95	**Free**
Total	$372.89	$372.89
		PREFERED

We see that customers are averse to paying for shipping even when the price between Method 1 and Method 2 is the same. However, the cost of shipping increases every year by about five percent. This conflict is a challenge for businesses to resolve. Amazon is partly to blame for this customer perspective.

Amazon. Amazon has been a disruptive force in the e-commerce marketplace. According to Statista.com, Amazon's gross market value of all e-commerce sales has grown from 34% in 2016 to 47% in 2020, with the estimate to be 50% in 2021 (Sabanoglu, 2020). It is suggested that this amount could be underestimated because Amazon reports only the charged fees as income and not the total sale. The sheer size of Amazon is disruptive.

Also, Amazon can be predatory to third-party sellers and will begin selling like products that reduce sales for these sellers (Wang, 2018; Zhu & Liu, 2018; Khan, 2017; Reimers & Waldfogel, 2017). Amazon has more information than other companies about product opportunities because they are constantly examining data. This company will continue to be a disruptive force on the Internet.

I mention all these disruptions to businesses that occurred before the onset of COVID-19. Researchers were concerned about small businesses because of these disruptions. A survey showed that 40% of small businesses are profitable, 30% break even, and 30% continually lose money (Mansfield, 2018). An estimated 7,795 retail stores in the United States closed for good in 2017 (Fisher, Gallino, & Netessine, 2019).

Digital marketing is growing faster than any other segment in retail, and retail managers are failing to adjust to the new market (Bonsu & Kuofie, 2019; Fulgoni, 2018). These managers are failing to adjust to the differences in the digital channel from traditional retail, and these businesses stand to learn and potentially gain from Amazon's strategies (Bonsu & Kuofie, 2019). Amazon has changed the customers' mindset to demand more choices, lower costs, and fast delivery (Fulgoni, 2018).

Before COVID-19, digital marketing was the only segment that was growing. COVID-19 only accelerated what was already happening, which was a migration by retail to the digital marketplace. This is the foundation with which we examine marketing today. JCPenney, Sears, Macy's, Radio Shack, National Geographic, Circuit City, Abercrombie & Fitch, Toys"R"Us, and Sharper Image have all failed to navigate the digital marketplace and to effectively adjust marketing strategies that work in today's changing market. Consumers who were quarantined were forced to order more products on the Internet, and many will continue to reduce brick-and-mortar shopping. The next section will discuss marketing attribution of channel performance and tracking the results.

Tracking Performance and Attribution

Digital marketing has changed over the years. When I started in business, we gave the credit for a sale to the last click before the purchase. If an email was sent to a customer and the customer clicked through the email, the credit for the sale went to the email channel. We would examine the cost of all the emails sent, track the click-through rates, and tally the total orders and revenue to obtain a return on investment (ROI). Email performance would be tracked for each email, and the email channel would be tracked as in table 13. (See next page.)

Table 13: Example of Email Performance Tracking

Email performance by campaign   by send

Send date	Promo description	circ	orders	sales	AOV	RR%	$/email	GP$	GP %	Delivered	Opened	Clicked	conversion
8/30/2020	Labor Day sale	162,572	257	$32,954	$128.23	0.16%	$0.20	$18,499	56.10%	162,572	25,199	2,041	3.00%
9/1/2020	Labor Day sale RM	100,395	-	$0	$0.00	0.00%	$0.00	$0	0.00%	100,395	24,998	1,825	5.60%
9/3/2020	New model kits	104,377	16	$1,606	$100.36	0.02%	$0.02	$866	53.90%	104,377	31,626	3,384	0.60%
9/5/2020	New lower prices	171,531	59	$7,503	$127.17	0.03%	$0.04	$3,699	49.30%	171,531	30,704	1,996	1.60%
9/7/2020	New lower prices RM	107,573	-	$0	$0.00	0.00%	$0.00	$0	0.00%	107,573	29,152	1,691	1.60%
9/10/2020	$10 sale	162,772	430	$18,833	$43.80	0.26%	$0.12	$13,164	69.90%	162,772	27,183	2,419	8.80%
9/12/2020	$10 sale RM	100,451	-	$0	$0.00	0.00%	$0.00	$0	0.00%	100,451	24,510	1,642	9.60%
9/14/2020	Halloween 1	97,378	25	$2,422	$96.88	0.03%	$0.03	$1,366	56.40%	97,378	26,292	1,762	1.40%
9/17/2020	15% off	162,614	593	$66,647	$112.39	0.36%	$0.41	$30,150	45.20%	162,614	27,319	2,240	5.60%
9/19/2020	15% off RM	89,381	-	$0	$0.00	0.00%	$0.00	$0	0.00%	89,381	25,027	1,602	6.80%
9/21/2020	15% off RMM	100,177	-	$0	$0.00	0.00%	$0.00	$0	0.00%	100,177	22,840	1,439	8.30%
9/24/2020	New arrivals - silhouette	96,884	30	$3,631	$121.03	0.03%	$0.04	$1,675	46.10%	96,884	31,294	3,317	0.80%
9/26/2020	Close-outs	171,088	161	$11,403	$70.83	0.09%	$0.07	$4,567	40.10%	171,088	30,796	8,500	1.70%

In table 13 the promo description shows the name of the email. If the name includes "RM" it is a remail or a duplicate email, and the performance is not tracked. The circulation is the number of customers who were sent the email. Orders per email, sales, average order value (AOV), response rate percentage (RR%), and gross profit (GP) are tracked.

The example also shows the number of emails that were actually delivered, the open rate, the click-through rate, and the conversion percentage. These monthly campaigns are tracked and summed to create quarterly and yearly comparisons, as shown in the example below.

Table 14: Example of Year-on-Year Email Campaign Comparison

Promo Description	circ	orders	sales	AOV	RR%	$/email	GP$	GP %
Year 2019	18,306,600	13,253	$1,394,304	$105.21	0.07%	$0.08	$711,919	51.10%
Year 2020	19,826,496	17,955	$1,769,435	$98.55	0.09%	$0.09	$916,525	51.80%
Qty var	1,519,896	4702	$375,131				$204,606	
% Var	8%	35%	27%	-6%	25%	17%	29%	0.70%

Table 14 shows the total number of emails sent (circ) up by eight percent and the number of orders and sales up. The example shows AOV down but RR% up 25%. All these numbers are based on the last-click attribution to credit the marketing channel.

However, the last-click method of attribution is flawed because it does not take into account all the influence of all touchpoints except the last one (Zhao, Mahboobi, & Bagheri, 2019; Nisar & Man Yeung, 2018; Moe & Fader, 2004), and it does not account for the array of different marketing that may have contributed to the sale. The crowded efforts of digital marketing today include search, emails, social media ads, retargeting ads, triggered emails based on customer activities, and much more. These multiple touchpoints, if part of the purchase journey, all contribute to the last-click and sale.

Marketing professionals struggle to derive attribution models that accurately represent the purchasing journey. The problem is how to accurately apply the credit for the sale. If marketers can determine the attribution, they can better adjust the areas in which money is spent to increase sales. Four different models exist to account for these multiple touchpoints. We will describe them briefly in this section.

Table 15: Attribution Models

Time Decay	3 -tep journey 1:3:6 is 10% or initial, 30% for 2nd, and 60% for last-click.
Uniformly Distributed Attribution	3-step journey is equally distributed credit at 33%
The Position-Based	Last and 1st steps more important; 40% for initial, 20% for 2nd, 40% for last-click
The Statistics-Based	Uses statically values of game theory.

(Nisar et al., 2018)

For me, these attribution models can get complicated quickly, and just tracking all the channels and attribution could be a lot of work. Conversely, I like to track last-click and total attribution. Only one channel gets the credit for the last-click sale. Many channels get credit for the journey attribution model.

Table 16: Example of Facebook Attribution

Month	Cost	Reach	Impressions	CPM	CTR	Clicks	CPC$	Sales	Website Purchases
Nov	$10,350	1,345,981	1,903,452	$5.43	2.87%	55,200	$0.18	$20,462	$59,734

In the case seen in table 16 the total last-click sales were $20,462. However, of the customers who clicked through at one point in time, many of them later went back and purchased. This is indicated in the website purchases at $59,734. In this example, the CPM is the cost per 1,000 impressions. The CTR is the percentage of click-throughs from Facebook to our website. The CPC is the cost per click.

Summary of the Current State of Marketing

We have discussed the current state of marketing, including the disruptions and new challenges marketing has faced, and the issue of attribution in tracking marketing performance. The disruptions included e-commerce sales tax collection requirements, Prop 65, tariffs, changes to the Google product feed, the issue of free shipping, and the disruption of Amazon. We also discussed the challenges in marketing attribution in today's economy.

9

Marketing Today

"Without promotion, something terrible happens—nothing."

—P. T. Barnum

Old and new companies have to navigate the digital marketplace to survive in today's market. At the same time, traditional marketing still has a place. In this section we will discuss digital marketing and then examine print and catalog marketing and end the discussion with brick-and-mortar marketing.

In the previous chapter we discussed the many challenges that businesses have faced in recent years. We also discussed the failures of many companies to adapt to the new digital marketplace and that those failures have led to closures.

Digital Marketing

Digital marketing is the only area of retail that's growing. But as we have discussed, many managers are having trouble navigating the digital marketplace. The Internet has reduced the cost of entry into retail to essentially a zero-dollar investment (Wang, 2018). However, many of these sellers lack the skills and knowledge to provide an adequate web environment (Xiao, 2016). In this section we will discuss best practices for the website, search, paid advertisement, social media, influencers, and short message service (SMS).

Website. Researchers have not agreed upon a definition for a website. Olsina, Covella, and Rossi (2006) said that while the quality of a website is easy to recognize, it is difficult to define and quantify, saying, "The meaning of quality is not simple and atomic, but a multidimensional and abstract concept" (p. 109). Semerádová and Weinlich (2020) said that despite the numerous studies that have been conducted on websites, a uniform definition of website quality factors has yet to be derived.

While numerous approaches have been developed within the area of software quality, no one has defined specifically for all the stakeholders' measurable attributes a quality website (Morales-Vargas, Pedraza-Jiménez, & Codina, 2020). With this confusion, even in a basic platform like a website, professionals must find a way to communicate with customers. We will provide our best offering for a quality website.

The quality of the website is critical to display the competitive advantage of what your company offers. Best practices say that quality and unique content, readability, images and videos, social media connections, and service quality are critical (USAS, 2019). Quality content includes text descriptions, videos, images, or sound, and all content should be to provide purpose to satisfy consumer needs (Bulygo, 2019).

Quality Content. SearchMetrics (2018) says that high-quality content gives websites a higher ranking on search engine queries. Good-quality content will develop loyal users who will return to the website. Some research suggests that websites with more than 1,000 words are more likely to have the number-one ranking in Google search (Hoque, Alsadoon, Maag, Prasad, Elchouemi, 2018). The length of the content can vary depending on the purpose of the website. Other research shows that the length of the content should be 2,500 words to gain search engine optimization (SEO) (USAS, 2019).

Readability. Another issue that determines a good website is the readability of the content. The content should be easy to read and understand. The suggestion is to use short sentences and remove all unnecessary content that is not related to customer goals (QuickSprou, 2019). Good readability will help content to be shared by other platforms (Sheats, Royal, Kedrowicz, 2019).

Images and video. Good creativity, including quality images and videos, is critical to a website. Also, alt tags or named images can help a website get better SEO page ranking, and the top websites have around seven named images (Bulygo, 2019). A viewer on your website will be drawn to the images initially before moving to other information. Pictures and video quality are important and are representative of the brand (QuickSprou, 2019).

Social media. Your website should have button links to Facebook, LinkedIn, and other social media channels for the customer's easy access (QuickSprou, 2019). These buttons allow customers and influencers to connect with their audiences, pushing your brand to more potential customers (Raguseo, 2018; Sharif, Troshani, Davidson, 2018).

Service quality. Service quality is the response to website services like live chats, interactivity, or security (Tandon, Kiran, Sah, 2017). The site should be secure and responsive. Customers have come to expect quick response and the customer experience will develop loyalty and retention of customers (Tandon et al., 2017). The website quality involves more than content today and includes system and service quality as a requirement (Shiller, Waldfogel, Ryan, 2018).

Digital marketing is continually changing. The website has evolved into a more consistent best practice. The thing that does evolve is the platform for the website. Shopify, Magento, BigCommerce, and others provide a solid platform to build your website. For a professional website, you will need to hire a developer if you are not one yourself. For an early website, you can do it yourself with Squarespace or Wix.

These sites allow you to add features to your website easily and add more later. In my view, the key to an effective website is not innovation; it is convention. Shoppers have become used to some simple standards in order to be comfortable with purchasing. The experience should be intuitive to navigate and click to the desired section.

1 Home > Mini Power Tools > Saws > MicroLux® Mini Tilt Arbor Table Saw

MicroLux® Mini Tilt Arbor Table Saw

2 Item #: 80463

List Price $537.9

Our Price $349.95

Add to

Add to

A Micro-Mark **Exclusive!**

The World's Best Hobby Size Table Saw with Features and Precision You Need

High Quality . . . Made in Japan

3 The MicroLux® is more powerful, more accurate, and smoother running than any other saw its size. And it's the world's first variable speed table saw, so it will cut metal and plastic, as well as wood. This is without a doubt the most feature-packed machine ever designed for the scale modeler. Includes a self-aligning rip fence, calibrated miter gauge, blade guard and an 80-tooth fine-cut blade for balsa and basswood up to 1 inch thick, hardwood up to 1/4 inch thick (hardwood up to 1 inch with optional carbide blades . . . to purchase optional blades, see below). Blade dia. 3-1/4 inches with 10mm hole.

Download Instructions

6 OUR NO-RISK GUARANTEE
Order the MicroLux® Table Saw in the usual way by sending full payment or charging to your credit card. Then examine it risk-free for 30 days. If you decide not to keep it for any reason, simply return it (in resalable condition, please) via courier or insured Priority Mail for an immediate refund.

4

5 Features:
>High torque, electronically rectified DC motor produces more torque and power than many motors rated at 1/2 hp and higher. And torque remains high, even at low rpm.
>Variable speed, from 3,600 to 7,000 rpm. Lets you cut plastic, aluminum, brass, and other non-ferrous metals without overheating.
>Tilting arbor for angle cuts up to 45 degrees.
>Cuts a full 1 inch at 90 degrees, 3/4 inch at 45 degrees.
>Blade height adjusts from 0 to 1 inch.
>Two miter gauge slots for cutting from left or right side of blade.
>1-year warranty.

7 People Who Viewed This Item Were Also Interested In

Customers Who Bought This Item Also Bought

8 Customer Reviews of This Item Average: 5 Stars ★ ★ ★ ★ ★ **Click to Read Reviews**

each page except the checkout page. The search bar should be on the top right of the home page and travels through to the product page. Search should include the item number and fussy versions of the product name. The product page should be clean. and easy to follow as shown.

The example product page is of one of Micro-Mark's best-selling items, the MicroLux® Mini Tilt Arbor Saw. The example product page has numbered sections to help with the discussion of best practices. Number 1 is the breadcrumbs. This allows the viewer to see the progression of the page, and the viewer can review the navigation. Number 2 is the product name and item number with the pricing. Notice this listing includes the list price and the website price. Also, this area is the "Add to Cart" button, which directs the customer to the shopping cart to purchase. This section also includes an "Add to Wish List" button. Additionally, the banner "A Micro-Mark Exclusive!" shows that the product is unique to Micro-Mark.

Item Number 3 is the copy written in concise form but thorough enough to get a customer comfortable with a purchase of over $300. The section has a link to more information in the "Download Instructions." Number 4, below the hero photo of the product, includes additional images of the product, and the arrow icon indicates a video. Unfortunately, for the purposes of the book, I could not find any peer-reviewed literature that indicated that videos help product sales. I did find that Renfro (2015) said the videos increase the AOV by 50%. Videos obviously help to sell the product. In my experience the video does not have to be studio quality on the product page. A video shot with an iPhone can make a big difference. Hopefully you can shoot videos to help sell your product on the product page.

Number 5 is the features of the product. These features should center on the benefits to the user. "This feature makes it easier to cut thin plastic or wood" is an example. Number 6 is the guarantee. People are suspicious and do not want to be taken. A clear guarantee significantly lowers the barrier to purchase.

Number 7 shows other items that people who visited this site were interested in, plus other items purchased by customers who purchased the featured product. This feature will help add to the shopping cart and provides customers validation of what other items they might need. Number 8 is the final item, which provides product reviews and ratings. This gives customers some comfort that others like the product. All these items are best practices, and all are essential to a good product page.

If you are not selling a product but are providing services or consulting, the page is different than the product page. The key to this website is to gain the viewer's interest quickly and to acquire to potential customer's contact information. The rules in table 17 are what to consider when creating a service-oriented website.

Table 17: Key Elements of a Service Website

1. Clearly state the value of the service for the customer.
2. Highlight what makes your service unique.
3. Keep the website simple.
4. List other companies that you have worked with.
5. Provide testimonials, photos, and case studies.
6. Show LinkedIn contact information.
7. Include an obvious CONTACT button.

If your website is going to have a functioning checkout cart to handle transactions, the key is to keep the cart simple to keep the transaction moving along. Many customers will shop using the cart and then abandon the cart or leave the site. Keeping the cart simple will lower the probability of an abandoned cart. Numerous software apps can be used to reconnect via email or text with customers who leave abandoned carts. We will discuss software apps later.

Your website should be able to take Visa, Mastercard, American

Express, Discover, and PayPal. You will work with a credit card processing company like Chase, Cybersource, Solupay, Flagship, or others to process the cards. Fees can be negotiated and vary based on the company and your amount of processing. You will work directly with PayPal. PayPal is slightly more expensive per transaction, but the issue of fraud is removed if you use PayPal.

Building and running a website is competitive. Proper management of a site with thousands of products needs daily attention. Newsweek rated the Micro-Mark website as the number-two site in the U.S. for the hobby and leisure category in 2020.

Newsweek's Best Online Shops for 2020 for Hobby and Leisure

Hobby, Leisure items

amainhobbies.com	8.83
micromark.com ★	8.13
rcplanet.com	8.10
jrcigars.com	8.07
thompsoncigar.com	8.00
modeltrainstuff.com	7.95
horizonhobby.com	7.90
telescope.com	7.81
towerhobbies.com	7.67
kellycodetectors.com	7.66

Newsweek also recognized a former company I led a few years ago as the eighth best in the category of flower and plants. I am proud to be associated with these organizations and the organizational expertise to run top websites.

Newsweek's Best Online Shops 2020 for Flowers, Plants

Flowers, Plants

globalrose.com	8.17
sendflowers.com	8.11
burpee.com	7.97
whiteflowerfarm.com	7.96
dutchbulbs.com	7.89
florists.com	7.81
michiganbulb.com	7.81
jacksonandperkins.com ★	7.75
brighterblooms.com	7.72
starkbros.com	7.66

BEST ONLINE SHOPS 2020

Search and Paid Ads. Queries on search engines are used by potential customers to find products or services online. "Search engine optimization" (SEO) has become the term used for optimizing website content. The goal of SEO is to improve the search results returned by a search engine to increase the chances that users will view relevant content (Palanisamy & Liu, 2018). A higher ranked website in search engine results pages (SERPs) will result in increased users of the website. The purpose of SEO is to improve the quality of the web pages that are reviewed or crawled by search engines to rank the website based on the terms in the query (Visser & Weidman; 2014). SERPs are based on organic search results and paid search results (Palanisamy & Liu, 2018). Organic search rankings are obtained by search engines that examine the website's web pages and the keyword or words provided for correlation (Palanisamy & Liu, 2018). The higher the correlation and accuracy of the web pages, the higher the organic search ranking. Paid advertisements are positioned based on the keyword searched and sponsored by sellers in competition for the more visible location (Palanisamy & Liu, 2018). The sponsor pays once the ad is clicked, even if the results do not end in a sale.

Search engine rankings are based on the review of the website and the web pages. We know that engagement is measured in how long a user is on a web page and how long a user is on the entire website. Increased time on a web page and time on a domain shows user engagement and correlation to the keywords searched. Other issues that impact organic search are page title, meta descriptions, keywords, content, and off-page factors. We will discuss each of these areas in the next several paragraphs.

Page Title. The World Wide Web Consortium suggests the web pages use the title element to identify the contents of the page. They recommend that the title provide content-rich wording. The title should be an overview and not an introduction to the page.

Meta Description. The meta description is a short blurb description that appears below the page link. This blurb is a short description that you use to describe or summarize the web page. The meta description should be used to encourage users to click on the links.

Keywords. Keywords are critical to identifying and optimizing the web page. A keyword analysis should be performed to make sure you are using the strongest keywords to obtain positive results. Too many keywords will lose relevance and cause confusion on the web page. The density of the keyword on a web page is also important. Using the keyword too often on a page will not improve the rankings. The density of a keyword on a web page should be three to five percent of the total words (Palanisamy & Liu, 2018). A main keyword in the page title can be helpful.

Content. One of the most important elements of the website is to provide trust for the user. The website should include a privacy policy, a description of the company, a contact link, and a method to receiving feedback. Improving the user experience should be the focus of the content on the website. Quality images and videos will improve the user experience and capture the user's attention.

Off-Page Factors. Off-page factors include links from social media to your webpages. Social media links will increase web traffic and the value of the website while creating interest to attract potential buyers (Zhang & Cabage, 2017). These external links indicate to Google that these third parties approve of your webpage and website. Also, links from other quality websites are helpful to improve rankings.

PLA. In the 20 years of my career in selling products on the Internet, a lot has changed. We have seen even more changes in search recently. Recent changes include the change from paid ads to product listing ads, or PLAs. A PLA is a sponsored or paid-per-click ad that goes to a different domain when clicked.

Micro-Mark's Mini Arbor Saw PLA

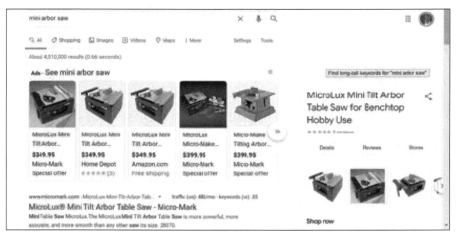

Above is a print screen of a Google search of a mini arbor saw. Micro-Mark's arbor saw shows as a high rank in this search. The ad at the top left is Micro-Mark's ad for our best-selling saw. The second ad is by Home Depot, but it is still our saw sold through Home Depot. The third image is our saw sold on Amazon. The fourth image is our saw included in a package with related accessories sold with our saw. The fifth image is another mini-saw that Micro-Mark sells.

Another change that Google has made recently is to include more information in the product feed that provides the information for organic search. These changes include restrictions on images without any promotional text. They also include the need for accurate shipping information. Finally, the feed is different for different countries. Micro-Mark has product feeds for the United States, Canada, and Australia because those countries are our top markets.

We track paid search weekly, monthly, quarterly, and annually. We divide key metrics between Google and Bing search engines. Table 18 is an example of a quarterly report for non-branded paid search in PLA.

In this case we see the number of clicks for Google, Bing and combined. The click-through rate (CTR) is also shown. The cost is the total cost of the clicks. Average cost per click is shown in the top row. Also shown is the total number of orders and total revenue. A/S is the average cost of the sale. In this example we are ranging between 19% and 24 %. This represents paying $.19 to $.24 in marketing cost for each $1.00 of revenue. Some companies will not have the product margin to absorb that much marketing cost per revenue dollar. If so, you must adjust downward how you bid.

Table 18: Example of Non-Branded Paid Search Tracking

Date Range	Clicks			CTR			Cost ($)			Avg CPC ($)		
	Google	Bing	Total	Google	Bing	Total	Google	Bing	Total	Google	Bing	Total
Sep 1-30, 2020	53,225	12,153	65,378	1.31%	1.20%	1.29%	14,836	3,781	18,618	0.28	0.31	0.28
Oct 1- 31, 2020	51,551	13,085	64,636	1.25%	1.57%	1.31%	13,491	3,787	17,278	0.26	0.29	0.27
Nov 1-30, 2020	125,137	12,031	137,168	1.08%	1.85%	1.12%	30,905	3,795	34,701	0.25	0.32	0.25

Date Range	Orders			Revenue ($)			A/S			AOV ($)		
	Google	Bing	Total	Google	Bing	Total	Google	Bing	Total	Google	Bing	Total
Sep 1-30, 2020	902	162	1,064	63,812	15,539	79,351	23.25%	24.81%	23.55%	71	96	75
Oct 1- 31, 2020	976	158	1,134	75,173	15,531	90,704	17.95%	24.38%	19.05%	77	98	80
Nov 1-30, 2020	1,597	185	1,782	145,811	17,969	163,780	21.20%	21.12%	21.19%	91	97	92

Google and Bing. Tutorials exist to help guide you through the learning process. Also, nowadays Google assigns you a Google representative. When Google started offering representatives, the quality of advice was not very good. Google has improved since then, and a representative relationship can be of value. Micro-Mark has gained a great reputation with the current website.

Email Marketing. Email marketing is a commercial message sent directly to customer's or potential customer's email address (VanBoskirk, 2007). The cost is lower, and speed of delivery is faster than traditional marketing tools and has been used for several decades. U.S. companies spent $400 million on email marketing in 2006 and $1.5 billion in 2012, in comparison to $64 billion on television, $34 billion on print advertisements, and $39 billion on online advertising with an estimated ROI of 4325% (Wu, Li, & Liu, 2018).

Email marketing performance tracks the length of customer's shopping history, recency of purchase, the average order value, average number of items per order. Research shows a strong connection between the length of time from the last purchase and response to an email promotion indicating that more inactive customers respond to promotional offers (Wu, Li, & Liu, 2018). Email marketing allows a company to acquire new customers, build lasting relationships, conduct surveys, and acquire sales (Kowalska, 2018).

Micro-Mark Opt-In Notice

To be compliant in email marketing, you must acquire email addresses with an opt-in agreement. There are many forms of the opt-in language, but the core of the language is to notify the customers that they agree to future marketing emails or texts and that they can unsubscribe anytime.

In this case we are giving the customer a 10% offer for opting into the email and text promotions. Also, each email and text must include an unsubscribe link that will remove the customer from the file. I highly recommend that you stay compliant with emails and texts within U.S. federal laws. The U.S. Department of Justice provides oversite over emailing and texting marketing. Shoppers who think they are being spammed can complain to the Internet Crime Complaint Center. which is a joint venture of the FBI and the National White Collar Crime Center. Penalties for noncompliance include fines and other potential suspensions of marketing.

For many years email marketing has been a very profitable marketing channel. Most of the companies I have been involved with had a pace of two to three emails per week. It does require some time for the creative department to create the email, which is then sent through a list service company. I have worked with Mailchimp, Cheetah Digital, Listrak, and Yesmail. We are currently using an Oracle product called Bronto. There are hundreds of these types of companies, which contract based on the annual number of emails sent. If you are starting out, I recommend Constant Contact, which provides easy-to-follow directions to begin email campaigns.

SMS and MMS. For approximately 25 years now, SMS (short message service) and MMS (multimedia messaging service) have been used to connect with customers. The SMS is text-only and limited to 160 characters to send to customers' mobile phones (Wouters & Wetzels, 2006). MMS allows images to be included in the phone message. These customers must opt-in just like email marketing.

In my experience, SMS and MMS are great ways to connect with customers. At Micro-Mark, customers are opting in by the thousands per week, and we see this marketing channel as having better open rates than email marketing and better return on investment. The cost of SMS and MMS is similar to email marketing, which is very inexpensive per contact.

Social Media. Research shows that audience response to business-initiated posts on social media can impact brand equity. Companies obtain increased brand equity with engagement by customers and followers with comments and sharing (Shay & Van Der Horst, 2019). Likes and views provide a lower level of brand equity and too many posts by a company can have negative brand equity (Shay & Van Der Horst, 2019). Social media has become an important part of customer engagement. For example, Adidas said the digital engagement is so important that they will focus on digital and social channels exclusively (McCarthy 2017).

Table 19: Social Media Information Guide

Company	Facebook	Twitter	YouTube	Instagram	TikTok
Owned by	Facebook, Inc.	Twitter, Inc.	Google, LLC	FaceBook, Inc.	BryteDance, Ltd.
Founded	2004	2006	2005	2010	2018
Media Form	Text, Image, Video	Text	Video	Image, Video	Video
Users*	2.5 B	386 M	2 B	1 B	800 M
Avg Age	40 years	42 years	NA	34 years	27 years

From Statistica.com/statistics

The effectiveness of digital programs is usually assessed with social media monitoring tools using metrics that includes the number of shares, likes, comments, opens, views, followers, and clicks, as metrics for engagement (Voorveld, van Noort, Muntinga, & Bronner, 2018). Table 19 shows the dominant social media companies, the owner of the company, when the company started, types of media, number of users, and the average age of the user.

This table shows that not all social media are equal. Pinterest is not included in the table because, despite the fact that Pinterest can generate a lot of click-throughs to your website, the traffic does not convert to sales because the user is not relevant. Relevancy of the traffic is key. Recently a Sherwin-Williams student employee was fired for using company time to shoot videos for TikTok of mixing paint. The student had 1.2 million followers (Chen, 2020). Sherwin-Williams fired him when they learned that his videos were shot while he was on the clock. Many think that Sherwin-Williams just does not understand social media, and that view could be correct. However, I would like to know the relevance of his Tok-Tok traffic. Do these viewers buy paint? If they were watching just because the content showed amazing colors mixing together, then the majority of the viewers were not likely paint buyers anytime soon.

More than just gaining followers and brand equity, companies can deliver advertisements on social media, which is an instant platform for instant and interactive marketing on a global scale (Hudson, Huang, Roth, and Madden, 2016). When Micro-Mark first started on social media, we worked toward finding audiences who were interested in the skills and hobbies that we supported with unique tools and supplies. We showed videos of how the tools were used and the results of the work. We were able to build relevant audiences slowly, increasing followings on Facebook and Instagram. We also loaded these videos on YouTube. All these posts would show in organic search based on keywords with some number of views. We were allowed to boost the viewership to reach a broader like or an audience similar to our following.

Later Facebook and Instagram allowed companies to post advertisements that could be viewed by not only your audience but other audiences' filters by demographics. This has proven for us and many other social media advertisers to be an effective source of new customers with this different marketing channel use.

We do well on Facebook because we have a narrow customer demographic base. Now social media is an important part of our marketing efforts, and we track weekly, monthly, and annually. See table 20 for a sample social media tracking of key performance indicators for Facebook.

Table 20: Social Media Monthly Performance Tracking

Month	Cost ($)	Impressions	CPM ($)	CTR	Clicks	CPC ($)	Landing Page Views	Cost/Landing Page Views ($)
Nov	10,594.46	1,947,904	5.44	2.86%	55,663	0.19	44,587	0.24
Oct	11,320.07	2,171,560	5.21	2.65%	57,583	0.2	45,681	0.25
Sep	11,060.63	1,768,227	6.26	2.68%	47,372	0.23	38,206	0.29

Month	Post Engagement	Cost/Post Engagement ($)	Website Purchases	CVR	Website Purchase Revenue ($)	RoAS ($)	CPO ($)
Nov	61,845	0.17	542	0.97%	47,822.60	4.51	19.55
Oct	66,255	0.17	648	1.13%	54,938.89	4.85	17.47
Sep	52,880	0.21	580	1.22%	40,583.85	3.67	19.07

The monthly tracking shows the monthly spending, impressions, cost per 1,000 impressions (CPM), click-through rate (CTR) percentage, total number of clicks, total cost per click (CPC), landing page views, and cost of each landing page view. The second part shows post engagement, which are customers who clicked through and then came back to the Micro-Mark website via retargeting in an advertisement we posted for them personally and the cost of that advertisement per click. It also shows the total number of orders, the conversion rate (CVR), and the total revenue from the campaign. The return on ad spend (RoAS) is an item we examine closely. For every ad dollar spent, we received back around $4.50 in revenue returned. The cost per order (CPO) is also a number that should be aligned with your AOV. For us, our AOV is around $100.

Another tactic in social media is to find a non-competing company with similar demographics to run a joint promotion campaign. In this strategy you would post the other company's promotion on your feed in exchange for similar posts on their feed of your promotion. This equal exposure brings in new customers, and the exposure to your customers is appreciated if the company you have partnered with is relevant to your causes.

For now, we see opportunities on Facebook and Instagram. We use Pinterest images for web traffic. We post heavily on YouTube and identify keywords for Google organic search value. We do not yet see ROI in TikTok as of yet. However, many of these platforms took years before they created opportunities for advertising that could bring an acceptable return. I am a member of several groups of CEOs and CMOs, and no one whom I am aware of has yet to see ROI on TikTok. However, TikTok is making changes all the time, and I think it is likely that sometime in the future TikTok will be a viable source for capturing younger customers. Many times the social media market and the influencer market cross paths.

Influencers. The influencer market has grown significantly in the last few years. Now influencers can build their own brands or public opinions about something. Nedra, Hadhri, and Mezrani (2019) highlighted the main benefits of social media like sharing videos or images, writing feedbacks, using hashtags, engaging with other users, and engaging with other trademarks or brands. Research shows that high influencer-product connections drive improved consumer response, and followed-up interactions elicit higher customer purchaser intention (Ilyoung & Chen, 2019).

Influencer marketing will top $10 billion in 2020 and has become of increasing relevance for many companies in the B2C industries (Haenlein, Anadol, Farnsworth, Hugo, Hunichen, & Welte, 2020). Most businesses today in the fashion, beauty, food and beverage, and travel industries are using influencer promotions on some platforms like Instagram and TikTok (Haenlein et al., 2020). However, many marketing managers have a less-than-adequate knowledge of influencer platforms as compared with knowledge of more traditional channels and have difficulty navigating these rapid-moving environments (Haenlein et al., 2020).

Marketing managers have difficulty reaching younger customers using traditional marketing channels. However, influencers on Instagram and TikTok provide access to these younger potential customers. Sixty percent of users on Instagram in the U.S. are younger than 34, and 40% of users on TikTok are between 10 and 19 (Haenlein et al., 2020). The influencer influence on marketing is growing quickly. By all accounts, the channel will be more important in the future. Here are some current facts:

Influencer Marketing Fact Sheet

- Average earned media value per $1 spent has increased to $5.78.
- Three hundred percent more micro-influencers are now utilized by large firms than in 2016.
- Only 14% of influencer posts sampled were fully compliant with FTC guidelines.
- Nearly 90% of all influencer campaigns include Instagram as part of the marketing mix.
- Large companies have nearly doubled the number of creators they activate per campaign in the past two years.
- The majority (55%) admit to having a stand-alone budget for content marketing.
- Ninety-one percent of our survey respondents believe influencer marketing to be an effective form of marketing.
- Sixty-five percent of our respondents measure the ROI from their influencer campaigns.

(Influencer Marketing Hub, 2020)

Despite the potential and popularity, influencer marketing is still an activity run by younger staff, interns, or outside agencies. This situation is a great opportunity for younger employees, but in some cases these employees are not yet aligned with the organization's priorities.

Many of the young followers of influencers are following people like Kim Kardashian West (@kimkardashian), footballer Cristiano Ronaldo (@cristiano), and Kylie Jenner (@kyliejenner). These three are just examples to show the sheer number of followers these celebrities have free access to in marketing products they endorse. The following is a screen show of their Instagram profiles. Kim Kardashian has 195 million followers, Cristiano Ronaldo has 247 million, and Kylie Jenner has 205 million. The influencer channel might seem to be new and emerging, but the history of influencer marketing dates back many years.

Three Top Celebrity Influencer Instagram Profiles

Frank Sinatra and Jack Daniels. The first influencer could have been Frank Sinatra. Sinatra was an iconic international figure in music with a career from the 1940s through the 1980s. He was one of the few singers who can be referred to by just his first name, such as "Michael," "Elvis," "Madonna," and "Beyonce." "Frank's" medium was records, radio, television, and concerts. He was known to end his shows with an amber liquid in a glass for his last number. The story goes that one day a reporter asked what was in the glass. Frank said that it was "Jack Daniels, nectar of the gods." Jack Daniels at the time was a regional supplier of Tennessee whiskey. The story hit the newspapers, radio, and television. Every time Frank ended a show, it was an influencer promotion of Jack Daniels. The influence of Frank's disclosure provided viral marketing that grew Jack Daniels into an international company.

Jack Daniels

Social media has provided celebrities with instant access to millions of fans and followers twho are interested in the habits, day-to-day life, and products preferred by the celebrity lifestyle. I have a friend who graduated with a bachelor of science degree from Seton Hall University in New Jersey (and an MBA from Pace University, Lubin School of Business, in New York City). Lori Mariano started her career in the health and beauty industry, working for well-known brands in a corporate environment. She later broke off to form a company with two partners to "disrupt the health and beauty industry" and has made remarkable progress. Through their company, Hampton Beauty has shown the health and beauty industry the power of influencer marketing.

Kim Kardashian Perfume in Unique Bottle

The product development process includes working closely with celebrity/influencers to ensure that the product brings to life their vision, captures their DNA, and is a product that they're passionate about. As Instagram moments are important, attention to detail is a top priority when designing and developing products. Unlike traditional marketing methods, digital marketing strategy includes managing social platforms, content posting, and community engagement all in an effort to reach millions of fans and potential customers. Traditional PR and advertising are also still beneficial and can include TV appearances, print media, out-of-home events, and many other forms that reach a broad audience. Reach and impressions gained from these activities can be both paid and earned media value.

Celebrity brands are not new to the beauty category, but the business side has evolved. Celebrities that have built wildly successful brands through licensee/licensor relationships, include Elizabeth Taylor, Britney Spears, and Paris Hilton, to name a few. In recent years many celebrities and influencers have taken on a more entrepreneurial role with interest in brand ownership. Standouts among celebrity beauty brands today include Kim Kardashian West (KKW Fragrance and KKW Beauty), Rihanna (Fenty Beauty), and Kylie Jenner (Kylie Cosmetics). Celebrities who own their businesses are typically more hands-on and involved every step of the way, inspiring, designing, collaborating, marketing, selling, and making final decisions. On the front end, awareness-building tactics include, pushing out content via social media to connect product, fans, and sales. On the back end, fulfillment, distribution, and customer service complete the cycle to help digital first brands gain a competitive advantage in the health and beauty space.

Another company that uses influencers is Luvo, a company that sells healthful and tasty frozen food. The frozen food space in a grocery store environment is called the "morgue" because the space is shrinking with the trend to local and fresh foods in the marketplace today. The CEO is Christine Day, former CEO of Lululemon Athletica who spent 20 years with Starbucks. She invested in Luvo in 2014 after an unexceptional launch in 2013. She changed the menu to include ethnic dishes with robust spices and low calories.

Luvo Gourmet Frozen Food

She also acquired brand ambassadors like Derick Jeter, formerly of the New York Yankees, former Olympic swimmer Natalie Coughlin, and current National Football League player Russell Wilson, to invest in the company. Each of the brand ambassadors has large social media audiences whom Luvo has access to daily. This novel strategy has allowed Luvo to take competitive space in the frozen food sections of grocery stores nationwide.

Not all companies can obtain celebrities to help in marketing efforts. At Micro-Mark we find micro-thought leaders. Our influencer efforts are to find users of our tools who have as few as 20,000 followers but with high engagement. We look for influencers who use tools and supplies to make high-end creations, influencers who shoot high-quality videos of how they make certain creations; these are key to getting the influencer connection with Micro-Mark. In some cases we provide free products to the influencer in exchange for a product review. In other cases we have a more formal relationship that includes a promotion code that tracks to the influencer, which results in a return to the influencer of a percentage of sales.

We have had some success with what we call affiliate marketing. We provide tools and supplies for builders with engaged audiences to shoot videos of our products. We give the affiliate a promotional code that can be used by customers to obtain a discount when ordering on Micro-Mark's website. This networking type of marketing can spread quickly, even internationally. Influencer marketing is relatively new to widespread marketing programs.

Catalog

Catalogs were once a major part of marketing in the United States before experiencing a decline in the 1990s and 2000s. However, we now see an increase in brands using catalogs. The catalog is a method of marketing that captures the customers' attention longer than most other methods of digital marketing. Also, catalog advertising does not necessarily need a discount to obtain sales, unlike most forms of digital marketing. Cataloging has a history that goes back farther than most might think.

Catalog History. The first catalog was published in Venice, Italy, by Aldus Pius Manutius in 1498 (A visual history, n.d.; Gibbs, n.d.). Manutius had a printing press and wanted to distribute a list of printed offerings of Aristotle, Theocritus, Virgil, Dante, Homer, Aesop, and more for sale throughout Europe (Gibbs, n.d.).

Aldus Pius Manutius

From wmf.org

In 1667 William Lucus published a seed catalog and distributed the book throughout England (A visual history, n.d.; Gibbs, n.d.). The idea caught on, and Lucus's seed catalog started numerous seed and plant companies to follow suit throughout Europe and into North America for several centuries.

Some credit Benjamin Franklin with the invention of the mail-order concept in a catalog of valuable science books. Franklin asked customers in remote areas to mail orders to him in Philadelphia (A visual history, n.d.; Gibbs, n.d.).

Benjamin Franklin's Catalog, 1774

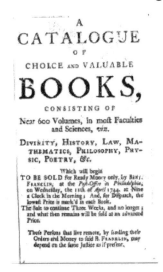

From flipsnack.com

Most credit the first commercial catalog effort in the United States to Tiffany's blue book, first published in 1845. This catalog has stood the test of time is and is still printed in the light blue cover today. Tiffany became well known worldwide for offerings of high-quality jewelry and related products. The iconic cover has become part of the Tiffany brand and is recognized by customers everywhere as a direct marketing pioneer.

This commercial effort was soon followed by many of the other giants in the catalog industry. The catalog movement from the mid-1800s allowed companies to offer products that were not readily available in the local brick-and-mortar stores. The development of the U.S. Post Office allowed the efficient delivery of the catalog, the mailed orders, and the product. Sears, Roebuck and Company became a well-known brand for large offerings of diverse products.

Tiffany's Blue Book

I remember receiving the Sears and Roebuck catalog as a child in the 1970s and spending hours flipping through the many pages of the book. Unfortunately, Sears discontinued the catalog in 1993, right before the beginning of digital marketing. This well-known company was a multichannel marketer with the catalog and with brick-and-mortar stores throughout the country. They never mastered the next layer of Internet marketing. I think some of the problem was bad timing as Sears in full strength would have been formattable online. Their stores continued to struggle, and the company filed for bankruptcy in 2018 but did survive. We will see if Sears can layer in best practices of digital marketing to survive into the future.

Sears & Roebuck Catalog, 1922

Sears & Roebuck

American catalogs were popping up everywhere. Montgomery Ward developed a catalog in 1875 for farmers in the United States to trade and cut out the middleman (Gibbs, n.d.). The company had a big impact in the catalog industry until it quit publishing catalogs in 1985. It also had brick-and-mortar stores throughout the United States. However, like Sears, it was the catalog that grew the company's brand recognition and allowed the stores to eventually enter the market. Sears and Montgomery Ward struggled to obtain a competitive advantage after failing in the brick-and-mortar and catalog environments. The companies have name recognition, but now that awareness is not associated with success. Also, despite both having large treasure chests at one time, neither of these companies adapted best practices in online marketing—highlighting the need for continuous improvement and learning.

Montgomery Ward Catalog, 1875

Montgomery Ward

Twenty years ago, the power of the catalog was still strong, and direct marketers or multi-channel marketers viewed websites as a method to lower transactional costs (Opportunities and Benefits, 2002). The popularity of catalogs and direct marketing was undoubtedly due to convenience, as research has shown for many years (Gehrt & Yale, 1996). Gehrt and Yale (1996) found that the convenience regarded more than simply time and included spatial and effort convenience as well.

The catalog business reached a peak in the 1990s and, with the introduction of digital marketing, saw a dip in the early 2000s. However, as stated earlier, in the past several years a resurgence of catalogs has occurred. In recent years digital marketing companies Wayfair and Amazon have included print catalogs in their multi-channel marketing efforts. The dip in catalog production and the resurgence have created a new demand for professionals who understand the complicated business of catalogs. However, many of the catalog professions have retired.

Consequently, researchers are rushing to provide information about the needs and qualifications of catalog professionals in the digital age (Park, Lu, & Marion, 2009). These researchers say that technological advances provide pressure for cataloging professionals' skills and knowledge to include electronic resource management, metadata creation, and web applications (Park et al., 2009).

You can outsource your catalog but I have found the cost to be very expensive. Hopefully you have a staff with expertise in images, copy, and publication. Good creative teams are hard to find. But the quality of your product will be substantially determined by the quality of your staff. Next, we will discuss some of the details of making a catalog.

Paper and Binding. Although print catalog skills have changed slightly in the digital age, some of the tried-and-true processes are still relevant today. The creation of a catalog will take more detail and can be provided in this document. However, basic brand issues need to be determined. One is the size of the actual catalog. Many catalogers are tempted to use a shape that is unusual. However, the basic 8.5 inches by 11 inches is the most efficient and financially effective. Another decision that you will need to make is the type of paper, which can be glossy to flat and the paper thickness ranging from 80# weight to 100# weight. The quality of the paper will be highlighted by the intensity of the white background. Good-quality paper will be whiter and the text will be easier to read but the cost can be significantly more. Also, a heavier weight paper will increase the weight of your catalog and increase the cost of mailing it. You must balance the look and feel of the brand with the cost and expected ROI.

Micro-Mark Catalog Page, Saddle-Stitch

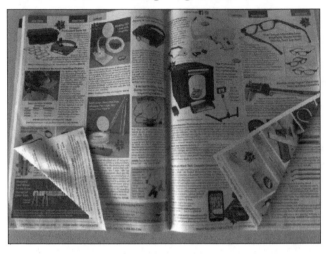

When a typical catalog is printed, one sheet of paper composes four different pages. These pages are placed strategically to create the catalog based on the type of binding. A common and less expensive type of binding is saddle stitch.

The stitch is commonly three staples in the middle of the catalog. The pages are stacked together to create the order of the pages.

The side of a saddle stitch looks like the image below.

Saddle Stich-Bound Catalog

A more expensive and higher quality binding is the perfect bind, shown below.

Perfect-Bound Catalog

Finally, less expensive than saddle stitch and perfect bind books is the spiral-bound book. Yes, this photo is of a book I wrote in 1989. I try to write one every 30 years.

Spiral-Bound Book

Space Allocation. Another challenge is the allocation of space in merchandising catalog products. Catalog managers must manage the space to expected sales in regard to placement location in the catalog, the total space allotted for the image and text (Sokolick & Hartung, 1969). Different allocation of space will result in significantly different catalog sales totals (Sokolick & Hartung, 1969). Another critical decision is the space, including image size and the amount of copy, given to a particular product on each page. Some big sellers might warrant an entire page for one product. Other products can be listed as one line. If more space is used to promote a product, the product will likely sell more units. However, the cost of the page is an important element. If, for example, the cost of a page in a 100-page catalog is $2,500 to produce, publish, and mail and you want your advertising cost to be $.25 per $1.00 in revenue, each page on average should obtain $10,000. However, the first few pages and the last few pages in the back of a catalog are important areas to provide space to top-selling products.

Many catalogers will develop a square-inch analysis that measures the allocated space on each space to the product. Six square inches of space should sell twice as much as three square inches of space. The square-inch analysis will include a projection and track the results of each product by the square inch by page.

I like to place new products at the beginning of the catalog to inspire old and new customers and to highlight the new items. These pages might be less dense with the number of products per page. As the new product is introduced in a few catalog publications, the space allocation is reduced, and the location would move to the appropriate category location within the book. Next we will discuss circulation.

Circulation. In many catalog companies the circulation manager occupies a full-time job with the staff. This team works with the customer mailing list service provider. These are companies that manage your customer file, similar to the way Mailchimp manages your email file. These are companies like Experian, DirectMail.com, Caldwell List Company, and Conquest Graphics. We use a smaller company, Ryan, that provides the detail we like. Direct mailing does not have the same opt-in requirements similar to email and SMS. However, these customer service providers help to reduce address duplication, improve address validation, and can find addresses of customers who have moved.

The circulation manager will divide the customer file list primarily by recency, frequency, and monetary value (RFM). Recency is the last time of the order, and frequency is the number of orders. We break our file by recency and frequency and the AOV to divide the customers into segments. Customer segments with sooner recency, higher frequency, and higher AOV might receive more catalogs on an annual basis than one that is lower. Once the preliminary circulation plan is mapped, the circulation manager will then work with a consulting list manager to hone the list for improved addresses and lower duplication. These services can also provide options for buying a prospection list of customer files of brands that have similar demographics to your company. Circulation is real science, and I would recommend getting a manager, even a consultant, to work with your file and to work with one of the top consulting firms to manage your customer file and prospecting.

Printing. Several companies can provide catalog printing services. These companies will take the electronic file of the catalog you created, the specifications on the paper, binding, and circulation to print your catalog. We use a company called Dingley Press. But you have several options with QuadGraphics, Xerox, AastroNova, Cenveo, and many more. Many of these companies have numerous locations. Your catalogs have a go-to print time, and once in print, no changes can be made. These companies also provide the bulk mailing of the catalogs.

I do not go into postcards here because I have difficulty seeing the value of them. Most postcards have to have some kind of discount or offer to work. The difference in cost between a postcard and a 100-page catalog is not much. The cost of a postcard to create and send, including the mailing cost, is about $.38. With enough circulation, the cost of mailing a 100-page catalog is $.59 or less. The catalog is much more likely to get an order and is considerably better for your brand connection with the customers.

Freight Chart, Guarantee, Order Sheet. Some catalogs have an information page that includes a freight chart, the firm's guarantee, and in some cases an order sheet. An order sheet is common only in companies with older customers who prefer true direct mail orders. In most cases, the catalog acts as an information tool, and customers eventually go online to place the order.

The freight chart or freight cost disclosure is critical because many new customers will examine the freight cost before considering shopping. If your freight charges are out of line, the customer will not continue to look at the catalog. I call this page the "trust" page because it is one of the first pages a customer will go to understand the company and to lower the risk of this business transaction.

Example Trust Page

This page shows the guarantee, the freight chart in grey, shipping information, forms of payment, and the no-risk guarantee. Next, we will discuss the importance of the cover of a catalog.

The Cover. The cover of a catalog is the first thing a customer or potential customer will see, of course. If the cover is not compelling, the customer will not open the catalog, and you will not get a sale. If the cover is compelling enough, you will get several "page turns" before the customer will decide if he or she wants to go through the catalog. Many loyal customers look forward to the arrival of their favorite catalog and spend time perusing the entire book. Therefore, the cover is an important image. Over the many years I have been involved in the catalog industry, I have always given significant time and effort to improve the cover.

MCM Gold Award

The cover can be a brand image that conveys a lifestyle. It can also be a product shot. I have seen the revenue numbers on a good cover product image go up by 30 to 50%. The cover space is a good seller. It is also treated with honor by professional marketing associations. The Multi-Channel Marketing Association gave us the Gold Metal award (shown above) for the best catalog cover in 2008 while I was president of Jackson & Perkins.

While covers can win professional awards, the most important issue with covers is if they work for the customer. Everyone can have an opinion about covers, and rarely can we find out who was right. I personally like to input on the concept because in many cases we are trying to get across something about a product or something about our brand. The right image can make a big difference.

Park Seed Cover, 2007

This cover is not going for beauty or selling anything in particular; it was a brand effort. The lady in the image was one of the owners of the company. A catalog can be seen by millions of people, and sometimes a cover shot is desirable. However, the cover should speak to the brand's demographics. This brand's demographics were garden enthusiasts, almost 60% women, in the 50- to 65-year-old age range.

As you can see, however, this cover provides a 20% discount from any order and a free seed packet offer, which is a pretty rich offer. We highlight the company's 125-year history in the bottom right corner. We also have a $3.00 price tag at the top right corner. We rarely charged $3.00. We were showing value to those that received the catalog.

With the Jackson & Perkins brand, we took a different approach. This company was about roses because we were the largest ornamental rose grower in the world at the time. We carried many different types of roses, but the focus was on the new introductions in the rose breeding program. We introduced three to eight new roses each year that took eight to ten years to breed and evaluate. The new characteristic about the roses were the key features. The fragrance could be sweet, chocolatey, fruity, spicy, and musky. Other characteristics are repeat bloomers, large blooms, straight stems, and more. So, the catalog covers highlighted the new rose introductions each year. The following cover performed exceptionally well.

Jackson & Perkins 2011 Spring Catalog Cover

Jackson & Perkins sold bareroot roses in the spring and small container roses in the fall. However, the company built from that base of garden enthusiasts a following of customers for gift giving of holiday flowers. These holiday buyers were the same customers who purchased roses. The nice thing about the holiday business is that in many cases the gift buying is repeatable. We would change the look of the pot and change the arrangement each year using the best bulbs available. At one point Jackson & Perkins was the number-one bulb buyer in the world—and we were really a rose company.

Jackson & Perkins Holiday Gift Catalog, 2010

This cachepot was a top seller with the color and the cardinals. If you can leverage your file to provide a holiday gift offering, the opportunity is to improve the number of orders per year. These customers are already trusting of the brand, and the line extension is good if the quality of the gift offering matches the core offering quality, which in this case was high-quality roses.

Wayside Gardens was a little different. Wayside Gardens was a plant introduction company that had been responsible for the introduction of many key plants into the industry. A reknown gardener, John Elsley, was responsible for evaluating and selecting winners, as was the heart and soul of Wayside. This niche company had a major impact on what was hot in horticulture. If a plant was on the cover, garden enthusiasts bought up all the supply that was available for years.

Wayside Gardens Cover, 2011

When I arrived at the company, John was working privately but lived in the area. I knew him previously, and he had been a neighbor of mine. I was able to talk John into resuming as head of Wayside Gardens. Plant breeders were constantly improving on new types of plants, and John introduced the first herbaceous perennial Paeonia with a fragrance in 2011 on the Wayside Gardens cover. We reached an agreement to buy all the available stock of this plant for two years. We leveraged the cover to get exclusive agreements for other unique plants that we later introduced.

When I became the CEO of Micro-Mark, we did not leverage the covers or use the covers as selling tools. We had a skilled creative team, but leadership gave little focus to the product or brand; the emphasis was on *who* was on the cover. We eventually began using the cover to highlight products and to integrate the logistics, and leverage the vendor relationship to get the most out of our covers.

Micro-Mark Catalog Cover, 2017

In this cover we are showing a particular tool in action. Customers want to see what the tool can create. Inside the catalog we discuss the feature of the product but the interest is initiated by the results of using the tool.

Micro-Mark Catalog, Winter 2017

In this case we introduced a 3-D printer by connecting the product made by printing a replica of *The Thinker* by Auguste Rodin on display in Paris. The limitations of what you can create are the limitations of your mind.

Another cover of interest was Micro-Mark's Cosplay cover. We design and sell unique tools that are expensive but provide precision to skilled craftspeople. These craftspeople might work with wood, metal, plastic, or other materials. They could be making anything. We found that many of our new customers were making costumes and props for Cosplay or other types of hobbies. These craftspeople were making costume replicas of comic book characters and movie heroes and villains.

Micro-Mark's Cosplay Cover, 2019–2020

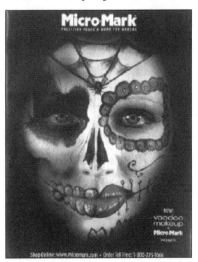

We started attending related tradeshows like New York Comicon, which had over 300,000 attendees, of which at least one-third were in full costume. Not all the costume wearers were highly skilled craftspeople, but many were. We knew we needed to reach these potential customers.

Print Advertisements

Print advertisements are a shrinking form of advertising but should be discussed. PricewaterhouseCoopers says that print advertising is currently 25% of the advertising spent on the Internet in the U.S. and is expected to be reduced by 10% over the next four years while Internet advertising is expected to grow by 25% (Global Entertainment, n.d.). However, print advertising can still play a role in your marketing efforts, especially if you serve enthusiasts' market.

Print advertisement has the constraints of space due to the cost of the medium, similar to catalog space. The cost of print advertisement varies dramatically depending on the circulation of the magazine. Some hobby or niche magazines only have 10,000 or so circulation every quarter, while other more prestigious magazines have millions in circulation monthly. These ads are sold as a full page, half page, or quarter page.

The race to obtain attention in the advertising space is highly competitive. Consumers see every day an average of 360 commercial messages across television, radio, the Internet, newspapers, and magazines (Johnson, 2014). One study showed that a competitive advantage could be reached by including human faces in the print advertisement (Guido, Pichierri Pino, & Nataraajan, 2019). Another study showed that print advertisements with animals or humans would improve the response rate (Trivedi & Teichert, 2020). However, this study showed that having both animals and humans in the ad will reduce the response rate (Trivedi, & Teichert, 2020).

Tracking the ROI of a print ad can be difficult unless the ad includes a unique promotion code for the customer to receive a discount if used. The code is generally to a specific magazine ad. Such a code includes a discount for the customer, so the cost of the ad is increased. Some research suggests that print ads should be treated like social media ads as a path for purchasing. This research advocates for some attribution for stages in the purchasing journey. They say if advertising spillovers are not included in some attribution, the impact of the ad is underestimated (Vardanyan & Tremblay, 2006).

Micro-Mark does some print advertisements in small production magazines for enthusiasts. We include a promotion code to track ROI intermediately and use the average to obtain an overall ROI per magazine. One problem with these small circulations is that many of the subscribers are already Micro-Mark's customers. Next we will discuss trade shows.

Trade Shows

Most industries have B2C and or B2B trade shows. These trade shows or exhibits allow small businesses to show products to consumers and other potential business buyers. The shows also allow B2B purchasers to find new products and vendor relationships. Several studies showed that not much academic research is available on trade shows and performance outcomes (Gerschewski, Evers, Nguyen, & Froese, 2020; Lovett, Chi, & Little, 2020).

Gerschewski et al. (2020) said that trade shows are a tactic that small businesses can take to develop networks, especially international networks. Lovett et al. (2020) said that trade shows are effective for the procurement of merchandise with a wide variety of types of trade shows available in the U.S. Other research showed that trade shows are good for relationship building and that they are a source for learning what is happening in the industry (Shih, T. Y., & Yang, C. C., 2019).

Virtually all the companies for which I have led a financial turnaround were not participating in trade shows prior to my arrival. I find it hard to obtain a short-term ROI on trade shows. In some cases, attending the show to find new products, ideas for new products, and new manufacturer relationship is worthwhile. In other cases, the trade show allows the exhibitor to sell products. In these cases, the cost of the show can usually be covered by the sales revenue. In other cases, exhibiting the show is to obtain more B2B relationships. At Park Seed and Jackson & Perkins, we started exhibiting B2B shows to obtain new wholesale customers.

NY Comicon 2019 Micro-Mark Booth

At Micro-Mark the company had not exhibited at trade shows for many decades. We started to exhibit at shows slowly and grew the number of trade shows to over 20 before the pandemic. We exhibited at tool shows, model train shows, and modeling exhibits. We also dived into the Cosplay world by exhibiting at the NY Comicon and a few other regional shows.

When exhibiting at a B2C show, we try to gain interest at the booth with a discussion. However, the primary goal is to obtain contact information so we can reach the potential customer later. We also use potential customer social media and images to spread Micro-Mark across many followers.

We look at trade shows as a means of engagement. We try to be selective about how many shows we can attend and how much we spend. We always learn many things at trade shows, and the event is a source of continual learning.

Micro-Mark Backdrop for Trade Show Images

Brick and Mortar

Family-owned retail stores have been a fixture in retail stores since the 1700s in the United States. These stores appeared as small towns popped up during the move west. Micro-Mark's origins were from a small family-owned store in Newark, New Jersey, before we moved a few miles west to Berkeley Heights, New Jersey.

Scientific Model Store in Newark, New Jersey, 1928

Department stores started appearing in the late 1800s, culminating in large numbers of iconic stores like Sears, Roebuck, and Company; Macy's; JCPenney; and many more. Cash registers, the invention of the credit card, and eventually the debit card made retail brick-and-mortar stores more convenient. Malls began appearing in the 1950s, soon followed by the big-box store concept of Walmart in 1962. As we moved into the 1990s e-commerce began to appear. Many brick-and-mortar retailers have not been able to move to the digital marketing space.

Since 2014 Sears has closed 218 stores, or 25% of their total number of stores; Macy's has closed 135 stores, or 24%; and JCPenney has closed 218 stores, or 20% (Tokosh, 2019). Retail bankruptcies and store closings have increased rapidly over the last few years, creating what some call "retail apocalypse" (Peterson, 2017; Rushe, 2017; Kline, 2017). Brick-and-mortar stores are still an important element of retail sales. However, the extent of the decline and new role for brick-and-mortar is still to be determined.

Some research shows that traditional retail has been under stress since the multi-channel business model appeared in the 1990s (Jocevski, 2020). Jocevski says that the lines between physical and digital space are blurred and that five new innovations will enter the modern retail store, including in-store technology, the role of sales associates, the use of the mobile channel, data analytics, and collaborations. The role of the brick-and-mortar store can be that of a hub. Companies that can pull off the integration of the store with the five new innovations will win the retail battle (Jocevski, 2020).

Aninday Ghose wrote *Tap: Unlocking the Mobile Economy* in 2017. I have a signed copy of his book, which highlights the connection between smart phones, brick-and-mortar stores, and the future of retail. He emphasizes the smart phone as the key to future retail. The phone provides customer data in regard to location, even within view of a billboard or retail store to serve up texts and promotions to market based on proximity (Ghose, 2017). Some retailers are embracing this technology.

Consumers are spending more time on the phone than any other device and the information this time can reveal is detailed consumer information (Ghose, 2017). Some might not like the access to individual information that the smart phone can reveal. This information cannot be used without consent. So now in many malls, as you walk in you might receive a text that says to opt in to receive mall store promotions. Why would you not consider getting discount promotions? You accept. Then you shop in a store and walk away. You soon receive a text that gives you a discount at the store you just left. This is the state of brick-and-mortar retail today, according to Ghose (2017).

Summary of Marketing Today

We have discussed the many changes that have happened in recent years. We examined digital marketing, including current research and professional best practices in websites, search and paid advertisements, and email marketing. We also discussed SMS and MMS, social media, and influencers.

This section also reviewed catalog and print advertisement. The catalog review included the history of the catalog and the integral parts of developing one. The catalog creation discussion included paper and binding, space allocation, circulation, printing, the trust page, and the details about the cover. Then advertisements and trade shows were scrutinized. Finally, the marketing section discussed the current research and the state of the brick-and-mortar retail industry.

10

Amazon Marketplace

"There are two kinds of companies: those that work to try to charge more and those that work to charge less. We will be the second."

—Jeff Bezos

Amazon was founded in 1994 and began selling books on the Internet in 1995, and the initial public offering (IPO) was in 1997 (Reimers & Waldfogel, 2017). Bezos started the company as an online bookseller, shipping from a warehouse, and expanded to sell less popular books through third-party sellers' inventory, which was the start of Amazon Marketplace (Cusumano, 2017). Amazon's book offering soon grew to over two million, which was far more than that of any other competitor (Cusumano, 2017). Soon Amazon began selling many other products. Bezos's goal is not for profits; it is for Amazon to sell everything (Stone, 2013). Amazon's dominance of the Internet is undeniable.

The Amazon Marketplace provides Amazon products and third-party sellers' products. Today these products include books, music, DVDs, unboxing videos, downloads, VHS, magazines, newspapers, video games, software, Amazon shorts, electronics, audio, video, camera and photo, cell phones and service, computers, hardware, office products, musical instruments, outlets, and home and garden items (Bezos, 2007). Amazon also sells bed and bath items, furniture and décor items, gourmet food, kitchen and housewares, outdoor living products, pet supplies, automotive supplies, tools and hardware, industrial and scientific items, apparel and accessories, shoes, jewelry and watches, grocery items, beauty and health items, personal care products, sports and outdoors items, toys and games, and baby products (Bezos, 2007). FBA (Fulfillment by Amazon) provides warehousing and fulfillment of products to consumers and businesses. This line of business competes with UPS and Federal Express to deliver the last step of fulfillment.

In June 2017 Amazon acquired Whole Food Incorporated (Whole Foods), a national grocery store chain with almost 500 locations, for $13.7 billion (Cusumano, 2017). Amazon will continue to expand product offerings and third-party access to customers via 147 warehouse locations throughout the United States. Amazon is committed to low or no shipping costs to the customer (Zhu & Lui, 2018; Khan, 2017; Bezos, 2016). This commitment comes at a high cost of billions of dollars of negative net freight (Khan, 2017; Bezos, 2016). Amazon is poised to provide one-hour shipping to 35% of the U.S. population with the proximity of Amazon warehouses (Soper, 2019; Khan, 2017; Bezos, 2016). Amazon will also enter the shipping business to compete directly with UPS and Federal Express in the U.S. (Bezos, 2014).

Any company that sells a product has to have some kind of Amazon Marketplace strategy. There are several different strategies, including not selling within the Amazon Marketplace. We will discuss some of the threats of the Amazon Marketplace as well as the massive opportunities in using the Amazon Marketplace.

Definition of Amazon Terms

Amazon Marketplace. Amazon began as an online bookseller and soon opened the online offering to third-party sellers, which was the beginning of the Amazon Marketplace (Cusumano, 2017). The Amazon Marketplace offers products from Amazon and third parties competing on the same platform. The Amazon Marketplace consists of FBA and Seller Fulfilled.

FBA (Fulfillment by Amazon). In a letter to the Amazon shareholders, Bezos (2007) said that FBA was a set of web server interfaces that convert warehouse fulfillment centers into a computer peripheral. FBA allows third-party sellers to ship products to the Amazon fulfillment warehouse to store prior to the sale to the Amazon customer. Once the product is purchased on the Amazon website, Amazon handles the fulfillment to the customer and charges the third-party seller a fee. FBA allows third-party sellers access to Amazon Prime customers. Amazon Prime is defined below.

Seller Fulfilled. Seller Fulfilled products are those sold on Amazon's website and fulfilled from the third-party warehouse (Hartley, 2019).

Amazon Prime (Prime). By 2018 Prime had over 100 million members who pay a fee to access free two-day shipping for many products sold on the Amazon website (Bezos, 2019). The membership also provides free unlimited access to digital content, including movies and series (Reimers & Waldfogel, 2017). Prime was introduced in 2005 and has been a key Amazon strategy for customer loyalty (Reimers & Waldfogel, 2017). As of 2018, Prime offered free one-day shipping in 8,000 cities worldwide (Bezos, 2018).

Seller Fulfilled Prime. Seller Fulfilled Prime allows third-party sellers to ship directly from the third-party warehouse to Prime consumers (Bezos, 2016). Amazon sets a high-quality standard for on-time shipping and consistency for third-party sellers to qualify for Seller Fulfilled Prime (Bezos, 2016).

Prime Now. Prime Now offers one-hour delivery to select cities worldwide (Bezos, 2016). By 2018 Prime Now offered free one-hour shipping in 50 cities in nine countries (Bezos, 2018).

AWS. In 2005 Amazon launched AWS to sell excess storage and computing capacity from Amazon's data centers (Cusumano, 2017). AWS is the most profitable line of business for Amazon (Cusumano, 2017).

Star Ratings. Star Ratings are ratings on Amazon.com based on reviews from buyers of third-party sellers and provide the percentage of positive feedback from the last twelve months (Wang, 2018). Many customers use the ratings to decide which seller to select and will pay more for more stars (Wang, 2018).

The Opportunities of the Amazon Marketplace

Amazon stormed onto the digital marketplace selling books online and has since changed the retail market as we knew it. Amazon Marketplace growth is the fastest of any company and continues to grow at an astounding pace. The company has focused on growth with narrow profit margins and has grown in revenue every year since its inception with indications that it will continue to grow in the future.

Amazon.com focused on growth over profit, and the company first made a profit in 2001 at five million dollars on $1 billion in sales or 0.5 percent in net profit (Reimers & Waldfogel, 2017). The company has since fluctuated between losses and narrow profits for years (Reimers & Waldfogel, 2017).

Table 21: Amazon's Revenue and Profit by Year

	Revenue	Net Profit	Net		Revenue	Net Profit	Net
1997	0.2	0	-19%	2009	24.5	0.9	4%
1998	0.6	-0.1	-19%	2010	34.2	1.2	4%
1999	1.6	-0.6	-38%	2011	48	0.6	1%
2000	2.8	-0.9	-31%	2012	61.1	0	0%
2001	3.1	-0.4	-13%	2013	74.5	0.3	0%
2002	3.9	0.1	2%	2014	89	-0.2	0%
2003	5.3	0.3	5%	2015	107	0.6	1%
2004	7	0.6	8%	2016	136	2.4	2%
2005	8.4	0.4	4%	2017	173	3	2%
2006	10.7	0.2	2%	2018	233	10.1	4%
2007	14.8	0.5	3%	2019	280.5	11.6	4%
2008	19.1	0.6	3%				

Amazon.com, 2020, Revenue and Profit in Billions $

This growth of Amazon provides opportunities for you. Today the Amazon Marketplace provides access to more customers than any other platform. Amazon Marketplace is the largest online marketplace in the United States, with opportunities for third-party sellers to reach digital customers (Hartley, 2019).

In the first year Amazon Marketplace operations third-party sellers accounted for five percent of the total units sold on the Amazon website, and in 2014 third-party sellers accounted for 40% of the total sales and two billion units sold (Bezos, 2015). By 2017 over 50% of all items sold on Amazon were from third parties (Bezos, 2018).

Table 22: Percentage of Amazon's Sales by Third-Party Sellers

Year	% of Sales	Year	% of Sales
1999	3%	2009	31%
2000	3%	2010	34%
2001	6%	2011	38%
2002	17%	2012	42%
2003	22%	2013	46%
2004	25%	2014	49%
2005	28%	2015	51%
2006	28%	2016	54%
2007	29%	2017	56%
2008	30%	2018	58%

Note that Amazon has not provided data about percentage of third-party sales in 2019 or 2020 to date. Third-party sellers can participate in the Amazon Marketplace via FBA or Seller Fulfilled channels. Also, third-party sellers can distinguish from other sellers using Star Ratings, which rank sellers based on customer feed. This section will examine FBA (Fulfillment by Amazon), Seller Fulfilled, and Star Ratings.

In 2006 Amazon introduced FBA, providing warehousing, picking and packing, logistics, and deliver services for third-party sellers (Bezos, 2007). FBA offers these third-parties services through Amazon Prime or free two-day delivery (Bezos, 2007). The use of FBA has inserted Amazon directly into the business of its competitors. Bezos (2015) said that FBA is the glue that links the business strategy of the Marketplace to the business strategy of Prime. Third-party sellers' products and Amazon's products can be ordered together and combined into the same package for savings (Bezos, 2015). By the end of 2014 Amazon had 109 fulfillment centers with 15,000 robots that move inventory (Bezos, 2015).

In 2014 Bezos (2015) launched free two-hour delivery and one-hour delivery for a fee of $7.99 available in the Manhattan, Brooklyn, Miami, Baltimore, Dallas, Atlanta, and Austin markets. Using FBA allows third-party sellers to have one-hour delivery in some parts of the world. Amazon has leveraged the online dominance to negotiate favorable terms in the delivery sector and to build warehouses and delivery vehicle logistics, establishing physical delivery to the consumer (Khan, 2017).

One perspective is that retail competitors are left with two undesirable strategies: to try to compete directly against Amazon or be reliant on Amazon to deliver to the customer (Khan, 2017). Another opinion is that third-party seller use of FBA has additional advantages (Mitchell, 2016). For example, third-party sellers using FBA will rank higher in Amazon search results than third-party sellers not using FBA (Mitchell, 2016). Amazon sells slightly more third-party products than direct Amazon-sold products, and approximately half of the third-party sales are FBA while the other half are Seller Fulfilled (Hartley, 2019).

Seller Fulfilled products are those sold on Amazon's website and fulfilled from a third-party warehouse (Hartley, 2019). Amazon has demanding requirements to qualify for Seller Fulfilled Prime with high standards for shipping speed and consistency (Bezos, 2016). Amazon and eBay have grown in part because they connect third-party sellers and consumers with a safer environment to conduct transactions (Xiao, 2016).

Seller reputation through **Star Ratings** is important to obtain a large number of sales, and a new seller could take many months or years to develop a large number of good ratings. Consequently, a market for selling businesses with good ratings has developed (Xu, 2018). A seller could enter the marketplace using the strategy of developing a new account in Amazon, or a seller could acquire an existing account with a good reputation (Xu, 2018). Obtaining and maintaining a good seller reputation is a critical strategy for third-party sellers on Amazon (Xu, 2018).

Amazon Prime. One of the primary strategies of Amazon's growth was through Amazon Prime. In 2005 the company introduced Amazon Prime, which provided customers free shipping and unlimited access to digital content for $79 per year (Khan, 2017; Reimers & Waldfogel, 2017). Amazon has added other perks like free books, videos, one-hour delivery in certain areas, and more television programs to obtain customer loyalty (Khan, 2017). As with other Amazon programs, the company lost money for many years to obtain growth in membership in Amazon Prime (Khan, 2017). The loss estimates on Amazon Prime are as high as $2 billion annually (Khan, 2017).

By 2018 Amazon Prime had over 100 million members globally, purchasing 5 billion items annually, with over 50% of items sold by third-party sellers and 25% across borders (Bezos, 2018). Membership to Amazon Prime allows access to Prime Video with a vast number of television shows and series with numerous awards, including Golden Globes and Emmys (Bezos, 2016). Amazon Prime only recently started advertising, but one researcher said that the position of Prime and recent Amazon moves could substantially change advertising in the future (Lipsman, 2019). The current configuration of advertising is that 60% is about branding and 40% is about the sale of a product (Lipsman, 2019). The primary reason for the configuration is that advertising is challenging to track attribution to a purchase of a product, and the return on investment is unclear (Lipsman, 2019). Amazon recently acquired the digital advertising server Sizmek Incorporated (Sizmek) (Slefo, 2019). Sizmek is a direct competitor to Google Marketing Platform, which helps companies place digital advertisements and provides tracking of performance (Slefo, 2019). With the acquisition of Sizmek, Amazon will get paid to send web traffic to Amazon.com (Slefo, 2019).

The acquisition also will change advertising to flip from 60% branding to 60% product sales because Amazon will have more insight to acquire attribution (Lipsman, 2019). Amazon will bring in more data from brick-and-mortar locations like Whole Foods, Amazon Go, Amazon Books, and Amazon Four-Star. With the advertising data, brick-and-mortar data, Prime Video data, and Amazon's website data with over 100 million members in Amazon Prime, Amazon will have 360 degrees of individual shoppers' buying habits across all channels (Lipsman, 2019).

Amazon Prime bundles perks like renting e-books, streaming music, videos, free rapid delivery in one-hour, or same-day delivery to create membership loyalty (Khan, 2017). According to an analysis, customers who become Prime Members increase by 150% annually (Stone, 2013). Amazon Prime members also spend considerably more each year on Amazon.com. The average Prime member annually spends $1,500, compared to the non-Prime customer at $625 (Rubin, 2016). As a result, Amazon Prime members are more loyal and more likely to shop at Amazon.com than other websites (Khan, 2017).

AWS is now the biggest provider of cloud services in the world and has more market share than the next three main competitors combined, which are Microsoft, IBM, and Google (Bromall, Mishra, Draus, & Stewart, 2019). Cloud technology began in the early 2000s and is now, in one way or another, involved in every business (Bromall et al., 2019). AWS began operations in 2010, and in eight years it was the Linkedin selection for top companies to work for professionals (Bezos, 2018). AWS includes Amazon Aurora, WorkDocs, WorkMail, AWS Lambda, EC2 Container Service, AWS Marketplace, and Mechanical Turk (MTurk) (Bezos 2015). AWS provides speed and agility but also reduces customers' information technology (IT) costs (Bezos, 2015). Netflix chose AWS in 2009 as a storage solution because of speed, capacity, scalability, and cost (Bezos, 2016). In 2017, AWS introduced SageMaker, which allows third-party developers to build machine learning (Bezos, 2018).

Bezos (2019) said that today AWS customers, which range from startup to enterprise, including government and nonprofits and users, include developers, operation managers, chief information officers, digital managers, chief information security officers, and more. With AWS, Prime, and FBA, Amazon can make money on any part of the retail chain. Amazon can also not make money in some areas to increase growth with reduced cost to customers. Amazon Marketplace is the largest e-commerce platform retail market on the Internet and gives third-party sellers access to the biggest customer pool in the world (Khan, 2017). But this access is not without real threats. We will discuss those potential threats in the next section.

The Threats of the Amazon Marketplace

Amazon has shown the use of the strategy of predatory pricing, or pricing below costs, to forgo profits to gain dominance (Wang, 2018; Khan, 2017; Reimers & Waldfogel, 2017). Some have found that small retailers have complicated choices to enter the Amazon Marketplace, and more research is needed to provide retailers information about the different strategic outcomes in the marketplace channels (Xu, 2018). Amazon can be predatory to third-party sellers and will begin selling like products that reduce sales for these sellers (Wang, 2018; Zhu & Liu, 2018; Khan, 2017; Reimers & Waldfogel, 2017). Amazon has considerable influence over the success of third-party sellers, and many third-party sellers with successful products are pushed out of the market because Amazon begins to compete directly (Zhu & Liu, 2018).

Amazon will copy only products that have shown success, and it is less likely to copy products that will take greater effort to sell (Zhu & Lui, 2018). This strategy by Amazon discourages the affected third-party sellers from pursuing growth in the Amazon Marketplace, but Amazon justifies the practice because of the product demand and the subsequent reduction of shipping costs for consumers (Zhu & Lui, 2018). It is recommended that third-party sellers use a strategy not to sell blockbuster products on Amazon and to engage in continual new product development to leverage the Amazon Marketplace (Zhu and Lui, 2018).

Regarding product sales, Amazon is committed to low prices, even to the point of low or no profit (Wang, 2018; Khan, 2017; Reimers & Waldfogel, 2017; Bezos, 2006). The company is determined to keep costs low in order to grow business. Amazon is also committed to innovation (Galetti et al., 2019; Bezos, 2018; Rossman, 2019; Rossman & Euchner, 2018; Bezos, 2017; Bezos, 2016). This innovation comes not only from core competence like the need for data storage and the development of AWS (Bromall et al., 2019; Bezos, 2018; Cusumano, 2017). Amazon's innovation includes areas that are new to Amazon, like the introduction of Kindle (Reimers & Waldfogel, 2017; Bezos, 2009).

Amazon is a learning organization at the core of the business (Galetti et al., 2019; Fulgoni, 2018; Bezos, 2017; Khan, 2017). The company will continue to piece together more data about consumers. Data from Whole Foods and other physical stores will be combined to provide better understanding of individual customer needs and desires (Lipsman, 2019; Soper, 2019; Fulfoni, 2018). This data will then be accessed to deliver a more personal experience for the customer on the Amazon website, in communications, and in the physical retail locations (Fulgoni, 2018; Bezos, 2011).

One of the key issues with using the Amazon Marketplace channel is the many frustrations that third-party sellers experience. The relationship with Amazon is unbalanced, and Amazon is not interested in making the relationship fair. The types of frustration that third parties experience is with communication, penalties and fines, shipping issues and restrictions, pressures to fulfill, and returns.

Communication with Amazon is frustrating because the company communicates primarily through email. Amazon's decisions in favor of the customer are made mostly through email, and it rarely replies to the third-party seller's side of the story. After the company suspended Amazon Shipping, Micro-Mark had no satisfactory method to communicate with Amazon.

Amazon is quick to apply penalties and fines to third-party sellers. The penalties include the suspension of Seller Fulfilled Prime for reasons outside of the third-party seller's control. I have seen Amazon suspend many times from Seller Fulfilled Prime status primarily for long-time in transit deliveries. In these cases, the transit delays were out of the control of the third-party seller once in the hands of the transit company.

To regain the Seller Fulfilled Prime status, the third-party seller would have to develop a corrective plan of action to submit to Amazon. In each case, Amazon rejects the plan and does not reinstate the Seller Fulfilled Prime. Usually, a resubmission of an edit of some minor changes will cause Amazon to approve the plan. The fines include sending packages over 50 pounds to FBA without a team lift sign on five sides of the package. The fine is $50 for each violation.

These themes should be taken into consideration when designing a strategy to enter the Amazon Marketplace. A third-party seller should look for ways to leverage the Amazon strategies for the benefit of the third-party seller. The data shows that Amazon will continue to have success and will likely continue to use predatory tactics to third-party sellers. Additionally, Amazon appears to be in a good position to avoid antitrust issues. Bezos's strategy from the beginning was to provide lower costs and more choices for the consumer. Amazon's success appears to be sustainable.

Strategies to Consider for the Amazon Marketplace

Products that you can consider for the Amazon Marketplace are those for which you have at least a 45% product margin between the selling price and your cost. Amazon will take fees in many forms, including a selling fee, shipping fees, advertisement fees, FBA fees, and many more. These fees are complicated and non-negotiable. Your profit will come from the difference in the selling price, your product cost, less the Amazon fees. This amount can come at a loss to you. However, most sellers make between 5 to 35% profit on the Amazon Marketplace. The price for which you sell the product on Amazon can vary. In highly competitive products, you will see price-cutting to get higher visibility on the Amazon website.

Higher visibility comes not only from the lowest price. Higher visibility on the Amazon website can come from higher Star Ratings, using FBA, and running advertisements on the Amazon website. We try to run advertisements at around 15% of the price initially for new products. Once we get higher visibility, we run ads at around 9–10% of the selling price.

If the product is one you created, I recommend getting a Universal Product Code (UPC). To obtain a UPC, go to https://www.barcode-us.info/. If you are selling a product that is made by another company, use their UPC code. If it does not have a UPC code, you can generate an Amazon number for the product within Seller Central.

I recommend Jason R. Boyce and Rick Cesari's book *The Amazon Jungle* (2020). They provide some additional information about how to set up products on the Amazon Marketplace. This information includes cope, images, and videos.

I have been astonished at the number of sales that can come from one product. The Amazon Marketplace is massive, and you will likely also be surprised at how much you can sell if you follow specific strategies. We lay out some strategies that we know have worked for us and others.

Strategy One: FBA. To implement Strategy One, you need to go to Amazon's Seller Central on their website and follow the instructions for loading products. If the product you load is accepted, you will receive a notice as to how many units you can send to FBA. You can send up to the limit based on your packaging. Amazon will provide you a UPS label to send your products to FBA. You have no choice as to which Amazon FBA warehouse your product will go. In some cases your products will go to multiple locations. Amazon normally will have your product available to sell within a week of shipping.

The benefit of using FBA is that your product will be available to millions of loyal Prime customers. Amazon is responsible for shipping the product to the purchasing customer. And your product will get to customers with Amazon's rapid shipping time. You get paid every two weeks. The more you sell, the more Amazon will allow you to send to FBA. If the product does not sell after several weeks, Amazon will send it back to you and charge your account.

Strategy Two: Seller Fulfilled. The Seller Fulfilled strategy is different only in that you are responsible for shipping the product to the Amazon customer. The listing is the same as in FBA. Amazon requires you to ship within one day, and in some cases, you must ship the same day. If you fail to follow Amazon shipping guidelines, you could face suspension. It is not uncommon for third-party sellers to get suspended. A good third-party seller can be upgraded to **Seller Fulfilled Prime**. This means that you have access to Prime customers with products shipped from your warehouse.

Strategy Three: Both FBA and Seller Fulfilled. The combination of FBA and seller fulfilled can take many forms. You could use Seller Fulfilled to determine if a new product will sell well enough to send to FBA. If the product sells well enough, you could ship it to FBA. If it does not, you could continue to sell in Seller Fulfilled to get the sales that are available.

Strategy Four: Do Not Sell in the Amazon Marketplace. The last strategy involves not selling on Amazon. This strategy in some situations could make sense. If you have a good product that is easily copied, selling on Amazon would likely shorten the time before the product is copied.

Not selling on Amazon does not just eliminate access to the largest digital marketplace. If you have your own website, you will not get the traffic from Amazon. Many Amazon customers will look at the product owner's website. Many of these customers will become your customers.

This is the ultimate reason for selling on Amazon, according to Jason R. Boyce, a top seller on Amazon (Boyce & Cesari, 2020).

—11—

Other Marketplace Channels

"The secret of successful retailing is to give your customers what they want. And really, if you think about it from your point of view as a customer, you want everything: a wide assortment of good-quality merchandise; the lowest possible prices; guaranteed satisfaction with what you buy; friendly, knowledgeable service; convenient hours; free parking; a pleasant shopping experience."
—Sam Walton, 1918–1992

Walmart.com, HomeDepot.com, eBay, Etsy, and Alibaba are discussed after the section on Amazon. Amazon is so much more impactful than these other channels, but these channels are other places to market digitally and find new customers.

Walmart.com

Walmart.com was founded in 2000 with headquarters in the Silicon Valley area to have access to digital experts (Walmart.com history, n.d.). Walmart is the largest retailer in the world with $524 billion in annual revenue in 2019, 11,500 stores in 27 countries, and the company is growing at 10% annually (Walmart, 2020). In contrast, Amazon had only

$280 billion in 2019 with 21% growth.

Walmart has the advantage of the number of stores over Amazon, but they have not leveraged that advantage in the digital space yet. Walmart.com operates separately from the brick-and-mortar operations except that a Walmart.com customer can return an order through the stores. Walmart.com is far behind Amazon in digital sales.

Micro-Mark sells products on Walmart.com, and the channel is second for us in marketplace channels in revenue. Walmart.com is also growing quickly on an annual basis for Micro-Mark. Walmart.com is more selective in regard to third-party sellers, whereas Amazon will let virtually anyone sell on their platform.

Also, Walmart.com will not blame the third-party seller for in-transit issues from carriers like UPS and FedEx. Amazon's rationale behind suspending third-party sellers for issues out of the control of the third-party is frustrating. Walmart.com does have strict requirements behind shipping the same day. Micro-Mark was contacted in December 2020 and asked to participate in the new FBA version of Walmart.com. We are currently trying out this channel.

Micro-Mark Product on Walmart.com

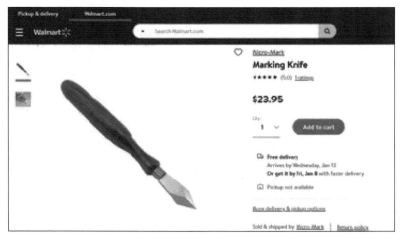

Micro-Mark expects to see sales continue growing on Walmart. com. We were able to easily integrate Walmart.com with our NetSuite ERP to have inventory and transaction flow. We found this integration to be significantly easier to integrate with Amazon or HomeDepot.com. Next, we will discuss HomeDepot.com.

HomeDepot.com

HomeDepot.com began operations in 2000 (History of HomeDepot, n.d.). The company has over 2,200 stores worldwide and had sales of $110 billion in 2019 with 3.5% growth (HomeDepot, 2020). I started selling on HomeDepot.com in 2005 using the Park Seed Company. We saw success and then started selling plants using the Wayside Garden brand. In 2007 we also began selling plants and supplies using the Jackson & Perkins brand. We grew the business into a multi-million-dollar enterprise. HomeDepot.com operates with an integrator called Commerce Hub. Commerce Hub is difficult to integrate with other ERP channels. The business grew to have dedicated employees to manage the orders and customer service. The orders were fulfilled similarly to the core business orders. At Micro-Mark I expected similar results with our power tool and hand tool offerings. We have seen growth in the channel, but not like with Walmart.com or even close to Amazon. We have integrated Commerce Hub to our NetSuite ERP system. However, this integration took a significant amount of custom scripting.

Micro-Mark's Arbor Saw on HomeDepot.com

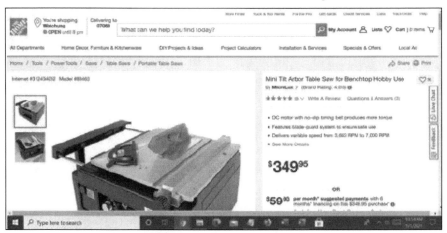

Next we will discuss eBay.

eBay

During Labor Day weekend in 1995, Pierre Omidyar spent the weekend writing code on his personal computer that led to the launch of AuctionWeb (Our History, n.d.). Two years later the company changed the name to eBay, and in 2002 eBay purchased PayPal (Our History, n.d.). In 2014 eBay and PayPal separated to become two companies traded separately (Our History, n.d.). eBay had revenues of $10.8 billion in 2019, up one percent from the previous year and the company had 183 million active buyers on the website (eBay Financials, 2020).

One innovation that eBay provided to buyers was to establish a reputation mechanism to both sellers and buyers for monitoring and to improve trust (Cabral & Hortacsu, 2010). Traditional retail relies on trust developed by repeated interaction and personal encounters. Digital markets had to create trust mechanism with sellers and buyers that remain anonymous. Cabral and Hortacsu (2010) found that when a seller received the first negative feedback, the seller growth rate drops from positive five percent to negative percent. Also, once a seller receives the first negative feedback, he or she is more likely to receive subsequent negative feedbacks, and the impact is not much as with the first negative feedback (Cabral & Hortascu, 2010). Finally, sellers are more likely to exit eBay once they receive multiple negative feedback responses.

For small sellers who have time to give individual buyers attention, eBay is good. The buyers pose questions in the form of email that has to be answered within a reasonable amount of time. Many of the items sold on eBay are one-of-a-kind, sometimes used, and need detailed explanation and images.

We sold several hundreds of thousands of dollars in revenue at Park Seed. I have sold several items personally on eBay. Unlike Amazon, eBay tends to let the buyer and seller resolve disputes before stepping in. Micro-Mark does not currently sell products on eBay.

Third-Party Selling Micro-Mark Product on eBay

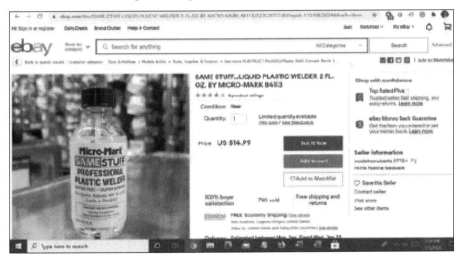

Etsy

Etsy was founded in 2005 by Rob Kalin, Chris Maguire, and Haim Schoppik in a Brooklyn apartment (Majewski, 2015). The original vision was to create a platform that would function as a place for craftsmen to sell their goods (Majewski, 2015). Etsy's annual revenue at the end of 2019 was almost $5 billion, and growth for the last few years has been 26% to 35% year over year (Etsy Annual Report, 2020).

Church and Oakley (2018) found that microenterprises that emphasize core competencies around customized and handmade products command higher sales prices on Etsy. Etsy exposes small business to a large customer base to allow critical mass for profit in niche areas of the economy while providing expanded amounts of products and product lines (Church & Oakley, 2018).

I have not sold on Etsy but we buy some products there. We have found good craftspeople on Etsy to perform custom work or to contract for high-end piece work. Etsy is growing and is a good place to get started if you are making a product yourself. Next we will discuss Alibaba.

Alibaba

The Alibaba Group was founded in 1999 by 18 individuals led by Jack Ma, a former English teacher from Hangzhou, China (Company overview, n.d.). The stated goal of Alibaba is to provide a platform that will allow small enterprises to leverage innovation and technology to grow and compete efficiently in domestic and international economies (Company overview, n.d.). In the Alibaba fiscal year ending in March 2020, Alibaba generated $1 trillion in revenue (Company overview, n.d.). Alibaba has grown quickly into a major player in the digital marketplace worldwide in both B2B and B2C marketplaces (Anwar, 2017). Alibaba has become the largest B2B firm in the world and is planning more international expansion (Kim, Zhang, & Zhang, 2016). While Alibaba's B2B platforms are the largest in the world, Alibaba maintains ten distinct B2B and B2C internet platforms available for small businesses and consumers worldwide (Anwar, 2017).

In September 2014 the Chinese-owned digital company issued shares on the New York Stock Exchange, making Alibaba the world's largest initial public offering at the time (Burke & Eaton, 2016). Alibaba's platform consists of sellers, buyers, third-party service providers, strategic alliance partners; investors and the company's revenue are primarily from online marketing services, commissions on product sales, and fees from the sale of memberships in wholesale marketplaces (Burke & Eaton, 2016). Alibaba does not engage in direct sales or hold inventory (Burke & Eaton, 2016). Its revenue comes from pay-per-click, display ad services, and commissions from product sales and memberships. Substantially, all of Alibaba's revenue comes from transactions in China (Burke & Eaton, 2016). China has seen economic growth, and the market is expected to grow even faster in the future.

At Micro-Mark we have used Alibaba to connect with manufacturers to produce small-batch custom manufacturing runs. The platform is good for finding small manufacturers that specialize in niche products. We have not yet used the platform to connect B2C transactions with Chinese customers—although with the growth of the Chinese economy and the increase in Chinese wealth, the market should be a target for Micro-Mark in the future. In the next chapter we will talk about freight and the many changes that have taken place in freight in recent years.

12

Freight

"Anyone can deliver packages—from the small boy in the neighborhood on up to the most extensive delivery systems in the land. The one thing we can have to offer that others will not always have is quality."
—Jim Casey, founder of UPS.

"The riskiest strategy is to try to avoid risk altogether."
—Fred Smith, founder of Fed Ex

We discussed earlier the increased demand for customers' desire for free shipping and the annual increases in shipping costs from the major carriers. Many years ago, direct mail companies made a lot of money on the difference between the cost of shipping and the revenue charged to customers for shipping. This net freight amount has dwindled over the years. This section will examine some of the issues with package delivery and freight. We will examine the importance of understanding dimensional weight. We will also discuss fraud before examining USPS, UPS, FedEx, and international shipping.

Dimensional Weight

All the major carriers except USPS use a dimensional weight factorial. The factor is a three-digit number that is the base dimension before additional fees are added. The baseline dimensional weight factor is 139 and can be negotiated with UPS or FedEx to well over 200. To show you how this factor can make a difference, we will review the three most commonly used box dimensions at the company I currently run, Micro-Mark.

The three boxes are close in size. The smallest box is a Baby Box at 8" x 6" x 5", the middle box is Box 19 at 11" x 8" x 5", and the larger box is Box 14 at 12" x 8" x 6". Assuming each box weighs 1.1 lb., most carriers will round the rate up to 2.0 lb. However, dimensional weight can be a factor. We will use a fictitious base price of $6.32 for the base shipping cost to ship to a nearby location.

Three Box Sizes

Table 23: Example of Dimensional Weight

	Actual Weight lb.	Carrier Round Up	Dim	139 Dim	Weight Charged lb.	215 Dim
Baby Box	1.1	2	8 x 6 x 5 = 240	240/139	2	240/215
Box 19	1.1	2	11 x 8 x 5 = 440	440/139	4	440/215
Box 14	1.1	2	12 x 8 x 6 = 576	576/139	5	576/215

As you can see by the chart, if your dimensional weight is 139, the charge is 5 lb. for a Box 14, even though the actual weight is 1.1 lb. If your negotiated dimensional weight is 215, the charge is only 3.0 lb. This difference can be $2 or more, and multiplied by thousands of packages, that can make a big difference in cost.

Fraud

One issue with shipping packages to consumers is that there are some bad people out there who will commit fraud. Just as shoplifters pilfer brick-and-mortar stores, people will attempt to steal packages from your business. The most common method is to provide a different billing address than the shipping address. Mastercard, Visa, American Express, and Discover will not honor different billing and shipping addresses if the customer later appeals. As a merchant, you will have no recourse. I understand that this seems unfair, but such is the way with commerce today. The credit card companies will eventually suspend the credit card of a consumer who has garnered multiple complaints. However, these criminals will likely just get another card.

Another method of fraud is to redirect the order in route. Both USP and Fed Ex will default to allow customers to go online and redirect the order to a different address. These are cases in which the credit card is probably stolen, so the transaction is later canceled while the criminals receive the package. The final most common method to steal a package is to take the package from the customer's porch. The customer, of course, will claim that the packaged did not arrive and the company is out the payment. Nobody advocates for the company. You are on your own. The carriers, the credit card company, and the customers do not take any responsibility. It is a cost of doing business.

I have found that different products have a greater likelihood of fraud cases. High-priced electronics are more likely to get fraud cases than other product lines in my experience. As the seller, you have to price in the cost of fraud or you can get hurt badly. Next, we will discuss the carriers and the differences between the carriers. We will discuss UPSP, UPS, and FedEx. The issues to consider when examining these carriers is the time in transit and the cost. I also think the brand can be an issue. Which of the carriers will represent your brand better?

Throughout my career I have negotiated with each of these organizations for better rates on particular types of services. If you are a large-enough shipper, you will have a representative (rep) from each organization. The rep's job is to understand your business and then provide services that fit your need at a competitive price. These reps will spend some time with you understanding your specific issues and then design a contract to obtain your business for one or two years.

Your location, the type of shipper, and the timing of your packages all determine how much they will negotiate for your business. My company, Micro-Mark, ships a lot of packages in the first quarter of the calendar year. Most carriers have excess capacity in the first quarter because a lot of shipments are in the fourth quarter during the holiday season. The carriers build up capacity for the holiday that they cannot fill outside the holiday season.

The negotiations with the carriers are important because the terms and pricing will impact your bottom line. Additionally, the time in transit can impact your customer's experience. The experience will determine whether the customer orders from you again.

USPS

The United States Postal Service is a United States government organization that is unionized. They have lost money for many years. USPS regularly increases prices for the different methods of shipping they offer. Despite losing money, USPS is a solid carrier, and for some sizes of packages, they are the most efficient.

If you are sending a package or envelope under 13.5 ounces, UPSP First Class is the least expensive and fastest method for delivery. Micro-Mark uses First Class whenever possible. Another service that USPS provides is Priority Mail, which is above 13 ounces up to 70 pounds with a 105-inch restriction from the longest side plus the girth of the box. I find Priority mail is good for packages that are between 13.5 ounces and 2 pounds.

UPSP also has a Priority Mail Flat Rate that can be negotiated below list prices if you have some significant shipments. USPS provides a Flat Rate box that comes in three small sizes. This solution is good if you are shipping a lot of similar-sized items repeatedly that are over 13.5 ounces and just over 1 pound.

UPS

I have done more business with United Parcel Service than with any other carrier, and I think the "brown" is a good brand. UPS SurePost is an economical residential service that partners with USPS to provide the last-leg delivery. This service is in competition with Fed Ex's SmartPost. Depending on the rates and dimensional weight factor you can negotiate, the service can provide a solution for packages that are over 1.5 pounds and up to about 10 pounds. For anything over 10 pounds it is going to be more economical to use USP Ground. UPS Ground can ship hazardous items like some kinds of paint or aerosols. UPS also has at Next Day and Second-Day Air rates that are negotiable.

FedEx

FedEx and UPS have similar services. FedEx's SmartPost® is similar to SurePost® although FedEx claims they do less last-leg delivery with USPS. FedEx also has ground service, next-day, and second-day delivery. FedEx and UPS compete directly and will go after the same business to obtain one- to two-year contracts to lock in the business with minimum volume to obtain discounts.

FedEx also has a robust Flat Rate shipping program that provides boxes. This program is good for small items that are repeatedly shipped. Most of the companies I have managed have had too many different product sizes to take advantage of these programs.

Amazon Shipping

Amazon started last-leg delivery to consumers in 2013 in the United Kingdom (Bezos, 2014) and now owns 65% of the last-leg delivery. Bezos (2015) discussed the three characteristics that a business strategy must have to be considered at Amazon, which include that customers must love the concept—the business can grow considerably large and have strong returns on capital for many decades. Amazon is going after the last-leg delivery of consumer freight in the United States, including UPS, FedEx, and USPS. The company will use these three services to game against each other and to help Amazon become the dominant delivery service.

Amazon rolled out Amazon Shipping in a trial form in March 2020. Micro-Mark was one of the few companies that were given the opportunity to try Amazon Shipping. We were told that it was because we were a good shipper and excelled as a Seller Fulfilled Amazon Prime shipper. The experience was good with regard to cost, convenience, and time in transit. The trial lasted approximately three months before Amazon suspended the program due to COVID-19. I fully expect to see

Amazon Shipping back in the near future to go after the UPS and FedEx businesses.

International Shipping

If you plan to do international shipping, you need to find the right shipper for your business and package sizes. In my mind there are three choices: UPS International, Asendia, and DHL. I ship a lot to Canada, Australia, and Europe and currently use Asendia. However, you should shop this service if you plan to include international shipping.

ShipStation

Regardless of what carrier you use, you have to create a label for the package. You can go to each of the carriers and buy shipping directly. However, this requires moving from the website to find the best rates. I use ShipStation because it allows Micro-Mark to shop the best rates from all the carriers based on the shipping address, weight, and dimensions. ShipStation can access your negotiated rates from each carrier, and ShipStation provides its own rates. The website allows seamless shopping. The company also provides some tools for address correction and bulk shipping. ShipStation has similar competitors like PaceJet, Shippo, ShippingEasy, and ShipWorks.

Returns

Returns are a part of doing business on the Internet, and you should count on a certain number of returns as factored into the cost of doing business. Returns are costly because in many cases you pay the expense of shipping to and from the customers. Some companies are able to charge the customer for the return or obtain a restocking fee that can range from 10% to 30%. Many companies do not charge for returns in order to lower the barrier to order or to reorder later. My company, Micro-

Mark, has a return order form on the back of the sales order. This form makes receiving the return easier to process. It allows the customer to provide customer identification information and the reason for the return. It also allows the customer to indicate if he or she desires a replacement or a refund. The form also has an area for adding to the order if desired, including credit card information. Finally, it provides the Micro-Mark guarantee and product liability disclaimer. In some cases, if Micro-Mark was in error, the customer will call to get a shipping label email from us to ship the package back. In most cases the customer pays for the return shipping.

Example—Return Form

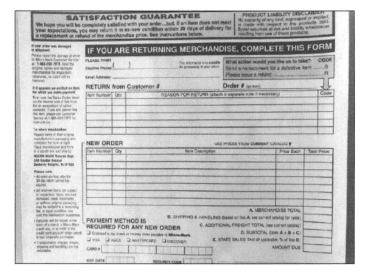

On the other side of the return form is the actual order listed, so this form will not be missed by the customer. If the form is filled out correctly, this form will help to process orders quickly and efficiently. Once you receive the item back, the item has to be inspected to see if the issue was actually what the customer claimed.

Summary of Freight

We discussed the importance of understanding dimensional weight and the need to negotiate the dim factor properly for your specific business. We also discussed the issue and frustration of fraud. You can try to avoid fraud, but it will likely happen in the course of doing business.

13

Finding and Managing Employees

"Hire character. Train skill."

– Peter Schutz

As the leader of your business, you are responsible for everything: product development, logistics, merchandising, marketing, customer service, fulfillment, government compliance, and much more. However, nothing will determine more about your success or failure than finding the right people and building an effective organizational culture. Pivotal decisions that you and your team make every day will determine the future of the company and the employees. If you hire the right employees and align their interests with the strategy of the company, you will have a much better chance of success in making the right decisions. The culture of your company will determine your future.

Leadership Style

Understanding your leadership style is important in finding the best process for leading your company. A big part of leading is developing trust between your employees and your customers.

Honesty. The first step to building trust is honesty. Employees and customers are constantly watching how you lead and how the company operates. You have to be honest 100% of the time. Once you break honesty, your role as a leader is cracked and very difficult to repair.

Trust in a leader stimulates positive work outcomes, and it helps employees to be more willing to listen to the leader and disclose their perspectives (Afsar & Shahjehan, 2018). Also, customers must be comfortable and trust your company before they will purchase products or services (Hess & Cameron, 2006). Hess and Cameron (2006) said that the goal of a value chain organizational structure is to maintain that every employee and customer is valued and treated with honor. The key to building the organizational culture starts with the leader and accountable leadership (Bäckström, Ingelsson, Snyder, Hedlund, & Lilja, 2018). The core strategy to obtaining loyal employees and loyal customers is honest leadership.

Servant Leadership

My leadership style is servant leadership. Robert K. Greenleaf introduced servant leadership in a 1970 essay (Spears, 1996). Spears has developed a list of ten characteristics of servant leadership, which include listening, empathy, healing, awareness, persuasion, conceptualizing, foresight, stewardship, commitment to the growth of others, and building community (Spears, 2004).

Several academic researchers have focused on servant leadership and organizational performance. One study showed that servant leadership provided a role model of serving that not only improves the performance of the employee but also impacts the improvement of the culture of the organization (Linden, Wayne, Chenwei, & Meuser, 2014). Jones (2012) said that servant leadership improves profits because of reduced employee turnover, increased trust, and enhanced employee satisfaction. Other studies showed that servant leadership builds a healthy workforce with cohesiveness and collaboration skills (Jit, Sharma, & Kawatra, 2017; Schwepker & Schultz, 2015). Finally, other research found that reduced self-interest found in servant leadership can increase performance, employees' collaboration, team cooperation, and can result in reduced conflict (Grisaffe, VanMeter, & Chonko, 2016; Tang, Kwan, Zhang, & Zhu, 2016). This section will address some of these areas of servant leadership.

Listening. One of the first tenants of a good leader is the ability to listen. Sometimes listening is difficult with the day-to-day difficulties that a business leader faces. There is a balance to listening. Employees have personal issues that generally are not part of work activity. Sometimes employees need an ear. But the main listening that is important at work is to make sure you are listening to different perspectives. If you shut employees out, you will miss a lot of good ideas. You will cut off a valuable resource to the company. Not all ideas can be implemented. However, you will get more perspectives if you are a leader who will listen to employees.

Also, you have to listen to your customers. Some operate under the saying "The customer is always right." I disagree. The customer is not always right, and sometimes customers will take advantage of your company. However, make sure that you are in touch with your customers. Customers will tell you when there is a problem with a particular product or carrier services, customer service, and every other aspect of the customer touchpoints.

As the CEO and president of several e-commerce companies, I have always made myself available as the last point of settlement with a customer problem. In most cases our customer service representatives can solve the problem. In cases they cannot resolve, I am the last level. Sometimes the problem is a misunderstanding. Each of these conversations provides information about our company.

Empathy. Empathy for your employees and for your customers is another key to servant leadership. Your employees need to know that you value them as individuals and not just people who provide labor. The sign of empathy can be from time to time but must show up when necessary. Looking at the business from the customer's view is another form of empathy in leadership.

Awareness. Another key to servant leadership is awareness. I always spend some time doing every job in the organization to gain awareness. Even in performing what is perceived to be the lowest job in the company, you can become aware of new ways of improving the processes. Assuming is the opposite of awareness and will eventually result in failure. As a leader, you should assume that you do not know and make all efforts to be aware.

Humility. Humility is another aspect of being a servant leader. A leader cannot let the trappings of the position clutter his or her thinking. If you assume a humble attitude, you will be more aware, have more empathy, and be more likely to listen to your employees and customers.

The Christian Perspective of Servant Leadership. Greenleaf and Spears were presenting servant leadership from a secular perspective. There is also the Christian perspective. According to the Bible, Jesus came to earth as the son of a carpenter, not as an earthly king. He came to serve humanity and washed the feet of His disciples. He was not arrogant, and He listened to those around Him. He also sought out to the right people to work with Him as His disciples.

Finding the Right People

As we mentioned before, finding the right people to work on your team is the key to your success. Over time I have improved in finding the right people. The thing I look for is the willingness to step up and learn new skills. We have a rapidly changing business environment with constant changes. People in general do not like change.

When I look at a résumé, I look to see progress in learning new software, certifications, or processes. A person who shows the propensity to learn new things will always be valuable to an organization. Also, the inclination to learn is not in every employee.

When I take over the leadership of an organization, I like to observe the interactions between employees. In most cases employees tend to drift into groups. These groups can sometimes be rivals and cause unneeded disruption in the organization. In many situations a key personality type or skill is missing from the organization that will be central to the strategy. If that person is not yet on the team, you will need to recruit to fill in the gap.

The first source for me to find qualified employees is through my professional network. LinkedIn has become a great source to this. The key is to write a job description that is appealing and describes the qualifications and needs for the job. If I am looking for a key executive, I will use an executive search firm because of the importance of obtaining a qualified fit.

Once you realize that an employee is not a fit, the best thing to do for the company, the employee, and yourself is to let them go. Sometimes a candid conversation will lead to the employee resigning. If you have been clear about your expectations and order of priorities and the employee cannot get on board, he or she likely never will. I have had to part with many employees. In most cases a logical discussion can make the transition easier for all parties. Helping as much as possible to achieve a smooth transition can go a long way. Remember that your employees will see and talk about how you treat other employees.

Compensation and Performance Reviews

A fair compensation plan can drive company performance, reduce employee turnover, and attract talent from outside the organization. The type of compensation plan and performance review should depend on the state of the company. If the company is in a financial turnaround or if the external business environment is uncertain, the compensation should be a fair base salary, modest increases, and bonus compensation for personal and company performance. Large salary increases are difficult because you are locked into that payroll going forward in the uncertain future.

Bonuses should always be achieved if the company is meeting the overall financial goals. If you are leading a rapidly growing company, you have to reward the performance of existing employees with raises and bonuses. This strategy will also attract outside talent to the organization. A rapidly growing organization can also reward employees with promotions from within to those who perform well. Sometimes this strategy is better because the employee understands the organizational culture and has a perspective from within.

Performance reviews weigh in heavily in human resource decisions in regard to layoffs, promotions, and merit pay, which can be contentious if employer and employee disagree (Martin, Bartol, & Kehoe, 2000). Performance reviews also help in the retention of strong workers and help to improve customer service by identifying problems and problem solvers. Employees should expect annual job reviews and obtain clear expectations for the coming year within the review. A policy that is in compliance with the law can be helpful in a contentious, expensive lawsuit.

Managing the Culture

Managing the culture of your company should include formal management and informal management. The formal management should be in performance reviews and the employee handbook. The informal should be in everyday life with a little bit of fun.

One reason to have the performance review and clear criteria outlined in the employee manual is to get all supervisors reviewing under the same process to also avoid conflict and to attempt to achieve standardization in evaluation. The importance of clear legal guidelines in the employee manual is that the documentation is helpful if the Equal Employment Opportunities Commission (EEOC) investigates the company. A clearly written policy and manual are evidence that the company is taking the equal opportunity seriously.

Academia defines the protected class as a group who suffered discrimination and are given special protections, including African Americans, Latinos, Native Americans, Asian Americans, and women (Gómez-Mejía, Balkin, & Cardy 2016). According to the EEOC, over 90,000 discrimination claims were filed in the U.S. in 2016 and the average settlement was over $125,000 in claims and legal expenses (Beemer, 2017). The best way a company can protect against discrimination is to institute a written policy that includes the following statements, described in Table 24.

Table 24: Statements in the Employee Manual to Consider

A statement that asserts that discrimination is illegal and that the company will not tolerate such
Examples of discrimination that include sexual, racial, religious, and others to demonstrate what is not acceptable
Explanation of how to report a discrimination complaint
A statement that encourages complaints of discrimination if they exist
A statement that the employer will conduct a prompt and thorough investigation and take appropriate action
A statement that the company will not retaliate against an employee who makes a complaint

Beemer, 2017

If the statements are in the employee manual or handbook, it does not mean the company is completely protected, but it demonstrates that the company is serious about discrimination. Employee handbooks, or policy manuals, are the best source for information provided by the human resource department, and they inform both the supervisor and the employee (Gómez-Mejía et al., 2016). All parties involved, the organization, the supervisor, and the employee have rights and responsibilities. One of the purposes of the policy manual is to avoid disputes and conflict (Gómez-Mejía et al., 2016).

While the employee handbook provides formal management of the organizational culture, just having fun can manage the culture informally. A company-paid meal, ugly sweater day, and other special events that bring the company together can have a real impact. I like to encourage managers and employees to develop and try events that are fun and relationship-building.

Giving Back to the Community

Another way to acquire and keep good employees, provide a sense of purpose to your organization, and improve your company's stakeholders is to give back to the community.

Many years ago, before the term *entrepreneurship* was used, India coined the term "Vaishya" to represent the business community as a part of varnashradharma (Jayaraman, 2020). Varnashradharma has a bad reputation within the caste system, but some of the system had positive potential. Jayaraman (2020) argues that the concept of the business community, which is still existing in India today, can be a model for business worldwide.

Most Indian companies I have worked with embrace community action as part of the organization's mission. Our digital ad agency, NetElixir, is headquartered in Princeton, New Jersey, but they also have operations in India. The CEO, Udayan Bose, and his wife, Tulika, run the company providing digital services. NetElixir also supports rural Indian girls who have little chance of higher education. If the girls do well in school, NetElixir will pay for their further education in high school and college.

This concept of supporting the community is widespread in Indian firms. The causes can be education, nutrition, women's issues, and many more. This form of giving back is a natural part of business in India. As we discussed earlier regarding the recent growth of the B Corp in the U.S., India has had this form of organization for centuries. Consequently, many U.S. corporations look to hire CEOs and executives from India.

Indian CEOs of U.S. Companies

1. Sundar Pichai—Google
2. Satya Nadella—Microsoft
3. Niraj Shah—Wayfair
4. Shantanu Narayen—Adobe Systems
5. Arvind Krishna—IBM
6. Anshuman Jain—Ex-Co-CEO, Deutsche Bank
7. Rajeev Suri—Nokia
8. Indra Nooyi—PepsiCo
9. Ajaypal Singh Banga—Mastercard
10. Punit Renjen—Deloitte
11. Ivan Manuel Menezes—Diageo
12. Sanjay Jha—Global Foundries

Indian CEOs leading U.S. firms far outnumber CEOs from other emerging countries like China and Japan. These CEOs instill a sense of belonging because the companies they run give back to the communities and the employees and shareholders appreciate the efforts. This effort is not just charitable; it has selfish intentions also. These companies realize that the communities surrounding their business will have to provide employees, customers, and support of the business operations (Mahapatra, 2019). The areas that surround the business have to retain and attract talent for the business to survive (Mahapatra, 2019).

The Importance of Diversity

Several studies show that inclusion and diversity in the workforce impact the organization to strongly improve global competitiveness

(Rahman, Turpin Jr. & Phelps, 2020; Mollel, Mulongo, & Market, 2015; Raatikainen, 2002). One reason is that organizations with an inclusive work environment will attract and retain the top talent that generates innovation that drives customer response (Mollel, et al., 2015; Raatikainen, 2002). Diverse groups tend to make better decisions and foster trust with customers (Raatikainen, 2002). However, a CEO's words and actions are not sufficient for the implementation of diversity management practices in an organization, and managers must view the CEOs as being committed to diversity in order for diversity management to be realized (Ng & Sears, 2020).

Setting aside the ethical and moral issues associated with discrimination over many centuries in many countries, from a pure business standpoint I want my team to be at least as diverse as my customer base just to get a balanced perspective. We discussed earlier the importance of obtaining different perspective from your employees; in order to get diverse reflective perspectives, you have to have diversity on your team. Throughout my career I have tried to hire diverse employees, and in all cases I have never regretted the hire.

Change and Employee Resistance to Change

Many studies have shown that employees resist change of any kind (García-Cabrera & García-Barba Hernández, 2014; Sasikala & Victor Anthonyraj, 2015; Yu & Lee, 2015). In doing financial turnaround of companies in stress, I experienced employee resistance to change. Employees can see only what they are allowed to see. Sometimes the view of the employee is narrow and does not include many of the aspects of the organizational operations. Also, when a company is under stress, naturally rumors will spread that cause disinformation. The employee stress level is understood because jobs could be on the line.

When I take over a financially stressed company, the first thing I do is to conduct personal interviews with key employees to obtain perspectives, a review of the financial records, and I observe the day-to-day employee interactions. When I became president of Park Seed in 2005, the company had been losing money for 15 years. The company needed to transition from a catalog-centered company to a digital company, which meant some changes.

While observing the first few weeks, I noticed that every day the staff would gather in the lunchroom to celebrate someone's birthday. Park had over 500 employees, which meant that there was a birthday virtually every day. These celebrations would include a birthday cake and punch and lasted about a half hour. Some days there were two birthdays on the same day. Instead of combining the celebrations, they had one in the morning and one in the afternoon. The cake-eating had become the primary focus of the company. The culture had evolved to be unaware of the negative impact of daily cake to the detriment of the financial condition of the company and to the health of the employees. I ended the daily cake fest. It was met with open resistance. Even as something so obvious, the employees did not want to change. We celebrated on the first of the month a short party for the employees born in the month as a substitute for the daily parties.

Employee resistance to change can be in the open, or it can be passive, but it is destructive to survival. The best way to lower the resistance to change is to include key team members in the analysis process. In chapter four we discussed examining your company for competitive advantage. We examined using the balanced scorecard, SWOT, VRIO, and other tools. Including key employees in the process will produce a better examination. The result is a clear strategy with priorities for time and other resources. The inclusion will also bring that team together, and they will be advocates of the new priorities. These new priorities are changes in everyday activity.

Once you have the advocates, the resistance to change is harder to implement. The resistance is not based on a strategy—it is based on "that's the way we've always done it." People will rally around the strategy, and the changes will make more sense.

Also, don't make changes just for the sake of making changes. If I'm used to a process in a previous company, I don't just make that change in the new company. Know that for some people change is difficult. Make changes only when necessary, which will lower the pain of the transition.

14

Product and Services Development

"Creativity is the process that gives life to a new product."
—James Taylor

"You don't get new product out of sameness."
—Jane Jacobs

In marketing it is new product, new content, or discount. If you rely on discounts only, it is a race to the bottom. New content is good and can obtain more views, but it is repackaging or reframing. In my world nothing beats new product. However, to create something really impactful takes innovation and work. Even if you create something special, you have to get the manufacturing perfect and the instructions impeccable.

New product is king. So, whenever I get involved with a new company, I want to understand how they develop new products. I like to find a diverse group of employees who understand the brand's customer needs to build the new product development team.

Academic literature recognizes the importance of new product development, and many studies have chased professional best practices. Some studies show that business relationships are essential for acquiring business opportunities, and international and domestic business relationships can positively influence new product development because firms accumulate knowledge and start new ventures (Fernhaber, McDougall-Covin, & Shepherd, 2009; Lin, Lu, Liu, & Zhang, 2016).

New technologies in design and manufacturing have improved and reduced the time necessary to create new product ideas. 3D printers and materials and design resources lower the prototyping cost and time, lower material consumption, lower production cost, and allow lower production runs (Achillas, Tzetzis, & Raimondo, 2017; Niaki, Mojtaba & Nonino, 2017).

At Micro-Mark we have used 3D printing for the design of prototypes and in production. We sell 3D printers, and we use them for manufacturing. The technology is improving every year, and we want to stay on top of what is happening in the 3D space. We also use many of the new design technologies that can translate into production programming.

I also agree that new product ideas can be found with third-party interaction. I see new product development happening in five methods, and I suggest that you use all five to introduce new products. We will discuss each of the methods, some new product concepts, and a summary of new product development in the next sections.

The Five Methods of New Product Development

The five methods of new product development include finding market-ready product, improving products on the market through collaboration, collaborating to create new products, developing new products in-house, and add-ons. Each of these methods requires different internal resources to achieve.

Market-Ready Product. Some products are available to purchase and ready for resale. Sometimes these products have good copy, images, and videos. Most products sold B2B will have minimum purchases, and many times you can receive additional discounts for increased purchases or commitments.

This following graphic shows a new product that Micro-Mark introduced to the U.S. hobby market last year. This desktop laser cutter can cut and engrave cardboard, wood, bamboo, leather, and acrylic. It can engrave fabric, steel, cement, glass, and many more materials. Micro-Mark worked with the manufacturer, Flux, to improve the instructions and some of the packaging. However, for the most part this product was ready to sell right out of the box. Micro-Mark sells primarily unique products, but we do sell some products that can be purchased in other locations. We offer these products because they are valuable for the customers we serve.

Beamo 30W Desktop Laser Cutter

One of the best ways to find market-ready product is at trade shows. I generally attend five to ten trade shows every year. These shows are in several different countries annually. The pandemic has slowed down some of these shows, and many have turned to virtual trade shows.

Improving an Existing Product. Another method of product development is to take an existing product and make it better. We found the Wondercutter at the Las Vegas tool show. The novel product was manufactured by a South Korean company, Cutra. The Wondercutter uses 40,000 ultrasonic vibrations per second to make precision cuts in wood, plastic, rubber, fabric, acrylic, and more.

We liked the product and the concept, but it needed some improvements to work in the U.S. market. Luckily, this startup company was willing to work with us to develop these improvements. Together we improved the instructions to be more English friendly; we worked to improve the collets, and we helped develop an improved cycle time and a few more items, including helping to navigate the Department of Energy (DOE), California's DOE, and Canada's DOE to obtain certifications.

You can find products that need some additional changes to fit into your market by attending trade shows. Sometimes you can find new products on the Internet and you can see that the idea is good but that some minor changes are necessary to access your market.

The Wondercutter, by Cutra

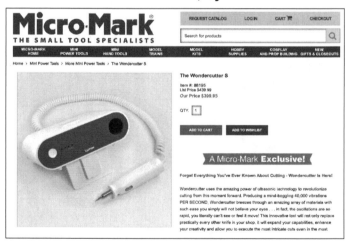

Collaboration to Create New Product. Another method used to create new products is to collaborate with another company to design, test, and manufacture a product. This is the primary method Micro-Mark uses to develop new products. We get an idea for a new product and discuss the concept with our new product development team. If the team is in favor, we create drawings or visuals of the concept. We also will create a video of what we envision about the product. That material is passed on to one of the product design engineering companies we work with regularly. They will develop drawings and get information back from potential manufacturers.

One of the issues that can increase the cost of a product is if the product needs tooling or dyes to make a part. Tooling can range from a few thousand dollars to hundreds of thousands of dollars. Sometimes the cost of the tooling is not worth the risk of the success or failure of the new product.

If we can agree on the costs and the risks, we have the manufacturer make a prototype. Usually the prototype needs some changes. Sometimes once you see the prototype you find that the actual design might need to change. These changes are kicked around for a few months before a prototype is finalized. You would think that once the prototype is developed, the manufacturing of the product would be a simple step. But inevitably the first run of the manufactured product is somewhat different than the prototype. These issues have to be worked out. The entire process could take 2 to 12 months, depending on the product.

Designed by Micro-Mark and Manufactured in Collaboration

Micro-Make Doctor Dry Booth was developed in six months in collaboration. The concept was developed by Micro-Mark and we worked with our design engineer and a manufacturer to bring the product to market.

In-House Development of New Product. Some products can be designed and manufactured in-house. Micro-Mark has been increasing manufacturing in the U.S. because our customers like "made in the USA." We have developed a design-build section that has over 200 products in production. Some are just components that are assembled.

Micro-Mark's SMI Keddie Roundhouse Kit

The Keddie Roundhouse was an actual building on the Western Pacific train line in the Sierra Nevada Mountains. Micro-Mark designed and now manufactures this kit for the hobby industry.

The Keddie, like some other Micro-Mark projects, was an intricate project that took months to design and prototype before going to production. Micro-Mark sells a line of model kits called SMI that have become popular in the hobby industry. These kits are either 3D-printed or laser cut and are either plastic or wooden. The design of some of these kits are replicas of actual buildings that existed. In many cases the actual architectural drawings are used to replicate the building on a reduced scale. Some of the buildings are quite large and take real skill with which to create an authentic replica.

The Add-On. The add-on is one of the most powerful strategies in new product development. Take a successful product and add an accessory to the product to improve the value. Customers like these types of values, and the new innovation keeps your product development moving. I have always used this strategy in product development.

Micro-Make Tilt Arbor Saw Super Value Package

At Micro-Mark we took our best-selling product, the Micro-Make tilt arbor saw, and created an add-on. The saw had sold for decades at Micro-Mark and the product was a success. We packaged together accessories like additional blades and fences to create a value package. The arbor saw value package idea soon became the new best-selling item for Micro-Mark. So, we created value packages around every best-selling power tool, and soon the page of value packages became the best-selling page in our catalog.

The add-on can continue. The Micro-Mark arbor saw is powerful and provides precision cuts for the user. The only knock on the saw was that it was small. It is used in modeling and diorama building, but it can be used for many other types of woodworking and finishing.

We took the one perceived knock on the saw, which was that it was small, and highlighted the fact that it is mobile. We created a heavy-duty carrying case to show the saw's mobility. The add-on idea can continue to reframe your products and to make customers rethink the usefulness of your products. Showing the new ideas for the product in action provides the customer a visual with which to see the product in new light.

Micro-Make Arbor Saw and Package

The add-on can be to many different types of products. At Jackson & Perkins we sold bareroot roses. The company sold bareroot roses for many decades. The breeding of a rose takes many years, and the company introduced one to four roses per year. These roses were bred to have improved fragrance, increased bloom time, a greater number of stems per rose, and more characteristics.

Jackson & Perkins aligned several of the roses in honor of an individual like Pope John Paul II, Princess Diana, and Nancy Reagan. Jackson & Perkins had agreements with the Vatican and the estates of the famous individuals. When we purchased Jackson & Perkins from Harry

& David, we were able to keep the agreements intact. What was nice was that the cause received a commission or a royalty to be paid to a cause of their choice. This arrangement led to the additional marketing that the Catholic Church would undertake to support the cause. The estates would also provide some publicity that would increase sales and allow us to increase the price.

J&P's The Pope Rose

For example, when we introduced the Pope John Paul II, we had 20,000 bareroot roses in stock for the year. We created a plaque to be planted with the rose to identify the rose in the garden. We sold the 20,000 units immediately for $150 each because of the relationship. This rose would normally sell for only $25.

This version of the add-on created increased profit margin and increased sales. While it was not my idea, it was intelligent marketing. We did create another add-on at Park Seed Company. The company had seed that had been in inventory for years. The seed was still viable and germinated at high rates. We found out that we had some seed from the original strain of the tomato call Park's Whopper Tomato. The strain had changed over the years and we also found that some old-timers preferred the older strain of the Whopper. We repackaged the seed to call it the Classic Park's Whopper, increased the price slightly, and sold out within a few weeks. People like a good story, and the Classic Park Whopper story was good.

Back to Nature Shitake Mushroom Log

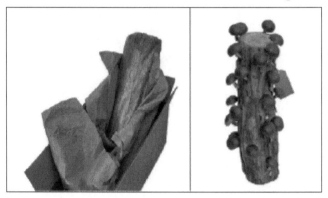

Another way to add-on is to create a line of products that are easily added for line extension. While at Back to Nature, we created a line of Living Gifts for Brookstone. The line was printed in their catalog and sold online. We started with a few nicely packaged gives and grew the like to be over 15 items.

The log was inoculated with Shitake fungi and sold packaged with directions. The log was then placed in the garden, and with natural rain, it began to grow and produce Shitake mushrooms—easy to grow and fun to harvest and eat. The edible nature of the product was another key element to the Living Gift program. Give a log as a gift, and the recipient has a mushroom garden soon without any work.

The Living Gift program also had a proprietary technique to ship fully planted terrariums. My team designed a packaging method to ship fully planted terrariums that could easily be unpacked to display a beautiful living gift. We packaged the terrarium so well that it passed what I call the "drop kick test." This test is performed by dropping the packaged terrarium to the floor and then kicking the box. Once we were sure that the packaged terrarium was able to pass the "drop kick test," we were ready to ship.

Back to Nature's Living Gift Terrarium
Shipped Fully Planted for Brookstone

We have discussed the importance of new product development and the many ways you can develop new products, including finding market-ready products to resell, improving existing products, collaboration to create new products, in-house development of new products, and the add-on method. Each of these methods can work, and I suggest trying all of them if you can. Also, know that new product development does not always work out. Sometimes you run into design challenges or absorbent tooling costs. Other times you find out you misidentified the need in the marketplace.

At Micro-Mark we have introduced over 600 new products in the last three years. We have had a few that did not work, but the total sales of these products are 40% of our total sales. Micro-Mark customers have grown accustomed to knowing that new and interesting products will be just around the corner. The anticipation of the new "reveals" also increases the sales of the existing products.

—— 15 ——

Brand Management

"A brand for a company is like a reputation for a person.
Reputation is earned by trying to do hard things well."
—Jeff Bezos

Academia likes to define and quantify business terms, and organizational brand is no exception. In professional practice we use terms like *brand equity, brand loyalty, brand image, brand awareness, brand identity, brand ambassador,* and *brand strategy.* The branding concept has developed its own terms within large organizations, media firms, business schools, corporations, advertising agencies, and business schools (Drawbaugh, 2001). The term *brand* has become so used that its meanings have become blurred, and the very existence has been questioned (Stern, 2006). Some define *brand* as the visual and verbal representations associated with organizations and products or services (Drawbaugh, 2001). Others consider it as defined by consumers' collections of perceptions (Foumier, 1998).

The word *brand* first appeared in Germanic languages that evolved into Anglo-Saxon, appearing as a noun around 1000 A.D. in the epic poem *Beowulf* (Heaney, 2002). Later the word appeared as a verb in 1400 A.D. in Wycliffe's *An Apology for Lollard Doctrines* (Todd, 1842). The

Germanic origins of the word are from the word *burn* (Oxford Dictionary Online, 2020). It later evolved into a distinguished marketing word used to identify ownership (Oxford Dictionary Online, 2020). The word was used widely to market ownership of farm animals or cattle. Somehow we jumped from cattle to Coke. We must also add a few other concepts to the topic of brand. Brand is considered important, and without strong brand loyalty, organizations will have a hard time increasing sales revenue (Lin, Wu, & Wang, 2000). Also, there is an emotional tie of customers to a brand that binds the relationship. Veloutsou (2009) stated that there are different emotions towards a brand. He also argued that consumers could develop strong emotions toward an organization that improves brand loyalty.

Recently efforts to build a strong and competitive brand from the perspective of the customer has become one of the key priorities in the organizational environment (Christodoulides, Cadogan, & Veloutsou, 2015). However, brand development is complex and subjective, difficult to measure, and is challenging for professionals to manage (Christodoulides et al., 2015). Corporate brands are an intangible strategic asset that can create a sustainable competitive advantage (Barney, 1991) for both large firms and small companies. However, branding research has focused on large companies (Balmer, 2012; Urde 2003). Very little research has considered brand management for small companies (Centeno, Hart, and Dinnie, 2013; Krake, 2005).

For the purpose of this book, we will focus on brand management. Brand management is the positioning of the company on the market in a way that it will attract and satisfy incoming consumer needs (Djordjevic, Cockalo, & Bogetic, 2016). This positioning of the company uses the strategies employed by management to create a sustainable strategic advantage.

Brand management consists of internal management and external management. Large corporations manage internal efforts and external efforts separately (Urde, 2003). Small companies tend to rely on the role of the founders and a close-knit management team to manage the brand (Inskip, 2004). These companies tend to manage both internal efforts and external efforts concurrently (Abimbola and Kocak, 2007). With that framework, this section will explain the current academic thinking in regard to brand management. We will categorize the different strategies to show the differences.

M'zungu, Merrilees, and Miller (2019) divided brand management into four different strategies. These strategies are Brand Identity-Driven, Brand Image-Driven, Operationally Driven, and Opportunistic Driven. Each has a focus either internally or externally.

Table 25: Brand Management Strategies for Small Companies

	Brand Identity Driven	Brand Image Driven	Operations Driven	Opportunity Driven
Focus	Internal position focus	External position focus	Internal position focus	External position focus
Action	Manage company culture	Customer focus	Operations focus, brand perfunctory	Exploit perceived opportunities
Measurement	Returning customers	Growth, new customers	Efficiencies	Growth, line extension
Brand	Strong	Strong	Weak	Weak

M'zungu, Merrilees, and Miller (2019)

M'zungu, Merrilees, and Miller (2019) provide categories of brand management strategies based on internal or external focus and priorities of the company. The Brand Identity Driven company is focused on internal culture and processes to gain a competitive advantage and customer loyalty. The measurement for the success of the Brand Identity Driven company is returning customers and lifetime customer value. The Brand Image Driven company is focused on the customer and the customers' perceptions. The is an externally positioned and focused company. The company measures success with growth and the addition of new customers and a key metric. The Brand Image Driven company will examine internal capabilities and shy away from opportunities because they could be a distraction.

The Operations Driven company is focused on internal processes to deliver customer satisfaction. This company is a well-oiled machine that is trying to improve with efficiencies like improved inventory turnover ratio, less waste, and lower return sales. The role of brand is perfunctory and considered only with a logo. The Opportunity Driven company also has an external position focus. The company is constantly looking for opportunities in the marketplace to exploit. This company will measure success with the expansion of new markets and products, including line extensions.

According to M'zungu, Merrilees, and Miller (2019), the Brand Identity Driven and the Brand Image Driven companies will create strong brands based on their style of brand management. They also say the Operations Driven and Opportunity Driven companies' brand management strategies will result in weak brands. My personal take is that the lines between these strategies are blurred. The same company can be viewed differently by different customers despite the employed strategy.

When I led the acquisition of Jackson & Perkins from Harry & David, I learned a lot about the Harry & David story. Samuel Rosenberg founded Harry & David in 1910, originally as Bear Creek Orchards in Medford, Oregon. Bear Creek Orchards grew amazing pears and other fruit. In 1914 Rosenberg's sons, Harry and David. The company eventually sold gift-packaged upscale pears and other fruit directly to consumers. When I arrived in Medford in 2007, Harry & David was still selling packaged pears in gift baskets. However, the number-one-selling item was their Moose Munch, a mixture of popcorn, caramel, nuts, and chocolate.

Harry & David had a large campus where they made and packaged the products they sold. However, their management told me that they sold so much Moose Munch in the holiday season that they had to begin making it in January and cold-storing it the entire year to meet the demand for holiday shipping.

Harry & David's Moose Munch

My view of brand comes from one of the iconic brand creators of all time. A long-time friend of mine, Brad Merkle, introduced me to Pat Farrah. Brad and I played football together at Furman University, and he is one of the best networkers I have ever met, much like Rev. Dr. Sidney S. Williams Jr.

Pat Farrah was one of the founders of Home Depot. He along with bankers Bernie Marcus and Author Blank teamed together to create the company. Pat was the merchant. His vision made Home Depot what it is today, and these guys really changed retail to what it is now known as. At one point, according to Pat, Home Depot was building a new store every 48 hours. Just imagine all that goes into building a store, hiring, and everything else.

For some reason Pat and I got along, and we worked on several projects together. He is a great storyteller, and I was eager to learn as much as I could from him. Pat said that one day he was standing in a Home Depot next to a customer in the water heater isle. Pat was always in the stores learning what customers want.

While both were looking up at the shelves of water heaters, Pat asked the customer, "What heater do you have at home?" The guy said, "A GE hot water heater, I think." Pat knew his water heaters, and he knew that at the time GE did not make a hot water heater. This interested Pat and he began asking other customers what brands of hot water heaters they had in their houses. It turns out that a lot of people thought they had GE. He then started videotaping these conversations with customers about hot water heaters.

Path then met with the CEO of GE at the time, Jack Welch. He showed him the videos and said, "Jack you own the hot water heater category, and you don't even make hot water heaters." GE soon bought a hot water heater manufacturer, added some of the GE touches to the product, and soon GE had the number-one-selling hot water heater in the U.S. with Home Depot as their top reseller. GE stayed in the hot water heater business until 2016, when they sold the business to Rheem, who is now the number-one seller of hot water heaters with Home Depot as their top reseller.

16

Franchising

"The most stunning thing you can do is go to Riyadh [the capital of Saudi Arabia] and walk around the streets downtown. . . . After you have had lunch at McDonald's, coffee at Dunkin Donuts, and have shopped at Saks Fifth Avenue, you have to wonder if they actually hate Americans or not."
—Thomas Lippman, Middle East journalist

"Franchising is the single most successful marketing concept ever."
—John Naisbitt in *Megatrends*

Not everyone agrees as to how and when franchising started. Many say it started in ancient China, in churches in Europe, or in the distribution of alcohol in Germany and England. Several say that the first franchise in the United States was by Benjamin Franklin as the franchisor in Philadelphia and Thomas Whitmarsh as the franchisee in Charleston, South Carolina, in 1731 over a printing business (*The History of Modern Franchising*, n.d.; *A Brief History of Franchising*, n.d). Seid (n.d.) says that the first franchise was truly in 1852, when Fredrick Henry Harvey opened restaurants on the Atchison, Topeka & Santa Fe Railroad with restaurants every 100 miles.

The International Franchise Association says that the first modern-day franchise was started by a woman, Martha Matilda Harper, who franchised the Harper Method Shops in 1891 to franchise hair care training and branded products and provided advertising and insurance to over 500 locations. The last location closed operations in 1972 (*The History of Modern Franchising*, n.d.).

General Motors sold its first franchise to William Metzger of Detroit in 1898, and Coca-Cola issued its first franchise to the Georgia Coca-Cola Bottling Company in 1901 (*The History of Modern Franchising*, n.d.). From there, many franchises opened throughout the United States and worldwide.

Table 26: United States Franchise History

Franchise	Opened
Rexall Drug Store	1902
Western Auto	1908
White Castle	1920
A&W Root Beer	1924
Hertz	1925
Kentucky Fried Chicken	1930
Authur Murray Dance Studios	1938
Dairy Queen	1940
Avis	1946
Dunkin Donuts	1950
Burger King	1954
McDonald's	1955

(*The History of Modern Franchising*, n.d.; *A Brief History of Franchising*, n.d).

The International Franchise Association (IFA) was founded in 1960 to address some of the problems in franchising, and today the IFA represents more than 1,300 franchisors, 10,000 franchisees, and more than 600 consultants and suppliers to the franchise industry (*The History of Modern Franchising*, n.d.). In 1979 the federal government issued the franchise rule from the U.S. Federal Trade Commission, which established minimum disclosure requirements for franchisors in the United States (Seig, n.d.). Currently there are over 3,000 franchisors and over a half-million franchisees operating in the United States with increased growth year after year (Seig, n.d.).

Some research shows that franchises perform better than non-franchise operations (Lafontaine, Zapletal & Zhang, 2019). However, this improved performance is between six and nine percent, according to research (Lafontaine et al., 2019). On one side the franchise business has brand awareness and the know-how behind the franchise that could save in advertising and the learning curve. Most franchises offer a supply chain that is efficient from bulk purchasing (Lafontaine et al., 2019). On the other side, franchisees must pay ongoing franchise fees, have less autonomy, and have less ability to adapt to local markets and changing markets (Lafontaine et al., 2019).

Another aspect of the franchise business is that franchisors screen applicants and therefore should eliminate applicants who are not a good fit or qualified (Lafontaine et al., 2019). This element could account for the difference in the success of franchises and non-franchise businesses.

Table 27: Partial List of Existing Franchise Categories

Automotive parts, accessories, and tire stores	Vending machine operators
Furniture stores	Direct selling establishments
Home furnishings stores	Traveler accommodation
Electronics and appliance stores	Full-service restaurants
Building material and supplies dealers	Limited-service eating establishments
Lawn and garden equipment and supplies stores	Special food services
Grocery stores	Automotive repair and maintenance
Specialty food stores	Electronic equipment repair and maintenance
Health and personal care stores	Personal and household goods repair and maintenance
Clothing stores	Personal care services
Shoe stores	Dry cleaning and laundry services
Jewelry, luggage, and leather goods stores	Other general merchandise stores
Sporting goods, hobby, and musical instrument stores	Office supplies, stationery, and gift stores
Bookstores and news dealers	Electronic shopping and mail-order houses

(Lafontaine et al., 2019)

As you can see, almost any product or service can be and is franchised. Also, the business models can vary just as much. Some franchises can be part-time while others require full-time commitment. Some require working weekends and others are not as regimented. I have several friends who own franchises. Many NFL players own franchises. Athletes are used to leading teams and following the game plan. That type of mentality is what franchisors are looking for in a franchisee.

Just as the range of products and services and time commitment can vary, so does the investment amount and the potential payoff. One model that is intriguing is Chick-fil-A. Today there are over 2,000 Chick-fil-A stores in the U.S. (*Own Your Franchise*, n.d.). I know several people who own Chick-fil-A franchises and they tell me that the process to be accepted to own a store is very difficult and most do not make the cut. They say that you can list three states where you would relocate to in order to run a store, and you must be willing to move to a store in those states. Also, if you make the cut, the fee to obtain a franchise is $10,000. Chick-fil-A will select the location and pay for the building and capital investment for the equipment and furnishings. A poorly performing store achieves $3M in revenues a good store can achieve $8M. The profit margins are between 8% and 15%. The franchisee splits the profit with Chick-fil-A. Not a bad return of between $120,000 to $600,000 annually. However, a franchisee can own only one store, and Chick-fil-A expects full-time involvement in it.

Chick-fil-A

There is a reason that at lunchtime most Chick-fil-A stores have a line—but they've figured out how to make the line move fast. Some are not willing to be under the control of others who want to try to make more money. So, Chick-fil-a is not for everyone. I have heard many great franchise stories and many horror stories. I think the key is to find the right franchise for your personality and to settle on the right location.

From time-to-time franchise stores fail because of poor management, poor location, or stiff competition. Sometimes these failed franchises are available for repurchase. Before considering a repurchase of one of these failed businesses, one should closely scrutinize it to understand why and how it failed.

Mariel Miller is a franchise consultant and founder with the Franchise Advisor, a national franchise search and coaching firm whose focus is to match franchisees with franchisors. Mariel will spend time understanding the personality, habits, goals, strengths, and weaknesses of a franchisee. She and her firm have intimate knowledge of many emerging franchises. *Emerging franchises* was a new term to me. I thought a franchisee would want a well-known franchise. It turns out that a franchisee makes more money by obtaining an *emerging* franchise. Mariel says, "If you know the name of the franchise, it's too late." Her focus on emerging franchises with solid and experienced franchisor management teams gives the franchisee the best chance of success. Another reason to look at emerging franchises is to negotiate to buy entire territories. In some cases, a franchisee can buy entire states or regions and build individual stores over time.

Mariel's success rate is high because she finds the right franchisees for the type of franchisor. She delves into your personal interests before ever presenting franchising options. Do you want to be a millionaire, or are you interested in part-time work? Are you buying your way into a job? Once she gets to know you, she presents several options to consider based on your profile. Mariel ranks franchises higher if they are in a category that is not highly competitive, and the franchisor's management team has documented previous success. I would not consider a franchise without talking to someone like Mariel Miller.

—17—

Continuous Learning and Innovation

"Continuous learning is the minimum requirement for success in any field."
—Brian Tracy

"Learning and innovation go hand in hand. The arrogance of success is to think that what you did yesterday will be sufficient for tomorrow."
—William Pollard

I strongly believe that an organizational culture of innovation and continuous learning is critical not only for growth in today's business environment—it is critical for survival. Business is changing more rapidly than ever with new technologies, new processes, and changing customer needs and tastes. In years past, companies could remain the same with technology, processes, and products.

Figure 9: Possible Company Growth Trajectory

In today's business environment, you are innovative and continuously learning and growing or you are shrinking. There is no middle ground. I believe so much that learning is important that I earned my master of business administration (MBA) and my doctor of business administration (DBA) later in my professional career. I did not get my MBA and DBA to advance my professional career or to obtain higher pay. Rather, I know that the academic exercise made me a better professional because of the additional knowledge.

The constant change in business is due to globalization, technological improvements, and evolving market advancements, creating a turbulent environment to manage (Sakas, Vlachos, & Nasiopoulos, 2014). To deal with this instability and maintain success, business leaders develop learning organizations to create and acquire new knowledge (Fang & Wang, 2006). Academic research shows that organizations that are continually learning are more productive and more profitable (Marsick & Watkins, 2003). Developing a learning organization culture is the best strategy to sustain a competitive advantage (Jamali, Zanhour, & Keshishian, 2009).

Innovation is what supports and drives the progress of our society

(Roy, 2018). In a continuous change environment, a learning organization is better positioned to orient employees to adapt and efficiently obtain perceptions that lead to increased job satisfaction (Varshney, 2020). Job satisfaction leads to employee retention and lower employee turnover in the company.

Amazon is an example of what can be achieved with a learning organization committed to innovation. Amazon's obsession for the customer has allowed it to focus on innovative products and services (Galetti et al., 2019). Amazon's obsession for innovation is the top accomplishment of the organization (Garner, 2018). The company achieves innovation with isolated teams focused on significant improvements to products and services (Rossman, 2019).

Bezos (2016) is open about innovation and said a willingness to fail and learn by failing is critical at Amazon. Amazon is also committed to innovation by all accounts (Galetti et al., 2019; Bezos, 2018; Rossman, 2019; Rossman & Euchner, 2018; Bezos, 2017; Bezos, 2016).

Many methods are available for leaders to help develop a learning organization. One method I have used is assigning a research goal for key employees to investigate regarding a subject that could impact the organization. Then the employee will report on the subject to the team, which evolves to a question-and-answer period. Sometimes these presentations lead to additional research and presentations.

Also, when an employee visits a trade show, I ask him or her to take images and create a PowerPoint of the trip for the management team. This allows the management team to get a quick peek at the show and adds different perspectives to the conversation.

Additionally, Google, Amazon, Facebook, Instagram, and other channels are constantly changing and making our management team keep up with the changes or be left behind. Companies that do not keep up are indeed left behind. If you do not adhere to Google changes, your product listing will not appear. These platforms change to advance their goals and the result is a divide between the companies that continuously learn and companies that are left behind.

The innovation needed for new product development requires keeping up with the competition and what is new in the marketplace. Active research is necessary to keep abreast of what is coming next. Pushing your team to find the next great product introduction will drive your employees to continuously research and learn. If you can obtain an innovative team who is constantly learning, you have the best chance to keep a sustained competitive advantage and grow wealth for your company, you, your employees, your stakeholders, and your community.

Much of this is about enabling yourself and your team to see what is possible. We are inhibited and restrained because we cannot see past what we can see. Roger Banister broke the 4-minute mile in 1954 when he ran it in 3 minutes and 54.4 seconds. In the next 18 months 12 more runners broke the 4-minute mile barrier. Now even a few high school athletes can run under a 4-minute mile.

Another company that has created a company culture of innovation and continuous improvement is Costco. As I mentioned before, I have managed several programs for Costco. To land a deal with Costco, you have to go to their offices in Issaquah, Washington, to pitch your deal. Costco brings in three vendors to compete for the same space and product line. They purposely put you in the same waiting room with your competition to make sure you know the deal will be competitive.

In the waiting room is a bronze plaque with a salmon figure and the Costco salmon story. The story is that Costco initially did not sell salmon or other seafood. Soon the company saw an opportunity to sell salmon, but they knew nothing about salmon. In the first attempt of a salmon program, Costco was disappointed in the quality of the fish and undertook to improve the quality each year, seeing the sales increase with each improvement in quality. Today Costco has great quality salmon and sells a unique cut called the "F trim," which removes the skin and a layer of fat that is the first part of the salmon to go bad. Today Costco sells more salmon than any other company in the world. They also sell more wine, almonds, and many more products with their culture of continuous learning, innovation, and improvement.

Costco Salmon

That's not the end of the story. With Costco's culture in mind, the company will put the onus on the vendor to bring more value each year. Even if the program the year before was profitable for both parties and a great success, to win the account again the vendor must bring increased value the next year. The increased value to the Costco customer could be more quantity, improved quantity, better packaging, lower price, or some other factor.

Each competing vendor will make its best pitch. Costco will request some changes and then make a decision as to who gets the order. In many cases it is the largest order in the world that year for that particular product. Costco gives an award each year to whoever creates the most value for Costco customers.

We can learn from companies like Costco and Amazon and people like Pat Farrah. We can review history to see the evolution of many elements of business. We can review academic tools that can be applied to business today. However, we cannot stop there. The quest for survival and success are the same. They require a continued search of new ideas and innovations. If you can create an organizational culture of continuous learning, you and your team will be successful.

Conclusion

*"Winning is not everything but, it sure beats
anything that comes in second."*
—Bear Bryant

My sports background is the foundation for how I like to manage the organizational culture. When things are going well, going to work is fun, interesting, and fulfilling. When employees see that the company is growing, they are happy to be a part of a winning culture. Success breeds success.

I saw firsthand the creation of a winning culture in my college football years. I went to Furman University in Greenville, South Carolina, and the team had just begun having winning seasons. Our teams came together to win four conference championships, and we set the tone for a total of 14 championships. The 19 seniors I graduated with are all successful and lifelong friends. And we are 19-0 with no divorces. Winning translates to other areas of life.

Furman Seniors

When I took over Micro-Mark five years ago, the company was shrinking, and employee morale was low. I implemented the fundamentals in this book, and now we have a completely different culture. Our team members used to worry only about their jobs. Now anyone is willing to do what is necessary. We have created an innovative learning organization for new products and new programs. We have learned many new skills and built new programs to be growing and profitable in the core business, Amazon, Search, Social Media, and more.

More than anything, we have created together a fun place to work and win. Nobody would want to go back to what we were five years ago. We also know that we have many opportunities before us that will allow us to continue to grow. If you do the right things as a leader, success will soon follow.

About the Author

Early Years

I grew up in a military family with a father, mother, and three younger sisters. The military requires families to move often, and our family moved approximately every three years. We lived in numerous states and in the United Kingdom and Germany. These moves provided an experience to learn to adapt to new environments to survive the jungle of adolescence. To survive, I learned to observe the new environment first. Identifying the norms and the key influencers were essential to navigating the path successfully in these new environments.

I was brought up as a Christian in several different Baptist churches in many locations. My parents were committed Christians. However, my Christian perspective ebbed and flowed over many years. My time at home was with a middle-class upbringing with supporting parents. My father retired from the U.S. Air Force as a brigadier general. However, my upbringing was not rigid or militaristic.

Sports

I moved with my military family to Hampton, Virginia, from a station in Germany and entered Eaton Junior High School. The school was primarily African American. No worries, I thought. I tried out for the football team. To cut to the chase, I was good in football and drafted in the fourth round in the NFL in 1986. But we did not anticipate this at the time, of course.

The first practice showed that I was good. But the other players did not like that. After practice, walking out of the locker room, I was met by much older, larger, practice mates. They surrounded me and said that I needed to quit, proceeding to kick, punch, and beat me. I just covered up my face. Eventually they stopped. They said this would happen every day until I quit. I told no one.

The next day I had a really good practice. Afterward I was met by four of these practice mates. They again said they would beat me every day until I quit. I told no one. The next day I had another great practice. Outside there were three practice mates, and I took my beating—but it seemed to be less intense.

The next day at practice, I sensed that that the opposition was over. I played a position that was not normally considered a position a white player would play. Eventually the guys who had earlier surrounded me to beat me became good friends.

This background created a strong desire to succeed in different environments. One way to adapt and fit in was to play sports. I played little league sports when I was younger, which provided a platform to stand out. I found that the better I was in sports, the easier it was to fit into a new place. I moved to South Dakota for high school and focused on football and track. This drive pushed me to spend time training to be a better athlete. The training I focused on was speed training, which paid off with a college scholarship to play football at Furman.

I balanced academia with sports throughout college and continued speed training at a high level and obtained a bachelor's degree in business administration. Another important part of my education was learning to win. I was a part of four conference championships and learned that the formula for winning was teamwork. I was drafted by the Kansas City Chiefs of the National Football League (NFL) as a wide receiver and return specialist and spent the next three years bouncing around the league from St. Louis to Buffalo to Kansas City.

The NFL experience was enlightening. It seemed to me that most teams had equal talent. The differences between the NFL teams' records were the strategies employed by the coaches. I realized that the strategies you use in applying your resources were critical in the field and in life.

Another lesson from my sports experience was the benefits of preparation. In college football and the NFL, we watched films of every play multiple times. In the NFL we even watched practices on video. And, of course, every play of the competition was reviewed over and over again. Attention to detail at all levels was discussed, analyzed, and refined.

The need to develop precise strategies and the benefits of preparation carried on in my mind to other areas of my life. I saw how important they were in sports and knew they would be important in life. Playing in the NFL and living in many different locations also provided exposure to diversity. After playing in the NFL, I married my college sweetheart and started a family and a business.

Professional Experience

I started my first real business in 1990, selling plants delivered by mail and other delivery methods. I expected to find instant success in a new business because of my previous success in sports and school. However, it was not as quick to appear as I thought. I experienced a tough learning curve, and the business took much longer to achieve success than I expected. The experience was confusing to me, and it felt as though many unknown obstacles were appearing out of nowhere. Eventually the company grew to profitability, and I sold it.

I did another start-up company that was focused on a new technology. In this company I learned to raise capital and manage investors and bankers. From there I led the financial turnarounds of two national brands.

They were the rose company Jackson & Perkins Company (J&P) and the seed company Geo Park Seed Company (Park). These companies were mid-sized with hundreds of employees and combined annual revenues of over $100 million.

Developing and managing the changes in the strategies for J&P and Park provided firsthand experience with employee resistance to change. These companies had been losing money for 15 years, and yet few employees embraced the changes that were needed to survive. The experience of financial turnaround juxtaposed against the fun of running a company that is growing and thriving highlights the need for companies to operate withing the principles of this book.

Now

I continue to practice the tenets of this book and am humbled by the many blessings I have been given. I continue to lead Micro-Mark's team and build on the innovations and learning culture. I have also begun work as an adjunct professor at Seton Hall University's Stillman School of Business. I hope this book helps you with your business, and I trust you can experience the fulfillment of growing a business for you, your team, and your community.

The Story of Chas Against Hall of Famer Lawrence Taylor of the NFL

It may not be obvious to everyone, but for me, sports have provided a platform for lessons in my business career. In my brief time in the NFL, I encountered exceptional people, great leaders, and an expectation of attention to detail that helped me later in life.

In 1986 I played for the St. Louis Cardinals as a wide receiver. In my first start we were playing the New York Giants, who had a great defense and one of the most dominant players of all time—Lawrence

Taylor. Our offensive coaches were clearly concerned about Taylor, who is a Hall of Famer and might be considered the greatest defensive player of all time. In 1986 he was in his prime.

"L.T." was big, 6'4", 250 pounds, but he was also the fastest player on the field. He was a great pass rusher and could stop the run. One of the toughest things about him was that it was difficult to run away from him. If you ran to the opposite side, he was so fast that he would run down the running back from behind. You could not run *at* him, and you could not run *away from* him.

Our coaches were clearly concerned and decided to come up with a new play to deter L.T.'s backside stops. I will never forget our offensive coordinator, Jim Shofner, saying, "Fox, when we run the sweep right, you go in motion and 'redirect' Taylor." Notice he did not say *block* Taylor; he said *redirect.*

I was willing to do anything I was told, but I was also concerned that we had never gone in motion before and had only one play that now called for motion—the play I was supposed to go for against Taylor.

The first drive of the game we called *the sweep,* and I slowly jogged out to line up thinking, about how I was about to block Lawrence Taylor. And how *was* I going to block Lawrence Taylor? I knew he was not expecting me to block him, so I did have the element of surprise, but that was about the only advantage I had. Neil Lomax, our quarterback, signaled for me to go in motion, and immediately the entire Giant defense began yelling. They hadn't seen us go in motion all year, so consequently it caused quite a commotion.

I motioned by Lomax, not looking at Taylor, instead looking past him downfield. Just as I got even with Taylor, we hiked the ball, and I just put my shoulder into his shins and rolled him up, taking his legs out from under his body (only because he was not expecting it). As I lay on the ground with a smile on my face, I heard a terrible roar. I looked back and saw Taylor looking at me with animal eyes. It looked as if he had smoke coming out of his nose and mouth. Taylor pounded the ground and got up and started toward me.

The only thing I knew to do was run, and while the play was still going on, Taylor was chasing me and cussing me. I ran around and finally got behind my offensive linemen. Taylor was raging, and even while we were in the huddle for the next play, he was pacing and taunting and calling me out: "Fox, I'm gonna get you. I'm gonna *kill* you!"

The game continued, and we did not run the sweep again until the fourth quarter. It was a close game, and I had all but forgotten about the incident with Taylor. But lo and behold, Lomax called the sweep again. As I jogged out to line up, I realized that I could not just cut his legs out again as he would be aware and jump up and crush my back. As I was debating my options, I realized that he knew that I knew that I could not cut him again. So this time as Lomax signaled for me to go in motion, and as the Giants starting yelling because we had not gone in motion since the first quarter, I looked Taylor right in the eyes.

Taylor stared a hole through me as I motioned toward him. Smoke again puffed out his nose with each breath. As I got even with him, I positioned to deliver a typical block. Then right at the last second I dove to the ground. Because of his intense desire to kill me, I was able to cut him again. I heard the familiar roar, but this time, I did not wait and started running for dear life again. He was screaming, cussing, looking to the sky. It was like Mr. T's rant in *Rocky III.*

I made my way back to the huddle, feeling kind of good about myself. Taylor was again ranting and pacing and calling me out. As I leaned into the huddle, though, I could not believe what was coming out of Lomax's lips. "Sweep right!" The *same* play! My linemen even laughed as they jogged to the line, knowing my fate. It took forever to make it out to line up and even longer, to go in motion.

As I reached Taylor this time, I knew I had to block him straight up. I went back to the fundamentals, back to everything I ever learned about blocking from little league to the NFL. I made a good base with my feet. I got low. I exploded through my hips—and hit him with everything I had.

In the film room the next day they played back the play over and over again. I don't know if anyone had ever been hit so hard on the line of scrimmage before. I was literally flying backward parallel to the ground in the air. It looked like a cartoon. Taylor really blew me up.

When I finally landed on my back, Taylor was hovering inches from my face ranting, taunting, yelling, spitting. But as I lay there, assessing what might be broken, a smile came over my face. He killed me, but I "redirected" him. It is hard to brag about it, but *I went 3 for 3 against L.T.*

Things might not go exactly as you planned. And sometimes you need a little luck. *But preparation and innovation give you the best chance of success.*

References

A brief history of franchising (n.d.). Retrieved January 2021 from https://www. franchise-law.com/franchise-law-overview/a-brief-history-of-franchising. shtml.

Achillas, C., Tzetzis, D., & Raimond, M.O. (2017). Alternative production strategies based on the comparison of additive and traditional manufacturing technologies. *International Journal of Production Research, 55*(12): 3497–3509.

Afsar, B., & Shahjehan, A. (2018). Linking ethical leadership and moral voice: The effects of moral efficacy trust in leader, and leader-follower value congruence. *Leadership & Organization Development Journal, 39*(6), 775–793.

Al-Araki, M. (2013). SWOT analysis revisited through PEAK-framework. *Journal of Intelligent & Fuzzy Systems, 25*(3), 615–625.

Anwar, S. (2017). Alibaba: Entrepreneurial growth and global expansion in B2B/B2C markets. *Journal of International Entrepreneurship, 15*(4): 366–389.

Arnold, A. G., Ellis, R. B., & Krishnan, V. S. (2018). Toward effective use of the statement of cash flows. *Journal of Business & Behavioral Sciences, 30*(2), 46–62.

Arslan, A., & Wang, Y. (2015). Acquisition entry strategy of Nordic multinational enterprises in China: An analysis of key determinants. *Journal of Global Marketing, 28*(1), 32–51.

Bäckström, I., Ingelsson, P., Snyder, K., Hedlund, C., & Lilja, J. (2018). Capturing value based leadership in practice. *International Journal of Quality and Service Sciences, 10*(4), 422–430.

Beemer, J. M. (2017). Business owners must take steps now to prevent discrimination in the workplace. *Workforce Solutions Review, 8*(2), 25-2

Bergeson, L. L. (2017). Proposition 65 warning regulations must change—and soon! *Environmental Quality Management, 27*(2), 77–79.

Bezos, J. (2006). 2005 annual report Amazon.com Incorporated. Retrieved fromhttps://ir.aboutamazon.com/static-files/3178d8e9-24a9-4df1-b174-67ffd7812aff

Bezos, J. (2007). 2006 annual report Amazon.com Incorporated. Retrieved fromhttps://ir.aboutamazon.com/static-files/da2fdc31-ff4a-40c9-a2c4-be5d1fd52d5c

Bezos, J. (2009). 2008 annual report Amazon.com Incorporated. Retrieved from https://ir.aboutamazon.com/static-files/e1846da7-9425-42d9-add7-84218d7ee5e7

Bezos, J. (2011). 2010 annual report Amazon.com Incorporated. Retrieved from https://ir.aboutamazon.com/static-files/6f3c99ed-5094-4fed-a9ad-e18cdbf37478

Bezos, J. (2014). 2013 annual report Amazon.com Incorporated. Retrieved from https://ir.aboutamazon.com/static-files/1be0475a-fcab-4826-9258-17f11c208487

Bezos, J. (2015). 2014 annual report Amazon.com Incorporated. Retrieved from https://ir.aboutamazon.com/static-files/d6263104-b6fa-401a-aa29-3b66ec713f76

Bezos, J. (2016). 2015 annual report Amazon.com Incorporated. Retrieved from https://ir.aboutamazon.com/static-files/fdf51af3-79e0-4b3c-9868-19aa75aa0306

Bezos, J. (2017). 2016 annual report Amazon.com Incorporated. Retrieved from https://ir.aboutamazon.com/static-files/380785a4-779c-4252-897b-539d3ef70680

Bezos, J. (2018). 2017 annual report Amazon.com Incorporated. Retrieved from https://ir.aboutamazon.com/static-files/917130c5-e6bf-4790-a7bc-cc43ac7fb30a

Bezos, J. (2019). 2018 annual report Amazon.com Incorporated. Retrieved from https://ir.aboutamazon.com/static-files/4f64d0cd-12f2-4d6c-952e-bbed15ab1082

Bohórquez Arévalo, L. E. (2016). The absence of response of organizations to changing business environment conditions: a complex management problem. *Pensamiento & Gestión*, (41), 13–35.

Bonsu, S., & Kuofie, M. (2019). Small business survival. *Journal of Marketing & Management, 10*(1), 51–63.

Boyce, J. R., Cesari, R. (2020). *The Amazon jungle*. New York: Morgan James Publishing.

Bromall, N., Mishra, S., Draus, P., & Stewart, J. (2019). A case study-based analysis of innovative cloud technologies implementation: Challenges, tools and benefits of Amazon AWS. *Proceedings for the Northeast Region Decision Sciences Institute (NEDSI)*, 323–337.

Broome, O. W. (2004). Statement of cash flows: Time for change! *Financial Analysts Journal, 60*(2), 16–22.

Bulygo, Z. (2019). The elements of a high-quality website (infographic). Retrieved December 19, 2020, from https://neilpatel.com/blog/elements-highquality-website/

Burke, Q. L., & Eaton, T. V. (2016). Alibaba group initial public offering: A case study of financial reporting issues. *Issues in Accounting Education, 31*(1), 1–29.

Cabral, L., & Hortacsu, A. (2010). The Dynamics of seller reputation: Evidence from eBay. *Journal of Industrial Economics, 58*(1), 54–78.

Chen, T., (2020). A college student behind a massively popular paint-mixing TikTok page was fired from Sherwin-Williams. Retrieved from https://www.buzzfeednews.com/article/tanyachen/college-student-behind-a-massively-popular-paint-mixing

Christodoulides, G., Cadogan, J. W., & Veloutsou, C. (2015). Consumer-based brand equity measurement: lessons learned from an international study. *International Marketing Review, 32*(3/4), 307–328.

Church, E. M., & Oakley, R. L. (2018). Etsy and the long-tail: how microenterprises use hyper-differentiation in online handicraft marketplaces. *Electronic Commerce Research, 18*(4), 883–898.

Company overview (n.d.). AlibabaGroup.com. Retrieved January 2, 2021, from https://www.alibabagroup.com/en/about/overview

Coppola, D. (2020). Costco membership worldwide. Retrieved January 7, 2020, from https://www.statista.com/statistics/718406/costco-membership/

Cusumano, M. A. (2017). Amazon and Whole Foods: Follow the strategy (and the money) Checking out the recent Amazon acquisition of Whole Foods. *Communications of the ACM, 60*(10), 24–26.

Daft, R. L. (2016). *Organization theory & design* (12th ed.). Boston: Cengage Learning.

Dhillon, I., & Gupta, S. (2015). Organizational restructuring and collaborative creativity: The case of Microsoft and Sony. *IUP Journal of Business Strategy, 12*(1), 53–65.

Djordjevic, D., Cockalo, D., & Bogetic, S. (2016). The analysis of marketing concept implementation in domestic enterprises. *Journal of Engineering Management and Competitiveness, 6*(2), 120–128.

Drawbaugh, K. (2001). *Brands in the balance: Meeting the challenges to commercial identity*. London: Reuters.

Duncan, R. (1979). What is the right organization structure? Decision tree analysis provides the answer. *Organizational Dynamics, 7*(3), 59–80.

eBay financials (January 2020). Retrieved January 1, 2021, from https://ebay. q4cdn.com/610426115/files/doc_financials/2019/q4/Exhibit-99.1-ER-eBay-Q4-2019_FINAL.pdf

Employee stock ownership plans (ESOPs). (n. d.). Retrieved from https:// community-wealth.org/strategies/panel/esops/index.html

Esposito, M., & Tse, T. (2018). DRIVE: The five megatrends that underpin the future business, social, and economic landscapes. *Thunderbird international business review, 60*(1), 121–129.

Etsy Annual Report (2020). Esty.com. Retrieved from https://s22.q4cdn. com/941741262/files/doc_financials/annual/2019/Etsy-Annual-Report.pdf

Fang, S. C., & Wang, J. F. (2006). Effects of organizational culture and learning on manufacturing strategy selection: An empirical study. *International Journal of Management, 23*(3), 503–514.

Fernhaber, Stephanie A., McDougall-Covin, Patricia P., & Shepherd, Dean A. (2009). International entrepreneurship: Leveraging internal and external knowledge sources. *Strategic Entrepreneurship Journal, 3*(4), 297–320.

Fisher, M., Gallino, S. & Netessine, S. (2019). Retailers are squandering their most potent weapons. *Harvard Business Review*. January–February edition.

Fulgoni, G. M. (2018). Will digital commerce and analytics be the death of traditional brands? *Journal of Advertising Research, 58*(2), 146–150.

Galetti, B., Golden III, J., & Brozovich, S. (2019). Inside day 1: How Amazon uses agile team structures and adaptive practices to innovate on behalf of customers. *People & Strategy, 42*(2), 36–41.

Gamble, J. E., Peteraf, M. A., & Thompson, A. A. (2019). *Essentials of strategic management: The quest for competitive advantage.* New York: McGraw Hill Education.

García-Cabrera, A. M., & García-Barba Hernández, F. (2014). Differentiating the three components of resistance to change: The moderating effect of organization-based self-esteem on the employee involvement-resistance relation. *Human Resource Development Quarterly, 25*(4), 441–469.

Garner, B. A. (2018). Amazon in the global market. *Journal of Marketing & Management, 9*(2), 63–73. Retrieved from https://search-ebscohost-com. ezproxy.liberty.edu/login.aspx?direct=true&db=bth&AN=135820425&site=eh ost-live&scope=site

Gerschewski, S., Evers, N., Nguyen, A. T., & Froese, F. J. (2020). Trade shows and SME internationalisation: Networking for performance. *Management International Review (MIR), 60*(4), 573–595.

Global Entertainment & Media Outlook 2020–2024 (n.d.). Retrieved on December 29, 2020, from https://www.pwc.com/outlook

Gómez-Mejía, L. R., Balkin, D. B., & Cardy, R. L. (2016). *Managing human resources* (8th ed.). Boston: Pearson.

Greenleaf, R. K. (2002). Servant leadership: A journey into the nature of legitimate power and greatness (25th anniversary edition). Mahwah, NJ: Paulis Press.

Grisaffe, D. B., VanMeter, R., & Chonko, L. B. (2016). Serving first for the benefit of others: preliminary evidence for a hierarchical conceptualization of servant leadership. *Journal of Personal Selling & Sales Management, 36*(1), 40–8.

Guido, G., Pichierri M., Pino, G., & Nataraajan, R. (2019). Effects of face images and face pareidolia on consumers' responses to print advertising: An empirical investigation. *Journal of Advertising Research, 59*(2), 219–231

Gunasekaran, A., Yusuf, Y. Y., Adeleye, E. O., & Papadopoulos, T. (2018). Agile manufacturing practices: the role of big data and business analytics with multiple case studies. *International Journal of Production Research, 56*(1/2), 385–397.

Haenlein, M., Anadol, E., Farnsworth, T., Hugo, H., Hunichen, J., & Welte, D. (2020). Navigating the new era of influencer marketing: How to be successful on Instagram, TikTok, & Co. *California Management Review, 63*(1), 5–25.

Hall, A. T. (2019). The pros and cons of an ESOP for employee retirement security. *Benefits Law Journal, 32*(2), 24–31.

Hansen, J. R., & Jacobsen, C. B. (2016). Changing strategy processes and strategy content in public sector organizations? A longitudinal case study of NPM reforms' influence on strategic management. *British Journal of Management, 27*(2), 373–389.

Hartley, A. (2019). Exclusive: US state drags Amazon to court on platform sales tax liability. *International Tax Review*, N.PAG.

Heaney, S. (2002). *Beowulf. A verse translation*. New York: Norton.

Hess, E. D., & Cameron, K. S. (2006). *Leading with Values: Positivity, Virtue, and High Performance.* Cambridge, UK: Cambridge University Press. History of HomeDepot (n.d.). Retrieved January 1, 2021, from https://corporate. homedepot.com/sites/default/themes/thd/images/timeline/History-Of-The-Home-Depot.pdf

HomeDepot (February 2, 2020). Retrieved January 1, 2020, from https:// ir.homedepot.com/~/media/Files/H/HomeDepotIR/2020/2019_THD_AnnualReport_vf.pdf

Honeyman, R., Jana, T. (2019). *The B Corp Handbook* (2ⁿᵈ ed.). Oakland, CA: Berrett-Koehler Publishers.

Hoque, M., Alsadoon, A., Maag, A., Prasad, P. W. C., & Elchouemi, A. (2018). Comprehensive search engine optimization model for commercial websites: Surgeon's website in Sydney *JSW. 13*(1), 43–56.

Hudson, S., Huang, L., Roth, M., and Madden, T., (2016), The influence of social media interactions on consumer-brand relationships: A three-country study of brand perceptions and marketing behaviors. *International Journal of Research in Marketing, 33*(1), 27–41.

Influencer Marketing Hub (2020). Influencer marketing benchmark report 2020. Retrieved from https://influencermarketinghub.com/influencer-marketing-benchmark-report-2020/

Ivanova, A. I., Maher, J. K., Marco, G. J., & Reinbold, M. (2018). Moderating factors on the impact of B Corporation certification on purchasing intention, willingness to pay a price premium and consumer trust. *Atlantic Marketing Journal, 7*(2), 17–35.

Jamali, D., Zanhour, M., & Keshishian, T. (2009). Peculiar strengths and relational attributes of SMEs in the context of CSR. *Journal of Business Ethics, 87*(3), 355–367.

Jayaraman, P. (2020) Indian concept of entrepreneurship—Evolution and impact of business communities in Tamilnadu. Retrieved from https://papers.ssrn.com/sol3/papers.cfm?abstract_id=3643820

Jeong-Eun, P., & Morgan, R. M. (2017). Outsourcing marketing and organizational learning: Managing customer relationship management. *Journal of Marketing Thought, 4*(1), 27–44.

Jit, R., Sharma, C. S., & Kawatra, M. (2017). Healing a broken spirit: Role of servant leadership. *Vikalpa: The Journal for Decision Makers, 42*(2), 80–94.

Jocevski, M. (2020). Blurring the lines between physical and digital spaces: Business model innovation in retailing. *California Management Review, 63*(1), 99–117.

Johnson, S. (2014, September). New research shed light on daily ad exposures. Retrieved March 2015 from SJ Insights: http://sjinsights.net/2014/09/29/newresearch-sheds-light-ondaily-ad-exposures

Jones, D. (2012). Does servant leadership lead to greater customer focus and employee satisfaction? *Business Studies Journal, 4*(2), 21–35.

Ju, I., & Chen, L. (2019). Influencer marketing: Relationship norm moderates the effect of influencer-product congruence on social media. *American Academy of Advertising Conference Proceedings*, 68.

Kaplan, R. S., & Norton, D. P. (1992). The balanced scorecard—Measures that drive performance. *Harvard Business Review 70*(1): 71–79.

Karatop, B., Kubat, C., & Uygun, Ö. (2018). Determining the strategies on Turkish automotive sector using fuzzy AHP based on the SWOT analysis. *Sakarya University Journal of Science, 22*(5), 63–74.

Khan, L. M. (2017). Amazon's antitrust paradox. *Yale Law Journal*, 126(3), 710–805.

Kim, S., Zhang, X. A., Zhang, B. W. (2016). Self-mocking crisis strategy on social media: focusing on Alibaba chairman Jack Ma in China. *Public Relation Review*. doi:10.1016/j.pubrev.2016.10.004

Kline, D. B. (2017). Changing retail: Is everything you know about 'retail apocalypse' wrong? *USA Today.* Retrieved from ttps://www.usatoday.com/ story/money/business/2017/09/21/is-everything-you-know-about-the-retail-apocalypse-wrong/105809518/

Kowalska, M. (2018). *E-mail marketing. Research papers of the Wroclaw University of Economics*, 526, 99–108.

Lin, C., Wu, W.Y., & Wang, Z. F. (2000). A study of market structure: brand loyalty and brand switching behaviours for durable household appliances. *International Journal of Market Research, 42*(3), 277.

Lin, D., Lu, J., Liu, X., & Zhang, X. (2016). International knowledge brokerage and returnees' entrepreneurial decisions. *Journal of International BusinessStudies, 47*(3), 295–318.

Lindell, M. (2019). *What are the Odds?* Chaska, MN: Lindell Pub. ISBN 9781734283402.

Linden, R. C., Wayne, S. J., Chenwei, L., & Meuser, J. D. (2014). Servant leadership and serving culture: Influence on individual and unit performance. *Academy of Management Journal, 57*(5), 1434-1452.

Lipsman, A. (2019). How Amazon will revolutionize the future of television advertising. *Journal of Advertising Research, 59*(3), 259–262.

Lovett, M. G., Chi, Y. N., & Little, D. L. (2020). The development of a curriculum for the introduction to trade show buying. *Journal of Customer Behaviour, 19*(2), 127–141.

Mahapatra, M. (2019). CSR practices among public and private sector companies: A community development approach in Indian context. *Journal of Management & Public Policy, 10*(2), 33–42.

Majewski, T., (2015). A brief history of Etsy on its 10th anniversary. BuiltInNYC. com. Retrieved from https://www.builtinnyc.com/2015/11/04/brief-history-etsy

Mamadehussene, S. (2019). Price-matching guarantees as a direct signal of low prices. *Journal of Marketing Research (JMR), 56*(2), 245–258.

Mansfield, M. (2018). Startup statistics—the numbers you need to know. Retrieved from https:smallbiztrends.com/2016/11/startup-statistics-small-business.html

Marsick, V. J., & Watkins, K. E. (2003). Demonstrating the value of an organization's learning culture: The dimensions of the learning organization questionnaire. *Advances in Developing Human Resources, 5*(2), 132–151.

Martin, D. C., Bartol, K. M., & Kehoe, P. E. (2000). The legal ramifications of performance appraisal: The growing significance. *Public Personnel Management, 29*(3), 379.

McCarthy, J., (2017). Adidas chief casts doubt on TV ads: 'Digital engagement is key for us.' *The Drum.* Retrieved from http://www.thedrum.com/news/2017/03/17/adidas-chief-casts-doubt-tv-ads-digital-engagement-key-us

Mendes, E., Nile, M. (2006). *Web engineering* (2006 ed.) New York: Springer Publishing.

Meredith, J. R., & Scott, M. S. (2016). *Operations and supply chain management for MBAs.* (6th ed.). Hoboken, NJ: John Wiley & Sons.

Miles, R. E., Snow, C. C., Fjeldstad, O. D., Miles, G., Lettl, C. (2010). Designing organizations to meet 21st-century opportunities and challenges. *Organizational Dynamics, 39*(2), 93–103.

Mitchell, W., (2016). How to rank your products on Amazon—The ultimate guide, *Startupbros.* Retrieved from http://startupbros.com/rank-amazon

Moe, W. W., and P. S. Fader. (2004). Dynamic conversion behavior at e-commerce sites." *Management Science 50*(3), 326–335.

Mollel, E. R., Mulongo, L.S., and Market,L. (2015). Workforce diversity management and global organizational growth in the 21st century, *Journal of Scientific Research and Studies, 2*(7), 164–175.

Morales-Vargas, A., Pedraza-Jiménez, R., & Codina, L. (2020). Website quality: An analysis of scientific production. *The Information Professional, 29*(5), 1–21.

National Center for Employee Ownership. (n. d.). Retrieved from https://www.esop.org/#:~:text=Examples%20of%20Major%20ESOP%20Companies&text=Some%20of%20the%20more%20notable,our%20

Employee%20Ownership%20100%20list)

Nedra, B. A., Hadhri, W., and Mezrani, M. (2019). Determinants of customers' intentions to use hedonic networks: The case of Instagram. *Journal of Retailing and Consumer Services, 66*, 21–32.

Ng, E. S., & Sears, G. J. (2020). Walking the talk on diversity: CEO beliefs, moral values, and the implementation of workplace diversity practices. *Journal of Business Ethics, 164*(3), 437–450.

Niaki, K., Mojtaba, & Nonino, F. (2017). Additive manufacturing management: A review and future research agenda. *International Journal of Production Research, 55*: 1419–1439

Nisar, T. M., & Man Yeung. (2018). Attribution modeling in digital advertising: An empirical investigation of the impact of digital sales channels. *Journal of Advertising Research, 58*(4), 399–413.

Ontiveros, M. L. (2017). H-1B visas, outsourcing and body shops: A continuum of exploitation for high tech workers. *Berkeley Journal of Employment & Labor Law, 38*(1), 1–47. doi:10.15779/Z38QJ77X6H

Our History (n.d.). Retrieved January 1, 2021, from https://www.ebayinc.com/company/our-history/

Own Your Future (n.d.). Retrieved January 2021 from https://www.chick-fil-a.com/franchising

Palanisamy, R., & Liu, Y. (2018). User search satisfaction in search engine optimization: An empirical analysis. *Journal of Services Research, 18*(2), 83–120.

Patè-Cornell, E. (2015). Uncertainties, intelligence, and risk management: a few observations and recommendations on measuring and managing risk. *Stanford Journal of International Law, 51*(1), 53–67.

Peterson, H. (2017). The retail apocalypse has officially descended on America. *Business Insider*. Retrieved from http://www.businessinsider.com/the-retail-apocalypse-has-officially-descended-on-america-2017-3

Pitts, R. A., & Daniels, J. D. (1984). Aftermath of the matrix mania. *Columbia Journal of World Business, 19*(2), 48.

Quesado, P., Guzmán, B. A., & Rodrigues, L. L. (2018). Advantages and contributions in the balanced scorecard implementation. *Intangible Capital, 14*(1), 186–201.

QuickSprou (2019). The 22 key elements of a high quality website. Retrieved December 19, 2020, from https://www.quicksprout.com/the-key-elements-of-ahigh-quality-website/

Raatikainen, P. (2002). Contribution of multiculturalism to the competitive advantage of an organization. *Singapore Management Review, 24*, 81.

Raguseo, E. (2018). Big data technologies: An empirical investigation on their adoption, benefits and risks for companies. *International Journal of Information Management 38*(1), 187–195.

Rahman, M., Turpin Jr., L., & Phelps, L. (2020). Effects of inclusive national workplace diversity on global competitiveness: TSCS analysis. *International Journal of Business Insights & Transformation, 13*(2), 3–9.

Rasolofo, D. F., & Distler, F. (2018). Using the balanced scorecard to manage service supply chain uncertainty: Case studies in French real estate services. *Knowledge & Process Management, 25*(3), 129–142.

Reimers, I., & Waldfogel, J. (2017). Throwing the books at them: Amazon's puzzling long run pricing strategy. *Southern Economic Journal, 83*(4), 869–885. Renfrow, J. (2015). Videos increase average order value by 50%. *FierceRetail*, 1.

Rosen, C., & Rodrick, S. (2020). *Understanding ESOPs*. Oakland, CA: The National Center for Employee Ownership.

Rossman, J. (2019). *Think like Amazon: 50½ ideas to be a digital leader*. New York: McGraw-Hill Education.

Rossman, J., & Euchner, J. (2018). Innovation the Amazon way. *Research Technology Management, 61*(1), 13–22.

Rothaermel, F. T. (2017). *Strategic management.* (3rd ed.). New York: McGraw-Hill Education.

Rubin, C. (2016). The evolution of Amazon Prime and their followed success. *SKUBANA, 3*, Retrieved from https://www.skubana.com/evolution-of-amazon-prime/

Rushe, D. (2017). Big, bold… and broken: Is the US shopping mall in a fatal decline? *The Observer.* Retrieved from https://www.theguardian.com/us-news/2017/jul/22/mall-of-america-minnesota-retail-anniversary

Sabanoglu, T. (December 1, 2020). Projected retail ecommerce GMV. Retrieved from https://www.statista.com/statistics/788109/amazon-retail-market-share-usa/

Sakas, D., Vlachos, D., & Nasiopoulos, D. (2014). Modelling strategic management for the development of competitive advantage, based on technology. *Journal of Systems and Information Technology, 16*(3), 187–209.

Sangster, A., & Scataglinibelghitar, G. (2010). Luca Pacioli: the father of accounting Education. *Accounting Education, 19*(4), 423–438.

Sasikala, S. & Victor Anthonyraj, S. (2015). Self-Efficacy, Emotional intelligence and organizational commitment in relation to resistance to change among employees. *Annamalai International Journal of Business Studies & Research*, 30–35.

Schilling, M. A., & Steensma, H. K. (2001). The use of modular organizational forms: An industry-level analysis. *Academy of Management Journal, 44*(6), 1149–1168.

Schwepker, C. H., & Schultz, R. J. (2015). Influence of the ethical servant leader and ethical climate on customer value enhancing sales performance. *Journal of Personal Selling & Sales Management, 35*(2), 93–107.

Searchmetrics (2018). What is a ranking factor? Retrieved December 17, 2020, from https://www.searchmetrics.com/what-is-a-ranking-factor/

Seid, M. S. (n.d.). Where it all began. The evolution of franchising. Retrieved January 2021 from http://www.franchise-chat.com/resources/where_it_all_began_the_evolution_of_franchising.htm

Semerádová, T., Weinlich, P. (2020). *Website quality and shopping behavior: Quantitative and qualitative evidence*. Berlin: Germany, Springer.

Sharif, M. H. M., Troshani, I., & Davidson, R. (2018). Determinants of social media impact in local government. In media influence: breakthroughs in research and practice, pp. 141–164. IGI Global.

Shay, R., & Van Der Horst, M. (2019). Using brand equity to model ROI for social media marketing. *JMM: The International Journal on Media Management, 21*(1), 24–44.

Sheats, M. K., Royal, K., & Kedrowicz, A. (2019). Using readability software to enhance the health literacy of equine veterinary clients: An analysis of 17 American Association of Equine Practitioners' newsletter and website articles. *Equine Veterinary Journal 51*(4), pp. 552–555

Shih T.-Y. & Yang, C.-C. (2019). Generating intangible resource and international performance: Insights into enterprises organizational behavior and capability at trade shows. *Journal of Business Economics & Management, 20*(6), 1022–1044.

Shiller, B., Waldfogel, J., & Ryan, J. (2018). The effect of ad blocking on website traffic and quality. *The RAND Journal of Economics. 49*(1), pp. 43–63.

Slefo, G. P. (2019, May 31). Amazon aims to challenge Google after acquiring Sizmek ad server. *AdAge*, Retrieved from https://adage.com/article/digital/amazon-aims-challenge-google-after-acquiring-sizmek-adserver/2172801

SmallBizGenius (November 2020). Retrieved from https://www.smallbizgenius. net/by-the-numbers/small-business-statistics/#gref

Small Business Funding (November 2020). Retrieved from https://www. smallbusinessfunding.com/under-capitalized/Soper, S. (2019, September 20). Amazon expands two-hour Whole Foods delivery to catch

Stone, B. (2013). *The everything store: Jeff Bezos and the age of Amazon*. New York: Little, Brown, and Co.

Tandon, U., Kiran, R., & Sah, A. N. (2017). Customer satisfaction as mediator between website service quality and repurchase intention: An emerging economy case. *Service Science, 9*(2), 106–120.

Tang, G., Kwan, H., Zhang, D., & Zhu, Z. (2016). Work-family effects of servant leadership: The roles of emotional exhaustion and personal learning. *Journal of Business Ethics, 137*(2), 285–297.

The history of modern franchising (n.d.). International Franchise Association. Retrieved January 2021 from https://www.franchise.org/blog/the-history-of-modern-franchising#:~:text=In%20the%20United%20States%2C%20 many,franchisor%2C%20dating%20franchising%20to%201851

The Menke Group. (n.d.). Retrieved from https://www.menke.com/ esop-archives/the-origin-and-history-of-the-esop-and-its-future-role-as-a-business-succession-tool/#:~:text=The%20First%20ESOP%20 (1956),successors%2C%20the%20managers%20and%20employees

Todd, J. H., (1842). Introduction to *An apology for Lollard doctrines*. London: Camden Society.

Tokosh, J. (2019). Is the Macy's in my mall going to close? Uncovering the factors associated with the closures of Macy's, Sears, and J.C. Penney stores. *Growth & Change, 50*(1), 403–423.

Townsend, M., Coen, L., & Watson, K. (2017). From regional to global: Using a network strategy to align a multinational organization. *People & Strategy, 40*(2), 32–38.

Trivedi, R. H., & Teichert, T. (2020). Consumer reactions to animal and human models in print ads: How animals and people in ads influence the purchase-decision journey. *Journal of Advertising Research, 60*(4), 426–438.

U.S. Bureau of Labor Statistics (November 2020). Retrieved from https://www.bls. gov/bdm/bdmage.htm

VanBoskirk, S. (2007), US interactive marketing forecast, 2007 to 2012. Retrieved from https://member-west.expressscripts.com/images/pdf/Previewtest.pdf

Vardanyan, M., & Tremblay, V. J. (2006). The measurement of marketing efficiency in the presence of spillovers: theory and evidence. *Managerial & Decision Economics, 27*(5), 319–331.

Veloutsou, C. (2009). Brands as relationship facilitators in consumer markets. *Marketing Theory, 9*(1), 127–130.

Visser, E. B., & Weideman, M. (2011) An empirical study on website usability elements and how they affect search engine optimization, *South African Journal of Information Management, 13*(1), 1–9.

Voorveld, H. A. M., van Noort, G., Muntinga, D. G., & Bronner, F. (2018). Engagement with social media and social media advertising: The differentiating role of platform type. *Journal of Advertising, 47*(1), 38–54.

Walmart. *Bloomberg.com*, N.PAG. Stern, B. B. (2006). What does *brand* mean? Historical-analysis method and construct definition. *Journal of the Academy of Marketing Science, 34*(2), 216–223.

Walmart (May 20, 2020). Retrieved January 1, 2020, from https://corporate.walmart.com/media-library/document/q1-fy21-earnings-release/_proxyDocument?id=00000172-29ed-d3ff-a3f6bded2c350000#:~:text=With%20fiscal%20year%202020%20revenue,over%202.2%20million%20associates%20worldwide

Walmart.com history and mission (n.d.). Retrieved January 1, 2021, from https://www.walmart.com/help/article/walmart-com-s-history-and-mission/a62ce500758c4746a211d00d7c2acfcd#:~:text=Founded%20in%20January%202000%2C%20Walmart,Wal%2DMart%20Stores%2C%20Inc.

Wang, H. (2018). Pricing used books on Amazon.com: a spatial approach to price dispersion. Spatial Economic Analysis, 13(1), 99–117.

Williams, S. (2018). *Fishing differently. Ministry formation in the marketplace.* Grand Rapids, MI: Certa Publishing.

Wouters, J., & Wetzels, M. (2006). Recall effect of short message service as a complementary marketing communications instrument. *Journal of Advertising Research, 46*(2), 209–216.

Wu, J., Li, K. J., & Liu, J. S. (2018). Bayesian inference for assessing effects of email marketing campaigns. *Journal of Business & Economic Statistics, 36*(2), 253–266.

Xiao, Q. (2016). Managing e-commerce platform quality and its performance implication: A multiple-group structural model comparison. *Journal of Internet Commerce, 15*(2), 142–162.

Xu, H. (2018). To compete or to take over? An economic analysis of new sellers on e-commerce marketplaces. Information Systems & E-Business Management, 16(4), 817–829.

Yu, M., & Lee, M. (2015). Unlocking the black box: Exploring the link between perceive organizational support and resistance to change. *Asia Pacific Management Review, 20*(3), 177–183.

Zhang, S., & Cabage, N. (2017) Search engine optimization: Comparison of link building and social sharing. *The Journal of Computer Information Systems, 57(*2), 148–159.

Zhao, K., Mahboobi, S. H., & Bagheri, S. R. (2019). Revenue-based attribution modeling for online advertising. *International Journal of Market Research,* 61(2), 195–209.

Zhu, F., & Liu, Q. (2018). Competing with complementors: An empirical look at Amazon.com. *Strategic Management Journal, 39*(10), 2618–2642.